Heroine

Black & Blue #3

Heroine (Black & Blue #3)
By
Melyssa Winchester

This journey that is Matthias and Kimber's story, was affected in a lot of ways by people that were an active part of my life over the course of the year and a half it took me to write it. But there was no greater impact made than the one by Jonathan Good (Dean Ambrose). So, for everything you've done, and everything you will continue to do, this one for you.

"I refuse to let my past dictate my future. There isn't a person on the planet that should let a past nightmare dictate their future dreams." – CM Punk

Prologue

Matthias

Hey Bartender. Pour me another.

The last two forties of Jack Daniels haven't done the trick. I think I need a bit more before the events of the past two days can be completely erased.

I should be on top of the fucking world.

Friday night at the show, I speared my way straight to the top of the world. At least the top of the world as it's known in Harbor Front Wrestling Alliance.

I was the HFWA World Champion.

What makes it even more amazing is that it's the first time in two years the title has changed hands. And it all came about because the guys running the show laid five magical words on me.

"We've got faith in you."

Yeah, I can see how much faith they had in me carrying the company now.

I'm sitting in a dive bar surrounded by a bunch of drunks that I'm pretty sure are setting up for their next DUI.

My boy, the Nobel Peace prize-winning scholar, John Boyd Orr said it best.

Empires won by conquest have always fallen, either by revolt within or by defeat by a rival.

I'm the new guy, and in my experience in this crazy business known as professional wrestling, the lifers—guys that have been bleeding into the mat for generations—don't take kindly to the new guy coming in and owning them.

Davis Ripley, aka Socio Sniper for anyone who follows this business, has been on top of the promotion since he walked through the door two years ago.

He'd bled on the mat and come back from injuries that would have taken down lesser men. Earning the respect of the guys in the locker room.

Exactly what I attempted to do when I was scooped up by Reese and Bryan.

What I failed at.

Mutiny on the inside had taken my moment and twisted it until I was left right back where I started.

Nowhere. With nothing.

Well, no. That's not true. I've got this bottle of whiskey and the clothes on my back. With JD there to soothe all that ails me, I'm richer than I think.

Man, I really need to lay off the sauce. I'm starting to sound like a goddamned infomercial.

"Saw what happened tonight, Matty boy. You were robbed."

Saul, my bartender for the night—well, every night—always was an insightful son of a bitch.

I *was* robbed, but it was my own fault.

If I'd only kept my eyes on the end game instead of getting caught up in other interests, this wouldn't be happening now.

When you're going about your day, politics are just something you see on television or hear about on the radio. Prime Ministers and Presidents all duking it out, trying to prove once and for all who has the biggest balls of them all.

Always on the periphery, it never affects what you as an average Joe, need to do.

At least it doesn't until you get the bright idea to become a professional wrestler. Once you do that, all bets are off. The hot steaming brown paper bag of shit lands right on your doorstep, and no matter how hard you go out of your way to avoid it, you always step in it.

Tonight, well that was me opening my front door, taking a step out without looking, and stepping right into a gigantic pile of it.

The shortest championship reign in HFWA history.

If I look at it in a glass half full way, at least I managed to snag myself a place in the record books. But you know what? My shot glass isn't half full right now. It's empty.

Just like me.

If I had the good sense God gave me, I'd hail a cab and head home. Get some sleep. Another thing that hasn't been going so well lately. But I've been wrestling for almost twelve years. Getting my head kicked in for the entertainment of others. Sense, much less the good kind, left me a long time ago.

So Saul's it is.

"Another shot, barkeep."

Earning another pathetic look of sympathy from the man, he turns and starts doing as I ask. He doesn't have to tell me I need to knock it off, or I've drunk my body weight in booze tonight. I'm aware of it.

I just don't give a shit.

It's not like I've got anything worth staying sober for.

At least I didn't think I did until a thin arm comes out around me, grabbing the shot just as Saul places it on the bar and downs it before I can.

Twisting my head to meet the person with the balls to get involved in my quest for alcohol poisoning, I groan.

"Now that's a shame."

No way.

There's no way in hell this is happening right now.

I am not drunk enough for this conversation.

"What's that, sugar?" I spit out, disgusted by the slur I can hear in my words.

"I figured you for a beer guy." She responds deadpan and turning back to the bar beings to laugh.

"What's so funny?"

"Generally or do you mean right now?"

"Now."

"Well, *sugar*," she snidely mimics. "That would be you."

"If you don't like it, I'm sure there's someplace else you can be."

"Nope. I think I like it here. Thinking of making it my regular joint."

Jesus Christ.

Is it not bad enough that I had to lose my belt? Now I've gotta suffer through this with her too? Just who the hell did I piss off to deserve this?

Her, stupid. You pissed her off. Or in your inebriated state, have you forgotten your history?

"Have at it, sweetheart. I was done here anyway."

Sliding down off the stool, reaching out and gripping it as I start to feel the effects of the three hours' worth of shots I plied myself with, she laughs again. Effectively kick-starting the headache I've been trying to ignore for the better part of two hours, and making me wish I'd just gone home after all.

"Wasn't my walk of shame earlier enough for you? What the hell do you want, Kimber?"

"Aww, Matty. Since you asked so nicely, what I want is you."

"Well, little one, you got me, but that doesn't answer my question. What do you want with me?"

Fuck Matthias. Get it together. You're so blasted you're barely making sense to yourself.

"I want to save your life."

Part One
The Beginning

Chapter One

2003

Matthias

This is complete bullshit.

When I made the choice to bail out on the guys and head home early, the last damn thing I wanted to walk in on was the two of them going at each other.

I guess I shouldn't be all that surprised. This isn't the first time I've had to sit in here and listen to them go at it. It's been the same routine for the last three years.

Ever since the piece of shit known as my old man lost his job at the power plant and decided that drowning his shit in the bottom of a bottle seemed like a better alternative.

It's pretty obvious from the way my mom shrieks and the wall shakes, that just like the other night, he's drunk off his ass.

The break from shit I wanted is definitely not happening now.

Hoisting myself off the bed as another loud bang hits, I grab my jacket off the back of the chair and throw it on.

If they're gonna keep this shit up, they can do it without the audience.

Except when I make my way out into the hall and pass by the living room, my eyes catching hers, that's not at all what happens.

I've seen my mom react in a lot of different ways when she gets into it with my old man, but what I see when my eyes meet hers is a first. She's not standing toe to toe with him, shoving her hands into his chest and screaming at him to listen to her. She's not even flinching from the impact of the abuse he shoves her way.

No. This time she's quiet. Her eyes are dead.

He's finally stripped her of what was left of her will.

Fucking prick.

"Get the fuck off her!" I yell, crossing the room until I'm putting myself between them. Focusing his attention on me the way it should be.

If he wants to beat on someone, let him pick on someone that's damn near his own size.

The days of him putting his hands on her are over.

"Watch yourself, little boy." He sneers. "Go back and hide in your room. Let the adults handle their shit."

"Slamming your wife against the wall is what they call handling shit now?"

"Matty, do what he says." My mom interrupts quietly, her eyes still devoid of all feeling. Her words robotic.

"No! I'm sick of coming home and having to listen to the two of you do this shit. It ends now."

Turning back to the man I'm supposed to call dad and staring him down, I silently dare him to push me. To make me lose what's left of the little self-control I have so I can finally let loose all of the aggression I've been swallowing down for years.

Let him see what it feels like to be on the receiving end of what he loves dishing out.

"What exactly do you think you're going to do to stop it?" my old man demands and I just smile. "You're more of a girl than she is. At least she knows how to throw a punch."

"Matthias." My mom tries again, but my name falls on deaf ears because I'm on him before she even gets it all the way out.

My fist connecting with his face and knocking him back a few paces before he catches himself enough to stupidly come back for more. Hitting him with another jab and following it up with an uppercut, making him stumble again. Then, before he has the chance to recover, following it up by laying the steel toe of my boot into his gut, again and again until he finally collapses to the floor.

Sucking in a breath, I look over to where my mom is standing and holding out my hand, silently pray she takes it. But before she can, my old man groans and attempts to move and stepping back, I hit him with another hard boot. This time landing it in his side.

Turning my attention back quickly to my mom and catching her eyes flicker from him to me, I hold out my hand again and this time, she takes a trepid step forward and slips her hand into mine.

"We're getting out of here and we're not coming back."

Answering with a quick nod, we cross the room to the front door and after opening it and ushering her out, I motion across the grass to where my car is parked at the curb.

"Go. The passenger side is unlocked. Get in. And no matter what happens or what you hear, don't get out."

"Matty, you don't have to do this."

I'd be a complete idiot not to hear the plea in her voice, but after the dead look I saw in her eyes a few minutes ago, we're way past the point of her pleas working.

I'm ending this the way I should have three years ago and there's not a damn thing she can say right now to change it.

"Just do what I said, Mom. This shit ends tonight. He's not gonna lay another hand on you. I'll make sure of it."

Shoving my hand out and pointing to the car again, I level her with the same unwavering look I gave my old man before my fist connected with his face.

I meant what I said. I'm ending this.

That piece of shit laid out on the living room floor is never going to get another shot at hurting her again.

After a few minutes of attempting to stand her ground, she finally relents and turns away. Picking up the pace and making quick work of our front lawn until she's at the car and lowering herself inside. Which, once I'm content that she's securely locked away, lets me focus my attention back on the house. Back on the piece of shit waiting on the other side of the door.

It's time to give Jonathan Kemper a taste of his own medicine.

✳✳✳✳✳

"What the fuck—" Bryan catches himself when he opens the door and his eyes land on my mom. "I mean, what the heck happened to your face?"

"Long story. You think we can come in?"

Proving why he's my best friend, he steps back from the door, only moving back to close it once we're both safely inside.

"I'm gonna go let my mom know you're here." He smiles at my mom before heading up the stairs, and after a couple of minutes where I can make out the faint sound of voices, he's coming back down to us, but not alone.

His mom, Gretchen right on his heels.

Her face, despite the way we both must look, lit up in a smile. Almost as if seeing a busted up boy and his broken mom in her entryway is an everyday occurrence.

"Diane. Matthias. It's nice to see you."

I'm pretty sure it's not that nice to see us, but gotta love the woman for trying. Her gentle greeting is enough to get my mom to lift her head from the floor and replace the vacant look in her eye with one of actual feeling.

"Sorry for the intrusion, Gretchen."

"No trouble at all. I was only upstairs putting this one's laundry away." She says, swatting Bryan's arm. "I was going to make myself some tea. How about you join me and we leave the boys to it?"

With a delicate nod, my mom slips her hand out of mine. But before walking away, she leans in and kisses my cheek.

"Thank you." She whispers, and not wanting to let on how the sound of her weak voice guts me, I just nod and let her go.

"He was pounding on her again, wasn't he?" Bryan asks as soon as they're out of earshot and I heave out a heavy breath.

"It was different this time, man."

"How so?"

"Fucking asshole must have slammed her off the damn wall about six times before I finally had enough and ended it. Sick thing is, I was just gonna leave her there. I was sick of their shit. Figured I'd head over to the gym to let loose on the punching bag."

"Why didn't you?"

"I walked by the living room and saw her eyes. She's looked beaten down and broken before, Bry, but this time she looked dead. Like the last slam off the wall took what little life she had left and she was gone completely."

"Shit."

Bryan's been listening to me spout off about this from the day we met freshman year. He knows the crap I've been living with—what we've both been living with, but he never pushes. He listens, let's me vent, and then we screw off and do other shit. I can tell by the way he's looking at me now though, that the time for him being silent about shit is over.

"What did you do?"

"I used him as a punching bag instead."

"Matty..."

"Don't worry. I left the piece of shit breathing. Barely."

"Son of a bitch." He curses before turning and heading for the stairs. "Come on. There's a first aid kit in the bathroom, not that I think it will do much for the bruises you're sporting."

"You think I look bad, you should—"

"See the other guy." He finishes. "Yeah, I figured that."

Following him up the stairs and into his room, I head into the bathroom off to the side while he throws himself down on the bed. His eyes, despite being out my view still felt on me as I start working on cleaning up my face.

"How much longer are you gonna put up with this?" He calls out.

"Until Smith says I can train with him full-time. Once he does that, I'm getting the fuck out of here."

"So six months from now? You really think after what went down tonight, you're going back there again?"

"No, but mom says there's enough in her savings account with what I've been passing off, that we can stay at a hotel for a while."

"What's that gonna get you?" he calls out over the water as I turn on the tap. "A couple weeks?"

"Couple months with everything we've saved." I yell back, applying the bandage to the cut over my eye and shutting off the water before making my way back out into his room.

"You're still not gonna be old enough for Smith to let you in."

Throwing my body down on the bed, moaning and gripping my ribs after landing a little hard, I lean forward and nod.

"I know, but it's better than going back there and listening to them fight again. Wondering if the next one is gonna be the last."

Truth is, I've been getting the feeling that the end was near for a while when it comes to my parents. What started out as mild bickering years ago, quickly escalated into him laying hands on her. Slowly stripping her of whatever fight she had and leaving her nothing more than an empty shell of the mom I remember.

It's only a matter of time before she's taken out of the house in a body bag. I know this.

I tried letting her handle it. Tried keeping my nose out of their crap the way she asked. But tonight I couldn't do it anymore. I never should have let it get that bad in the first place.

That changes now.

I'm not the same midget kid I was when this all started. I'm not a string bean. It took me a year and a half, but I put on some weight and packed on some muscle. I'm stronger than him now, which puts me in the perfect position to end it.

For both of us.

"Stay here." Bryan offers, pulling me back out of my head.

"I'm not bringing you and your parents into this mess."

"Newsflash, bro. We're already in it. We've been in it for three years. If you think that my mom is letting yours walk out of here tonight, you obviously don't know shit."

Gretchen and Tom Michaelchuk are good people. From keeping me overnight when the fighting at home was at an all-time high, to feeding me when my mom's paycheck didn't carry over into the next one and we were low on food. They've done it all. Taken care of me—us—every step of the way.

Making what he's saying, the truth.

His mom won't let us leave tonight. She'll make sure I've got a sleeping bag in Bry's room, she'll put my mom up in their guest room, and no argument either of us make will work.

Can you tell we've been here before?

I'm starting to lose count on the amount of times Bry and his family have come to our rescue.

"This is the last time."

"Is it even worth mentioning that you've said those exact same words before?"

This is the first time they're putting someone other than me up, but again he's right. I said the exact same words the last time I showed up on their doorstep looking to escape, and knowing my mom and the damn hold my dad has on her, I'm going to be saying it again in the near future.

Which is the exact reason I'm never wasting time on love. If love makes you go back and get beat on until you can barely see, let alone walk, I want no fucking part of it.

"Six months, Bry. All I need to do is stay under the radar for six fucking months and I'll be rid of this shit once and for all."

"And what about her?" he motions to the door. "You know she's just gonna go back and you're gonna be over here bitching about it again. So what's your grand plan with her?"

That's the million dollar question, and one that try as I might, I don't have an answer to because until this very second, there is no plan.

I know what my mom's gonna do. She's gonna agree to stay when Gretchen asks her, but just like the time she took off to the woman's shelter and left me alone for the two days she was gone, she'll go back.

As much as I love the woman, love has made her lose what's left of her damn mind.

She still believes that if he could just get another job, he'd come around again and we'd all go back to the way things were when we were happy.

When what she needs to get through her head is that there's no intervention alive that will save that sorry sack of shit. Once an abuser, always an abuser.

"I don't know, alright? I know she's gonna go back and put up with his shit again. I just don't know what the fuck I'm expected to do."

"Nothing, Matty. You can't save her if she doesn't want to be saved. All you can do is try. If she doesn't get it, that's on her. You're only responsible for saving yourself."

Chapter Two

Matthias

For as long as I can remember, I've wanted to be a wrestler.

From the first time I sat down in front of the TV in our piece of shit apartment at five years old and saw Bret Hart and Shawn Michaels squaring off in the center of the ring, I knew what I was going to do with the rest of my life.

At five years old, I was in no position to actually achieve it, but with the way I sat mesmerized, my mom having to call my name ten times before I finally heard her and went to eat dinner, there was no doubt in my mind that when I was old enough, I was going to make my mark just like those guys did.

From that moment on, anytime it came on television, I was all over it. I devoured it the way some people do books and lately video games. I thought about it from the second I got up in the morning, all through the day while at school, and straight up until I went to bed at night. I ate, slept and breathed anything that had to do with a wrestling ring.

It became such a huge part of my life that as an early birthday present the year I turned seven, my parents went all out and splurged on tickets to a show taking place a couple of provinces away in Saskatchewan.

When Bret won the title that night in '92 from Ric Flair, I should have seen the way the business would go, but I didn't. I was a punk ass seven year old that didn't know *nothing about nothing* in terms of how the business was run or how champions were chosen.

All I saw was that guys like Hulk Hogan, The Ultimate Warrior and Lex Luger were dominating, despite the younger and smaller guys holding their own in main event level matches.

Big guys. Guys that could snap me in half like the twig I was.

Those were the guys I needed to emulate.

It's just too bad that when I did get old enough to actually do something about it, my body wasn't exactly in a cooperating mood.

I wasn't a midget or anything. I mean, I grew into my six foot frame pretty nicely, but the weight was a whole other issue. No matter how much I ate, how healthy or unhealthy the food was. How many sports I joined in school, along with the work I put in after it at the gym, nothing worked. I just couldn't seem to get any bigger than I was.

By the time I started freshman year, I'd all but given up on ever achieving what the guys before me had done, especially since by then, there were guys like Kevin Nash and the Giant on the scene making me feel even more inferior.

Enter Bryan Michaelchuk. Who, just like he's there for me now with all the shit with my parents, was there for me then.

At the end of my rope and ready to give up on this stupid dream of mine, he was thrown—literally—in my path and well, the fight was back on.

New to the area, having moved in down the street from me, he was an easy target for the assholes I spent the last nine years going to school with.

Being a smaller guy—even smaller than me—made him the perfect target.

Having already had his lunch money stolen, he was being shoved around and heading out of class, he fell right in front of me.

Shit wasn't bad at home then, so while I did have a lot of pent up aggression as it pertained to my failure to bulk up, I wasn't a super angry guy. I didn't have beefs with anyone in the school, because after trying to fuck with me in elementary, they learned real quick I wouldn't take their shit and left me alone.

There was something about the way he curled up into a ball at my feet that rubbed me the wrong way.

I didn't know the guy from a hole in the wall, but I knew that he wasn't supposed to be lying in the middle of the hall scared as shit.

It was when the heavier one of the group advanced on him, most likely to add insult to the very real injuries they'd already given him, something inside me snapped. All the tapes I watched, all the shows I went to, and wrestlers I was determined to emulate, it all came flooding out of me.

Stepping over Bryan, I blocked the asshole from doing more damage. And while he wasted time trying to figure out how to sidestep me, I landed an uppercut to his face knocking him back.

Stalking toward him, I'd wasted no time shoving him until he was the one with his back slamming off the metal frame of the lockers. The sound of it as it rebounded off the walls of the hallway, enough to put the fear of god into his buddies who took off and left us alone.

After landing another few punches and a knee to the groin, I set up to do it again and a hand gripping my shoulder stopped me cold.

Turning around, fully prepared to wail on whoever was stupid enough to try and touch me, I came face to face with the guy that minutes before had been in a heap on the floor. And within seconds, the need to physically hurt someone wilted away.

"It's all good, man. You can stop now."

Eight words was all it took to make me back off, and with a clipped nod and a grunt, I turned to walk away until just like before he stopped me.

I never understood that day why I got involved, or even why Bryan would have wanted to hang out with me after it was over. I mean, I'm pretty sure I looked like a rabid animal when I wailed on the guy that hurt him. What I do know is, everything happens for a reason.

That incident, meeting Bryan that way and becoming fast friends after it, the reason was clear.

Having an obsession with professional wrestling as I did, Bryan Michaelchuk was brought into my life to make sure I never gave up on my dream.

It just sucks that a year later on the field, in the middle of one of the biggest football games of his high school career, he suffered an injury to his neck that would keep him out of the ring indefinitely. Taking all of those hopes and dreams he had and pinning them solely on me.

"Kemper! Get your head out of your ass! And while you're at it, wake Michaelchuk up. The ring ain't gonna put itself together."

The gruff angry tone of the man that in a few short months would be my trainer, wakes me from my revelry and doing what he said, I shove Bryan.

"Wake up, jackass. You know how the old man is about sleeping on the job. You're making me look bad."

Grinning before finally opening his eyes, he slips his body effortlessly off the chair.

"Just because my eyes were closed doesn't mean I was asleep. I was just waiting for you to come out of your head."

"Sure you were."

"Where'd you go this time?" he asks as we make our way over to begin setting up the ring. "You looked a million miles away."

"Just remembering how close I was to giving up. How most days, I still feel like I should."

"When did Matthias Kemper become a quitter?"

"Grade Nine."

"That shit again? I still think you're full of shit. There's no way me getting beat on in the hall kept you from walking away. Wrestling is in your blood."

He's not wrong. It is in my blood. It just doesn't change the facts.

If it wasn't for him I wouldn't be standing here. I'm not sure I'd be standing at all, especially with the way shit has gone down since.

"Think whatever you want, but if you hadn't been as big a fan as I was, I'm pretty sure neither of us would be standing here now."

"Calling bullshit, bro. The need to see this through got us here. I'm just coming along for the ride."

After things started going to hell at home, I started spending a lot of time at Holt's Gym. When I finally filled Bryan in on where I spent most of my nights—even sleeping over there when I didn't feel like heading home—he'd done exactly what he said and come along for the ride.

All the aggression that we built up during school, we ended up releasing it there. At least we did until Holt came to us with tears in his big bear eyes, telling us he couldn't afford to keep the place open anymore.

Another moment in my life where I had to make a choice whether to keep going or just take the loss and call it a day. Truth is, I had a lot of moments like that over the last couple of years, but unlike the day I met Bry, I never backed down.

Which is why we're standing where we are.

He's right. I did this.

"Whatever, Bry. All that matters is that we're here and in six months, we're gonna finally get what we're after."

"Don't you mean *you're* gonna get it?"

"You're here, aren't you?"

Combat Pro Wrestling or CPW, is the place to be in terms of independents in the area, and after slapping down money on every show put on within a 25 Km radius for the last two years, it seemed like the next logical step.

Radley Smith, one-time champion and well on his way to hitting the big time with the promotion, was the owner. He also ran his own wrestling school for guys that were just as passionate as he was. As it turns out though, if I thought it would be easy to get him to take me and Bryan under his wing, I had another thing coming.

Smith, as he's known to anyone he deems worthy of giving the time of day to, is a brash motherfucker. He can spot a shit talker a mile away, but that isn't the worst of his traits. He's also a stickler for the rules.

Spoken *and* unspoken.

He didn't give two shits about how determined I was to do this for the rest of my life, or even what I was willing to put my body through in order to achieve it. Didn't even care about everything I had already put myself through or just how deep my dedication ran before landing on his doorstep that first day.

All he saw was me being sixteen years old.

Two years too damn young.

But what the old guy hadn't expected was just how annoying I can be when I want something badly enough. With Holt's officially closed and the shit at home getting worse by the second, I needed an outlet and I was determined this was it.

I wanted to get my start training under Smith with the intent of one day ruling CPW.

Willing to sit outside in the middle of a blizzard waiting for him or roasting my ass off in the summer in order to prove it.

Prove myself.

Determined to show him he wouldn't be making a bad investment by putting his faith and time in me.

Bryan was hurt at that point, so he wasn't going to be making leaps and bounds in the squared circle, but he was my biggest supporter. Pushing me in times when it was hazardous to his health to help me out. Spending hours training and working with me on meal plans and the right supplements to take that would give me some of the upper body mass I was so desperate for.

He did it all, which meant he was part of my team.

And after months of riding Smith until he couldn't take it anymore, he finally relented and gave us a slice of the heavenly pie we were after.

We couldn't train under him yet, but we could be his gofers until I aged out. Putting the ring together, dishing out popcorn and programs. Even driving the boys around.

We did it all.

Bringing us to where we are now. Assembling the ring for the show taking place in a few hours and loving every second of it.

"So when are we gonna talk about the elephant in the room?" He calls out after spending the last forty minutes working in silence.

"Nothing to talk about. You called it. She made the decision to go back even after I gave her the ultimatum. There's nothing I can do."

"You ever think about going to the cops?"

"Been there, done that. Twice. It never gets anywhere because he's smart enough not to leave marks, and she's gotten better at lying to people."

"I'm sorry, Matty. I know this isn't going down the way you expected."

"Actually, it is," I admit as he lowers his attention back to the turnbuckle he's working on. "It's like a fucking merry-go-round with her, ya know? I knew she was gonna go back. She always goes back. I just hoped that after last night, a light bulb would have gone off."

"Yeah, well, it still fucking sucks."

No argument there.

"As much as I want to help get her away, there's only so much I can do. It's like she's always telling me. I'm just a kid. I don't think I've been a kid in a long ass time, but I mean, legally she's right. I gotta leave her to fix her own mess and hope she does it."

Before Bryan can answer, Smith's voice booms loud and large over the enclosed space.

"Kemper! Do you think you can head over and pick up Daniels? Or do I need to let you girls finish having your heart to heart and do it myself?"

Yeah, there's no doubt about it.

Here in this space surrounded by my best friend, the angry son of a bitch promoter, and the ring we've just spent the last hour putting together, I'm home.

Chapter Three

Matthias

December 7, 2003, will go down in infamy as the day everything changed.

Gone, the days of setting up and tearing down equipment, driving wrestlers wherever the fuck it is they wanna go, and being at Smith's beck and call.

It's a new day and the minute I turn over in bed and slip the blankets off in order to sit up, the true reality of what today is sets in.

I'm officially eighteen.

Which means as per Smith's rules, I'm ready to become a student of the game.

An argument could be made that I've been a student since I was five, but considering the closest I've gotten to standing in the middle of the ring is the makeshift ones Bryan and I made as kids in our backyards, it's not the truth.

I may have sucked up every bit of information I could while doing tasks the old man assigned over the last two years, but it still paled in comparison to what would actually happen once I stood inside what he likes to call *his yard* and locked up with an opponent for the first time.

Despite my need to remain cool about the whole thing, it's hard to mask the smile that comes as I make my way from my bedroom to the bathroom and see my appearance. All the after-hours time I spent training finally paying off and giving me the body definition I'm going for.

This is it. This is what you've been busting your ass for.

Taking a quick shower and tossing on the last of the clean clothes from the duffel I brought with me, I load all of my stuff back into the bag and head for the door. More than a little eager to book it across town to what I just know is the start of my new life.

Sliding in and tossing the bag down on the passenger seat and turning the key in the ignition, the beginning notes of Def Leppard's *Rock of Ages* begins to play. Reaching over and grabbing it, I lean back in the seat, prepared for the onslaught of excitement I'm sure to get.

"Happy Birthday, you piece of shit!" he yells, and I just shake my head. In true best friend fashion, his next words nailing me to the letter. "You in the car yet?"

"Yeah, just started her up." I laugh. "It's scary how well you know me."

"We've only been waiting on this day for two fucking years, brother. Attacking the days on the calendar with that Sharpie you carry around with you like you're ready for the days of merch signing. It'd be scary if I didn't know what you were up to."

Memories of the calendars adorning his walls that we'd been putting X's on every day for the past two years flood me. The knowledge that the days of marking are over is filling me with pride.

By some miracle, I somehow managed to keep my shit together in order to see this through.

There's no going back now.

"You meeting me there?"

"Yeah, but I'm gonna be late. I need to head over to the school first. Mom's orders."

Where I walked away from my senior year in favor of following what my old man likes to call *this pointless dream of mine*, Bryan stayed in. His parents deciding that he would finish school before moving on to whatever it was he wanted to do with his life.

The complete opposite of the way my family looked at it.

Despite knowing in the end that it was my choices that landed me where I am, I can't help feeling a little jealous of him for that.

Maybe if my parents gave two shits about something other than getting drunk and fighting, I'd be there with him fixing to graduate, instead of living out of a decrepit motel and working my ass off as a bouncer at a strip joint to keep my head above board.

Fall back options.

For as often as I heard those words before dropping out, you'd think it would have sunk in. That I would have done what Bryan is doing, so that in the unlikely event that this dream of mine does crash and burn, it's not the end of the line for me.

But this is what people don't get.

I won't fail.

I will rule this business because I have something that not a lot of people have.

Heart.

Call me crazy, but when I've bled onto every mat across this country and obtained every title imaginable, I'll prove why I don't need a fall back option.

Why this is my only option.

Kimberlee

"Come on! You let Zach do it!"

I don't know why he's being like this. It's frustrating. I'm hoping that reminding him that he let my older brother Zachary wrestle will work in my favor.

I need him to see me differently than he does.

What can I say? He raised a weird kid.

William and Mary Parker have been married for twenty-five years. For eleven of them, they've been my parents.

For a whole lot longer than that wrestling has been a part of their lives. My dad fancying himself a wrestler from the time he turned ten and my mother coming along for the ride, doing it herself after they married.

Culminating in what they started four years ago when they opened up their own wrestling school. And what after hosting a bunch of people that in the years since have gone on to enjoy success in various different promotions, they let my brother try his hand at.

He's been doing it ever since and he's sixteen now.

For a long time it didn't interest me. Sure, I thought it was cool, but it wasn't exactly something I was chomping at the bit to do.

I had bigger dreams than a wrestling ring. Even if those dreams changed six times in as many years.

After bringing me along more times than I can count and letting me watch them train though; something happened to me.

I started looking at what they were doing differently. My heart would pick up whenever two people were going at it in the ring. I would even swing and kick right alongside some of the guys and girls doing it, thinking I was such a badass. Even stealing one of my brother's old blow-up dolls and power bombing it the way I saw one of the guys do in the ring.

It wasn't long after that when I knew I wanted to do. Who I wanted to be.

Which brings me to this conversation with my dad.

The fourth time I've tried and failed at getting him to see me as more than his baby girl, and instead, someone who can actually do this for a living.

Be good at it.

"No, Kimber. We've talked about this already and bringing your brother into it isn't going to change my mind. What happened with Zachary is a different situation."

Right. It's different because I'm a girl and he's a boy. Doesn't matter that I'm just as tough as he is. I'm a girl and his only one, so he's gonna say no every single time.

Sexist pig.

"The only difference between me and Zach is that he has a dick."

"What did I tell you about language like that?" he snaps. "You're lucky your mother isn't hearing you talk like that or you'd be having your mouth washed out with soap."

See what I mean?

I'm eleven, not five. After all the time I've spent surrounded by nothing but old sweaty guys that curse worse than sailors, you'd think he'd get that I picked up a lot of it. *But nooo.* Of course, he doesn't. He sees me as a little girl, but more than that, a lady.

'Ladies shouldn't curse.' He reminds me of every freaking chance he gets.

Bullshit. I'll fucking curse if I want to.

"I'm just as good as any of those guys you've trained, Dad! Just give me a shot to prove it. One chance. If something happens or I don't prove how good I am, I'll leave it alone. I swear."

"Now why don't I believe that?" he questions with a raise of his brow.

Maybe because you know its bullshit and that with or without you I'm gonna do it? I answer back silently, smart enough not to spit the words out loud and endure his wrath. If just saying the word dick is setting him off, lord only knows what that would do.

"Please, Daddy?" I bat my eyes at him sweetly, relying on past times I've used this and gotten my way. "I've learned so much from watching you guys. I just want to see if I'm good at it."

Pressing a hand into the heavy lines in his forehead; lines that are the result of all the blades he's taken over the years, he sighs and it's in that sound I know I've got him.

I'm wearing him down. He's going to say yes.

Woohoo! *Score another one for Parker!*

"Levi!" he calls out to the boy currently running the ropes inside the ring. "Get your ass over here."

Levi Springsteen. The cutest boy on the entire freaking planet is making his way over here. The one my father is obviously going to put all of his trust into work with me.

Did I pick the best day to do this or what?

"What do ya need, Will?" he asks once he's jumped down off the apron and made his way over.

"Kimber. I want you to work with her."

"Say what?" the boy with the sweetest green eyes on the planet asks in disbelief. "Work with her how?"

"Get in the ring and lock up. What do you think I mean?"

Oh boy. He's not happy.

"Nothing. Got it, boss."

Is it wrong that my heart turns to mush whenever Levi caves into my parents? He does the same thing with my mother and I swear I'm just a puddle inside when his voice drops a couple of decibels and it's all low and sultry like.

Chill, Kimber. Now's not the time to be going all doe-eyed. You wanna be taken seriously.

Turning away from my dad and motioning to the ring, I skip my way past him and up the ring steps. Jumping in between the ropes for the first time, and in my excitement, running around the ring as I wait for Levi to join me. Which, after watching him lean into my dad and his lips moving so quickly, I can't pick up, he does a few seconds later.

"You sure you wanna do this, Kimmie?"

Have I mentioned how much I loathe being called Kimmie?

I can't stand it. It makes me sound like a little kid, and since he's the same age as my brother Zach, he doesn't get to do that.

No way.

"Yep. Positive." I grin brightly, earning a scowl.

Maybe Levi isn't so great after all. You'd think someone who wants to do this for a living one day the same as I do, would be a little more supportive.

Jerk.

"Do you even know what you're doing?" he hisses, and even though it's childish, I stick my tongue out.

He's seen how often I'm here. Asking that question just makes me as mad as my dad seemed a few minutes ago.

"Can we just lock up already?"

Giving me what I'm after, but making sure I hear his displeasure with the loud groan he lays on me before stepping forward, we dive straight in.

Locking up, he pushes me back into the middle of the ropes and my dad from somewhere in the distance, after seeing me struggle to get out of it in order to reverse it, calls for a break. When Levi steps away, looking down at the mat and wiping his hand over his face, I wait for him to look up and when he does, hit him with a kick. One that takes him off guard. Making him stumble before falling to the mat, just like I hoped he would.

Skipping over to him and bending over, knowing it's going to cost me but trying to be nice since we're just screwing around, I hold out my hand for him to take, and as expected, I hear my dad swear right before Levi yanks on my arm, pulling me to the mat with him. Gripping me with his legs before twisting my arm back and making me scream out in pain as he pulls back on it.

"Little girl thinks she can play with the big boys, huh?"

I'll show him a little girl.

Shifting my legs just a smidge, I heave them straight into his nuts, and even though I know I'm going to pay for it when my father gets wind—since low blowing isn't a sanctioned move—I take the opportunity I'm given when he crumples back onto the mat, and pin him.

Since there was no referee for this and he was just seeing what I could do, there's no tapping on the mat or even a count of three. My dad just hollers out again and it's over.

This time when I get back to my feet, I don't even think to help Levi up.

Jerk got what was coming to him.

It's just too bad my dad doesn't see it that way.

"You want to explain to me what that was?"

"He was shit talking, so I shut him up."

"By low blowing him?"

"Whatever gets the job done, right?" I repeat back the advice he gives his guys. Making sure to blast him with a full megawatt smile at the same time.

One that just like when I bat my eyes, he's powerless against.

Sometimes being the only girl rules.

"Go on, Kimber. Go back to the house." He motions to the door. "I'm sure your mother needs help with something."

I don't bloody well think so. He's not gonna dismiss me that easy. Not when he owes me an answer about whether I can stick around and train.

"Not until you tell me I can wrestle."

"Kimber…" he sighs, but I don't quit. If he didn't want to deal with this, he never should have gotten mom pregnant and then let her wrestle that way. It's probably his fault I'm the way I am right now. In fact, I know it is. We Parkers are a stubborn ass bunch.

"No, Dad, don't Kimber me. I want to know if I can come back or not. I'm not going anywhere until you give it up."

"You're not going to give up on this even if I say no, are you?"

"Nope." I grin again and with a shake of his head and another motion to the door, he gives me the answer I'm after.

"Tomorrow after school. Be prepared to learn some moves that don't require nut cracking."

Yes!

Chapter Four
2005

Matthias

What are the odds that after what I heard, she's okay?

Slamming my foot down onto the pedal, swerving in and around all the cars moving slowly around me, I gun it as fast as I can to the house. Her words on the message playing over on a continuous loop in my head.

"Matty...my sweet baby boy. I love you so much."
Goddamnit!

Why did she have to go back after the last time? Wasn't a dislocated shoulder enough of a deterrent? What is it going to take for her to realize that the kind of love that my piece of shit father is selling isn't what she should be buying?

All he's serving to do is break her down just a little more until I'm pretty damn sure there won't be anything left of her.

Laying my foot down heavy on the gas when the light changes, I hear the squeal of the tires and focus on the skid marks I'm sure I'm leaving behind as I pull away. Sucking in as much air as possible as I drive the remaining half mile to the house of horrors. Refusing to believe I'm too late.

I can't be too late.

You never should have left her there to begin with.

How many times have I told myself that since I took everything I had and moved into the motel?

A hundred? A thousand?

Obviously not enough if my mind is choosing now to give it to me again.

I fucked up.

I always fuck up.

She's called me like this before. Even worse, she's said those words to my face after he beat her within an inch of her life. She tells me she loves me because every fucking time she finds herself on the receiving end of his rage, she always thinks it's going to be the last time, and wants to be sure I never doubt how she feels.

Pulling onto my street, I've got the car barely in park before I'm diving out and running over the lawn to the front door. Summoning up every bit of strength I've got when I find it locked and kicking it clear off its hinges. Greeted by the crunch of the jaded wood when I step over the threshold into the house.

Blood rushing to my head with my heart beating erratically as my body begins to shake, I survey the damage laid out in front of me.

The end table that's normally laid flat against the base of the stairs, now in pieces on the floor with the wooden legs nowhere to be found. The vase full of flowers she had on top of it a few days ago now a sea of colorful shards covering the front entryway. The water that filled it, soaked clean through parts of the carpet. The flowers completely DOA as they're crunched and scattered all over.

Just like I'm sure my mom is.

Looking away as my gut twists from the visual, I cross the room making a beeline for the living room. Where in the past, every damn one of the beatings has taken place. Almost as though doing it behind the closed doors of their bedroom wasn't good enough, and finding exactly what I expect when I step through.

Her body in a heap on the floor. Eyes closed and already swollen. With the monster from all of my greatest nightmares standing above her and alerting me even more to his presence by the string of obscenities now flying from his mouth.

What I think at first is directed at me for coming in on him in the middle of it, but when he doesn't so much as acknowledge my existence, I clearly see he's throwing at her.

"You piece of shit!" I curse as the rage takes over and I charge. His body lifting just enough to take me in before I land directly into his midsection, throwing him backwards. Both of us falling to the floor in our own heap, with the weight of my body blocking his in.

What do you know? I can execute a near perfect spear after all.

Pushing myself up and to my knees, I tighten their grip around his legs, blocking him in as I unload with a fury of fists. Taking every hit he's ever given her or tossed my way, and giving them back tenfold.

One. Two. Three. Ten. Twenty. Thirty.

I lose count the more I continue to pound on him. Flecks of blood flying from what I have to assume is his broken nose landing on my face, but the need to completely pulverize him for what he's done overriding my full acknowledgement of it.

It doesn't stop it.

It can't.

I didn't make him pay enough last time. This time, I'm gonna damn sure make it count.

Laying into him at least another dozen times, prepared to keep going even when I see his eyes roll back and begin to fade, it's the sound of a moan not belonging to him that awakens me.

Focuses me.

As much as I want to kill this son of a bitch, he's not the reason I'm here.

She is.

Slipping back off him and falling to the floor, leaning against the back of the sofa, I hear the moan again and stumbling toward it, crawl across until it's not the devil I know under me anymore, but the woman that despite her shortcomings is my angel.

"God, Mom." I hiss as I take her in. Her eyes so beaten in they're bloodshot and bleeding, beginning to swell up to the size of golf balls. Her lips fattened and purple, almost as bloody as her eyes. But it's the handprints around her neck, the grip that he had so tight they've left permanent marks that get me most.

Ugly marks.

Ones that if I had just gotten her to come with me when I left, she wouldn't be wearing now.

This is all my fault.

"Matty..." she chokes out, her face falling to the side as a string of saliva mixed with blood falls in a line from her half-parted lips to the carpet.

"I'm here, Mom. You're gonna be okay, I promise."

I'm lying. I know I am. There's no way with as badly as she's beaten, what I can now make out is her left leg twisted in a way it's not meant to be, slashes on her arms, and a gash at the back of her head, I'm going to be able to get her out this time.

He took it too far.

Pulling back, I frantically search the room for the phone, and not seeing it on the dock the way I'm used to, I release the guttural scream that ever since I came in and saw him cursing at her, I've been holding onto. It's loud. An animalistic release that doesn't do a damn thing to help curb the torture I'm experiencing with what I walked in on.

Crawling across the floor, still feeling the burn from the spear I'd given him, I struggle to my feet and race from the room. Not stopping until I'm in the kitchen and pulling the other phone off the base on the counter, punching in the three numbers that I know better than I should.

Praying that when the operator answers and I tell her what happened, begging her to get someone here quickly, that my earlier thought wasn't right.

Please don't make me too late.

✳ ✳ ✳ ✳ ✳

"I'm sorry, Matthias. There's nothing more we can do for her."

Her brain is bleeding. If the external bruising and cuts weren't enough, she's bleeding internally too.

Machines are keeping her alive.

The rest of her gone, with only the stem of her brain keeping her here. The reality being she died on the floor of our house hours ago.

Her message on Bryan's machine the only thing I have left of her now.

The voice that was frightened and alone, shakily whispering her love for me when she should have been using that energy to fight.

I never should have listened to it.

It's going to be that version of her on repeat and what will haunt me every day once I sign papers giving the hospital permission to turn everything off.

To let her die.

Fuck! I knew making me power of attorney on my birthday was going to come back and bite me. I can't make this decision.

I can't be the one that ends her life.

What the hell was she thinking putting me in this position? Especially since when it comes to her all I'm capable of doing is making mistakes. Getting shit wrong.

"There's no chance she can come back from this?"

"No, I'm afraid not. I'm sorry." The doctor repeats and I just nod in acknowledgment of his words.

We had a deal! My mind cries. *You weren't supposed to leave me until I'd made it! You said no matter what happened there was no way you were missing that! Why'd you go back on your word?*

Swallowing down the bile threatening to spill up and over in my throat at the realization of just what caused her to do it, I slam my fist into the wall after the doctor pats me on the shoulder and makes his way into the room.

Even after making the call and standing guard, making sure that piece of shit didn't move or so much as twitch in her direction, situating her, and bringing her to me when I heard the gurgling sound that I now know was her choking on her own blood, it still wasn't enough.

She's gone.

Gone as in never coming back.

Gone as in forever.

"Fuck!" I howl before smashing my fist into the wall again. Releasing the well of emotion that I've had in a vice since I walked into the house and letting it pour down my face as my body collapses and my cheek aligns with the chill of the floor tiles.

Welcoming the coolness. Needing it to tame the beast inside. The part that remained dormant during the ride in the ambulance, but that was now coming back fast and furious.

The anger. Rage so hot it's making me burn from the inside out. What the coolness from the tiles now seems to soothe even though I know nothing will ever take it away entirely.

I should have killed that son of a bitch while I had the chance.

He should be the one taking his last breath and rotting in hell where he belongs. Not her.

Not all I had. All I loved.

"Alright, boy. That's enough of that shit." A husky voice says from behind me before a pair of bare hands grab me up from my place on the floor. "I don't care why you're doing it, but the last damn thing your mama would want is your ass splayed out in a hospital corridor spilling snot on the floor."

"Pretty sure she doesn't want anything anymore, Smith." I bark out through my convulsions. "She's dead."

"Even more reason for your ass to be upright."

What the hell does this old bastard know?

Just because I spent the better part of two years wanting to train with him, doesn't give him the right to come in here and throw his opinions around.

"What are you even doing here?"

"Little pipsqueak you call a best friend called me. Said you bolted from his place like a bat out of hell and he was worried since you weren't returning his calls."

Bryan. Great.

In the insanity of taking off from his place and the trauma I walked into at mine, I completely forgot to fill him in.

Just another way I'm proving what a screw-up I am.

"Well, you got what you came for. You can leave now. I gotta go in there." I motion to the door. "I gotta go say goodbye."

"It's screwed up, ya know." he says, completely ignoring everything I've said. "Been years since I been in a hospital. Forgot how bad they smelled. And they say wrestlers stink."

"Is there a point to this?"

"Just stating observations, boy. But if you're looking for a point, let me shoot straight. The idea you got to go in there and say goodbye, screw it."

"Excuse me?"

Holy shit.

I already dealt with one piece of crap today and now the guy that's considered my boss is starting in. If the idea is for me to completely snap and end up murdering someone, he's succeeding.

"I've been where you're standing son, and if you think for a god damned second that I'm gonna let you walk in there alone, you got another thing coming."

"You didn't even know her." I spit out in an attempt to mask my surprise at what he's doing. I can say a lot about Radley Smith, but him being the guy that holds your hand through one of the toughest times of your life? That's not one of them.

"What do you mean you've been where I'm standing?"

"I lost a parent pretty violently myself."

"How?"

"You didn't screw with my daddy. All of us boys knew it, but my brother Thomas didn't give two flying fucks about the old man's wrath. He was gonna do whatever the fuck he wanted, regardless of the consequences. It ended up costing him his life, and because my old man wanted to be the one handing out the whooping and had gone after him, he paid too."

I'll be damned. Smith does get it.

"I spent years wanting to dig up that sorry ass brother of mine to make him pay for what happened to our daddy, and I'd venture to say given that it was your daddy that did this to your mama, you're feeling the same damn way about him."

He's not wrong.

"Channel that rage you got, boy. Put it where it belongs."

In the ring.

He doesn't even have to say it, I know that's what he means. I just don't agree. It doesn't belong there. If I bring this shit into the ring, especially against someone innocent, I'll end up with a murder wrap. As good as it would feel to release the fire raging inside, I can't do it.

"It doesn't belong in the ring."

"You gotta put it somewhere." Smith says, lifting a hand and bringing it down hard across his chest. "So do your worst."

"I'm not unloading on you, Radley."

"You sure as shit ain't going in that room and saying goodbye to your mother with all the pent up shit swirling around in ya. So like I said. Do your worst." He hits his chest again and this time I just stare at him as he continues to do it. "Here, I'll get you started."

I feel the sting of his hand before I've even placed what he's done, but what he wanted he got, because no sooner does his hand pull back off my face then I'm on him. Fists slamming into the same chest he just pounded into, each one harder than the last.

Over and over I repeat the same motion until after about forty or fifty hits and my breath completely stolen, I back up and sink against the wall.

"Feel better?"

"No." I tell him honestly, looking down at my knuckles and back up at him. One of my hits obviously hitting more than just his chest by the nasty looking mark I'd left along his cheek. "I feel fucking worse. Why did you do that?"

"Because she's still in there, Matthias. She might be gone like you say, but she ain't dead yet. I didn't do it to make you feel better. I guarantee you're gonna feel fucking worse than you do right now soon enough, but at least when you walk in there, she won't bear witness to it."

"Your plan backfired, old man. I screwed up your pretty face." I lamely joke, pointing to the mark now marring his skin.

"Nah, boy. You did me a favor. Made me prettier." He chuckles. "And if you walk in there wearing the shit I see in your eyes now, I got what I asked for."

What shit in my eyes? What does he see that I apparently can't even feel, much less see for myself?

"What are you talking about?"

"You're hurting because you love her. It's written all over your face. So we're gonna go in there now and tell her that. Say goodbye the right way. Don't let the last thing your mother sees be the anger, boy. That shit will have her rolling before she even hits the grave. Trust me on that."

Strangely enough, he doesn't even have to tell me to trust him. The way his eyes seem to trail off somewhere else; somewhere far from where we're standing now, speak to him having been through some shit. Radley Smith knows what he's talking about.

"This about what you told me before?"

"One and the same, but a story for another time."

"So if I don't go in there showing her the person I am, who the hell am I supposed to show her?"

"The boy she loves, and the boy that loves her just as much. That's what you want her last vision of you to be. Not the damn beast you'll end up becoming."

"Is that what you did with your old man?"

"No." he answers immediately. "And I've regretted it every damn second since we put him in the ground. Don't go in there and make the same mistake, boy. Life is too god damned short. Be better than that. Be better than me."

Chapter Five

2006

Matthias

"Do we really need to go over this again?"

This—what we're standing here to do—is the aftermath of what happened with my mom. Well, the fourth go-round of it. The first taking place the night she died—at the hospital no less, then the following two taking place over the months it had taken to get to where we are now.

About to go to trial.

Jonathan Kemper having exhausted every stall tactic imaginable and finally preparing to pay for the hell he put my mom through. What he put me through, even though I'm the lucky one getting to stand here after the fact.

Making me the unluckiest bastard in the place.

As masochistic as it may seem, my mom is actually the lucky one in all of this. She doesn't have to put up with seeing that son of a bitch's face every day in court the way I have to. The smug look he's been wearing, or the twisted glint in his eyes in the rare times we've made eye contact. The look he tries to hide behind the fake remorse he feels for being the one to strip my mother from the face of the earth.

God, I would give anything to be someplace else.

"I know the last time we spoke, I guaranteed you wouldn't need to testify given the history between your parents and the events of the night in question, but that was before I got my hands on the defense his lawyer is going to use."

"He's still pleading not guilty?"

"In a manner of speaking."

"What are you not saying?"

Lowering his body down onto the edge of his desk and bringing his hands across his midsection until they're locked together, he frowns.

"Your father is pleading not guilty by reason of mental disease or defect."

Defective is a good word to use when describing my old man, but there's no way in hell that him being a complete asshole is the reason my mother is six feet under. No, he was definitely in his right mind when he beat her so bad he made her brain bleed. I'm just sorry I didn't end him that night. He definitely deserved it.

If I had my way he'd been buried under the damn jail he's trying to keep himself out of.

"And how does going over what happened that night help?"

"It's not just that night I want to go over, Matthias. It's the timeline of abuse. When it started. What steps were taken throughout in order to distance her from it. A little insight into what made her continue to go back. What you witnessed. Those are what we need to focus on moving forward."

"How the hell am I supposed to testify to why she went back? I'm not her." I grumble, even more annoyed now that I'm aware of just how deep we're about to go.

"My apologies. I wasn't clear. You can't testify to her motivations, but you can testify to what was shared between the two of you during that time. What she may have said about it and why you believe she continued to go back."

"Easy. She was a love-struck moron. I mean, come on. If she didn't love that piece of shit, she would have left him in a heartbeat. You really want me saying that to a jury? Better yet, I might be a dumbass on a good day, but isn't anything she said considered hearsay?"

"In a manner of speaking yes, but we've already been through and won the motion regarding that, so what took place at its most basic is allowed."

Great. Not only do I have to relive the shittiest years of my life, but now I've got to go into detail about what we said to each other each and every time she tried to leave and stupidly went back.

"Way to go, Mom. Thanks for this." I mutter under my breath before focusing again on the prosecutor. "What do you wanna know?"

"When did the abuse start? And to expand on that, was it physical immediately or did things start verbally and then escalate?"

"Unbelievable! All day I spend out there pounding the fucking pavement. A warm meal the least of what I deserve, and this is

what I get? I'm supposed to live off this bullshit? Since when did I become the brat?"

"Jonathan, I just got home from work myself. When I saw that you weren't home, I made dinner for Matty first. I'm about to start ours now."

Swallowing down the noodles I've just shovelled into my mouth and gagging as a few of them get stuck on their way down, both sets of eyes turn to me and I immediately lower my gaze to the table.

"If you weren't so damn incompetent, you could have done both and had dinner waiting when I got here. Now, because you love that little fucker more than me, I've gotta wait. Can you be more useless?"

Damnit. Here he goes again. Hovering and intimidating her. Making her feel like shit because she took her time making me dinner. Third time this week. I'm getting sick of it.

Sliding the chair across the floor, I bolt over to where they're standing, slipping my way between them and shoving into him with everything I've got.

No one is gonna talk to my mom like that.

"Back off."

"Big words from such a little shit."

"Full sentences from the biggest idiot in the room. I'm impressed." I clap, and pulling her when I see his body twitch before lunging, I laugh when the rush of air escapes as he stumbles and his midsection connects with the counter.

Serves the piece of crap right.

"Obviously you haven't learned how to keep your mouth shut." He snaps, pulling himself back with a glare in our direction.

He hasn't hit her yet, but with the building rage I can see simmering in his eyes and the rigidness of his body, I know it's only a matter of time before he does.

Well, if he doesn't decide to take his shit out on me first.

"She's finished with me, okay? She's gonna cook your dinner now. So go to the living room, lay around in your boxers like you do every night and leave her the hell alone."

I know I'm only making things worse, but I'll be damned if I'm gonna sit here and let him berate her again. There's been enough of that already.

I know losing your job is shitty and it makes money tight and causes issues, but that's no excuse to treat us like shit under his shoes.

The only one he should be doing that with is himself.

*

"Matthias? Did you hear the question?"

Shaking myself free of the memory and focusing again on the question that had been posed, I nod.

"It was verbal for years before he finally laid hands on her. The first time was actually him trying to get to me but she jumped between us. She tried to protect me."

Damn, it's hot in here.

Pulling at my shirt, trying to open up and get some air, I shut my eyes tight and continue to breathe while at the same time attempting to keep the demons that are memories of what happened between them at bay.

I can't go there again. Not this soon. One memory has to be enough.

"I don't think I can do this."

"Matthias, I can't even begin to understand what you lived through. But if we want to get the maximum sentence, I need you to do it."

From sympathy to guilt-tripping. They're bringing out the big guns now.

Tightening the grip on my shirt and pulling on it, I repeat it over and over until I start to cool, giving the man what he's after.

"She tried to protect me when I should have been the one protecting her." I let the words tumble out and he shakes his head in a silent argument.

What the fuck does he know? He wasn't there. He didn't live this, so his argument means shit.

Same as every attempt I made to break my mom free of the hold Jonathan Kemper had on her.

Screw calling him my dad. He stopped being that the minute he looked at her in a way that wasn't completely driven by love.

"From all of the reports I've gotten from friends and outside agencies, it seems as though you did protect her. As best you could anyway."

"That's bullshit!" I roar, not willing to accept lies from another outsider.

"Tell me why you think that."

"You getting paid to be my shrink now?"

If I'd been a good son I would have ended the piece of shit the first time he laid his hands on her. Squashed him like the bug he is. Instead, I tried to do things the proper way, and look where it ended up getting us. She's dead and I'm alone.

"If it helps you get through what has to come next, then yes. Whatever it takes."

"Every time I got her out, I knew she was going to go back. I didn't do anything to stop it. I just let it happen. I've known for years that it was going to be me or her. Don't you get it? It should have been me! She actually meant something to the world! I was just the piece of shit he always said I was."

"Matthias..."

"No! Whatever line you're about to spout off, save it. The truth is, the wrong person died that day. It should have been me and there's nothing you or anyone else can say to change it."

✳ ✳ ✳ ✳ ✳ ✳

"We the jury in the above-entitled action, find the defendant, Jonathan Kemper, guilty of second-degree murder."

Six months.

One hundred and eighty days.

Four thousand, three hundred and eighty hours.

That's how long it took to get to this point. To hear those words spoken by the jury foreman.

Six months and a verdict that doesn't do dick all to bring her back or assuage my guilt over her being gone in the first place. The feeling that it should have been me still as strong as it was that day in the prosecutor's office.

I've been told by my court appointed shrink that whatever I feel is natural.

Some people feel relief when the verdict comes down. Some even feel happy because the party responsible is getting what they deserve.

Not me.

All I feel is sick.

Focusing my attention on the man standing at the table directly in front of me, as the rest of the gallery of observers and even my dad's lawyer begin making their way out of the courtroom, I shove my hand out in front of me the way I've seen people do on television and I shake the man who put my dad behind bars' hand. The tight grip when his hand makes contact doing nothing to rid me of the upset I'm experiencing as I see my father make his exit from the courtroom to what I know will be his permanent home.

"So it's really over?"

"Not yet, but with the verdict in and only the sentencing on the horizon, it's at the very least settled."

If only I could believe that. Too bad I know my dad a little better than this guy.

"He's going to appeal the verdict. What then?"

"We'll cross that bridge when we come to it, son."

There are two things wrong with what he said.

First, I'm no longer anybody's son, and that bridge statement is a copout. He'd get a much better response if he just admitted that the appeal would be coming soon and I'd be called on again. It might not be what I want to hear, but it's damn sure the truth.

"What's the maximum sentence he can get?" I ask, preparing myself for another vague brush off.

"Twenty-five years with the possibility of parole after he's served fifteen."

"What are the odds of that happening? Better yet, what are the odds of him winning on appeal and having the verdict vacated?"

In the weeks leading up to my testimony at trial, I've had nothing but time on my hands when I'm not training in the gym or working with Smith. The time I've spent pouring over every law website I can find and books I can pull out of the library.

Most of it not making a damn bit of sense, but the reading giving me just enough to be able to show the man in front of me that I know a lot more than he thinks I do.

"Slim to none. Every aspect of this trial was handled to the letter, so he doesn't have a leg to stand on. I'm aware that he will try and appeal, but it's not going to stand up. It's without merit, Matthias. All of the evidence that we presented, along with what you lived through, is more than enough to keep him behind bars for the duration."

"But you can't promise that."

"I can't promise anything, son. But justice was done here today and it will be again in a weeks' time. I know it doesn't bring your mother back, but it's all we have."

Easy for him to say. He didn't lose the most important person in his life.

He didn't lose anything at all.

"I don't presume to know how you must be feeling, Matthias, but I do know that all of these questions you have, this unsettled feeling you're presenting, it's not going to go away if I answer every question you throw at me. Only time can do that."

Am I really that transparent?

"Go home, Matty." He says before motioning back toward Bryan and his mother standing at the door waiting. "Go be with them and leave the rest to me."

He doesn't know me as well as he thinks because if he did, he might realize that as of the moment the verdict came down, I no longer had a home.

Sad reality is...maybe I never did.

Chapter Six

August 2006

Kimberlee

This is where I belong.

It had taken a lot of finagling, but once I'd proven my desire to do this and been put through my paces by my dad, there's definitely no doubt to be had.

I was born to do this.

Why nothing else seemed to work before, why I always got bored and jumped from one random pursuit to the next, it's all because from the moment I was born, here is where I was meant to be.

"Kimber, get your butt over here!" My dad hollers, and much like I've been doing since I got him to agree to let me train three years ago, I don't waste time hauling ass over.

The old guy could have said screw it to this entire thing and defended his decision by telling me again that he didn't want his only daughter getting hurt doing this, but he didn't. So because of that, and all of the ball busting I know he's been taking since agreeing to give me the shot, I don't keep him waiting.

"What's up? You gonna ask me to clean up after the guys again?"

Wrinkling my nose just thinking about what he had me doing apart from training, I silently pray he's not reverting back to it. More determined now than I was in the beginning to see this through and prove myself to not only myself and him, but everyone else.

Raising an eyebrow, he chuckles to himself before shaking his head.

"Even though the place has never looked as clean as it does when you work your magic, no. I called you over for a different reason."

"Well let's have it, old man."

Motioning with my hands when instead of cluing me in he just stands taking me in, he laughs again.

"Saturday. You and your brother are gonna be put in an intergender tag match."

"What?" I question, excited. Needing to be sure I heard him right and begging him with my eyes to repeat it. There's no way he just announced he's putting me in a match. Much less one that's gonna be televised, since the Saturday shows always are.

"You heard me."

"Nope. Sorry. I didn't hear a word you said. You're *definitely* gonna have to repeat it."

Laughing when again he raises his brow, he gives me what I'm after when he repeats what he just said, only this time, making sure to go full dad mode at the same time.

"You've more than proven you're ready for this, but I don't want to throw you to the wolves. So we're starting you off light."

Not sure what planet he's living on, but whether I'm alone or with a partner, it's just as hard. Maybe even more so. Even if the guy I'm teaming with is my brother, we still have to get ourselves in sync so we can sell the epic match we're gonna put on.

Yes, I said epic.

If this is how my dad wants my first time in the ring in front of a crowd to go, then I'll be damned if it's going to be anything short of perfection.

It's just too bad I know Zach won't feel the same. The last thing he wants to do with hopes of making it to the big time, working with his baby sister.

Another male in the Parker house that thinks I'm stupid for wanting to do this even though I've proven just how good I am. Makes me wish I could rely on the crotch shots more because if anyone deserves a good hard hit to the nuts, it's my brother.

Well, if he had any to hit anyway.

"How does Zach feel about working with me?"

"Believe it or not, he's the one that requested it. Apparently, he caught the match last week with Cam and wants to work with you."

Yeah. Right.

Last week Zach was taking bets on how long I'd last in the match with his best friend, and now my dad expects me to believe he thinks I'm awesome or something?

When is he gonna realize I'm smarter than he thinks?

"That's bullshit."

"Kimberlee! What the hell did I tell you about the language?"

"Mom's not here, Dad. And even if she was, I'd just blame it on you guys. Bad influences and all." I wink and grin bright when he reacts the way I hope and laughs.

"You might have a point, but don't ever let me hear you using that language around your mother. She'd whip me and not in a fun way."

"Gross, Dad. TMI."

"Do I even want to know what that means?"

"Nah. You can figure it out on your own later. Now, why don't you tell me how Zach really feels?"

"I *was* telling you the truth." He says before motioning across the gym to where my brother is unloading on a punching bag. "I know your brother is riding you even harder than I am, but that's only because until now he's only seen you working with me and some of the girls. Taking on Cameron last week was an eye opener for him. He didn't think you had it in you."

"Sounds familiar." I spit out bitterly. Hating that even though he's given me the chance, he still thinks I'm crazy for even wanting to attempt it.

"Yeah, and I already told you I was sorry for that. You're good and you've got it in your blood just as much as Zach does. He's seeing that now and wants to see how the two of you will work as a team. Question is, do you think you're ready? There's no going back once we book you in."

Am I ready? He's kidding, right?

I was born ready.

If Zach thinks he's seen all I've got, he's got another thing coming. I've still got a few tricks up my sleeve. One's that now that I know I'm going to officially get my shot, I'm going to get to show.

Stepping forward and placing a meaty hand on my shoulder, he squeezes gently as he meets my eyes. For the first time in the years since I forced his hand, he's no longer my trainer, but my daddy again.

"You can do this, little one." He offers up his support, though his use of his name for me makes me roll my eyes. "You've more than proven you can handle yourself."

Stepping back and pointing toward the ring, I notice my brother standing inside now, somewhere between the first look and this one having abandoned the punching bag in favor of leaning against the ring ropes. His expression the softest I've ever seen it as he smiles down at us, motioning for me to get in.

Maybe my dad wasn't lying after all.

"Before you get in and work on putting together the match, I'm going to ask again. Are you sure you're ready for this, Kimberlee?"

Meeting his eyes, I'm the one reaching out and squeezing him this time. Reassuring him in touch that what I'm about to say in words is true.

I have never been more ready.

"I'm ready, Dad. I just hope you are."

"Me? What do I need to be ready for?"

The answer to that is so simple, he should already know it.

"For me, Daddy. Because once I get in that ring, I'm going to own it. It won't be your house anymore. It's gonna be mine."

Kimberlee Parker is here to stay.

Matthias

"Remind me again why I ditched a workout for this?"

"Because all you do is work out, watch tapes, eat and sleep. You need to see how the other half lives." Bryan laughs as we make our way into the building. "And before you make up some excuse about Smith giving you shit, he's the reason you're here."

I wasn't going to say a word even though the thought had crossed my mind. If Smith wanted me to drive hours out of my way to watch some small promotions show, so be it.

"Wasn't gonna say a word."

"Sure you weren't. You forget I know you." Bryan tosses back before pointing across the room to the behemoth of a man standing beside the ring.

A guy that despite never having worked with him, I know on sight.

Will *"Renegade"* Parker.

A guy who after studying every magazine known to man, and devouring tape after tape, I know was a dude never slated to be anything more than a jobber. The guy booked to make everyone else look better, but who had risen to the top of the business with a style that was practically unheard of when he did it. His move set one that combined a little bit of everything, making him one hell of a beast in the ring.

High flying, slower technical style, he did it all.

Shit, with everything I've read and seen, he was the man everyone wanted to work with because he did just that. He made you work. Whether you were just starting out, a seasoned performer, or a veteran, you wanted to work with him because he would find a way to single out your strengths and bring out your best.

Seeing him with his hand in the air as he catches sight of Bryan, my eyes damn near bug out of my head when my best friend waves back.

What the hell is going on? Since when does Bryan know Renegade?

"You gonna explain how the hell you know Parker?" I grind out, shoving into his shoulder before he starts walking with purpose toward one of my idols.

Shrugging and laughing when he catches my scowl, he doesn't say another word until we've made our way across the room and we're standing in front of the man himself.

All 6 foot 5, three hundred pounds of him.

"I'm gonna let Renegade tell you himself." Bryan grins and I swallow the gigantic lump taking up residence in my throat.

I've been around a whole host of guys I dreamed about meeting when I first got into wrestling, but this one? This one is the biggest.

Bryan being the only person in existence that knows just how deep my adoration and respect goes for the man we're now standing in front of.

The very man that's made me feel like a teenage fanboy and he hasn't so much as acknowledged my existence yet.

When he turns and fixes his hard brown eyes on me after Bryan introduces us though, well that just makes it even worse.

Can a grown man piss his pants? Because I sure as shit want to right now.

"Kemper! Been hearin' good things about you."

I doubt that.

Ever since my mom died, I've been a pain in Smith's ass, let alone anyone else who's dealt with me. My matches taking on a whole new darker feel as my anger comes out and does more harm than good at the most inopportune moments.

Pretty sure the last thing anyone is hearing about me is anything good.

Honestly, I'm surprised Smith hasn't washed his hands of me yet. Bryan too for that matter. Especially with the way I went off on him a few weeks ago. The fading yellow marks across his face and down under his eye a painful reminder of just how messed up I've been.

"Smith tells me that you're well on your way to becoming CPW Champion."

"Pretty sure he's blowing smoke up your ass with that shit, Renegade." I finally find my voice to respond. With a slap to my back and hearty laugh that seems to be pulled straight from the bowels of his chest, he puts me at ease.

"So he's still the king of bullshit, is he?"

"Always."

"Some things never change."

"You did." I blurt out and I've never wanted to kick my ass faster.

William Parker was and is one of the best in the business. I've already been over that. What I haven't talked about is how he gave it all up to be a family man. That for the last seven years he's been running a small wrestling school and only here in the last few branched out into the promotional end of things. Keeping the whole thing family oriented by bringing his kid and wife on board.

"That I did. But change isn't exactly a bad thing. Speaking of change, he mention why I requested you be here?"

Looking from Renegade to Bryan, gauging their expressions and finding nothing, I linger on my best friend for a while before telling the man the truth.

"No one's said anything. Figured I was here to scout out your talent though."

"What if I said you're here because I want you to be one of my talents? Short term basis of course, since I know Smith has big plans for you."

"Did you know about this?" I lean in, hissing at Bryan and when he smiles, I'm given my answer. Of course, he did.

I'm here because Renegade wants me, and that knowledge alone is enough to have me both excited and wanting to shit bricks at the same time.

"You want me to come and wrestle for you?"

"Yeah. I reached out to Smith a few months back. Told him I needed a few guys for a weeks' worth of shows I'm doing up and down the east coast in a few months. Your name came up."

"And he was okay with this?"

"He is if you are. Said something about wanting to broaden your horizons. Figured it was crap at the time, but starting to see now what he was getting at."

Before I can ask him what he means, we're interrupted as a girl skips her way up, pausing at Renegade's side and leaning in close. My heart pausing momentarily when after studying Will, she turns her attention to me and Bry and I'm nailed head on by the deepest set of emerald eyes I've ever seen.

Eyes made only more potent by the dark black hair framing her face.

Holy shit.

"Mom's looking for you." She elbows Renegade with a smirk. "Said it's important, and if your ass isn't back there in two minutes, it's not gonna be anywhere for a long ass time."

Turning her attention away from the man I now realize is her father, I'm gobsmacked first by the smirk resting playfully on her face, and then by the penetrating stare of those eyes.

If my mom were here, she'd call them old soul eyes. Ones that right from the second they find yours, see everything. All the layers of bullshit, the mask you wear for the rest of the world, they bypass it all. They see you.

The real you. Or in this case...the real me.

Jesus Christ.

Flicking her attention from me and nailing Bryan with the look, I take the opportunity I've been given and finally swallow the lump of saliva that's hindered my ability to speak.

"Think on it." Renegade cuts back in, bringing my attention front and center. "Sit back, enjoy the show and when we're done, let me know what you think."

Slapping me on the back and throwing his hand out, I shake it, watching him do the same with Bryan before he turns and walks away. Completely stunned into submission with the knowledge that I just shook my idol's hand. At least I am until a warm brush of air envelopes me as the softest touch I've ever felt runs across my bare arm.

The hairs that had been resting and still, immediately standing on end.

"You're him." She says softly, studying me curiously.

"Him who?"

"The one I heard my Dad talking to my brother about. The guy with the issues." She air quotes.

A familiar edge rises, reminding me again why I never do this. Why I keep myself away from others when I'm not required to interact for a match.

What she's been told about me pretty much the general consensus since my mom died, and one I'm damn sick of hearing.

I don't give a shit how mesmerizing her eyes are or who her father is. No one is gonna sit around talking shit about me and get away with it. My issues are mine. Nobody else's.

"The only issue I have right now is the little midget who thinks I actually care what she thinks that's leeched herself onto my arm."

"Jerk." She bites softly under her breath before yanking her hand away as if she's been burned. Her name calling obviously not getting the response she's after when she scowls before her eyes fall after catching the smirk I'm sporting.

Son of a bitch!

The way her gaze lingers on the floor is *not* supposed to bug me. I can't afford to care about stupid shit like this, yet here I am watching it unfold and letting it twist me up.

I actually want to kick my own ass for taking my attitude out on a little kid.

"That's what they call me." I wink, my mouth clearly talking out my ass and making things worse until Bryan, seeing what's happening, wraps his arm tight around my neck and squeezes before attempting to pull me away.

Always trying to protect me, even when I don't fucking want it.

"Run along, little girl. Go find the other little kids and settle in for the show. Wouldn't want you sticking around so close to the action and getting hurt."

Why I continue to keep running my mouth I'll never know, but with the flash of fire I see billow up in her irises, I know I've definitely burned my bridge here. Something I should care about, but I'm having a hard time summoning up the fucks to give for.

"Nice to meet you, Kimberlee. Tell your dad we'll see him later." Bryan attempts to save the moment, offering up an awkward smile before pulling me away. Not stopping until he's full-on dragging me over and throwing my ass down hard into the metal seats two rows back from ringside.

"Way to go, jackass."

"What? Did you not hear what she called me?"

"Was she wrong?"

No, she's not wrong. That's half the damn problem. With everything I've put into wanting to do this, the last thing I want to be known as, is the guy with issues.

The one who puts his body on the line each and every night, that isn't afraid to get dirty and is more than willing to do whatever it takes to get to the top, those things I wouldn't mind.

My attitude issues? The loss of my mom and the aching hole she left there when she died?

Like I said before, that's for me only.

"Why didn't you tell me Smith was looking to unload me?"

"He doesn't want to get rid of you, Matty. Fuck. Do you even hear yourself? Kimberlee got under your skin pretty bad, huh? She's managed to make you forget everything her old man said. Renegade was telling you the truth. He wants you here because he wants to work with you. More specifically, he wants you working with the kid."

"What kid? The girl?"

I can't see that working out well. Though with as angry as I made her a few minutes ago, I can bet she'd lay one hell of a beating on me if she ever did get me alone.

The ones with fire in their eyes always do.

"No, not her. The son. Look, he's in an intergender tag tonight. So just put whatever the hell that was with Kimberlee out of your head and watch the damn match. If you didn't just totally screw your chances here, tell me at the end if you think he's someone you can work with, alright?"

Bryan's annoyance, the exasperation in his tone, I know it well. He's bossy and has no issue putting me in my place, but it's his way of watching over me. He's taking charge the way I need him to because if he didn't, I wouldn't have a career to look forward to at all.

"Fine, but if all these people are gonna do is look at me like I'm damaged fucking goods, they can find themselves another toy to play with."

Focusing my attention on the ring and watching as the people that were milling about finally start making their way to their seats, one question keeps playing over in my head. One that seems to haunt me almost as much as those damn green eyes do.

What the hell have I gotten myself into?

Chapter Seven

Kimberlee

Why are the pretty ones so mean?

First Levi, then Tommy a little over a month ago, and now this asshat.

Yeah, you heard me. Matthias Kemper is an asshat. Even if he is prettier than Levi.

I heard my dad talking to this Smith guy the other night on the phone. They were talking all about Matthias, and Dad said how badly he hoped a deal could be made so he could come here and work with Zach.

My brother is pretty amazing in the ring, but he's not well rounded like I'm proving to be. He sticks strictly to the mat, and while that doesn't exactly make him garbage or anything, you can totally tell that Zach wants to be more than that.

He wants to be like Matthias.

So while the two old guys reminisced about the old days and what they wanted to do with Matthias, I went online and checked him out. I knew who he was before I even made my way over to deliver my mom's message. I just thought that with the way his eyes seemed softer than the rest of him, he was one of the good ones.

It's just too bad that like I was wrong about the other guys I've been crushing on, I was wrong about Matthias too.

Damn him and that mussed up sandy hair and equally damning eyes. Ones that if I just close mine, I can bring up clear as day. Lightened blue like the sky, they're easy to get lost in. Especially with the earlier softness I caught when I first pulled up near my dad.

The softness I now know is a façade.

He's a trickster and I'm glad that his stupid face is away from mine right now or I might have to punch it.

Or kiss it.

Damnit. My body is a traitor. I hate this.

I've spent years around guys, what with Daddy training them, and never once has there been interest in anything but what they were doing inside the ring. Even with that, it took a long time to spark any interest. They were just people.

Then along comes puberty, and like the aftermath of a car crash, my heart speeds up, I sweat and certain parts of my body even thump and tingle.

I know, I know. It's gross to me too, but it doesn't make it any less real.

Matthias made all of that happen, same as Levi did, and even though part of me wants to smack the crap out of him for treating me like a little kid when I'm clearly not, I also can't help the urge I have to shut him the hell up by pressing my lips to his.

I wonder what they would feel like.

Get a grip, Kimber. He's an asshole. Remember that.

Swallowing down my annoyance, I head off in search of Zach. Praying as I go that once I find him, he can suggest something that will knock all thoughts of Matthias Kemper from my head completely.

"There you are!" Zach calls out before grabbing my wrist and pulling me to him, practically dragging me down the hall as he speeds off down it like his ass is on fire.

"Where are we going?"

"Dad's office. We need to talk."

Keeping pace so he doesn't have to keep dragging me and slipping my arm out of his, I don't say another word until we're pulling to a stop in front of our dad's office and he's shoving the key into the lock, allowing us entrance.

"Why? Shouldn't we be getting ready for the match?"

"This is about the match, Kimber."

"Okay."

"Where were you about an hour ago?"

"With Mom, why?" I ask as his face sinks in and he releases a shaky breath. Whatever's going on, it's obviously bad if it's got him reacting like this. My brother is usually the cooler head between us. Seeing him shaken up is troubling.

"Levi claims that you...fuck," he curses before raking a hand down over his face. "Levi says you messed with his gear."

See what I mean?

The guy can't handle being beaten by a girl, so now he's making stuff up to make me look bad. He knows how dad is about the story we're telling in the ring turning real outside of it. He's also aware of the crush I had on him and isn't against using it to his advantage now to get out of facing me.

Maybe this time I kick him in the nuts double because this is complete bullshit.

"Mom was freaking out over my gear so I've been with her making sure it all fit. I don't know why Levi's saying I'm the one that screwed with his stuff, but I wasn't anywhere near him."

Levi and my father aren't the only people that know how I used to feel about one half of the team we're facing tonight. It wasn't exactly a secret, which means the probing look Zach is giving me, trying to get in my head and make me crack, is expected. He thinks that because the guy isn't interested that I've gone completely loco.

"You believe him!"

"I didn't say that." He grumbles quietly, only serving to prove my point.

"You don't have to! You're staring at me like I did it, and when you try and deny it you're quieter than a mouse. That's a pretty dead giveaway, you know."

All of this is expected, but it doesn't make it hurt any less.

We're family.

Even if I had a 'thing' for Levi still, Zach should know me well enough by now to know I wouldn't do this.

Not to our dad, not to him, and definitely not to myself.

I'm better than that.

I'm better than Levi.

"Does he really hate the idea of fighting me so much that he'd be willing to make this crap up right before we're supposed to go out there?"

"The better question is what dad is gonna do when he gets wind of it. It's only a matter of time before Levi finds him and spouts off the same garbage." He sighs heavily. "I know you didn't do this, Kimber, but it looks really bad. We all know how into the guy you were not that long ago."

"Years ago! I had a little crush on the guy for a few weeks years ago, Zach. Am I gonna be crucified forever for a moment of stupidity?"

Plus, ever since Matthias showed up, it's more like Levi who?

"No. I'm gonna find dad and settle this. I just wanted you to know. I wanted to see for myself that you didn't do it. But when we're out there, if he thinks I'm gonna go easy on his ass after this stunt, he's got another thing coming."

Zach and I have never been super close. We basically tolerate each other, which has more to do with the age difference than anything we've actually done or any effort we might make to appease our parents. Until I started doing this, we'd always just done our own thing.

Standing here listening to him stand up for me though, believing in me despite his earlier comments to the contrary, is nice. It's one of those moments where I'm happy he's the brother I ended up with.

"Not if I end him first." I inform my brother and when his lip begins to quirk up, I grin.

Maybe we're not all that different after all.

It's time for Levi to learn an important lesson.

You don't mess with a Parker.

Matthias

The dynasty that Renegade has built is solid.

I figured it would be given the way he handled his shit in the ring during his heyday, but what he's put together, both in the tag team arena and singles matches, is better than I imagined.

Everyone I've caught sight of so far looks to be around my age or a little younger, yet the ease at which they move around the ring speaking to the way they've been taught. Making them all appear as though they've been doing it for centuries more than just months or years.

Absorbing their surroundings and the opponents they're going against and creating the best damn show they can possible to do in order to match it.

But it's not those guys I'm here to see. It's Will's son, Zachary. The guy that any minute is going to be making his way out with some random girl and putting on a show not only for the other people but for me too.

Time to see if the apple falls far from the tree.

"It's funny that of all the things you could have gotten into, you chose wrestling."

Looking up from the television and seeing her eyes locked on the action taking place on the screen before flicking her attention back to me with a soft smile, I return it with one of my own. Patting the floor, my smile widens when she actually takes me up on my offer and plats herself down on the carpet beside me.

"Why's it funny?"

"He'll never admit it, but before he threw his back out, your father used to wrestle. Not the way the guys on TV do, but he did win a few championships with his school when he was your age."

You're damn right he'll never admit it. Anything before his back went to shit is off limits. Even if it's something that in the long term might actually bond us.

"Apple doesn't fall too far from the tree, I guess, huh?"

"I wouldn't go that far, Matty. In a lot of ways, you're different than your father. It's only in this one that I see similarities."

Thank god for that. If there's one thing I know for certain, it's this.

I'm never going to be like Jonathan Kemper. No matter how shitty my life may get. I'm determined never to put the people I love through the hell that he has.

This apple won't fall anywhere near that god damned tree.

"He should be the one down on the floor with you, Matthias." She sighs and before I can argue that the right parent is with me, she continues. "I always knew this was the path you would take. I think we both knew it. From the moment you first saw it and we caught the gleam in your eye, we knew you would be here. I just wish he could see his way past the darkness inside himself so he could share it with you."

I spend the majority of my time disgusted by the way she takes up for him with the beatings he lays on her, but sometimes in moments like the one we're in now, I can also understand at least a little where she's coming from.

She loves him damn near as much as she does me, despite the ugliness of their relationship. She also knew the man before he turned into a monster. It's not exactly a bad thing that she wants to see the man she fell in love with again. Even if to the rest of the world it makes her look like a doormat. A willing participant in the abuse.

Truth is, I wouldn't mind getting my old man back either.

The light-hearted guy he was when he took me to my first wrestling event ten years ago.

"I want him to be a part of this too, but he doesn't want to be, Mom. He doesn't want to be a part of anything."

Reaching over as I see the tear slip its way out through her eye and wiping it away, sucking the watery substance from my fingers before leaning back on my hands and turning my attention to the television, I focus on the action taking place in the ring while attempting to swallow the urge I have to do the same.

Cry.

Sometimes remembering the way things used to be sucks. It makes you long for what deep down you know you'll never have *again. Where this is the first time in months my mom has been able to let her emotions out freely without fear of reprisal, I don't have the same luxury.*

I can't let her see how her breaking makes me crack. How badly I want to wrap my arms around her and hold her until all of this shit passes. I can't let her see me weakened because right now, I have a feeling I'm the only thing holding her together.

"So what do you think?" I turn and ask, motioning back to the TV where two of my favorites are going at it.

"I think that what they're doing to one another is all well and good…" she says, tapering off at the end before offering me a weak smile.

"But?"

"But the idea of you doing the same thing, getting your body beat on every night for the rest of your life, well, Matty, it scares the crap out of me."

Maybe what I said earlier is true after all. Only not for me and my old man.

The apple doesn't fall far from the tree in my case because just like she's scared, I am too.

Just not scared enough to give up and walk away.

Something else we share.

"Looks like that apple doesn't fall too far after all."

"Holy shit!" Bryan's voice breaks through the memory, bringing me back to the present. "Please tell me you're seeing this shit!"

"Seeing what?"

Following the direction of his hand as he points to the ring, I see exactly what it is he's talking about and my heart stops.

That little midget from before, the one Bryan referred to as Kimberlee, and the daughter of the man that wanted me here, is in the ring. But more than that, she's actually holding her own against a very *male* opponent. Something that while not unheard of in the world of pro wrestling, is a first for me since Smith wants nothing to do with it.

"She wrestles?"

"And well too!" Bryan exclaims, picking up his seat and dragging it across the floor until he's as close to the metal barricade as he can get. Completely mesmerized by the girl now executing a hurricanrana off the top rope.

A move she's obviously done before as she nails it to perfection. Capitalizing on her opponent and selling it to the crowd in the form of being completely stunned into submission as she pulls him into the pin.

I may have spaced out for a good portion of the very match I was supposed to be paying attention to, but it's definitely not Zach I'm interested in.

Maybe she's not the annoying little brat I thought she was.

"How old is this girl?"

"Fourteen, I think. Why?"

Following Bryan's lead and moving my chair closer to get a better look at the action as Kimberlee tags in her brother, I shrug.

"No reason. Just wondered. She's good."

"She's better than good, bro!" he slugs me in the arm. "Reminds me of someone though."

"Who?"

We've been in CPW for a while now, and even though Smith does employ his share of women, not a one of them compares to the one standing in the corner clapping her hands and motivating the crowd to get behind her brother.

I'm not sure anyone can.

"You really don't see it."

"See what, Bry?"

If he's trying to get me to see her quickness and ability, I already do. I've also seen just how into it she gets, going so far as to interact with the crowd in a way that has them nearly as pumped as she is. The sound reverberating back off the walls and making it hard to think, much less hear what my best friend has to say.

I'm just not sure what else there is to see. I've got it.

Kimberlee Parker is amazing.

"Matty, I know you're a little slow sometimes, but it's like looking in a mirror."

"Still not following. You're gonna have to spell it out."

"Matty, Kimber is you."

Chapter Eight
February 2007

Matthias

This is the stupidest shit I've ever heard, and considering who I share a locker room with, that's saying something.

I obviously didn't hear him right.

Since when is adopting a more aggressive style in the ring a bad thing? Isn't that the exact thing he wanted from me?

"Smith, I don't get it. So I knocked him out. It's not that big of a deal."

"There's a difference between ringing his bell for a few seconds and what you did, Matthias."

Says the guy that told me to beat the shit out of him in the hospital.

If he didn't want me doing things this way, why did he tell me to put the shit where it belongs?

I should have known it was too good to be true.

The offer from Renegade, how down with it Smith seemed to be. I should have seen it for what it was when it was offered. I mean, hell. Even Renegade's kid knew about my supposed 'issues'. If I had just listened to the brat instead of treating her like shit and blowing her off, maybe I could have cut this off at the pass.

"You damn near begged me to be aggressive! You said I was going too easy on the guys and you wanted to see what I could do unhinged. I gave you what you fucking wanted! And you're thanking me by sending me away?"

"I'm not sending you away. Renegade wants you there."

"Bullshit." I spit out, seething in anger. "He wants me there because you told him you wanted to get rid of me."

"Matty,' Bryan attempts to interject when unbeknownst to me he steps into the office. "That's not what this is."

"You can spare me, bro." I spin my venom around on him. "You knew what was going down the entire time. You're just as guilty as he is."

"I am." He agrees, and it's the opening he wants because with as pissed off as I am and with as many choice words as I've got for the both of these jerkoffs right now, I wasn't at all prepared for that. "I'm guilty because I saw you bust a guy wide open for real in the ring. I saw his blood pouring out onto the mat and you not letting up. Referee's pouring all over you, and you slinging them off like some kind of animal. That's not what you signed on to do."

What the fuck does he know?

Bryan's got the perfect damn life. He's set for life here with Smith because the old fucker knows what he's got in me and wouldn't dream of pissing me off by getting rid of the one person that despite it all has remained in my corner. He's got two parents that adore his ass and who will drop everything to be there for him. A girlfriend that half the fucking high school wanted but that he got.

He doesn't know shit about me and what I signed up for.

Except he does. He's the only damn one that does.

"I signed on to kick ass."

"No, son. You signed on to entertain. To wrestle. What you did out there, in case you need a reminder, wasn't entertainment. It was assault with the deadliest of weapons." Lowering his gaze to my fists and taking it a step further and drifting all the way down to my knees, I get the picture.

My body was the weapon.

I didn't go out to the ring and put on a five-star match wrestling aficionados would be creaming their jeans over. I went out there and threw every bit of anger I had into a match that I made sure turned into a blood bath. Taking a solid performer in Grant "the Pulveriser" Yates and breaking him. Making it so he was off getting a brain scan instead of outrunning spots with the guys where he should be.

Bryan is right. I took things too far. Lost control.

And now I'm paying the price.

Getting to spend any amount of time with Will "Renegade" Parker should make me the one unloading in my jeans, but given what it took to get it to happen, it's nothing but a punishment. I'm paying for the shit storm I created. For the match that people will be talking about for generations to come, but not for the reasons they should be.

"How long?" I whisper hiss as the steam billowing out of my ears finally begins to dissipate.

"A couple of months. Maybe three. Despite what you've talked your dumb ass into believing, this isn't a punishment, son. Renegade does want you there working with his kid."

His kid.

The only one of those springing to mind, not the guy, but the girl with the eyes. Eyes that even though they belong to a snotty little brat, still managed to seep into my subconscious and make themselves at home. Eyes with the power to heal. Haunt. Destroy whatever gets in their path. The fire I'd seen there calling her a little girl more than enough indicator of that.

Her I want to train.

If only to see if the fire I saw simmering there during our first meeting transfers over into the matches she's a part of. See once and for all if what Bryan said the day we were at the show is true and she really is me.

But you know, the better looking version.

"Zach is looking forward to it, Matty. Talking to Renegade, it's been all the kid's been able to talk about since you showed up."

"What about the girl?" I curiously ask, ignoring pretty much everything Bryan's said in order to get what really matters. "Am I training her too?"

"Not a chance." Smith interrupts. "You know the rules. No way in hell you're going there and fighting a girl. Any chance of getting you over after that would be shot to hell, no matter how good a pounding she can take."

He means nothing by it, but with the swiftness of my fist clenching and the swirl of rage I feel building in my brain that's threatening to change the dynamic of the conversation very quickly, I'm ready to strike.

I wasn't exactly nice to the girl when we met, but after watching what she can do when she's given the chance in the ring, I can't help taking offense for her.

Women have been looked at as pieces of ass for so long in this fucking business, that to see one with pure heart and a boatload of talent be denied the chance to work with someone her father thinks is worthy, is just plain wrong.

Making what I was initially against, now all I wanna do.

I will work with Kimberlee Parker, and when I'm done, it won't be just me and Bryan seeing what she brings to the table. What she means and will mean for the future of the Women's Division.

Everyone will.

"Book the ticket. I'm in."

Kimberlee

"You have got to be kidding me!" I shriek after my father delivers the news of Matthias Kemper's impending arrival. "He's a complete nut job! Why the hell would you want to do business with someone as unpredictable as him? Did you not see what he did to Pulveriser? He took him out of action indefinitely!"

My dad has always been one of the smartest businessmen I know. Okay fine. He's the only one I know, but that's really beside the point. All of the years he spent in the ring made his ability to pick and work with those worthy of being the best, unmatched. There hasn't been a guy—Levi aside—that he's brought through here that hasn't gone out to bigger and better things.

He still has to make a splash in a big way where the women are concerned, but that's what I'm here for. I'm his secret weapon. The world won't know what hit them when I'm through here and rising to the top. Bringing all of those other girls that come through here wanting to be something, some of them even being worthy of it, with me.

He'll get there when I'm there.

In every other way though, I've always admired his uncanny ability to see through egotistical bullshit, find the strengths in guys that seemingly have none, and bring them out for the rest of the world to see. It's a good part of the reason why in the end this is what I chose to do. I had two amazing role models to guide me. So did Zach.

Which is why this deal he's worked out with Radley Smith to bring in and use Matthias for the next few months is the craziest thing I've ever heard.

He's still young. He's got a lot of life left in him. I've seen it. But is it possible my dad has taken one too many kicks to the head and he's finally losing his marbles?

God. Of all the guys he could have told us about tonight, that crazy SOB wasn't one I expected.

After treating me like I wasn't worthy enough to breathe the same damn air as him and then ignoring me for the rest of the night, he'd dug his grave even more when he sat back with my dad a couple hours after the show and ripped Zach apart.

My brother and I might not always get along, but the only one allowed to attack his style in the ring is my dad.

Matthias Kemper can kiss my ass.

"I'm well aware of what happened with Grant. That isn't up for discussion, nor is there any dispute that he took things too far. The boy is struggling, Kimberlee. I wouldn't expect you to understand. There are some things about Matthias you don't know."

There are things about Matthias that I don't care to know either.

"Spare me, dad. We've all got shit going on. Doesn't mean we have to step in the ring and take it out on someone who we're trained to keep safe. Matthias is no better than the bullies you used to have to go to school and deal with for Zach."

"Young lady, what did I tell you about that language? Now, I didn't have to sit you down and tell you this. I could have easily just brought him in and forced your hands in working with him. I didn't. I had enough respect for the both of you to bring it to you so you were prepared. How about you show me and Matthias the same?"

"Respect is earned, Dad. Isn't that what you've been drilling into our heads for years?" I snidely respond, not backing down even when he levels his angry brown irises my way, lips straight, jaw hardened. I don't care if he's pissed off. He's not gonna change my mind on this stupid acquisition he's made.

I hate it. I'm always going to hate it.

Even if Matthias is hotter than some of the bands I've got posters off on my wall.

Yep. Not even then.

I hate him.

Hate this.

"It is earned, and from where I'm sitting, you're the only one being disrespectful, young lady. So don't make me say it again. Knock it off or I'll make sure you never take another step in a ring again."

There's only one way he knows of that can make me fall in line and of course he's using it.

With the struggle it took to get him to agree to let me do this in the first place, especially since I have another four years before I'm even legal to do it anywhere else, the last thing I want to do is piss him off enough so that he reaches out to all of those contacts he's made over the years and has me blackballed.

I can hear the wheels spinning in your head right now. *He's your father, he wouldn't do something like that to you.* You obviously don't know William Parker. He'll do whatever he wants, whenever he wants. Pulling me away from something I know I can be the absolute best at would be easy. Just another parenting decision done right for him.

Even if to me it would be so damn wrong.

"Kimber," Zach finally interrupts, taking a swallow of his water and turning to me. "Shut up."

"Dad!"

"He's got a point. You're taking things too far. Making more of this than there needs to be. Besides, your brother wants him here. You know after going over his performance lately, he wants to bring in as many different people as he can to help him change things up."

I'm *thisclose* to stomping my foot straight through the ground and I don't care how much trouble it would get me into or how childish I would look.

I'm fourteen, not five, and I know what I'm talking about. This is a mistake, even if it's what Zach wants.

Why can't they see that?

"You better not expect me to work with him." I mutter, forking another bite of dinner into my mouth and chewing as loudly as possible to block out whatever is next in their tag team effort.

"He's here for your brother, Kimber. You've made your feelings known, so I expect you to stay out of it. It doesn't concern you."

"You better not ruin this for me." Zach leans over hissing before I can even formulate a response for my dad. "He's good. One of the best. If there's anyone that can teach me how to be better, it's him. So listen to Dad and stay the fuck out of it."

"Zachary." Dad growls and there's no hiding my smug smile. It's about damn time Zach was treated like my equal. Screw the different rules for girls crap. It's all or nothing.

"Sorry, Dad, but it's true. This has nothing to do with her."

He's wrong. It has everything to do with me since this is a family operation. But if they want me to knock it off, I will. At least for now.

All bets are off when he shows up though.

Matthias may not work with me, may not end up anywhere near me during his time here, but he will pay.

No one calls Kimberlee Parker a little girl and gets away with it.

Chapter Nine

Matthias

Parkers Gym.

Where boys come to be made into men. Err—rather, boys come to have their asses whooped on hard by William Parker.

Same difference really.

For the next few months though, it's where I'm going to have my attitude adjusted.

Smith can say he's sending me here so I can get my head on straight, or even that it's happening because Renegade personally requested that I work with his son, but I know the truth. We all do. I'm here because if things had just gone down one smidge different than they did, I'd be in a cell right now looking at homicide charges.

I get where everyone was coming from now, wanting me away from everything that for the better part of the year I've spent living without her, continues to haunt me.

It's just a bitter pill to swallow.

There has been one thing that in being driven by pure desire to step into the ring and do this for the rest of my life, I've always prided myself on. Safety. Keeping the person in the ring with me as safe as he does me. Having the respect for the guys I work with and making sure that in putting on the best damn show possible, I'm also taking precautions against exactly what happened in the ring that night.

Losing my shit, pummeling him within an inch of his life, that's not Matthias fucking Kemper.

That's what's left after love, loss and death itself got through making him its bitch.

You see? I get it.

I screwed up, and this is a punishment that's more blessing than curse. It's a chance, not a write-off.

I just wish it didn't have to involve my best friend.

Smith shipping me off to parts unknown and making me pay for my mistakes, makes sense. Bryan knowing about it long before it was even dropped in my lap and then lying to me, selling it as something it most definitely isn't, that's where shit gets muddled in my head.

Since when did he switch sides? Work against me instead of for me?

Some would argue he is working for me still, but I just happen to not be one of them.

So not only is my family fractured and basically non-existent, but now so is my relationship with my best friend.

Staring at the door, I lift my hand to the raised golden plate bearing the name of one of my idols. Taking my time, I run one finger, then two, over the grooves and indents in the metal that make up the name and the place. Letting the magnitude of what I'm about to do and who I'm about to do it with sink in before finally dropping my hand with a heavy laden sigh to the doorknob, gripping it tightly before twisting and shoving my way inside.

Slinging my now slipping bag back over my shoulder, my eyes immediately gravitate toward the ring as they always do whenever I`m in a place as reverent as this. A church of sorts. At least to all that make their way into the building and the squared circle that awaits. What I find though, it's not expected.

Instead of Renegade center in the ring with his son, it's a much smaller form. Catching a height unknown to most of the ladies in CPW—men too—she flies through the air from the top rope and down hard in a splash to the poor idiot stupid enough to face her.

Kimberlee Parker.

The wicked little one with the penchant for making people eat their doubts of her.

Also the girl with the knee-weakening eyes that no matter where I've gone since our first meeting, are always there just on the periphery of my mind. Eating away at what's left of my tortured and fractured soul. The pieces that my mom didn't take with her when she died. Speaking to me. Informing me that she knows more than I've told and she sees it all. That nothing is hidden and I'm the open book my mother always told me I was.

Basically she's the bane of my current existence.

But shit, she's a talented one.

Moving toward the ring but keeping my steps slow and deliberate, not wanting to let on to my arrival, I study the three people in the ring as the person who had been flat on his back moments before demonstrates a kick up to Kimber and motions to the mat for her to drop and attempt to do it herself.

After watching her false start, she finally throw her legs back as far as they can from her position with her back flat against the mat, and in the time it takes me to suck in a breath and blink, she's on her feet. All the air stripped from my lungs as she does the strangest thing. Her lips curving up, her mouth dropping open just slightly, and her eyes coming alive as she grins.

This isn't your typical grin of happiness. This, what she's doing, is something more.

It's electric.

She's damn proud of herself, smug even. An innocent expression that even though it's been years since I've worn it myself, I'd recognize anywhere.

She just learned something she'll incorporate into the way she wrestles and is already mentally planning uses for it where it will have the most impact in the future.

She's a planner, this girl.

Bryan was fucking right.

She's me and even my body is aware of it. The fine hairs on my arms rising and goosebumps appearing as the rest of my body hums and damn near sputters to life like an old beater one expects never to work again.

Kimber's age, her innocence, is altering me.

She's breathing new life into what until I walked in the door a few minutes ago, had been a lifeless shell. Empty. Completely devoid of everything it takes to function.

Jesus. I've got my work cut out for me with this one.

Renegade, stepping back and over to the opposite corner of the ring spots me and winks before turning his attention back to his daughter and who after he calls the guy by name, I realize is one of ten trainers he's got under his employ.

Barking out in the same angry garble as Smith for him to run bumps with her, he slips through the ropes and down to the mats on the floor. Eyeing me suspiciously before making his way over and slapping his arm down hard across my shoulder blade.

"Thanks for taking the time."

Taking the time, my ass.

Pretty sure he's as aware of the reason I'm here as everyone else that was involved in making it happen. Swallowing down the urge to shred him the way I did Bryan and Smith before making my way here, I just grunt.

"If you're planning on working with my boy, you're gonna need some work yourself." He states, his voice even without the slightest tinge of annoyance. "For starters, lose the damn chip."

"Don't know what you're talking about."

"Sure you don't. So Grant ending up in the hospital, you know nothing 'bout that, huh?"

Well, I nailed that.

"I made a mistake. One. Goddamned. Time."

It's in the way I answer him and the smirk that rises on his face that I finally screw my head on straight and admit defeat. That damn chip he's talking about, it's still clearly there and as big, raw, and jagged as always. If this is gonna work, I've gotta can the bullshit. Even if my first choice of handling this is bringing the man beside me to the ground.

Clearly I need more work than even Smith thought.

"Look, son. Smith called me before you hit the road. Explained the reasoning you're coming in with for why you're here. What you need to get square with is that's all your own bullshit. I brought you here because Zach's been going on about ya for months now. Loves the fact that you don't stick to one particular style and like to dip into all the pots. Says I'm too old to get it, but it's exciting. Figure he might have a point, so here you are."

"So it really is like you said a few months back? You're not cashing in now because of what happened with Grant?"

"Truth be told, that fucker needed to be brought down a few pegs. Don't like the way you dealt with it, but can't go back and change it. Shit happened. So pick up your tights, strap in, and make sure the next time it happens, it has a different ending."

Motioning with my head to the ring and pointing, I laugh when he shakes his head. Almost as though he knows what I'm about to say next.

"That what you had in mind for a different ending?"

"Don't even get me started on that one, Kemper. She's my daughter and I love her, but there's no talking her out of this shit. Stubborn as her old man. Maybe even more so."

"She's good though." I admit honestly, which only seems to make the scowl beginning, fall deeper into his features. "How long has she been doing this?"

"Almost four years, despite her mother and I's insistence that she choose something more appropriate."

I know next to nothing about their family and even less about Kimberlee Parker, but something about the way he says it, the exasperation woven in his words, rubs me the wrong way.

How many times did my old man call me worse than a girl and make sure to knock into my head that what I wanted to do was a pipe dream destined to go nowhere?

Every damn day. Even worse, for a while there, I even believed the shit he was spewing.

If it wasn't for my mom and then Bryan later, I don't think I'd be standing here talking to Renegade.

Kimberlee just needs someone to be that way with her too. *Someone like you.*

Shaking and ridding myself of the nonsense my mind is spewing, I put my attention back on the ring again, but instead of seeing her in various stages of bump taking the way her father demanded, she's going toe to toe with her trainer, first blocking an aerial move and then delivering one hell of a shot of her own as her leg extends and damn near knocks his head off.

"Is this normally how you run things?"

One of the reasons professional wrestling seems to speak so easily to everyday people is because it's like a dance of sorts. Each person at any given moment in the match, able to predict the moves they've gone over, how they're gonna fall and take them in a way that lessens the impact. Watching Kimber now, it's as though Renegade has thrown that out in the window in favor of a rougher style.

One where every hit, every kick or spot, hits its mark. *Hard.*

"No, but she needs some sense knocked into her."

I'm not a parent. Pretty sure I'm never gonna be one either, so I really don't have the right to judge the way he does things with his kids. But having his daughter actually taking the full brunt of some of these moves, bringing her to her knees and damn near knocking the life out of her, doesn't seem like the way to go. If anything, it's only going to make her want it more.

That's how it went down for me and as she takes her opponent down, pulls his leg up and pins him, even using her free hand to hit the mat, something tells me we're not all that different in that regard either.

"Alright! That's enough!" Renegade barks out, slapping me across my back again before hopping back up onto the apron and getting back into the ring. Making his way over and pulling his trainer up and beginning to converse quietly, his back completely turned on his daughter.

Studying her reaction to what's taking place, I'm struck by the way her eyes sink in, her brow tightens and her lips go ramrod straight. But that's not all. If my eyes aren't deceiving me, her foot is also twitching. At least it is before she stomps it down hard onto the mat in annoyance.

She's being ignored.

She's got every damn right to react the way she is. Seeing the way it's all transpiring, I can actually feel some of the childhood adoration I had for the man known as Renegade begin to dissipate.

Kimber deserves better than this.

What are you waiting for, big guy? Get in the ring and make it better if you really think she deserves it.

Giving into the voice, the familiar burn inside to go my own way driving me, I do just that. Calling out to her father at the exact moment her voice filters across the ring and straight down to where I'm standing. My name falling bitterly as her hand extends and she points directly to me.

"You!" she sneers, to the chagrin of her father as he shakes his head. "You're supposed to be the best in CPW right? Unpredictable, erratic, but entertaining? Since Tom doesn't seem to want to fight a girl, why don't you do it?"

It comes out as a question but when she quickly follows it up with more heavily loaded words based on the reputation I've been building for myself over the last couple of years, it turns into more.

She's making a statement at my expense.

What she doesn't get is, I'm gonna let her have it.

I want her to have it all.

Me included.

"Wanna prove you're the best? Get in here and show me what you've got. That is, if you're not afraid of having your ass kicked by a girl the way the rest of this damn place is."

"Kimberlee Rose Parker!" Renegade attempts to admonish, and flipping him the bird, she steps closer to the edge of the ropes, her eyes falling down to my place on the ground, lip raising into a twisted grin.

"If Matthias is the one to beat, I want first crack at him. I wanna see if he's as good as he says." Smiling sweetly at her dad before turning back and leveling me with the coldest set of eyes I've ever seen, she smirks. "Surely if he's the God everyone speaks of, he won't mind working with me."

Turning to Renegade at the exact moment his head starts shaking emphatically, I'm drawn back to her when she stomps on the mat, following it up with a low growl at what she knows is going to be his refusal.

Come on, Renegade. I've got her. Let us do this. I plead with the man, albeit silently. Not wanting to rock the boat so soon after showing up, but wanting this almost as badly as she does.

This is why I'm here after all.

Her.

Batting her eyes sweetly and leaning her head on her hands, she waits him out and after a few seconds and a few choice curse words spit under his breath the same way I've seen Smith do, his shoulders finally sag in defeat and he gives in.

"Fine, but you go slow. Easy. I don't wanna see who has the bigger balls of the two of you." When no response comes from Kimber, his cold gaze turns to me and after a quick shudder from the intensity, I give him what he's after, nodding. "I see you pulling anything like you did the last time you were in a ring and you'll be going back to Smith in a god damned body bag. We clear?"

"Crystal." I whisper, shaking off the very real chill I experience from his words. My next words falling in a whisper. "I'll keep her safe."

"Good." He grumbles before turning back to his daughter. "No low blows this time."

When she grins and winks, an obvious story dying to be told behind his threat, he turns his back again and begins walking toward the door with Tom, leaving the two of us to our own devices.

"You gonna do this or what?"

Kimberlee

If my mom was here and saw the way I'm behaving, she'd be questioning just what the hell has gotten into me. Most likely believing that taking all the hits I have been today, I'd scrambled my brains.

Talking back to my dad, exerting a level of confidence so huge it's practically unheard of around here, and pushing myself on Matthias? It really is like I've lost my mind.

Parkers, more specifically the ladies, we don't behave like this.

Screw that, I say. I might be my mom's girl most days, but when I'm in the ring and fighting to prove my worth, I'm definitely Will Parker's kid. Equal parts stubborn and stupid, Zach likes to tell me. But since he's not here and Daddy's now turning his back and leaving me with Matthias, I'm gonna be as stupid as it takes.

Kemper needs a reality check. A wake up call. God, with everything I've read about him, he probably needs a hell of a lot more than what a beating can provide.

But that's none of my business. I just wanna kick his ass. Prove once and for all just what this *brat* can do.

First things first? Knocking that stupid ass smirk off his face. "Did you hear me or do I need to repeat myself?"

Keeping the smirk firmly in place, he answers me by jumping up on the apron and sliding into the ring, each step he takes once he's in, calculated. As if he's trying to get me even more riled as he stalks forward, stopping directly in front of me and shifting back and forth on his feet, waiting me out.

Blowing out a heavy exhale of air and shifting the stray tendrils of hair in his eyes away from his face, I inch closer. The warmth that follows once I've stepped so close I can actually feel the waves of heat just rolling off him, completely enveloping me and making me forget for a split second just how badly I want to lay a beating on him.

My mind and body reacting in a way that speaks to the opposite.

The tingling sensation making its way through my veins all the way up to my head as the blood rushes in heavy and warm, making me acutely aware of just how close he is. How easy it would be to press my body to his. How in just the time it takes to suck in a breath, my body aches with the need to wrestle him to the ground, but not to beat him.

To give in to him.

Groaning and earning a chuckle from the peanut gallery, I scowl, but unsure at what. Myself or him, I can't be sure. All I know is that this reaction, this awareness, isn't wanted, but oh so easy to give into.

We had the talk last week, my mom and me. What all of these feelings and reactions mean.

I'm becoming a woman she said. It's natural to feel all of these intense emotions toward members of the opposite sex. God, she talked to me like she was reciting lines from a self-help book, but with the way my body overheats, my breath catches and releases, and my heart seem to quicken and then beat in time with Matthias's own, it's the only thing keeping me grounded in place.

This is all biological.

I'm reacting because he's a guy, he's older, and he just happens to be gorgeous. Ice blue eyes, rugged jaw, defined body, and hair that just begs to be reached out and touched. Fingers running through, getting tangled and maybe, just maybe as his breath warms my face as he talks to me before bending down and giving into this ignited fire between us kissing me, hair that demands to be tugged on roughly as he has his way with me.

Breathe Kimber.

Shaking myself free of the hormones and swallowing down every indecent thought, I ball my hands into fists. Nails digging into the skin of my hands as I wait for his own arms to rise in an effort to lock up.

Come on, Matthias. Give me this. Put my head back where it belongs.

My plea falling on deaf ears as when he does finally shift his gaze to my face and away from my body as a whole, it's not a passing glance, but a full on stare. Intense. Heavy. As though just looking at me this way, every part of me is exposed. Every secret I'm trying to hold onto, ripped open like a favorite book and exposed for him to see.

He sees me.

Lips parting and a ragged breath releasing and falling over me, he smile. And even though I know I shouldn't trust it, there's something so genuine about it that makes it impossible to fight against. It's really as though with the intensity in his stare and the smile, he really does see me. Sees what it is I want and wants to give it to me.

Please God, don't let me be reading him wrong.

Raising his arms in the air, he nods in my direction and it's on. We're locking up and all of that angst—the hormonal overload—it's out the window as I push back against him. Ignoring as best I can how weak the lockup is from his end, but failing with as I finally let the anger I have for this guy and his accomplishments take over and I'm shoving everything I've got into him. Moving him back until I can feel his back bouncing off the ropes.

Releasing a series of chops across his chest, quick and impulsive in an attempt to keep him locked in place, I gear up for another round. But right before I can land the first of what will be many, his hands come up defensively and in surrender.

Pausing, his hand hanging in the hair between us, I use the moment to take a breath as he calls out for my dad.

"Renegade! Shit! I can't do this."

Oh no you don't, asshole! I silently scream, finally releasing the control on my arm and letting it come down across his chest again. Catching his gaze the second his eyes flick back to me, everything changes.

The air around us and what he's trying like hell to hide. It all comes out.

His anger. His rage.

The very things that once ignited inside him, he'd used to take out Yates.

Gifting him with a twisted smile at the sight, I giggle, and that's when nice Matthias breaks free of his final restraints and attacks. Ducking and slipping around me as I attempt to land another shot to his midsection, his arms are around my waist in seconds and I'm ripped straight off my feet as he brings me flipping over with a suplex. My body hitting the mat in a heap, the selling of his move easy considering the shockwave of pain now drifting swiftly through me.

Straddling me on the mat, he emulates chops across my chest, all while slapping his own and that's when I hear it. The raised voice of my father yelling Matty's name.

Meeting his eyes and finding the same look I'd seen before we even locked up, everything becomes clear. He really *is* doing this for me.

The reaction from my dad. The way he's landing chops quickly against his own chest where no one else can see. How he guides my body with his own to react—to sell—and I writhe around on the mat as if I've actually been hit.

He's making a point.

Matthias is not the enemy.

He's just a guy, seeing what I hoped would have been clear as day to my father, and giving it to me.

The attention I've spent the better part of two years trying to earn.

"I'm gonna stomp the mat. When I do it, sell it and when you're done, get your knees up in the air."

Breath hot against my face, I momentarily lose myself in the set of his jaw, the fire in his eyes and the warmth that floods me as his lips land a hairs breath from mine.

Gulping as he shifts away and stomps the mat as directed, I do what he says when turning his back, he heads for the ropes. I put together his next move and after making it appear as though I'm stunned by hit from his boots, I wait him out. Timing the raise of my knees with his move and the air he catches as he dives off the rope. Sucking in as much air as I can and lifting, having them hit their mark when I feel the pressure of his midsection heavy across my much smaller legs.

Summoning up as much strength as I can, I harden them against the pressure until I feel it being stripped away as he takes the hit and falls back hard against the mat. The breathless whisper of *elbow drop* heaved from his lips before his eyes closed and he gives into the moment. Proving himself to be the caliber of performer everyone says he is and making me eat all my earlier hate again as he sets me up for what I just know is going to be a win.

Stomping him with my boot a couple of times, I use the ropes to my advantage and ride them from one end of the ring to the other, gaining momentum and speed until after the second run back and forth, I deliver the move he asked for in a hard elbow. Quickly flipping to my feet and after climbing the ropes, executing a moonsault off the top, landing on him before falling backwards into my own heap.

"Three seconds," I hiss over, to which he twitches his acceptance. "I'm gonna kick up and set you in the figure four."

"Sounds good, little one."

Shoving my boot down hard into him after I've executed the perfect kick up, I continue to lay boots into him, laughing when he curls into himself.

That'll teach him. I'm not a little anything.

Grabbing his leg and twisting it in, just like I've been practicing for weeks, I slap on the leg lock, and after putting forth a valiant yet forced effort to break free of the move, he finally taps the mat.

"Little one can hit." His whispered admiration washes over me as I spring to my feet in victory. Making my way over to the corner of the ring and accepting the now waiting bottle of water from Tom as my father makes his way over to Matthias.

"You should see what I do when you call me a brat." I bite out, taking his extended hand when after skirting around my old man, he makes his way over and pulls me to my feet.

"I'm looking forward to finding out."

Winking, he makes his way back over to where my father awaits and watching the two of them as they begin to converse, the familiar rumblings from before begin to rear their ugly head.

Matthias may have been physically appealing before, but now, it's something more. Something much stronger.

There's admiration simmering. Respect growing.

And as he turns mid-conversation and our eyes meet again, both of us silent, our gazes lingering, it happens. It's small and foreign compared to the ones he's already given me since his arrival, but there's no mistaking it.

Matthias is smiling, as genuine a smile as I think he can give.

And it's in that smile that it happens.

I start to fall.

Chapter Ten

March 2007

Matthias

If there's one thing in pro wrestling that you can be assured of, it's that when you screw up you're paying for it.

Sure, the punishments may vary, and with all the talk these days of pro wrestling being more entertainment than sport, they definitely don't seem as hardcore as some other sports, but they're still there.

After what happened between me and Grant a few weeks back, I knew it was only a matter of time before Smith slammed the hammer down and dished out just what my punishment would be. So after working for a couple of hours with Renegade's son, Zach, with little to no interruptions and having Renegade bark out for me to meet him in the house, I know what's coming.

I'm about the pay the piper.

About time, I say.

It had taken about a week for me to lose the chip Will said I was carrying when I walked in here, but lose it I did, and for the last two weeks have stayed behind the scenes helping work with his two kids and a couple of the younger guys, minding my business and my place. I no longer looked at being here as the punishment I thought it was, and it seems now I know why it was so easy.

After making my way through the front door and stepping into his office, he wastes no time filling me in on just what I'm doing there the second my butt plants itself hard onto the metal folding chair.

"Matthias, you know how much I enjoy having you here working with the guys. You're an asset to me and this place." He motions around the room. "But I think it's time we discuss why you've been kept off the shows we've had. Why I've regulated you more to the background than you should be."

"It's Grant." I announce, not wanting to waste my time or his skirting around the real issue.

Let's just call a damn spade a spade.

"Yeah, son. It's because of what happened with Pulveriser." He easily admits. "But you gotta know that keeping you off wasn't what Smith wanted. He did it because of the pressure he was getting from Yates's family."

I respect Renegade a hell of a lot, but what he's doing is bullshit. I damn near ended a man's life. If Smith didn't deal with me, I would have found a way to deal with myself. It's what you have to do. I don't care if it really was pressure from Grant's family. At the end of the day, I took things too far and I need to own it. Even if it costs me food money for the next few months.

"You and I both know it was the right move, so don't pussyfoot around it, Renegade. I think I've managed to earn your respect since I've been here. I'd hate to have that messed with because you felt the need to placate me."

Humming under his breath, he rubs the stubble coming in across his jaw while staring me down. I've seen this response a lot since I've gotten here. Hell, it's familiar as fuck back home too. Bryan wears it a lot.

He's clearly surprised at the way I'm reacting.

I'm a hot head, I admit it. I've been that way for a while. I don't use outlets the way I'm supposed to and half the damn time, I block them out altogether. But, even knowing that's how I am, it doesn't last forever. There is always a time where the light bulb goes off, I pull my head out of my ass and think about things logically.

"How long?" I pull his attention away from his quiet studying of me and ask.

"Three months."

Well, I'm three and a half weeks through the first month of being here, so that's not too bad. I've only got a little over sixty days left in my exile and things will be square. At least they will be when I finally get home and stand in front of the man I hurt anyway. I'm not stepping back into a show for Smith until that happens. Grant is owed that much.

He didn't ask for what he got, same as I didn't ask to be filled with all the rage in order to make it happen.

I'm gonna make this shit right for everyone.

"How deep does it run, Will? What can I actually do for you?"

"You can be here and train, but when there's media you're regulated to the house."

In other words, I'm taking care of the shit he's slacking off on in his family life.

"You can't be anywhere near a show for the next nine weeks. I know its bullshit, Matty, but this was all they would agree on."

"Will there be charges?"

"No. Grant's awake and adamant that what happened wasn't your fault. He refuses to let his family take things any further than they already have. Considering what a shit brick he can be most days, I'd say he's giving you a gift with just the suspension."

That he is and when I get back, I plan on thanking him for it. Shit brick or not.

"Okay."

"Okay?" he eyes me suspiciously.

"Yeah. I knew it wasn't gonna be pretty, and it's not, but bitching about it isn't gonna change anything. I'll serve my time, do what I can while I'm here and make it right when I get home."

Raising my ass off the chair, I pause when his hand flies up before motioning back toward it.

"There's something else I wanted to talk to you about while I've got you here."

"Sure, boss. What's up?"

"Kimber."

Oh fuck. I should have bolted while I had the chance. His daughter is the last person I want to get into. Especially with the way things have been going between us since I got here.

Why so uncomfortable, Matthias? Afraid the man might know more about your fascination with his daughter than you thought? Come on, you know he does. He has to have seen the looks passing between the two of you. You never were good at hiding them. How about how hard you get when you've got her in a pin position?

"What," I gulp and swallow nervously, shoving the voice and its accusations down. "What about her?"

"I've been watching the two of you over the last few weeks." *Here it comes. He does know.* "Seen the changes she's made. She's come a long way under your tutelage."

Phew. Okay. Breathe Matthias.

"She's a quick study, Renegade. A sponge for this shit, really. Don't know how much more I can teach her."

Here's my chance. All of my internal bullshit aside, especially my physical reaction to a girl I know to be seven years too damn young, this is my chance to talk him around to seeing what the rest of the damn place does. Talk him into giving her a push.

Kimberlee has the ability to be main event player here and it's about damn time her old man realized it.

He's sitting on a goldmine.

"She's gonna have a rough road ahead of her, son. I don't expect to you to know what I mean, seeing as you're pretty wet behind the ears yourself, but I'm sure you're aware of how some of the other promoters will treat her."

He's right about that. For a long time women weren't taken as seriously in this business as their male counterparts. They were regulated to managerial positions or even ones where they were holding a microphone as they talked to the actual performers. It's only here in the last ten or fifteen years where that seems to be shifting. Especially since women previously thought of as tits and ass made a point of proving they could be more.

Smith is a lot like the older promoters. He's stuck in the Stone Age in terms of how he uses the female talent, but day by day, he's seeing the light. One day soon, I think he'll realize what I'm standing here wanting his buddy to get.

That his daughter is better than half the CPW roster.

"I know how things were run before, hell, how they still are, Renegade. But she's tough. She's got more balls than half the guys I work with back home. She can handle herself. Pretty sure with the ass whipping she enjoys giving me, she can kick it into their massively thick skulls."

I'm not expecting his boisterous and deep belly laugh, but there's no denying I enjoy it. It means I'm getting somewhere. Even if I've gotta make him laugh to do it, I'll get him to look past his daughter to the natural born performer underneath.

Maybe if you kiss her ass even harder, she'll let you see what lies beneath the gear.

"Fuck off." I hiss and lifting my head, realize by the widened eyes of the man currently allowing me under his wing, I've been caught.

"What was that?" Renegade probes, pretending as though he hadn't heard anything, but me knowing better.

"Nothing, sorry." I blow him off with a wave of my hand. "So was that all you wanted to say about Kimber?"

"As a matter of fact, no. I was going to ask you for a favor. I know after delivering the bomb about your in-ring suspension, you're probably not feeling in a giving mood, but I'd really like you to give it some thought."

"What did you need?"

"I know I brought you down to work with Zach and you've been keeping your end of the deal, but I think I wanna pull you off that for a couple of weeks. Have you work with someone else."

Here he goes again. He's beating around the bush. He wants me to work with Kimber. He alluded to it not two seconds ago, so leaving her name out now is stupid.

"You sure you're gonna be alright with me working with your little girl?"

Please say no. I silently beg, not wanting to pay any credence to the voice from earlier that sounds a hell of a lot like my old man, but needing to at the moment because, despite my annoyance with it, it's fucking right.

My body has reacted to her in the ring. Her eyes have been haunting me for the weeks I've been here. And the first thing I think about when I roll off the damn cot in the back room every morning *is* her.

Kimber is with me everywhere. Mind and body.

"To tell you the truth, she hasn't had the best track record with the guys around her age, and even if she did, I wouldn't trust half of them as far as I could throw them. I've seen you with the other girls, Matthias. You're quiet. Respectful. You take the time to listen to them. So to answer your question, there's no one else here apart from Zach that I do trust with her."

For fuck sakes. I'm screwed.

But instead of manning the fuck up and telling him I'd feel more comfortable sticking with the original plan, that's not what falls out of my mouth when I finally separate my dry as fuck lips to speak.

No. What I say is ten times worse.

"You make sure I manage to eat in order to stay alive over the next two months and you've got yourself a deal."

✳✳✳✳✳

"You two have been at each other's throats for weeks. Starting the match with a standard lockup is boring. So when she goes to lock up, meet her, Kimber, but keep it loose. Then, before she can tell the difference, kick her in the stomach. Knock her off guard. Rachel, when she does it, sell it. Hunch over, fall to your knee, whatever. But make a production of it so she can take a run at the ropes, charge you and hit you with a punt.

It's a long shot, but I can see it all unfolding in my head. Kimberlee, having already decided she works much better as a heel, needs to do something to make an impact, and with as over with the crowd as Rachel seems to be, hitting a move with that much impact off the top, well it would give her the heat she's after.

She'd be vilified by the crowd.

Of course, there's also the matter of what will happen if the move goes wrong or it's not sold the way it seems to be in my head. I need to tread carefully. Sure, they can go as hard as the guys sometimes, but they're still not built the same. Something Rachel must agree on with the scowl she's aiming my way.

"Are you trying to set a record for how fast a match ends?" she snaps and instead of feeding into her upset, I just smile and shake my head. My hair falling down across my eyes at the exact moment I catch Kimberlee cover her mouth with her hands in order to hide a laugh.

I guess the term Diva was coined for this girl. I can already see her being a problem for my vision for this match.

"No, Rach. She's gonna go for the pin but you're gonna kick out."

"Yeah," Kimber interjects, the smile now plastered across her face damn near mirroring my own. "That's when I'll pull you to your feet, give you a few chops across the chest, knocking you back against the ropes and before I get the chance to deliver another one, you slap me hard across the face. Sure, it's cheap and simple, but it will stun me just enough for you to take a breath before laying a full-blown assault on me."

It's easy to see that she likes the idea of getting the upper hand on Kimber. A lot of the girls have been like that since she started working one on one with me last week. It's like they've got something to prove not only to me but her and her father. They wanna lay an even heavier beating on her, shoot real, because of who she is and what she means.

"So I'll get time to showcase what I can do?"

"Yes." Kimber and I answer simultaneously, her breaking out in a fit of giggles as the smile deepens even more into my face.

"Kimber might be going over here, Rachel, but you're an integral part of that. It can't happen without you. And based on your last few performances before you and Kimber were booked together, we know you're hard to beat. Letting her win within the first couple of minutes would ruin all the work you've done. That won't happen. Not on my watch."

It shouldn't bother me, the way she reacts. Yet it does. It always does. Their eyes when I compliment them, even in the most backhanded way, get big and bright, and I swear if I stood there long enough, I'd catch lust and desire there too. Especially with ones like Rachel who are my age.

It's unsettling.

Yeah, of course it is. It's not the girl you want doing it, that's why.

Resisting the urge to tell the voice to fuck off, I shake myself free of its hold and focus my attention on both girls, again ignoring its accuracy.

"So do you think you can take a few minutes, come up with the rest of the match and let me see what you got?"

"Of course, Matty." She purrs, batting her eyes. What I almost miss because I'm turning my full attention to the only person that actually deserves it with the professionalism she's managed to maintain since we started this today.

"You cool with that, little one?"

Shoving me hard in the arm and laughing, she nods.

"I got this, Kemper." She grins, before realizing a mistake and quickly clearing her throat. "I mean, *we* got this. So sit your ass down and let us show you what real greatness looks like."

I've avoided this girl as much as possible. Turned my nose down at her. Done every damn thing in the book of staying clear of the obvious attraction I have to her and it's gotten me nowhere. It's because every damn time I try, she does something like this. With that flirty little wink of hers, and the way she shakes her ass when she turns around, basically giving me her version of a fuck you, I'm putty in her hands.

Damn her. Damn Kimber to hell.

She's making me like her. Worse yet, she's making me like her a little too much.

I'm a dead man walking.

Kimberlee

After going over the match two more times after the one we managed to throw together for Matty, getting his input and implementing the changes, he finally calls for a break and I'm able to jump down to the ground and over to the cooler to grab some water.

Taking one bottle and pouring the entire thing down over my head, I lean back down and grab two more, shaking myself free of the pool of water I'm now drenched in by shaking it off and heading over to where he's still seated ringside.

"Thought you could use one of these," I say softly when he looks up as my shadow hovers, tossing him the bottle before throwing my own body down into the seat beside him and cracking the lid.

"It's hard work sitting ringside." He deadpans and I laugh. Like really laugh. Not understanding what the hell is so funny, but determined to go with it because of the way his eyes twinkle when he offers a tiny smile.

"My dad told us about your suspension." I blurt out and when his eyes fall and his lips follow suit, I know I've done it.

Foot in mouth syndrome strikes again.

"Pretty sure everyone heard about it. It's old news."

"Why'd you do it?"

"Why'd I do what?" he tilts his head toward mine and asks.

"Lose it on Yates like you did."

"You wouldn't understand."

"Try me." I say a little harsher than I intended. "Just because I'm a kid doesn't mean I won't understand. I've been dealing with my dad and his shit for years."

"What shit?"

Crap. I've really stepped in it now. I opened the damn door blurting out what I did.

"My dad..."

"What about him?" he gently pushes.

"The rest of the world when they come to the shows, all they see is Renegade. The man of five hundred holds. One's he's built a whole career on using and mastering. They see the myth, not the man."

"Kimber..."

"My dad drinks, Matty. He drinks a lot. He tried for a long time to hide it from my mom, from all of us, but it didn't take long for that secret to come out." Laughing nervously, I look down to my feet, blinking back the tears I know are just threatening to break through and spill, before sucking in a deep breath and starting again. "He's not exactly nice when that happens."

"Since when is Renegade nice?" He asks and I can't help but laugh. He's been here for a month tops and already he knows my dad well.

"Honestly, since you got here. He hasn't taken one drink since you showed up. It's like he's trying to be on his best behavior or something. Impress you the same way that you working with all of us is to impress him. Anyway, him being that way, it's taught me a lot. So whatever the reason is for what you did to Grant, I bet I'd understand better than anyone."

"He insulted my mother." Matthias admits, fidgeting uncomfortably in his seat. "The match probably would have gone off without a hitch, but he made some backhanded remark about my mom. Since it wasn't like she was there to defend herself, and I was already pissed off at the world, the flip switched and I lost it."

"I'm sorry."

It seems like such a copout, apologizing, but what else can I say? I really wasn't expecting it to be something like that.

It means my dad was right all along. There *is* a lot more going on with Matty than I know.

I need to lighten things up. Fast.

"Do you have any brothers or sisters?"

"No. It's just me."

"What does your dad do?"

It's quick, gone in a flash, but there's no missing the way he tenses up, or the vacant look that filters through his eyes and down over his face. I've hit another grenade spot.

So much for lightening the mood.

"He doesn't really do anything. So what about you? Zach your only brother?"

Thank God. An easy question.

"Yeah. It's just the two of us. Doc told Mom she shouldn't plan on having anymore if she wanted to keep wrestling."

"Wait. Your mom wrestles?"

"Used to, yeah. She even did it when she was pregnant with me. Trust me, my dad never wastes an opportunity these days to tell her it's because of that, I'm doing this now."

"Does he really blame her?" Matty asks, and when I nod my head slowly, he exhales with a curse. "I'm sorry, Kimber. I had no idea he was like that. He always seems put together when we're working."

I don't know what possesses me to do it, but there's something in the sad sinking of his eyes and sluggish fall to his shoulders that has me reaching out and resting my hand there, squeezing until his eyes are once again lifting and focusing themselves solely on me.

Matthias doesn't need to feel sorry for me, the same way I can tell he doesn't want me feeling it for him.

We're a sorry ass stubborn pair, the two of us.

"It's okay. We've all gotten used to it. It's second nature now."

"It shouldn't be." He growls, the lightness in his eyes darkening as a storm seems to take over. "Will you promise me something?"

"Sure. Anything."

"The next time it happens, promise you'll tell me. Don't think of it as second nature or the new normal. Find me and tell me."

"Find you where?"

It's an honest question. I know he's not staying with some of the other guys at the motel down the road, so the only other logical place for him to be would be a car, and I know it's not that. I've spent many a day looking through the windows of his in an attempt to learn something about the mystery known as Matthias and found nothing.

Not even a stray candy wrapper.

If he's sleeping in his car, he hides it well.

Motioning his head backward and following where it leads, it hits me. He's been staying in the gym.

Geez.

"If I promise to come find you, you've gotta promise me something. I'm not giving you something for free. I'm not that easy."

"There's nothing easy about you, little one."

Where my head wants to rage at his newest attack on my age, it's my heart winning out as it actually seems to take flight inside my chest. This isn't like all the other times he's called me a little girl or a brat when I'm acting like a pain in the ass. No, this name is softer. Sweeter.

Calm yourself, Kimber.

Damn hormones.

Sometimes being a girl sucks.

"What do you need me to promise?"

"That you'll come home with me."

Oh my God.

"That didn't come out—"

"I know, Kimber. Breathe." He laughs, easing the awkwardness of the moment and pausing my cheeks mid blush.

"What I meant was, we have three spare rooms in the house. Dad usually puts up his buddies when they're in town, but since no one's come by for months, they're all just sitting there empty. You could have a real bed with blankets and everything. Something better than the damn cot with holes in the mattress."

"Can't argue with that." He chuckles again, though this time, with the whispered tone of his words, a response that seems to only be for him.

"So come home with me. I'll talk to my mom, she'll double check with Dad, but I doubt it will be a thing. Besides, it will be a lot easier to come get you for my promise if you're close."

Okay, so I lied earlier. I actually *love* being a girl, because right now, Matthias is as easy to screw with as my dad. Bringing up the promise he wants me to make is the smartest thing I ever did.

I'm going to get my way. He can't resist me.

No one can.

"If your parents say yes, you've got a deal. But before we go and find out, there's something I want to say. I should have said it weeks ago, maybe even earlier today. I'm sorry I waited so long."

"What's that?"

"You're good at this, Kimber. I know it seems like no one sees that because your dad's put his hopes and dreams onto Zach, but I see it."

"You really mean that?"

"I don't say things I don't mean, little one."

Cursing his name under my breath, I growl before hauling off and slugging him in the shoulder.

"You really hate when I call you that, don't you?"

"I'm *not* a little girl." I whine, my eyes hardening and growing colder when he laughs. "Not the way you mean anyway."

"How do you think I mean it?"

"Just because I'm not as tall as you or as old, doesn't mean I'm little, damnit."

"Actually, it does. But since I can clearly see that you wanna slap me into next week, let me try again."

He waits patiently for god only knows what and after a couple of minutes of absolute silence, he clears his throat and starts.

"Forget what you think you know about the name, okay? I don't call you it to offend you. It's my way of separating you from the rest."

"Separating me?"

"I like you, Kimberlee Parker. You're a pretty cool kid once you stop worrying about what everyone else thinks. And contrary to the way I may have treated you when I got here, I actually enjoy spending time with you. So the name is my way of saying you're special."

"You think I'm special." I repeat back, trying to make myself believe he's actually said the words my mind and my heart hear and want to react to.

"Yes, Kimber." Reaching over, he rests his hand on mine and my heart soars with the connection he's made. "I think you're the best."

Chapter Eleven

April 2007

Kimberlee

Walking through the gym doors, holding onto them as the wind begins to force its weight and slam them, I bring them closed as silently as possible before turning my attention to the ring and the two combatants currently going at it inside.

Matthias, as he ducks under the clothesline my brother is bouncing back off the ropes in order to deliver and turning it into one of his own. The move so fluidly executed it takes Zach clear off his feet. Even from this distance it looking as though his head was snapped clear around as soon as he connected with Matthias's arm.

So caught up am I in the action, I'm completely unprepared for what silently creeps up behind me.

"I wonder what your dear old dad would think about the way you two are."

Levi.

Of course it is. He must be looking for another low blow. God knows over the last few months he's deserved that and more. His whispered taunts and hate-filled words failing at every turn.

"Who? Me and Zach?" I shove him with a giggle. "Gee, Levi. I think he'd be proud."

"That's right, keep playing dumb. Oh wait. You can't play at it when it's what you really are." He smugly smirks, making me clench my fists at my side so I don't lose my shit and take his head clear off.

What I ever saw in this guy is beyond me. I don't think they make pricks the size of Levi.

Like it's somehow my fault he sucks.

"What do you want, Levi?" I quietly growl. A move that only seems to make the smirk on his face more prominent as he steps in closer.

"You and Kemper. I've been watching you and there's something going on there. Something I don't think Renegade will like much when someone finally clues him in."

"That someone being you?"

"Who else? Though, I don't see how he can be so blind. It's not like you hide the fucking drool or anything."

Don't play into this, Kimber. He's just trying to get a rise out of you. He has nothing and he knows it. Don't be the one to give him something.

Pep talk doing its job, I beam the brightest smile I possibly can his way before leaning in, slamming my hand down onto his shoulder and squeezing. My next words calculated and based on the scowl he wears when I pull back, hitting their mark.

"Go ahead and tell him what you've seen. I dare you."

"Fine." He spits out, the spray from the force of his ire landing across the bridge of my nose.

Gross. Definitely gonna need that shower now. There's no way in hell I'm getting in the ring with the spray of asshole all over me.

Looking toward the ring when I hear the slapping of hands hard down across the mat, I put Levi and his threats out of my mind entirely when I see both men turn toward us. Zach's expression clouded with anger and Matthias's curiosity.

Zach, the more concerned of the two, wastes no time climbing through the ropes and down. Scurrying across the room faster than I think he's ever done until he's hovering over me like the bodyguard over the last few months, he's become.

"We good here?" he asks, angling his head down to me, ignoring Levi altogether.

"Yeah, big brother. We're good." I beam before turning it on Levi. Waiting until Zach has completely turned his back and winking cheekily.

Let him run to Daddy with his lies. It's not like after the stunt he pulled at the show, he's going to be believed anyway. If anything he'll just be giving my father the ammunition he needs to rid himself of him once and for all.

Good riddance.

Sliding my arm through Zach's, I let him guide me silently toward the ring and what is now about to turn into Kimberlee Parker getting her ass handed to her by the much more seasoned performer.

Otherwise known as, a training session.

The closer we get though, the faster my heart rate picks up until it's full-blown racing as I grip the ropes and use them to hop up onto the apron and into the ring. The smile I'm greeted by as he makes his way over from the opposite corner, making everything Levi threatened me with real.

Sweat beading at my forehead and building on my palms, making them slick to the touch, along with the catch in my breath when he grabs me around the neck and pulls me in to ruffle my hair, all the proof needed to show that none of it was lies.

I do like Matthias.

A lot.

And if something doesn't change quickly, Levi won't be the only one that knows it.

My daddy will too.

There's no way that can happen.

So I do the only thing in the moment that I can to ensure it doesn't.

I put on my game face.

Turning to Matthias and grinning like a Cheshire cat, I motion for Zach to get his butt out, moving to the center when I see him slide through the ropes and jump back down.

It's time to focus on the only thing that needs to matter now.

Kicking my crush's ass.

✶ ✶ ✶ ✶ ✶ ✶

"What made you wanna do this?"

"This, as in wrestling?" he asks after taking a long swig from the bottle and tossing it back down on the apron.

"Yeah. So far, everyone I've met always has one story, an instance really, where they just knew it was what they wanted to do for the rest of their life. I guess I'm wondering, what was yours?"

"I don't know if it was just one thing." Running a hand through his hair, he leans back against the ropes and sighs. "I guess a lot of it came from me needing an outlet."

"An outlet for what?"

"More like from." He laughs softly, but not the way I've heard him do in the past. This laugh more forced. His face subdued.

"Okay. What from?"

"Things weren't always the best growing up in my house, so whenever it was especially bad, I'd turn to wrestling. Watch old tapes at first. Then later, mimic what I saw in the tapes alone in my room. The gym came later, when things were the worst. It helped me unload." Pausing and looking down at me as I ponder what he said, he releases another laugh-sigh. "I guess everyone says that, huh?"

"Maybe a little."

"What made you wanna do this, little one?"

He's doing it again and despite my every attempt not to let on that it affects me, the newest change to the nickname he's given me manifests itself as the heat begins building in my face and I can actually feel the burn of it against my cheeks, dying to be freed.

Can I be any more of a girl right now?

"Honestly? I don't know. I grew up with this. Wrestling has been in my family forever, what with my parents doing it. They made it their life and for the longest time, I wanted nothing at all to do with it. I was bigger than wrestling. My dreams were bigger. I wanted more."

"So when did it all change?"

"When I was eleven. I'd been watching Zach coming up for years and one day, I was watching him do a powerbomb to some guy and that was it."

"A powerbomb did it for ya, huh?"

"I guess so." I admit, laughing softly.

Tearing my attention from the rise to his eyebrows as he questions me and grabbing his discarded water bottle, I put all of my focus into draining it dry so I don't have to look at him again. Small tendrils of his hair falling down into his eyes calling to me and making me wanna reach out even more than I already did and touch them—touch him—in order to push them back.

It's been happening a lot like this lately. Innocent conversation turning into a battle of hormones as I put forth my best attempt at ignoring the urge to touch him. Feel him. God, even kiss him. That last one, occurring more and more lately.

I don't want it to be like this! I don't want to be *that* girl. The one who gets into something that by all rights every single man in her life believes she had no business being in, and then spending my time mooning over the guys I work with instead of laying them out on their asses the way I damn well know I can.

I don't want to be the starry eyed fangirl.

I'm Kimberlee Parker for fuck sakes. I wanna be taken seriously.

Matthias Kemper comes around though? My priorities shift until he's the only thing I want to be serious about.

"Little one?" he calls, leaning over into my space and nudging me.

"Yeah?"

"Where'd you go just now?"

I went to a place where I'm your little one, there isn't this horrible seven year age difference between us, and you actually look at me like I'm your equal. I answer, thankfully quietly. My answer changing in an instant when I finally look up and meet his sky blue irises head on. The softness in them, stunning me into complete silence and making me powerless against what I stupidly am about to do next.

"Mat—Matthias..." I stumble, stammering. "I..."

"You what, Kimber—"

He's barely got my name out before I'm on him, unleashing all of the pent up need I've been walking around with since he got here, pressing my lips awkward and dryly to his. Not even thinking enough to wet them before I jam them to his face, but too stunned by the move I've made to think of pulling away in order to do it or take it back.

Closing my eyes, I give into the surprising softness that's there to greet me in his own. Unmoving, probably as stunned in the moment by my reckless move as I am, but still in it, with no attempt to pull away. Making me, as my cheeks overheat, the one to do it first.

"Oh my god, Matty! I'm so sorry. I don't know what I was thinking."

Embarrassment overriding everything else, I look down toward the floor before jumping off the apron. My eyes locked on my wrestling boots and the mats there to greet me.

Anywhere but at the man I basically just accosted when he was only trying to be nice and pull me back out of my own head.

"Kimber, wait!" He calls when I finally find my footing and start taking off. The doors to the gym so damn close, yet still so far, and the concern mixed with surprise in his voice only seeming to make the disappearing act I want that much more difficult.

"I know what you're gonna say, Matty." I call back as I pick up the pace, the door now only a foot or so away and definitely within my grasp. But before I can reach it, get a grip on the handle that my fingers are now barely brushing across, I'm being pulled back. The distance becoming almost insurmountable as in the blink of an eye I'm being spun around to stare straight into the deepest balls of light I've ever witnessed.

Matthias Kemper, the storm in every instance we've been together, suddenly becoming the calm as he studies me silently for one beat, then two, straight into a count of ten before his lips descend down onto mine again. This time, my own ready as the softness of his mixes with my own.

"You," he manages, leaning in and pressing his lips to my forehead. "You have no idea what I'm going to say, Kimber. Not one fucking clue. But that, this, it can't happen again."

Releasing his hold on my body and completely stepping away, he's the one to look down toward the floor, fists clenched and jaw tight. Fighting an internal battle that if he's anything like me, he'll never win.

"What the hell have I done?" he looks up to the ceiling, questioning the sky. Any answer he might be after non-existent as the only sound for miles is the pounding of my heart and the heavy intake and exhale of his own breathing. "Fourteen. Fucking fourteen."

"Matty…"

"Little one, don't."

We're at an impasse. The guilt he so obviously feels for what happened between us, my age mixing with the respect he has for my father and what he's allowed him to be a part of taking over, while the knowledge of him returning my awkward kiss with one of his own and wanting to do it again, all I can see. The need to run away and distance myself from what I've done, now transferred to him as he's the first to move.

But instead of calling out the way he had and stopping him before he has the chance to leave me, I do the opposite. Knowing deep down that even if I did call out, he wouldn't turn around.

I let him go.

Matthias

Stomping my way through the locker room doors like a man on a mission, I grab a towel from my bag and head straight into the showers. Determined to drown myself under the spray of the hot water after the stunt I just pulled.

The hate, disgust and guilt sneaking up on me like an opponent well versed in my abilities gripping me in the tightest of chokeholds. Not letting up until not only can I see the dots beginning to appear before my eyes as the world begins to fade to black, but actually feel the breath being stolen straight from my lungs before I fall limp and broken to the mat—in this case the floor—below.

What in the ever loving fuck was I thinking?

Her kissing me the way she did? The awkwardness? The stunning she laid on my ass because I hadn't so much as seen it coming? I could easily explain that away.

She's a kid for Christ sakes.

It wasn't all that long ago I was the same way. Hormones taking over and making things appear one way when in fact they're another entirely. Need, desire and a fucking place to put it all running rampant inside a body that was too damn young to keep up.

Being a teenager is a mess, no arguing that.

So why the fuck did I have to stop her, throw every stitch of common sense out the window, and kiss her again?

Because I'm a fucking mess.

Renegade takes a chance on a guy that most would have given up on considering the damage I did the last time I was in a match, and how do I repay him? By taking advantage of his nowhere near legal daughter.

Real bang-up job I did with the thank you there.

I've never been so disgusted in my life.

Which means of course that instead of drowning myself the way I deserve, I head for the mirror instead. Needing to see the disgusting piece of shit I've turned into.

Pausing a few feet back and taking in the face of someone no better than the man that raised me, I resist the urge to hurl.

I don't even know this guy staring back at me. There's a deadness in my eyes. Literally nothing living and breathing beyond the blue orbs encased in white staring back. I'm a shell of my former self. Whoever that guy was. It's been so long since I've felt remotely alive that it's a miracle there's not a sign tacked to my face saying *'Danger! Dead Inside'*.

I'm so fucking twisted I can actually see my reflection changing. Lips quirking up on the one side into a half smirk, eyes flickering with pleasure as he shows how pleased he truly is by the events that have taken place. Pleased with the transformation from defender to the monster that was always there, just waiting for the moment of escape. One where he would be able to run free the way he was always designed to.

"You would be pleased with yourself, wouldn't you, you selfish piece of shit?" I admonish the monster. "Preying on an innocent girl would be your speed."

Don't you mean our speed? You were there after all.

"Shut up!" I roar, crushing my hands to my ears, determined to block him and his truth out.

What happened with Kimberlee wasn't me. I wouldn't do that. It goes against everything I was taught. Everything I know.

Admit it, Kemper. He taunts as his eyes begin to dance. *You enjoyed it. That kiss, you wanted it damn near as much as she did. You still want it. I just gave you what you've been craving for weeks.*

"No!" Shaking my head, allowing my hands to fall from my ears and using them to grip onto the sink for the strength to stand, I look away. Determined not to look up again and see the sliver of truth there that no amount of denials will ever be able to erase.

I had wanted it, otherwise I never would have done it.

He's right.

I'm right.

Giving into the fight, I look up and just as suspected, the internal battle being waged inside of me, is gone. I'm here, but there's no smug expression on my face. No eyes dancing in glee over what I've done. I'm just me again. A combination of the monster and the guy with a moral compass that's determined to fight it some more.

Fight a battle that based on my genetics alone, I'm never going to win.

That's right, Matthias. Admit defeat. Give in to what you feel. Who you are.

"Give in to this, you son of a bitch!"

Looking down to my now clenched fist and back to the mirror and sucking in a breath, determined as I do to wipe the smug as shit smirk from his face once and for all, I swing. Hearing the impact as it connects with the mirror and the cracks begin to appear before the glass shatters around me. Shards, little slivers, and other jagged pieces clinking as they drop and bounce off the walls of the sink below.

Cuts beginning to form on my hands, blood breaking through the openings, but nothing, not the pain or the blood as it pools and begins to drip, getting through. Only her face breaking through the haze and the silent promise I make once I focus my eyes on what's left of the mirror I left behind.

Kimberlee will never have to fear what happened before happening again because after today, she's never going to see me again.

It's time to go home.

Chapter Twelve

Matthias

"You sure about this, son? You still got time to ride out on your suspension. Better you do that here than back there."

No, I'm not sure. I want to yell, but digging my teeth down into my lip, I bite back the urge.

I *want* to be here. I feel more at home here than I ever did back home. I've been accepted, faults and all. The pressure building around my neck has been alleviated since I've been helping work everyone instead of working myself.

At least it was until I stupidly kissed the man's daughter.

No matter how good things have been, nothing is going to erase that. Or the temptation working with her day in and day out would present now that I know what it feels like.

So decision made.

It's time to go home.

"There's nothing more I can do for your guys, Renegade. They're already worthy opponents who can carry themselves and the promotion you're attempting to build. All that's left is to take a step back and let them."

Especially your daughter.

"There's always work to be done, boy."

He's right about that. Just because you're good at what you do, doesn't mean there isn't always room to be better. Unfortunately, that's gotta happen without me.

If I stick around after what happened the other night with Kimber, I'm only going to screw up again. And the whole point of this was for me to get my head back on straight and not do that.

Swallowing down the slithery voice I hear laughing at me from inside, I meet Renegade's gaze head-on, letting him see what I've spent the better part of the last few days talking myself into.

It's time for me go.

"And now it's up to you to make sure they do it." I chuckle awkwardly. "Besides, I think I've imposed on you and your family enough. It's time to let you get back to it."

Leaving Kimberlee to fend with the father she says appears when the cameras are gone.

Great. I'm breaking another promise to a female that's important to me.

"Wasn't an imposition, son. Honestly, it felt good having another guy besides Zach to shoot the breeze with. Talk shop."

Hearing that, knowing that just like him and his family have made an impact on me, I've done the same for him, it means a lot.

Call me a fucking fanboy all you want, but when your idol tells you that he likes having you around, some lowly kid determined to fill shoes as big as his, it's a definite ego booster.

"Meant a lot to me too, boss. Also meant a lot, you letting me set up in your house. I won't forget what you did for me here. What you taught me."

When his hand rises and he begins swiping at his eyes, I'm hit square between my own with a realization.

My dad spent the better part of my childhood telling me that real men don't cry. They don't show emotion, and anyone that did was a pussy. No better than a woman.

As Renegade stands here doing just that, like in some way roles are reversed and I'm actually the son—his son—and he's seeing me head off into the world, it's a gut check moment.

If a man like him can openly show that part of himself, maybe my dad *was* full of shit. Maybe I've been doing it wrong all these years.

Emotion isn't a sign of weakness. It's a sign of strength. One of security and acceptance.

"You sure I can't talk you out of this?"

"Positive." I nod respectfully. "Gotta go home sometime. Might as well be now."

Before I make a mistake with your daughter I can't come back from. I add silently.

"Well, okay then. Let me round up the guys so they can say goodbye. Not gonna lie, boy. Some of 'em are gonna be damn sad to see you go."

That makes two of us, but I can't let him do this. If I'm gonna make a clean break and head back to Smith, CPW, and Bry, I gotta do it without Kimber knowing.

Goodbye is already hard enough standing here with Will.

I don't think I can do it at all with her.

"Nah, man. Let them keep to their routine. It's not like I won't ever come back. I'll be back and forth so much you'll get sick of seeing me."

The lie falls from my tongue effortlessly. As much as I would love it to be true, it can't be. I know that once I walk out of here today, no matter what anyone else wants, I can't come back. I can't come back to her.

She's better off without me.

Just like everyone else.

"You sure?"

"Positive." I repeat and he grunts before slapping a hand hard across my back and pulling me into an embrace. Bear hugs in the ring aside, this is the first time since Smith reached through my haze in the hospital and showed me any form of affection, and I've got no idea what to do with it.

My mind is racing, thoughts spinning. My body wanting to give in so bad to the olive branch of feeling the older man is showing me, but what my upbringing really hasn't prepared me to deal with.

Do I hug him back? Show him with the small motion just what my time with him meant, or do I just grunt like he did, tap his back and turn and walk away?

Pulling back he eyes me hard before slapping me, lighter this time, across my back.

"You mind doing this old man a favor?"

"Anything."

"Let me know when you're back. Don't have much experience on the road these days, and with Zach and Kimber staying close to home, don't really have to worry that way. I'd feel better 'bout this whole thing if you'd give me a heads up when you're safe."

He's doing it again. Caring.

Shit.

If I didn't know there were definitely two sides to this man, I'd think he was too good to be true.

Maybe that's why he's my idol. Because he's not perfect but still gives a shit.

"Will do, old man." I laugh when he scowls at the name calling. "And if I don't, I'm sure you'll be hearing Smith's foot stomping clear across the country when I do get there."

"Expecting nothing less." His slowly laughs, before his eyes grow serious. "You keep your nose clean, you got me? This world," he motions around. "Is yours for the taking and I wanna see you take it."

"You got it." I tell him honestly. The most truthful statement I've made since I landed here.

He's right. I'm good at this. It's flowing through my veins and I might have let personal shit get the better of me before, but it's a new day.

Time for a new me.

One that not only Renegade can be proud of, but I can too.

Kimberlee

This isn't happening.

No way.

I know we shared a kiss, but it doesn't have to be like this. He doesn't have to leave because of it. It can be our secret. I'm good at keeping those. The best really.

Like when Zachary thought he hid all those magazines he stole from dad's stash in the garage and I came across them. I never once told Mom about it even though I should have with the way he treated me after.

I can't let him leave like this. Especially knowing I'm the reason.

Being here has been good for him. For me too. I'm more confident when he's overseeing my matches. When we're chatting and he's telling me what works and what doesn't. Ways to make myself even better than I know I am.

I can't let some stupid little kiss change that.

Except it wasn't stupid and it wasn't a little kiss.

It was, *it is*, the first and only kiss that matters.

He's the only thing that matters.

God, I really hate that I'm being like this. He's just a guy here helping dad. A guy that happens to be totally messed up in the head and seven years older than me.

And knowing all of that, it's not what my heart sees.

It's not what *I* see.

I see Matthias. The real one hidden beneath the bravado, violence, and insulting words.

I see the Matthias that sees me.

The boy who crumbled both of our walls when his lips met mine after I awkwardly attempted my first kiss against his. The one who stole my breath. Set my soul ablaze. Made my heart hammer straight out of my chest cavity while at the same time, bathing me in quiet serenity.

Matthias reached out, touched and took hold of a part of me that even knowing he's going to walk out of here in a few minutes, I don't ever want him to give back.

I fell that first day and now that I've fallen I don't want back up.

It's not wrong to feel this way. *It can't be.* Not when it's something so freaking innocent.

Matthias is my first love.

"Why so glum, chum?" Zachary's voice carries through, interrupting the very real confession I've just made. Bumping me in the side when I don't even so much as blink to acknowledge his arrival, he shifts until he's standing directly in front of me and I can feel his eyes penetrating through my own as he stares.

"Seriously, Kimber. You're freaking me out. Why do you look like someone died?"

Because someone did!! I scream at him.

Matthias is leaving. He's gonna hightail his ass out of here without as much as a wave in our direction. It is like someone died.

"He's leaving." I manage to say, albeit softer than I was going for and acknowledgement shines in Zach's eyes.

"I know."

Finally looking up and meeting my brother head on, eyes raging with the anger rising, I shove him hard, and as he stumbles back, I line myself up to do it again. A move he catches and prevents by grabbing me by the shoulders and locking me in place.

"How the hell do you know since he's just now telling Dad?"

"Because he talked to me yesterday. Said it was time to pack it in and head back."

"And you're just gonna let him?" I scream, no longer caring who hears.

My asinine brother had the chance to stop this before it even started and he didn't do it. He's lucky I'm not laying him out flat on the ground.

Zachary doesn't stand a chance against pissed Kimber, and I'm definitely pissed.

"How can you just let him go?" I cry and catching my body as it sags against his own, I hear him whisper under his breath.

"It's true."

"What is?"

"You and Matthias. There's something going on there. Levi said there was and I blew him off, but Kimber..."

No. No. No.

I can't let my brother know he's right. I have to change the way I'm reacting even though I think it's too late. He can't know. He'll never look at Matty the same again. Or me.

"Zach..."

Here goes. I'm gonna tell him that Levi is full of shit.

"Don't lie to me, Kimber."

"It's...There's...Shit."

"Did he hurt you?"

I can feel the grip he has on my body hardening. Growing tighter. This is my brother when he's being my brother and not the annoyance he enjoys being. He's protective. He loves me. Finding out about Matthias because I can't hide shit knowing what's coming the second he walks out of the house, has flipped his big brother switch hard.

"No. I hurt him, though. He's running because of something I did. You need to stop him, Zach. Please stop him." I plead.

"I can't, Kimber. He's made his mind up and he's not from here. He has to go back to Smith. He works for CPW."

Yes, all of this is fact and I know it, but I don't care. I'm emotional, I'm overloaded and I'm in-fucking-love. Rational is the last thing I want to be right now.

"Don't you think I know that?" I hiss, finally righting myself and pulling out of my brother's embrace. "He still has time though. He doesn't need to go back yet."

Where I expect Zach to argue or slam me with more facts, he lowers his gaze to the ground before rubbing his forehead and lifting again, letting his softened eyes fall on my own.

"Does he know how you feel about him?"

"Yes. No. I don't know. What does it even matter? He's still gonna leave."

Shaking his head and releasing a heavy sigh, he steps toward me and instead of pulling out of the embrace before it even starts, I fall into it and let the tears that have been threatening to fall finally drop.

"I don't want him to go."

"I know you don't. I don't know what's going on with the two of you or what could have happened that would make him wanna get the hell out of here, but I don't want him to go either. It's easier with him here. Dad, he's different."

So I'm not the only one who's noticed that.

"He is. It's nice."

"Hey," he whispers, tipping my chin up so we're again staring at each other. "Dad and Smith are like war buddies with how close they are. We'll see him again. Maybe we can talk the old man into taking a road trip."

Zachary is being a little too understanding right now. He was tense before when he found out I couldn't lie about what Levi spilled, but now he seems relaxed. Cool with it. I'm not sure what's going on. Can I trust my brother? Or is he just waiting for me to let my guard down so he can ruin everything?

"You—you're not mad?" I stammer out through my cascading tears and he shakes his head.

"I had a feeling this might happen. You were so pissed about him coming here. I mean, I don't think Dad is gonna be too thrilled that you went and fell for one of his favorite guys, but he doesn't need to know if you don't want him to."

"He can't know. Please don't tell him."

Rubbing his hands across my back soothingly, he presses me to him, hugging me.

"Not planning on it. Matthias has got a reputation, but he's cool. I want to keep it that way, at least with Dad. It's our secret."

The door chooses that second to open and turning toward the sound, we watch as Matthias walks out with our father quickly on his heels. His eyes reaching out over the lawn and finding both of us.

Flicking his gaze in Zach's direction, he waves awkwardly before letting himself linger on me.

My body immediately warming even with the distance and despite the rise to his face as his eyes widen in surprise.

He really was going to leave me without saying goodbye.

Closing the distance, he starts down the stairs and makes quick work of the lawn, stopping when he reaches Zachary and bumping fists and grinning before again turning his attention to me.

"Guess the secret's out, huh?" he whispers and looking from the ground slowly up to him, I nod weakly.

I'm not ready for this. I don't think I'll ever be ready.

Not for this goodbye.

"You're leaving." I state evenly, surprising myself with how calm I'm managing to stay despite the firestorm going off inside.

"Yeah, I gotta get back."

"Why?" I demand, an edge creeping into my tone. "It's not like you're gonna be cleared to compete."

"It's where I belong, Kimber." He answers back with just as much bite. His shoulders, which for weeks have been slowly becoming more and more relaxed and loose, tensing again. Another change I've caused in him.

This sucks.

It sucks so bad.

"No, it's not. You belong here." *With me.* "We're all better because of you."

Shaking his head, he reaches out and the second his hand makes contact with mine, I flinch, causing him to draw back as if I've burned him.

"You were already the best." He admits softly and even though I know he means everyone, my heart wants me to believe it's only for me. That in this moment, he feels exactly the same things—the same feelings—as I do and does believe I'm the best.

Blushing what I'm sure is a whole new shade of red not yet heard of, when his hand reaches out again and brushes ever so lightly against mine, I don't pull away. I lean into it, needing to feel his touch sear straight under my skin so that when he does leave, I'll never forget him.

His mark will be left on me forever.

"There's nothing else I can do for you—with you, Kimber. All of you, you're phenomenal. I need to go back to where I belong. Where I can be used."

Slipping my hand out from under his, it's my turn to touch him now. Running swirls over his hand and slightly up his arm where I can reach without giving away anything to my father and brother now waiting on the porch.

"Don't do this, Matthias. Don't leave me."

"Little one..." I hear him whisper before he stops himself and slams his lips shut, his eyes quickly following suit as I catch his chest begin to rise and fall.

He's holding back from me and I want to scream. Demand to know why. I just can't. If I do, the secret that Zach and I swore to keep, it won't be a secret anymore.

Everyone will know.

So I do the only thing I can. I use his own shit against him. Praying it works and it makes him stay.

"What about the promise you had me make? What happens when you leave and he starts drinking again?"

Chapter Thirteen

June 2007

Matthias

"What happens when you leave and he starts drinking again?"

"Kimber—" I start and am abruptly cut off.

"No, Matty! I don't want to hear excuses. You made me promise to tell you when it happened again, but you're leaving. So who am I supposed to tell now?"

I hate this.

Letting Kimber down feels like I'm right back in that house of horrors and am too damn late to save my mom. I swore I wouldn't do this shit anymore. I wouldn't promise anyone anything, get attached, or care at all.

It was supposed to be easier that way. If there is no attachments or promises to be kept, then when I let them down—which I will always fucking do—the sting wouldn't be as bad.

Yet here I am. I made this girl make me a promise that I can never really make good on.

Not when I'm running.

When she's the very thing I'm running from.

"You tell your mom. You tell Zach."

"Do you really have to leave?"

"I do." I lie to her just like I did her dad before.

"Is this because of—" It's my turn to cut her off. I can't let her say the word. Not when I've been doing everything in my power to move on from it.

"No."

"I don't believe you." She stamps her foot onto the ground and pouts. "I think that the reason you need to go home is because of what happened."

It is. I silently tell her, agreeing with her assessment. The image I have of her being a little girl no longer relevant as she's more insightful than people twice her age.

"Well, little girl," I cover up with a sneer, knowing just the right button to push with her and being just enough of a dick to use it. *"I know you think you're always right, but in this case you're wrong. It has nothing to do with that. My suspension is almost up and I need to get back home. End of."*

"Bullshit." She curses under her breath. *"You're a coward and a bullshitter, Matthias Kemper."*

You have no idea how right you are, little one. But if you could only see the reality of what's staring us both square in the face, you'd understand why I have to be.

"And you're a hormonal little brat with daddy issues."

I feel the sting of her hand as it impacts with my face almost the second my words are out. The force of the slap so harsh, I actually catch flecks of saliva as they're knocked straight from my mouth.

"You don't mean that."

No, little one. Of course I don't mean it. I just can't do this with you right now. If ever. You're too young. I'm too damn fucked up. It's wrong.

It's right. *My mind argues.*

I could easily tell her all of this, maybe enlighten her to the real issue standing like a third person between us, but I don't say any of it. I keep it only for me and continue showing her the mask of Matthias, the asshole. The one that's gonna get me out of here and out of her life for good with minimal bloodshed.

Sure, she'll hate me for the rest of her life, but some prices paid are worth it.

"I mean every word. Now," motioning with a flick of my head to my car, I steel myself against the pull I have to bring her to me, and finish this. *"I need to go. So run along. I'm sure your next crush is waiting."*

Dejected, her foot starts to turn and her body pivots as though she's going to turn and stomp away, but before I can react in kind and do the same, I feel her hand brushing against my own and with as much force as she can muster, she's pulling me to her. Wrapping her arms around my midsection and tightening the hold.

Her next words only lending to what I already knew to be fact.

She sees right through me.

"I don't know what happened before you got here or everything you've been through. I just know that this guy, the one that's being mean, it's because of it. It's not the real you, Matthias. I've met him. I like him. And even though he's running

away because of what happened a couple of days ago, I'm never going to forget him."

Pressing those feathery soft and small lips of hers against my cheek, she kisses me before releasing her hold and finally distancing herself. Walking away before I can get even get my head clear enough to respond.

Much like every other part of this goodbye, the words being spoken for me only.

Goodbye, little one. I won't forget you either.

Shaken from the memory of Kimber when a hand grips my shoulder, I look up to meet the person I'm here to see dead on.

"When Smith said that you wanted to meet up, I gotta say, I thought he was bullshitting me."

Grant.

True to my word, when I got back into town, after rolling through the remaining couple of weeks on my sentence for what happened between us, I'd asked Smith to reach out and set something up.

My promise of a new Matthias coming back after spending time with Renegade and his camp, holding firm.

"Thank for agreeing to it. Pretty sure I'm not your favorite person these days." Motioning to his head, where I can see the beginnings of the scar that I know without asking leads deep into the back of his scalp, I ask the only question I can. "That gonna stop you from getting back in the ring?"

"Not a chance. I'm looking at a few more weeks' recovery time and Doc says I'm good to go."

I might not have cared the night in the ring, but now that my heads been pulled out of my ass and I'm seeing things clearly, it makes me wonder just how smart that is. Even after being medically cleared to compete, how wise is it to get right back in?

I've had my share of injuries, but none of them have been as serious as one that affects the brain. Bruises and abrasions? Sure. But scarring and deep lacerations? No way.

"You sure that's smart?"

"Wouldn't you do the same if you were me?"

"A few months ago, I would have said yes. It's not the same these days."

Throwing his body down hard onto the porch swing and leaning back, heaving out a heavy breath, he eyes me before looking out over the front lawn.

"What changed?"

"I guess I did."

"Listen man, about that night. The shit I was spewing was wrong. I didn't know what the fuck got into me then, and I still don't, but I can own that what happened was my fault. I'm sorry."

"There was two of us there that night, Yates. I could have shrugged off the shit you were saying and I didn't. That's on me. Not you."

"I'm sorry about your mom, Kemper. I used it because I thought it would add a different element to the match. Kinda like you'd been doing with some of other guys. I didn't think it out as much as I should have."

I can't let him keep doing this.

We're both at fault, sure, I can concede that much, but I was the one that took it to the next level. I took it out of the stratosphere. He didn't have a part in that. It's all on me.

The blame has to fall where it belongs.

Aggression and the monster I let loose that night aren't the same thing. They're two different beasts, and I'm just glad that after spending time with Renegade and channeling it in the right way, I now know the difference.

"I'm the one that's sorry. If I hadn't been pulled off you when I was, we wouldn't even be sitting here having this conversation. I was that far gone and that's unacceptable. That's not what this is supposed to be about. I fucked up and I know it doesn't mean shit, but I really am sorry."

Sorry for my mom.

Sorry for Grant.

Sorry for Kimber.

Geez. I'm a sad sorry fuck.

"It's cool, brother. I'll get my revenge when I'm cleared." He winks and grins, and despite the uncertainty, not knowing just how far his revenge is gonna run or how serious he really is, I return it with a laugh.

"And I'll let you. I deserve it."

"So," he puffs out, shifting himself forward and leaning on his hands. "You gotta tell me how it was working with the almighty Will Parker."

I've been asked that question a lot since I've been back, but have successfully been able to avoid answering it in depth. The most anyone has been able to get a sentence or two.

All mention of Renegade just brings his daughter to the forefront of my mind and with the way she's been seeping into my every damn waking and sleeping thought, I'm in desperate need of a break.

Kimberlee Parker has to stay in the past.

I've gotta put my eyes on the prize. In this case, the prize being working my tail off to get back to where I deserve to be.

Owning CPW—being the top guy—the way Renegade wanted me to.

"It was surreal."

"He run things like Smith?"

Shaking my head, he laughs and I join in easily. No one runs things quite like Smith and Marie do. They're in a class all their own.

"Both his kids compete. Shit, according to the daughter, his wife was even a wrestler at one point. It's a real family business down there. Definitely not the way Smith runs things."

"Maybe not with everyone else, but it's like that with you."

Arching my brow, he chuckles before leaning back again and throwing his arm around the back of the swing, the weight pulling the back and forth motion to a stop.

"You really don't see it, do you?"

"Obviously not."

"Smith is a hard mother fucker. He doesn't give two flying fucks about much, but there are two things besides wrestling that he does, and I'm looking at one of them."

He can't be serious. Sure, Smith and I have a bond that not a lot of the other guys have, but the same could be said for me and Bryan. It's just because we've been together so damn long and been through some pretty hard shit together.

"Bullshit, man. He's as hard on me as he is with the rest of you."

"That might be true, but it's for a different reason."

"And what reason would that be?"

Tapping his fingers against the wooden structure, he sighs.

"You really think that if Smith hadn't gone to bat for you, all you would have gotten was a three month suspension? Come on, man. You can't be this fucking blind. You got off as light as you did because to the rest of the damn locker room, you're his."

"I'm his what?"

"His kid. He's harder on you, pushes you and expects more from you, because you're the son he never had."

I hear everything he's saying but my brain, it's stuck on what he said about the suspension. Was it going to end up being worse and Smith really did use whatever pull he has to turn it around into what it became? Did Radley and Renegade do this together? And how much did Bry know?

We haven't so much as spoken two words to each other since I got back, but hearing the way Grant is talking, it seems like I'm the only one that was kept out of the loop.

Just how deep does this shit run and better yet, just how close had I come to losing my career altogether?

"What was I looking at before?"

"The end. Between me admitting that I brought it all on, and Smith going to hell and back with pretty much everyone, we fixed it. But brother, you would have been done."

After a few seconds of letting his words sink in, the impact of them doing a number on me internally and twisting me in knots that I'm not sure I'll ever be able to fully untangle, I clear my throat and find the words that much like the apology I offered earlier, need to be said.

"Thank you."

"Don't thank me, man. It was the right thing to do, considering the gum flapping I did about your family. If you really wanna thank someone though, I think your next stop should be Smith."

He's right, and after shooting the breeze for a few more minutes and saying our goodbyes with the promise of seeing each other in the ring, I slide behind the wheel with that in mind.

All this twisted shit with him, why I had the chip buried so deep on my shoulders when I showed up to Renegade, it's because what Grant said is true.

A father isn't a title you're given because of biology. It's one that over time is earned. And for every way I am Jonathan Kemper's son, I'm also Smith's.

I'm Radley Smith's prodigy and it's about damn time I acted like it.

He deserves nothing less.

Now it's time to prove it.

Part Two
Journey to the Top

Chapter Fourteen

September 2014

Kimberlee

You're not in Kansas anymore, Kimber.

I was never in Kansas, but that's beside the point.

After spending the last eleven years working exclusively with my parents promotion—other than a few shows outside of it—where I'm standing now is as far from that as it gets.

Home being my Kansas and this; well this might as well be another planet.

Anyone who is anything in this business knows about CPW. Even more about the husband and wife team that run the joint.

Radley Smith and his wife Marie having made quite the name from themselves, not only off his days on the road as a performer, but what they've done in the years since he had to give it up.

CPW is the top of the indie scene.

And officially my new home.

"Will wonders never cease?" The familiar voice of my family friend turned boss says as he saddles on up beside me, slinging a meaty arm tight around my shoulders and crushing me to him.

Spend a night sitting at a fire while the two old guys shot the shit about their years on the road together and apparently it makes it okay for the guy to get up close and personal.

Though, if it wasn't for that weekend six years ago, I don't think I'd be standing here.

But before you think I'm shitting on my ability or trying to dumb it down, I'm not. I'm just being real. It's because Radley Smith and William Parker go way back that I'm standing here now.

It's my ability that's going to *keep* me here.

"Hey, Radley."

"What did I tell you about that?"

He hates when people call him by his first name. To hear him tell it, I'm showing him disrespect. What he doesn't get is that I happen to like his first name a whole lot better and don't plan on changing it. He's just gonna have to deal with it. Even if it ends up earning me shit on my first day here.

"Why would you wanna be called Smith when there's about a million or so people with the same name?"

When he isn't quick with a response, I smirk and he laughs.

"I'm gonna have my hands full with you, aren't I?"

"Depends how literal you're being."

"Marie would slice off my balls and feed them to me for dinner if I even so much as thought about you that way, sweetheart."

Can't argue with that. I'd only met the woman once for about twenty minutes when I was sixteen, but what I had gotten wind of, I liked. She was even more of a ball buster than her husband. Which in my eyes, made them the best damn team in the business.

"In that case, yes you are. But considering what you said before even offering me a spot, I'm pretty sure that's exactly what you're after."

"Well, in a few weeks at the showcase, you're gonna have your chance to prove it."

The CPW Superstar Showcase.

My parents have been talking about it for months. Ever since he dropped the call that he was looking for talent and was gonna stop in for a scouting visit.

Which, considering all of the years I'd put in already; the blood I poured into the mat before my dad banned gigging, I was more than ready for.

If Radley wanted a real female athlete; one that did more than prance around in short skirts and shirts with more skin showing than actual fabric, that's exactly what he was going to get.

Even if he lived to regret it.

"Actually, I'm glad you brought that up. I had an idea I wanted to run by you."

Motioning down the hall, we start walking and after turning down into another corridor and walking in silence for a few minutes, he pulls to a stop at a door.

His name etched in gold across it.

"Ladies first."

That's new. Since when is Smith a gentleman?

I realize it's been a while since I've seen him, but not enough time for that particular leopard to change his spots.

Pushing the door open and stepping in, I waste no time throwing my body down into the chair across from the large metal desk that takes up the majority of the room and waiting while he made his way around to do the same. Leaning across the table, hands locked together, open to whatever it is he's about to hear next.

"I was thinking that instead of just going out there as Kimber the way I did with my dad, we could do something a bit different."

"Different how?"

Two years ago, after branching away from my father and reaching out to a few smaller promotions, I'd gotten booked in a match. It wasn't anything super special, there were no titles on the line or anything, but the booker talked to me when I got to the club and asked my name. Instead of giving Kimber the way I have every other time, I answered with Wycked.

There was something about it that when paired with my quicker paced wrestling style and gear, made it perfect. And even though it was only for one night, I'd been looking for an excuse to use it again.

CPW now that excuse.

"I was thinking a name change."

"Well, don't keep an old bastard in suspense. What'd you have in mind?"

"Wycked."

"The name you used in ASWA?"

Holy shit.

Considering it was a stretch to say there were a hundred people at the show that night, I have no clue how he even knows about it. Much less knows the name I used. I didn't even talk to my parents or Zach about it.

That night in ASWA being my dirty little secret. One that year's later still brings the biggest damn smile to my face, even with the loss I suffered.

"Yeah."

"Well, let's run with it. See how the crowd takes to it."

"Really?"

It's not unheard of for a promoter to hear out one of their talents, but for one to do it with someone they just brought in it can be. I had no expectations coming in here, and I still don't, but Radley being willing to hear me out about this, much less letting me do it, well, it makes my night.

"Yeah, but if it bombs, the next name you go by will be one I choose. We clear?"

"Crystal."

Reaching across the table and shoving his thick callused hand out between us, he smiles when I slip mine into it and grip it tighter, shaking it hard.

"Welcome to CPW, Wycked."

Chapter Fifteen

October 2014

Matthias

"Word is, the girl Smith brought in to shake things up in the Women's Division is from across the border."

"Bullshit, Ortiz. I heard it's just some random Goth chick whose daddy worked with the boss man, and he's doing the guy a favor."

Not that my mind needs the push to think about her, but hearing the way the guys are talking about this new acquisition, there's no denying there's only one girl that comes to mind.

Kimber.

It's like this every time Smith brings in a new girl, though. The guys even before they meet her, hash out why she's there. What she looks like, who's gonna be first to nail her, and just how many of the guys she'll let in her pants before she finally attempts to be a legitimate performer.

Doesn't even matter to these jackoffs that they're all legit performers.

If I had to take bets this time around, I'd say it's gonna be a race to the finish for Ortiz and the guy that is nowhere to be found, Gavin Fortune.

Come to think of it, since he came in, I don't think there's been one girl on the roster he hasn't gotten his claws into. He's been through them all and we've all had to deal with the fallout after it goes south. The worst, him and Melinda. That one, what with her being back and thrown back together with her ex, Jackson, still fresh as a god damned daisy.

"Hey, Kemper!"

Looking over at Ortiz with a scowl, I ready myself for what I know is coming.

They're gonna wanna pull me into their little gossip session. Something that even after working with some of the guys for the past six or seven years, still haven't learned I want no part of.

"What?"

"You and Smith go way back, right? Think you can get the deets on the new girl?"

That's new.

Everyone knows that out of all the guys here, I've been here the longest. In all that time not once has anyone asked me to use my relationship with Smith to get information. I gotta hand it to her. She's got these guys so spun with the mystery surrounding her that she's got them reacting in ways I never expected.

I'm actually surprised it took them nearly ten years to pull this card.

It's just too bad it doesn't change the response.

"No way. I'm staying the fuck away from this."

"Never figured you to be scared of a girl, Kemper."

"Not afraid, Ortiz. Just smart."

"Come on, man! You're always the first one here and the last damn one to leave. You're so far up Smith's ass, it's hard to see where he ends and you begin. Don't you ever get sick of it?"

There it is.

This I'm used to. Just because I stay focused and as far from women and all other temptations, I'm not one of them.

"Ask Fortune. He likes breaking in newbies." I offer, not even giving the time of day to what Ortiz said.

Tossing my discarded clothes into my bag and glancing at the time glaring at me from the face of my phone, I toss it inside and zip it shut before heading for the door.

The guys may have forgotten about what we're here to do tonight, but I haven't. I've got a showcase match to prepare for, and the mental psych up I need to give myself isn't going to happen here.

Not with these women going on.

"Just once, Kemper." Reid speaks under his breath as I pass by, making me pause and turn my attention to him.

"Got something you wanna add, Reid?"

Carter Reid came in a few months ago and quickly glued himself to the other guys. The complete opposite of the way I am. Until now, I've likened him to a mosquito. Basically an annoying buzzard, but harmless. He never speaks directly to me, but with what he's doing now, it looks like that's all about to change.

"Actually, I do." He announces, puffing his chest out in a lame attempt to appear like something other than the puppy he is.

"All ears."

"Remy has a point. I've only been here for a few months and I can see you're not a team player. Whenever we see you around, you're as far from other people as you can get. Sure, you work with us when we're put in matches, but that's as far as you take it. Even when you end up at the bar, you're always off in a corner all broody and shit. For once, I'd like to see you actually be the team player Smith claims you are."

Says the guy that two nights before we landed in New York spent the night in his hotel room pouting over a fight with his girlfriend. One that despite my aversion to all things relationship, I'd actually been a part of pulling him out and away from.

A night that ended with some girl's legs wrapped around him in the men's room and memorialized on video for the whole damn locker room to see after the fact.

If that's how you become a team player, count me the fuck out.

"Let me guess. After I run and get you the info you're after on this new girl, you're also gonna wanna team up and bang her together, right?"

Judging by the sour puss expression on his face, the idiot might have a bullshit line after all. It felt disgusting enough hearing myself say it.

"That's the dirtiest thing I've ever heard you say, choir boy." Ortiz pipes up. "Is that why you never partake of the chicks that are ready willing and able after the shows? Is tag teaming some bitch what gets you off?"

Not even dignifying that with a response.

"You want info on the new chick? Try growing a set and getting it yourself. I'm outta here."

There's no way in hell I'm telling these two pieces of shit that I know who she is. They'd never let up. I'm keeping the identity of the new girl mine a little longer.

Longer, as in forever right, Matty boy?

Shaking myself free of the reoccurrence of the voice, I slam my way from the room, making sure as I do that the door slams hard behind me. The only method I have these days of letting my anger show.

Leaning against the wall and sucking in a breath when I'm free and clear of the bullshit, I allow the tension of the last few minutes to dissipate, only moving when I'm sure I'm past the worst of it.

Weaving through the sea of people backstage, I head down one hall after another, thankful for the reprieve that just this short walk is giving me from what's about to come next.

I've still got time before my match, so I'm gonna do exactly what Reid accused me of, and run away to be all broody someplace quiet.

A feat that becomes damn near impossible when after passing by a set of soda machines and turning the corner, I'm met with a vision that not only has the hairs on the back of my neck standing at attention, but the tension before flooding straight back, even more powerfully than before.

There's a woman crouched on the floor with her head buried someplace between her hands and knees. The guttural sound of her sobs, ones I'm all too familiar with, calling to me and taking what was supposed to be my escape from the bullshit and gluing my feet in place on the floor.

Great.

Here we go again.

Kimberlee

My daddy may have trained me, molding me into the competitor I became, but I've done a lot since then.

Branched off and done my own thing. Become my own person.

Become Wycked.

No one here knows that though.

To every single person I pass, male or female, talent or the guys that put the ring together, I'm the new girl.

The newbie with a connection to the owner.

Which, if you don't understand the way this place works, means they think I'm going to be handed everything without having to work my tail off and earn it.

I've passed three behemoths since I got here already that have sneered as I passed. Flipping their noses up like I'm filthy and even so much as aiming their nostrils in my direction is going to flood them with a stench they can't wash off.

It's off-putting sure, but it's not like I haven't been in this exact place before.

Multiple times if we're pulling out the scorecard.

So imagine my surprise when after wandering around and getting a feel for my surroundings—my first time in Madison Square Garden—I end up coming across a scene the complete opposite of what I've already encountered.

A guy crouched down on the ground with his back to me, leaning in to a girl that looks about my age. Her eyes, even from here, swimming and seemingly drowning in tears, as the dark angry lines from whatever makeup she'd been wearing testifies to as it streaks its way down her face.

His voice, while deep and rough, is also soft as he attempts to get her to open up. Lame jokes and what I have to believe are silly expressions—seeing as he has yet to turn around so I can make him out—taking what otherwise would appear to be a heartbreaking scene and breathing life back into it.

The woman, based on the tag I can make out around her neck is a member of the truckload of press here tonight, but the guy, based on his build and the gear he's already sporting, definitely belongs here.

He's one of us.

I can't tell who he is from here, but what I do know is, he's different.

He cares.

Okay, before you all go off, hear me out.

Not all of the people I work with are dogs. Some of them are decent people. Married men with families that are doing this because they truly love it. Single guys with a love for a sport that for years has been labeled as something else entirely. Soft-hearted people with a sense of honor, integrity, and respect.

So it's not like in that way, this guy is anything all that different.

It's just normally you see it with a lot of the older guys and not someone that looks as young as he appears to be from where I'm standing.

Those guys, at least in my experience, while maybe doing this because they love it the same way I do, are also doing it for the reputations and perks they'll get.

They're sleeping with whoever willingly parts their legs, taking what is given, in some cases even demanding it, and letting the hunger to be the best and at the top of the game, turn them into complete and utter dickbags.

Maybe this guy is one of them, but with the almost tender way he is with the girl, my instincts scream that it's more.

He's more.

"Enjoying the show?"

Jumping back from the hot blast of air as it makes its way over my neck to my ear, I let out a squeak. Pivoting around and coming face to face with the very last person that given the reputation he's earned, I want to have anything to do with.

Gavin Fortune.

"Do you always sneak up on people or am I just special?"

"I could ask you the same thing."

"Are you doing that?"

"Am I what?"

Pretty may be the only thing he has going for him if he can't follow along with a conversation he started in the two seconds it took me to respond.

"Asking me."

Lips curving into a smirk, I resist the urge to reach out and smack it off his face.

Gavin is not my first go round with a champion. This is exactly what I was talking about earlier. This guy is the epitome of believing his shit doesn't stink.

Does that smirk really work on girls?

"I don't need to ask. I've been watching you stalk them for the last few minutes."

"Aww, Gav. I didn't think you had it in you to focus your attention on someone for that long."

This gets him. He's not on his game anymore.

"Who are you?"

Stepping toward him, I give him a bit of his own medicine back as I lean in, resting my hand on his shoulder, lips quirked up.

"I'm not interested."

"Who says I am?"

Nice play, Fortune, but I see right through you.

"The fact that I have tits says you are."

Whistling under his breath he backs upbringing both hands up in the air in some form of lame surrender, and despite my need to not let the two people a few feet away catch on to my presence, I laugh.

With everything I've heard about this guy even before I landed in town, I thought it was going to be a hell of a lot harder to get him to back down.

There's a champ in the building sure, but it's clearly not him.

"You seem to know a hell of a lot about me. So how about we stop playing whatever this game is and you tell me who the hell you are?"

"Wycked." I spit out, eyeing him for any sign of recognition of the name and finding none as his eyes only seem to pull in more.

"Right. Okay. I can believe that." He covers, letting his eyes start to roam down from their position on my face and over my chest with ease.

Gross.

The only thing he's missing in his perusal is letting his tongue fall out and wag like a dog.

Wait, no. That's an insult to dogs everywhere.

Reaching out and gripping his chin in my hand, I tighten the hold and yank up until his eyes are locked on mine.

"My eyes are up here."

"You didn't have to pull away. It's kind of hot the way you took charge and grabbed me."

Unbelievable.

Figures that something as simple and pulling his attention away from my tits would give this guy a hard-on. Makes me wish I could snap my fingers, have him vanish and turn my attention back to the guy down the hall.

The one that helps women instead of ogling them like they're dinner.

"Whatever it is you're trying to do here, pretty boy, you gotta know by now it's not gonna work. So why don't I do us both a favor and leave so you and that ego of yours can be alone."

Shifting my attention quickly in the direction of the two people I'd been watching and finding a third person joining them, I quickly look away and turn the other way. Starting to walk without so much as another glance in Fortune's direction. Getting a few steps away before a hand reaching out destroys my great escape.

Deep down, my mind willing it to be the sandy-haired guy from the hall coming to my rescue, but what reality ruins when I see it's just more of the same.

What the hell is this guy's game?

"Unless you're looking to get your ass laid out before it happens in the ring, let go of my arm."

Doing as I say and again bringing his hands in the air in surrender, he takes a step back and this time, the look I'm met with is different.

Cockiness stripped away until all that's left is what I imagine is the sheepish boy underneath the asshole he became.

"Look, I'm sorry. I was a prick. It's just, you're fucking gorgeous and you seem to know a hell of a lot about me. I just wanna know how that is, seeing as up until now I've never seen you around."

"I told you who I was."

"No you didn't. You shoved your gimmick at me."

"I think you mean I gave you my in-ring name."

"Same shit. Whatever way you wanna spin it, it's not what I'm after."

"I'm well aware of what you're after." I laugh. "You showed me as much with your little display before."

Before Gavin can mount any form of comeback, a shadow looms heavy over us, and turning instinctively toward it, I'm met by the very person I'd been hoping would come to my rescue.

Those eyes.

No. Freaking. Way.

It can't be.

"Is he bothering you?" my savior asks, and that's all it takes. Sure, it's deeper than it was the last time I heard it, but it's just as seductive. Now that it's closer and less muffled than it had been with the girl, there's no mistaking it.

My savior is Matthias Kemper.

Breathe, Kimber. You can't let either of them know that you know.

Looking from me to Gavin when no response follows from either of us, his eyes harden until the clearing of my throat breaks him free.

"He's not, but thanks for the save. I really should find Radley. I've been wandering around long enough."

Shifting his body, Matthias takes a step toward me at the exact moment I turn in an effort to leave, causing me to brush against him. My body completely unprepared for the way the hairs on my arm begin to stand on end with the accidental touch, but a reminder of every reaction I've had with him in the past.

It's definitely him.

Holding myself still, I suck in a breath as goosebumps begin to form in the exact area he touched. Only releasing it when after a few seconds where he appears as stunned as I am, he shifts again and breaks the connection.

"That's actually why I'm here, Kimber. He asked me to find you."

If I wasn't dealing with the way my body seems to be betraying me, I might be able to focus on the fact that he knows it's me.

As it stands though, all I can focus on now that my name has fallen from his pursed lips, is how to get him to repeat it. How to bridge the short distance that now exists between us just to see how far this visceral reaction I'm having to him is willing to go before it peaks.

It's clear that seven years doesn't mean shit when it comes to him. My body has clearly decided he owns it now just like he did then.

The race to my pulse and the quickened beat of my heart damn near making my mouth want to pop open so I can pant the same way I called Gavin out on.

Get a grip, Kimber.

"Thanks for that, man. I've been trying to get her to tell me who she is."

"Pretty sure you were after more than her name." Matty grounds out and I react. A giggle snort laugh that not even slapping a hand over my mouth is able to stop.

Taking what had until now been his attention on Gavin and turning it straight back to me. The beginnings of a scowl that present whenever he so much as flicks his attention to the third party of the group, twisting around until there's a slight lift to his face.

My laugh obviously pleasing him and making my heart do the wacky in the process.

"You said Smith sent you to find me?" I remind him, still determined to play dumb even with my body giving me away.

Stepping around from his position at my side until he's blocking me from Gavin's view completely, the other side of his face rises until he's offering me a full-on smile.

One I haven't seen in years. Also, one that the second it happens, he has to go and add fuel to the fire by following it up with a wink. One I have no problem returning.

Okay Matthias. I'll play your game.

"Yeah. You've got a match coming up and to quote him 'she's gonna be walking out to dead air if she doesn't get her ass back here and tell me what entrance music she wants.'"

Crap. I knew there was some things we still needed to settle up on.

"Let's go." I tell him, reaching out and grabbing hold of his hand, fully prepared to use him for the reprieve I'm after. "He's probably pulling out what's left of his damn hair by now."

Expecting him to untangle our fingers, he doesn't. Instead a gravelly sounding laugh booms out as he does the opposite. Tightening the hold as he takes control and starts pulling me away.

Looking back over my shoulder, I throw my free hand in the air in the lamest kind of wave before giving in and letting him pull me down the hall as fast as he can go. Only slowing him when we've made our way around the corner, but making sure not to release the hold, as the warmth that is now radiating straight through my arm and directly into my chest is too pleasurable to give up.

I can't even remember the last time I reacted like this toward someone.

Wait. Yes I can. It was with him.

"Thanks again for the save." I mutter as we turn down another hall to where Smith's office is waiting.

"Anytime."

"Did Smith really ask you to come find me?"

"No, but I overheard him bitching earlier, and since tonight seems to be the night for me and damsels in distress, I figured I'd step in. Assumed with the look I saw before I got there that you weren't looking to be another notch."

Slowing to a complete stop, I look toward our hands, studying the way they seem to fit together so perfectly, not even the slightest sliver of space between them.

Like they were made for each other.

My eyes lingering there until the soft clearing of his throat pulls my attention back.

Please don't pull away. I plead silently, closing my eyes and taking it so far as to wish before opening them and looking up to meet his, stormy as they are.

"I wasn't. So I appreciate it."

It's his turn to lower his gaze to our hands and despite the pull inside to tell him the same thing I told Fortune before, I can't do it. There's something about the way his head tilts and his eyes seem to lighten before softening that keeps me mum.

He's definitely as affected by me as I am by him.

Good.

"Little one..."

Even knowing I was right the second his eyes met mine earlier, it's still a jolt to my system when he uses the nickname. Solidifying what I know. Who he is.

The boy that when he first landed at our place had looked straight through me, and who a few short weeks later had become so caught up in whatever it was that was happening between us and returned my first kiss with his own, stronger one.

It's really him. It's really Matthias.

My biggest crush.

My first *and only* love.

He's really standing here.

"Matthias Kemper..." I whisper, finally dropping the act and admitting what I've known all along.

"Kimberlee Parker."

Chapter Sixteen

Matthias

Green fucking eyes.

Eyes that have haunted me from the first day I saw them over seven years ago. Ones that even with our time apart, I couldn't let go of and had to frequently check in with.

Calling Renegade for the first few weeks, maybe months with as often as I did it, and then finding other ways to follow her from afar. Reading up on her matches, results and interviews she did, all in the name of furthering herself and her father's promotion.

God, I even hounded Zach, and at that point I knew he knew it wasn't just a fascination because I worked with them.

It was because she had weaseled her way under my skin and not even distance and years apart could change it.

Her eyes see things. They see everything.

They see me.

Kimber the only person past my mother and Bryan that saw through my bullshit. Saw what lay underneath all of the layers of crap I've tacked on over the years.

And eyes that as they bore their way into me now, can probably see all of the new layers since our last encounter.

Kimberlee "Little One" Parker is finally here and looking anything like the little one I deemed her to be when she was barely fourteen years old.

She fucking grew up.

I can't fucking do this.

I can't fucking go there with her. I can't go there with anyone.

But god, do I want to go there.

Girls are a distraction from my goal. They're also nothing but trouble as evidenced by the way I'm reacting to seeing Kimber again.

I've managed to go this long without a woman. Singularly focused on my pursuit to make it to the top of CPW before moving on and owning the top of the business as a whole someplace else. I can't let the way my body responds to this girl pull me away from that now.

Even if I enjoy the way her hand rests in mine.

How soft her pale skin feels as its brushing up against the more hardened feel of my own.

She'll be my ruin if I give into this.

It's time for me to be the asshole she remembers. Break free of her and this overwhelming feeling threatening to sweep me away.

Kimber's power like a tidal wave.

One that *will* pull me under.

"You remember." She says softly and I look away, willing my ears to close up so I don't have to hear whatever she's going to say next. Her voice almost as hypnotic as the rest of her. The pull I had when she was a kid, no longer feeling like the dirty and shameful secret it was now that she's here all grown up.

Curves replacing every inch of her that as a young teen hadn't grown into itself, and making me no better than Gavin standing here with what is quickly turning into the hardest reaction I've ever had to a member of the opposite sex. Also what if I don't excuse myself right now and adjust, she'll notice as easily if I pulled it from my trunks and shoved it in her damn face myself.

Groaning at the visual of Kimber with my cock in her mouth, I shake myself free of my perversion at the exact moment as she scowls.

"I'm that memorable huh?" she asks dejected before attempted to harden herself. What fails as those eyes of hers betray her.

"Yes," I admit truthfully before catching myself and attempting to change it. "I mean, no. Not in the way you're thinking. All I remember is the little brat that thought she had what it took to be a wrestler."

Yeah, there you go, Matty. Pulling the brat card and making light of the very real ability she has should nail this coffin closed.

Ripping my hand harshly from hers, I swallow down the urge I have to pick it up again as the sting of my move causes her to react, her eyes dropping to the floor like Avery's earlier. Her body slinking backwards, just as dejected.

Looks like I can only handle one damsel per night. Avery was my limit.

I can't be Kimber's knight.

Jonathan Kemper and his fucking DNA made sure of that.

You see…what lies underneath what you see on the outside is frightening. There's a monster in me. A darkness I can't cure. What only wrestling has been able to tame since I found it and made it my great escape.

I let her close once. Almost let her see the demon within because god, when we were together, everything just became so incredibly easy.

But it can't stay that way forever.

At some point that pitch black darkness inside, what has turned my heart ice cold and my soul as black as sin itself, it will make an appearance. I *will* taint her with it.

I am my father's son after all.

So arm's length it has to be.

"And you clearly still have those same issues that had Smith suspending your ass and kicking you out." She gives back, and even though the truth of her shot stings, I don't so much as flinch.

She can't know she affects me.

That even seven years later, she's the only damn one that does.

"Didn't seem like you had a problem with my *issues* when I was saving your ass back there." I throw my thumb back the way we came. "Before it had the chance to land flat on its back."

Her hand swings out and the sting of it as it connects with my face should have been more expected than it was, but I can't deny that it's exactly what I was after when I said it.

It's safer for her this way. Even if doing it this way tosses her right in the path of vultures.

Gavin, Remy, hell, even Carter. They might use her, maybe even hurt her, but at least they wouldn't ruin her.

She'll survive them. She'll survive being here.

Something that with me, as she pulls back and moves around, quickly escaping inside the office, I know beyond a shadow of a doubt, she never would.

I'd ruin her the same way I did the last person I cared about. *I'm sorry, little one.*

Kimberlee

Seven years.

It's been seven years and there isn't much about his time with my family that I can't remember.

He's different now. His hair is messier and he's packed on more weight, but not in a sloppy way. It was done with purpose. He bulked up to be able to compete in the heavyweight division.

Matty wasn't exactly small when I knew him, but the definition to his body, how much wider he is from the way he was when I was fourteen, it's really no surprise I didn't realize it was him when he was with the girl.

What guts me, especially with the way I reacted to him once we were face to face, is that I should have known it then.

Matthias, contrary to what I tried selling the world, is unforgettable.

Even if he wasn't, I knew the entire roster by name. I even knew he was a part of it. Knew it was only a matter of time before we came across each other. And with the way he was when I was younger, listening to me and consoling me when I needed it, seems only right that it was him at the end of the hall helping the girl with the broken eyes.

Our meeting was inevitable.

I just didn't go out of my way to actively search him out. I couldn't. I wasn't ready to. Not when I had no idea how it would all play out. If the same feelings that drove me then, would manifest themselves again.

What I really hoped wouldn't, only because of his own words. Words that haunted me for months, years, after he left and came back home.

He'd been right in what he said when he left, even if his words had been cruel.

I did move on with my life.

He was wrong about me getting another crush though. That never happened.

All that did happen was the memory of the boy I met and subsequently fell for, staying with me. No matter what I did in order to block him out. And believe me, I tried.

I tried so damn hard it led to one of the worst experiences of my life.

Meeting a random guy at some party one of Zach's friends had thrown and mistakenly giving myself to him in an effort to forget. To move past the vice-like hold Matthias had on me.

To forget.

An event that after that night, sparked a change in me so powerful that no one could get through. Least of all another guy. The guilt I felt waking up the next day, sober and completely coherent, realizing what I'd done, not something I was willing to relive ever again.

Not when the one I really wanted to be with was a million miles away.

The one I still want.

Matthias—his memory—it manifested itself in every facet of my life even more after that.

When I decided in that strangers bed that I would give wrestling my sole focus. I would stop pretending I could be the party girl all my friends wanted me to be. The studious and good daughter my parents wanted. Even the brat Zach expected.

He became a part of it all.

He was the one silently pushing me when my father got caught up helping Zach make a splash in the independent scene. The one congratulating me after every win and holding me close after every loss. After every new move acquired and woven into the fabric of my wrestling style, he was there with that smile. The one only for me. He was there through every single step, cheering me on. Watching me rule what I know I was born to do. His imagined embrace getting me through the harder times. His promise to protect me when we as a family all banded together and sat my father down for the world's shittiest intervention, guiding me through it all.

An intervention that if he hadn't turned so cold toward me, I would have wanted to share most with him, since he was a big part of the reason it even happened at all.

So no, Matthias Kemper was never forgotten.

Leaning against the wall of Smith's office, I don't even bother checking to see if he's there. I wallow in the past and the pain I feel now in the present after what just happened out in the hall. It's only in the clearing of his throat and the heavy laboured breathing that follows that I bring myself around and finally acknowledge that I need to get myself together.

"You alright?" he heaves out from across the room, sounding awfully breathless for a man sitting in a chair while his performers are all out there tearing the house down.

"Yeah...Yes, I am. Just needed a minute." I admit, though the truth of the matter is, I'm not in the least bit okay.

How dare Matthias act that way? Especially after all this time. Why is he acting like this when we both know he's better?

Shaking it and him off, I give my boss my full attention. Matthias's words from before, as much as I would love now in the moment to block them out, reminding me of my reason for even standing here at all.

"You need music for me, right?"

"Unless you wanna be rolling out there to dead air."

"Who you got running the audio?"

"Mark. He's in a production truck out back. He's expectin' you."

"Good."

When I walked in here, I honestly had no idea what music I wanted to be playing when I made my way out for the first time. I knew I wanted something with an edge to go along with the name, but past that, there just hadn't been anything that came to me. Call it me remembering what it felt like to be a fourteen year old girl on the receiving end of disbelief, mean spirited words, and an opinion I had to prove wrong, but after my run-in with Matthias, I had it. It was an older song, couple of years since it had been released, and it was by a band that Zach was determined I had to hear live to believe, but there was nothing more suitable than it.

Demons by Sleigh Bells it is.

"Anything else you need?" I think to ask as I make my way over to the door but hesitate to go all the way through.

"Nope. You handle the shit with Mark, make sure you're ready to go out there and work, and we're set." Turning my attention back to the door and the escape it would provide, he pauses me mid-step when he calls out. "Just go easy on Richardson tonight, would ya? She's needed later for Jackson. I don't want her pretty face kicked in."

Smiling, thankful that he's more than a little aware of my ability and my reputation working under my father, I nod and head out.

Matthias Kemper and the influx of lust mixed with genuine feeling he brought alive be damned.

It's my time to shine and no one, not even him, is going to stand in the way of that.

Debut here I come.

✴ ✴ ✴ ✴ ✴ ✴

"We got off on the wrong foot before."

Oh, God. Not again.

Wasn't my altercation with Matthias enough? Can't I be left alone? I mean, surely the heavyweight champ has better things to do than follow some random girl around the place. Interviews. A match. Last minute details to go over with Smith. Something. Anything to get him the hell away from me and back amongst his kind where he belongs.

I am definitely not interested in buying whatever it is Gavin is selling.

"Actually, I'm pretty sure we got off on the right one."

Whistling low he takes a step back, thankfully not crowding me in despite the scent of stalking I can smell in the air, crossing his arms across his chest.

"I wasn't trying to hit on you. I saw you watching Kemper and the girl and was just calling you on it. That's it."

"Why don't I believe that?"

Smirking but managing to think better of it—something new for him I'm sure—he wipes it almost as quickly and stares me down.

"Because like I said before, you know more about me than I do about you. My reputation isn't exactly a secret."

"And what reputation would that be? That you chase anything in a skirt? Or the one where you throw your weight around because of that belt?" I point to the shimmering gold beauty hanging over his shoulder. "Assuming it means you should get whatever the hell you want whenever you want it?"

"I guess I deserve that."

"No denial? You really don't care that's how people see you?"

Shaking his head and looking quickly down to his foot, silencing the tapping he'd been doing since I acknowledged him, he takes a step closer to me and meets my hard stare head-on.

"If I denied it, would you believe me?"

"Not a chance."

"Exactly. You don't seem like the type of person I can bullshit the way I do with others around here. So I'm not gonna waste my breath. I do take advantage of my role as champion. I own that. I think everyone before me, and who'll come later, will do and has done the same. It's addictive, what you're given the second they strap the belt on you."

"You mean, high caliber matches, non-stop riding the road, and the overwhelming pressure to succeed? You think of those as perks?"

I'll give him his due. When he showed up again, I never expected him to agree with my assessment of him. Much less sit here and say something besides a typical flirty come on. I still think he's a first class prick based on everything I've seen and experienced tonight, but definitely a little less of one.

Even time with Gavin beats being shredded by the only boy I've ever loved.

Leaning back against the wall and settling in as comfortably as I can, I wait him out. Despite knowing it can get me into trouble later, I'm actually interested in what he has to say after what I just threw at him and once he sees my lack of attempt as bolting the way I did with Matthias earlier, he wastes no time getting right to it.

"No. Those aren't perks. But you can't tell me that in your time with other promotions that you didn't get addicted when you were handed the brass ring. Tickets to events, women—men in your case—at your beck and call. Free stuff. Every material possession you ever dreamed of at your fingertips."

Oh boy. If he really thinks that even after holding the newly implemented Women's Championship in my dad's promotion that I became addicted to anything, he's got another thing coming. This, what we do, is not supposed to be about what we can get. It's supposed to be what we can do. Just how many we can entertain and for how long.

Gavin Fortune needs a reality check.

"You don't deserve to be called champion."

Smirking and enraging me so much I have to lower my eyes to the floor and clench my hands to my sides to protect myself from the strong urge to assault him that's rising, I take a deep breath and laugh at his cockiness.

He's definitely in a class all his own.

"Why do you say that? Because I freely admit that I like the other side of being who I am? I enjoy indulging in what this world wants to give me?"

"No, you admitting you're in it for what you can get out of it was actually expected. Though, I will admit for a second there, I wondered if you would actually have the balls to admit to being such a disgrace to the title you're holding on your shoulder." I motion to his arm with my own smirk. "Not many would. Not when it could cost them."

"Ahh, princess! You gonna run and tell Smith what I said?" he laughs, devil may care attitude holding firm. "He is your daddy's best friend after all."

Oh hell no. He did not just bring my dad into this.

"Seems you do know something about me."

"Just what I went and looked up after our little introduction earlier. Trying to fill some pretty big shoes, aren't you, Parker? Not many can match Renegade."

"You want a medal for knowing how to work the internet?"

"No," he smirks again. *The bastard.* "I just want you to admit that you and me, we're not so damn different. You're here because of your daddy, and well, I'm here because...have you seen me?"

Running a hand over himself like I need direction to his body and the toned physique he's sporting, I roll my eyes. I'm well aware he's god-like. It's just too bad I don't care. Looks fade and they won't be what keeps him going when his body fails. Neither will the attitude he's sporting thinking his shit doesn't stink.

I take back what I said earlier. I'd much rather have another go-round with Matty again. At least with him, there's history and it's familiar.

"Well, this has been real, but some of us actually have to go out there tonight and bust our asses. We're not handed our perks on a brass platter." Pulling my body back off the wall, I go to make my way around him, but before I can escape, his hand flies out and blocks me in.

"Are you always like this?"

"Like what?" I purposely sneer, knowing it's only a matter of time before he questions aloud if I'm always a bitch.

It always goes down this way.

When a woman challenges them, the ones that aren't secure enough in their manhood to look at us like equals and still only see us as pieces of ass, it always turns into us being bitches. Fortune seems exactly the type to do it.

Like Levi before him and look where he is now.

Unemployed.

"This combative."

Well, that's unexpected.

"No, actually I'm not. I've been saving it up just for you."

"I'm honored." *Say what?* "But what I really wanna know is, who you are when you're not busting balls?"

Is this guy for real?

Clearly what's left of his brain cells spilled out in the last match he had if we're back on this again.

"Down boy."

I've clearly tripped him up as his arm falls back to his side and he takes a step back, eyes widening in what if I'm not mistaken is genuine surprise.

"What is your problem with me, Kimber? Did I shut you down before and you've got those pretty little panties in a bunch over it?"

I can't help myself. I've tried really hard to keep my wits about me through this entire thing, but he's clearly so into himself it's made him one of the blindest people on the planet.

After my laughter subsides, I lean in and placing a hand on his chest, beam the sweetest smile I can his way. Telling him what I've been dying to say since he basically admitted he's only in this business for the money and the ass it provides him.

"Newsflash, pretty boy. Not every female wants what you're selling. Some of us were born with more self-respect than that. Especially when it's not exactly a secret where it's been. And that title? I wouldn't get too comfortable with it if I were you."

"A—and why's that?" he manages to choke out, his voice barely a whisper. My verbal assault obviously hitting its mark and getting through his thick skull.

Finally.

"Because I might just exploit that friendship you accused me of using, in order to take it from you. Seeing as where I come from, it's raw talent, heart, and an uncanny ability to always get back up that make the man. Or in this case, the woman."

Shoving the hand resting over his chest hard and laughing when just as I hoped, I take him off guard and cause him to stumble, I blow him a kiss before turning and skipping off down the hall.

Mission piss off two of CPW's biggest performers, is a success.

I'm off to a great start.

Matthias

I should have known it would go down this way when we ended up in the same place again.

I'm not talking about me pushing her away and making her hate me the same way I attempted and clearly failed with when she was a kid.

No, I'm talking about what's going on in the ring.

Who she becomes when she slides between the ropes and puts on a show.

She did exactly what I knew she would.

Kimberlee owned her environment. Flipped the script and became the game changer.

All it takes is one look at her from my place behind the curtain after her and Melinda have locked up to see it.

The hunger, the deep in the gut desire she had when we were younger to be the best at this and prove herself. It's all still there. Except as she catches and flips Melinda over her back, the latter landing unforgiving to the canvas and selling it the way she's perfected, with Kimber quickly following it up with a run to the ropes and a diving double kick to the face when Melinda begins to sit up, it's more.

She's not proving herself anymore because this version of her, the one I always knew she had in her, is secure in her ability. Every move she makes as she bounces back up to her feet and runs for the ropes as Melinda struggles on the mat, is fluid. Done with ease. A confidence that when she was fourteen, she hadn't fully tapped into.

That's right, little one. Make me eat my words.

And eat my words as I do, when after a lame attempt at a comeback, no doubt Smith's punishment for all of the shit she's been pulling around here lately, Melinda is again taken off her ass and driven down into the mat as Kimber turns the momentum of the match around in her favor, landing a damn near perfect running bulldog on her.

The women of CPW don't stand a chance.

Just like I didn't.

Kimberlee Parker has done it.

Seven years, a few dozen cities, and three different promotions later, she did what she set out to do.

Own this business.

The same damn way she's always going to own me.

Chapter Seventeen
December 2014

Matthias

This is what I live for.

The second the lights in the arena fall. When you can hear a pin drop from the hush of the crowd in the seconds that pass before the opening bars of your entrance music begin. The rush of adrenaline that builds with each step taken toward the curtain, and the breeze that hits, seemingly lighting a fire under your ass and shutting down everything else going on, as you walk through it and hit the ramp.

Hair on my arms standing on end from the electricity coursing through my veins as I make my way to the ring, prepared to work my ass off for every morsel of attention this crowd is willing to give me. Which tonight, alongside none other than my greatest adversary Gavin Fortune, is sure to be enormous.

Blowing the roof off the response both Merrick and I received before our run came to an end.

It wasn't always that way.

Up until a couple of months ago, Gavin wasn't even on my radar. I was the Middleweight Champion, and he had his heavyweight duties. Shit, radar isn't even the right word. We weren't on the same planet.

Smith, though, perceptive old bastard that he is, saw something building between us and before I knew it, Jackson Merrick was the new Middleweight Champion and I was thrown into Gavin's stratosphere.

He's always been a good judge of character, Smith, but working with him as long as I have and never once entertaining the offers I received from more prominent promotions, has allowed him to know me better than anyone else. All it took was me reacting to something that even though I brought it on myself, I'd been blindsided by, and here we are.

It's her of course. All of this shit is because of Kimberlee Parker.

Only, she's Wycked now. Literally *and* figuratively.

She's also Gavin's girlfriend.

It all happened a few weeks after our moment outside Smith's office and it's only grown exponentially since.

Where a few years ago, it was all about Gavin and Melinda, these days it's Gavin and Kimber. They're the King and Queen of the locker room and the rest of us peons just bend to their will. For all the talk that surrounded her coming in and taking the Women's Division by storm, she sure as hell took the women's title and ran with it.

It was handed on that silver platter and Kimber had no problem accepting it, even with the backlash that quickly followed.

Backlash that's still happening. Even if she's closed herself off from hearing it.

Attacks on her talent that haunt me almost as much as she does.

I tried not to be affected. I shut my shit down and set my sights on my matches, and the training of the newest developmental talent that I was asked to be a part of.

I spent every waking hour in a match. One of my own design or one in order to train, with my body sporting the soreness and bruises to prove it. Doing everything I could until I had the temptation that Kimber presented under control.

At least as under control as it could be considering she was still anywhere and everywhere.

It was good. I was handling it. At least I was until the day I walked past as she admitted to one of the girls that Gavin asked her out and she accepted.

"It was the sweetest thing, Cara. He flew out to my parents and asked my dad if he could take me out. Then he showed up at my place with daisies. I mean, he showed up with my favorite flower. How could I say no?"

I had to hand it to Gavin, he sure as hell turned her mind around.

His reputation has never been a secret. In fact, I'm pretty sure with the way he adds new layers to it, he feeds off it. But leaving the States in order to go to Canada and ask permission to date Renegade's daughter? That was a new one. I didn't believe for a second that the guy labelled the pussy master, had changed. He was the same snake underneath. Still using his looks and that damn title to his advantage in order to screw with the female talent the second they were brought in. Breaking a little bit more of their spirit, the parts that wrestling and Smith didn't already wreck, in the process.

He sure as hell played it different with her though.

Word from a few of the guys is, he's changed. He's looking toward the future and not just a future in the ring. Unless by ring you mean the one he's going to end up putting on her finger.

Now you see why I'm gunning for the title.

If he gets to have the girl when I know for a fact he doesn't deserve her, I'm not letting him have that too.

I'm taking that belt and once I do, I'm not giving it back.

"Just the man I wanted to see."

It's never a good thing when Smith is actively looking for you. Even worse when the scowl is gone and he's grinning from ear to ear.

I'm gonna hate whatever comes next. Guaranteed.

"What's up?"

"Gonna need you to take one for the team out there tonight, son."

Considering the plan to have Gavin and I teaming up against River and Ross, furthering our hatred for one another when after reaching out for the tag, my partner is going to jump down off the apron and head for the back, I have no clue how I can further take one for the team.

"With Melinda and Jackson running their course, and the way the crowd seems to respond to the feud between you and Gavin that we're building, I want to capitalize on it going into the championship match."

"How?"

Please don't say you want to use Kimber. Say anything but that.

"We'll get to that, but first, I need to you tell me just how deep this shit runs between you and Wycked."

"What shit?" I feign confusion, not wanting to let on to there being anything between us. It's not like it's a total lie anyway. There really isn't anything going on. I made sure of it. "I've got no issues with her."

"Matty, what are the two things I absolutely despise my guys doing?"

"Lying and dating, not necessarily in that order. What does that have to do with this?"

"You're doing both right now," he pauses, holding a meaty hand in the air when I step forward ready to argue. "Save your breath. Whether you want to admit it to me or not, I'm not fucking blind and you're transparent. You're wearing that shit openly. Whole damn roster knows."

Bullshit, they do. To everyone here, I'm as morose as I've always been.

"I told you. I don't have an issue with Wycked. I have a few thoughts about the game Fortune's playing with her, but that's not on her. That's on him and me."

"I had a little chat with Renegade the other day and he said some stuff about your time there. So Matty," he pauses, staring me down. "I'm giving you one more chance to can the shit and give it to me straight."

There's only one thing Will Parker could have told Smith that wasn't public record all those years ago, and it's something that until now I thought no one knew but the two people involved. Since I didn't say a word, choosing instead to bury it down deep the way it needed to be with her age at the time, it means she talked.

Kimberlee told her father that we kissed.

Son of a bitch.

The worst part of all of this is, if I hadn't screwed my damn head on straight when I did, it probably would have ended up worse. I wouldn't have stopped at a kiss.

Since I'm still here breathing, she must not have figured that out.

Will Parker doesn't exactly seem like a guy to go easy when it comes to his daughter and sex.

"She had a crush on me, Smith. She kissed me and I pushed her away. The same way I did when she showed up here a couple of months ago. Haven't given her much thought since. It was nothing then, and it's nothing now."

If there was an award for sheer amount of actual horseshit slung, I'd be crowned the winner by a landslide. Not one bit of what I said even holding even the tiniest sliver of truth. But with the way his stance seems to relax and his arm comes out gripping my shoulder as he smiles, it looks like at the very least, he bought it.

"Good. That's what I wanna hear. You always did have the clearest head when it comes to that shit. One of the reasons you've stayed as long as you have. You know where your head needs to be at."

In other words, I've swallowed down the need to have it buried between Wycked's thighs and kept it in the ring. Successfully earning his respect.

If he only knew how unworthy I am.

Visuals of all of the ways I want to be with Kimber dominating my quiet moments just as much these days, even with her dating Gavin, as they did in the past. So powerfully that even standing here with the king of anti-romance, I could get carried away with.

"Now that we've cleared that up, you wanna tell me what you need me to do out there tonight?"

"She's going to run down during your match. When Fortune goes to leave, she's going to come out, but not for him. For you."

Son of a bitch.

If she gets within a foot of me tonight, I won't be responsible for what happens. Especially with the beast I roused awake thinking about being buried between her thighs. I'll ruin everything. Something that unless I want to be called out on the lies I just told, I can't bring up now.

I'm screwed.

"How far you taking it?"

"That's up to the two of you. I want you getting together and deciding what works. But Matty, it's gotta be enough to further the feud between you and Gavin. Enough to have him coming into the fight like an unhinged animal."

Has Smith been getting in the ring against Marie's orders again? He must if he thinks his pretty boy champion is gonna be able to pull off unhinged.

Has he forgotten who he's talking to?

"Smith..."

"Yeah?" he asks, lips curving up into a grin.

It's clear now. I wasn't entirely sure before, but everything I thought I sold him on about our past, he's seen right through it. This isn't about trying to turn Gavin into a beast for our title match.

This is about using what he knows and turning *me* into one.

I can't do that. Can't admit to something I can never act on. No one else needs to know there's something between Kimber and me. It's bad enough I know it. I'm not gonna put my very real shit on display and force something that none of us can come back from. Not for the man that signs my checks, and definitely not for a crowd of people that don't really give two flying fucks about me.

He should know better than this. Look how well it turned out the last time I lost control.

"I can't do that."

"You can and you will."

"Or what?" I challenge, knowing it's only going to end badly, but needing to fight despite it. I'll take my lumps. Even if it means I'm turned into a jobbing joke.

"If you don't play this out the way I need you to, consider yourself stripped out of the title picture permanently."

So be it.

I've spent years playing this game with Smith. Absorbing almost as much of the business as I did moves, matches, and the opponents I went up against. If he wants to pull me out of the title picture or worse, fire me and blackball me in the industry, let him.

There are other options. Other places.

This, what it would end up causing for Gavin, Kimber and even me, I can't do it.

For the first time in eleven years I can't be the company bitch anymore.

Smith doesn't need to know that though. At least not yet. Not until I've done the other thing he's asked.

"I'll talk to Wycked."

Kimberlee

"Hey, Kimmie!" Cassidy calls from the doorway. "You got a visitor."

That's it. The next match I want is with her. There's only so many times I can be called Kimmie before I go homicidal.

Tossing my e-reader down onto the bench and running a quick hand through my hair, thinking it's going to be Gavin, I make my way over, pulling it all the way open when she steps away.

Coming face to face with the last person I ever expected to be standing here for me.

Standing here period, with everything I've come to learn about him since I got here and a lot of the other girls filled me in.

Matthias Kemper doesn't play well with others. He's a loner. Broody on a good day. Downright nasty on a bad one. He spends more time alone in his room than he does out with the other guys when we're moving from town and town, and as far as I've been able to tell, hasn't been on one date since he started here eleven years ago.

"You needed something?" I ask, leaning back against the door and he nods.

"Yeah. You got a few minutes?"

I want to tell him no. Say I was in the middle of a really good part of the book I'm reading, and that not even the almighty Matthias Kemper, god among wrestlers, is pulling me from it.

But I don't, because despite my need to treat him the same way he does me, fourteen year old Kimber won't let me.

Releasing my grip on the door and letting it close behind us, I take a few steps away and lean back against the wall, waiting for him to follow and when he does, lowering himself to the floor, I join him.

"I was beginning to think you were avoiding me." I admit honestly, reminded as always of just how out of his way he goes whenever we're on the same show together to run in the opposite direction.

"I was. Avoiding you that is. I had to."

"Who told you that?"

"I did. Kimber..." he trails off and swallowing down the fourteen year old with stars in her eyes for the man with the striking blue eyes, I shove my body into his. Knocking him off his slightly elevated stance until his ass is firmly planted on the ground.

"Don't Kimber me, jerk. You know what? On second thought, I don't care what you have to say. I don't have time to hear it anymore."

Sliding to my knees, he's on me before I can even begin to lift off the ground, hands gripping my arms. His strength based on what I've seen him execute in the ring, definitely not running high. His grip halting not hurting.

"Please don't leave. I know I'm acting like an asshole, and I deserve a whole lot more than that shove but hear me out."

The plea in his voice and the pain in his eyes is my undoing. My reaction to it so strong, I can physically feel my own ache beginning to form. For whatever reason he needs to talk to me and even though the way he treated me when I got here was deplorable, I have to do what he wants.

I have to listen.

"Matty, what's wrong?"

"Smith wants you involved in our tag match tonight. That's not the problem. It's what he wants to happen that is."

I spoke with Smith *ad nauseam* earlier and not once did he mention wanting me to play any sort of part in their match. The fact that Gavin already told me the way it was supposed to play out should have been enough. A guy bailing on his partner would add fuel to the feud already taking place, making their match in a few weeks even stronger. The need for Matthias's revenge enough to watch on its own.

What the hell could they possibly need me for?

"He didn't say anything when I talked to him."

"Because he just thought of it. Gavin doesn't even know yet."

"So what does he want me to do?"

His eyes fall to the floor and after watching him hone in on a particular portion of the flooring without so much as a twitch to let me know he's still with me, I slug him again.

"He wants you to come to my aid, but in a physical way. Kimber..."

There he goes again. The sound of my name so raw yet soft coming from his lips, it's causing my stomach to flip.

I'm not annoyed that he trailed off this time. Now I'm just reacting. Just like it seems I'm always going to when it comes to this man.

"We need to get physical. Something that would piss off Gavin and make him even more determined going into the title match."

That didn't seem so hard. I think to myself, though it does seem like a move Smith would make. Especially with what he thinks he knows about me.

The same way that Matthias wears everything he's feeling so openly, I do too.

Smith has been after me for weeks now, wanting to know exactly what it is that's made me so aggressive in the ring and sad outside of it. He even went so far as to reach out to my father in order to get answers. I've got no doubt that after he'd gotten an earful about Matthias's time with Renegade, he was more than ready to act on what he figured was going on here.

He might not have come right out and asked if there was something between the guy he considers a son and me, but something tells me he doesn't have to. We're making it too easy.

"So basically he just wants us to kiss, right?"

Grunting something I can't quite make out under his breath, I get ready to elbow him in order to make him give it up, but he beats me to the punch.

"He knows that a kiss wouldn't just be a kiss with you, Kimber."

Oh.

Ohhh.

Now I see why he looks like death. Knowing it doesn't stop what happens next though.

The way my hand seems to move with a mind of its own until it's finding his and curling itself around it, squeezing. Or the way his eyes seem to lift with the contact until we're both surrendering to the need that always seems to be there to look at one another. The worst though, being the way my heart seems to respond to his admission, even with the knowledge that given my current relationship status, is all sorts of wrong.

Matthias isn't speaking to the rational Kimberlee anymore. He's speaking to the girl that placed her lips on his and never wanted to let go.

"Matty, you uhh..." I stammer over my words, his gaze lowering to my lips rendering me incapable of cohesive thought. "You need to do it. See it through."

Right now! My heart screams.

"I can't. I've done a lot of things for Smith, Kimber. I would do a lot more. But I can't do this."

"Why not?"

Shifting himself on the floor and bringing himself to his knees, he moves until he's hovering over me. His shadow drinking me in.

Lifting his hands, he places them on either side of my face and as he leans in, so close I can feel the warmth of his breath across my skin, he pulls me in with him.

He's going to kiss me. My mind readies itself, repeating it on a loop until his lips parting and him speaking slams me back to reality.

"I think you know why not. One kiss. One touch. It's never enough, Kimber. If I kiss you like I want to right now, it will be the end. It will be ruin for all of us."

Unable to withstand the betrayal of his words reflecting back on me through his pointed but pained gaze, I attempt to break the connection by flicking my eyes to the side, but his finger slipping over and tugging on my chin stops me. Brings me back.

Brings me where I know I belong, even if the choices I've made say different.

"You scare me, Kimberlee." Running a finger over my bottom lip, he lingers for a breath before tracing the outline of my top one. "When I look into your eyes I see the future and what we could be. It scares the fucking shit out of me."

"Why?" I whisper when he finally pulls his finger back, but thankfully keeps his body close.

"The last time I saw two people that way...it ended badly." He admits with an ease I didn't think he was capable of. Something in the way his eyes seem to cloud over, making me believe he's just given me a glimpse into a life not many are aware of.

Making me feel special.

Trusted.

"And you think because of what happened to them, the same could happen to us if we acted on whatever this is?"

"I know what this is, Kimber, and no. It's not something that could. It's something that *would* happen and I don't want that for you. I don't want it for anyone."

In every interaction we've had since I was a kid, none of them have ever been this open or honest. He has never exposed himself this much. Allowed himself to be vulnerable. It's a lot like I thought earlier. Matthias is a god among wrestlers, at least he's been built that way. He's very guarded. Never allowing himself to get close enough to feel much of anything past whatever he feels when he gets into the ring. There's a fortress built around him to keep all others out. Even the ones, like me, that desperately want to be let in.

"Who was it? Who got hurt?"

Shaking his head, he pulls back and I instantly feel the change in the air. The loss of the moment as a rush of coolness settles over my face and makes me long for the warmth I lost by pushing things too far.

"My mom, Kimber. It was my mom. Their love was so strong, so fucking toxic, it got her killed."

"Matthias—"

"No, Kimber." He interrupts, again bringing a lone finger to my lips and letting it linger. "I've spent years trying to understand why out of all of the people I've worked with and spent any amount of time around, it was the piercing emerald eyes of a fourteen year old that got through. Why it was those eyes that wouldn't leave me alone. Those that haunt me every second of every day. I gave up trying to understand it when you showed up here four months ago. When you looked at me and took my hand and held it. I wanted it. I wanted you. I still fucking want you, and I can't even explain why. I just know that whenever I'm with you, my body fires on all cylinders. I can actually feel a buzz, hear it whirring underneath my skin. You bring me to life. But I can't have you."

Yes, you can! I silently scream as my heart takes over again. Matthias putting to words every feeling, every experience, I've ever had with him in a way that my younger self couldn't do at the time.

"He had her, and even though it took years, he slowly took everything about her that he loved—that I loved—and he broke her. He took her life long before he killed her. I want to succumb—*give in*—to the girl that brought me back to life, but not if it means being the one to eventually take hers. So as much as I want to touch you, kiss you, and strip away every layer of ourselves—the layers no one else can see—I can't do it. I care too much."

I've heard people speak countless times of the way it feels in the moment their heart breaks, but not one of them ever prepared me for what the physical feel of your chest splitting apart, and your soul bleeding out, would actually feel like. The agony that one experiences—that I experience—as he explains how he really feels. I can actually feel the split taking place as he tries to set me free. The slicing and then cracking as he breaks me wide open. The pain excruciating, but pain I'm too stubborn to fight feeling because in stopping it, I'm denying it happening at all.

I'm never going to forget this feeling.

Forget him.

He can believe he's saving me later, setting me free now, but he's not.

What he's doing is only bonding me to him more.

"Don't do this." I weakly attempt to stop him as his body moves again and he's bringing himself so close we become one.

As his lips graze my forehead, I'm powerless as I melt into him. Every one of my senses on high alert, breathing him in. Committing the sound of his voice and the feel of his lips on my skin as it brands me, to memory. Knowing instinctively this is the last time I'll ever experience it.

Experience him.

"You're with Gavin. He's playing a game, I just can't figure out what one yet. He will hurt you, Kimber, but he won't destroy you the way I will. Forget this. Forget me. Go live in the moment with him. Please."

"Matthias..."

"In another life, I would have loved you, little one. Loved you so recklessly, so powerfully, and so completely there would never be any doubt about who held the key to my heart. Our love would have set the world on fire. The same way you've already managed to do to me here." Taking my hand, he places it over his heart. "It burns for you, Kimber. In this life and the next. It will always burn for you. It just has to burn alone."

I can feel him moving as my hands fall from his chest and back down into my lap. The coolness of the hallway settling in as the warmth fades away, but I can't reach out fast enough to stop him because I can no longer see him. Between the tears clouding my vision and what feels like my soul bleeding out onto the arena floor, I'm stuck. Unable to move. Unable to produce sound.

I'm stuck, he's gone, and even though we were never officially anything more than two people working for the same wrestling promotion, what's left of my heart knows it was so much more.

Because in walking away, he not only took a part of me with him, but he also left a pretty big part behind.

The haunting and debilitating memory of what could have been.

Chapter Eighteen

Matthias

When I think back over the years and who it is I have to thank for being able to stand here now, there's only one name that comes to mind.

And it's not Radley Smith.

We may have gotten separated when Bryan, wanting more than to be a manager-slash-mouthpiece for me, walked away in favor of starting his own promotion. I may have even grown a shit ton in the time since, but there's no denying that he's the reason any of this is happening.

So facing one of the biggest dilemmas of my life, it's him I call.

If there's anyone that can stop me from making what could possibly be the single biggest mistake of my career, it's him.

"I don't know how many times I can say this," He says when after the rings going in at least a dozen times, he finally picks up. "What we shared was explosive, but I'm just not ready for a relationship. I'm sorry."

With what just happened in the hall, the last damn thing I'm in the mood for is this bullshit, but after all the mud that's been slung his way over the years, the name-calling, labels and beatings he's lived through all in the name of seeing me succeed, I'm not about to deliver a curb stomping of epic proportions to his current attitude.

It sounds good on him.

"But, Bry. The earth moved that night. I know you felt it. How can you turn your back on that? We could *be* something."

"I always knew you secretly had a hot nut for me, man."

"You know it."

"Piece of advice. If you ever want to make a relationship work, you gotta return calls. And not just when you want something."

Not exactly in the mood to admit that he's read me perfectly again, I keep slinging the bullshit.

"Who says I want anything? Maybe I was calling because I missed that explosive night you're talking about."

"Kiss my hairy ass, Matty. You forget I know you. So stop yanking my chain and let me have it."

"I need advice."

"Don't pick anyone up when you're drinking. They're gonna look a whole lot different in the morning. Believe that. But if you're hell-bent on it, at least wrap that shit. Don't want your dick falling off before your pretty ass has the chance to make some little Kempers for me to train."

Little Kempers.

He's fucking with me, I know this. It doesn't stop the visual from becoming real in my head though. The complete opposite of the help I was coming for considering the only person I can imagine that happening with, I just walked away from in the hall.

"You done?" I bark out, swallowing down the visual of Kimber's tearstained face and focusing on the escape that this call was supposed to be.

"With you? Never. It's too damn fun screwing with you. But because I know steam is about to start billowing out of your ears, I'll stop for now. What's going on, Matty?"

"Kimberlee Parker."

Groaning, I hear a scuffling before a series of knocks filters its way over the line.

"Bryan, what the hell is going on?"

"If you must know," he laughs. "I was knocking my phone against my skull because you can't possibly be bringing this shit up again."

For a good six months after I came back from working with Renegade, I complained about Kimberlee. I was relentless in the amount of bitching I did. Mainly because just like she's doing again, she'd gotten under my skin and I couldn't make sense of it. Then last week, after seven years without so much as a peep about the girl even though her eyes continued to haunt me, I brought her up again when he blew through town scouting talent.

His last words on the subject being that I needed to pull my head out of my ass and do something about her or put her out of my mind completely. No in between. No other answer.

As done hearing about my issues with this girl as I was talking about them.

"You want my advice?" he finally asks when after a few minutes its apparent I'm not going to be answering.

"It's what I called for."

"I know all about your stupid fucking rules, and I even get why you have them. I don't agree, but it isn't my life. I also know that for the last seven years, you've let some little girl get under your skin, and now said little girl is all grown up. You're being forced to acknowledge that there may be more there than you want there to be. Act on it, Matthias. Stop fucking overthinking shit and for once in your life, allow yourself the right to be happy." Taking a breath, he starts up again, only this time, his voice is more subdued. "She wouldn't want you living like a monk out of some sense of misplaced guilt over what happened."

"Are you done?"

"No, not really. I mean, you called for my advice right? Which means this is my stage right now."

"Far be it from me to stop you."

"I told you last week how I felt about this, but apparently you've got that brain of yours sealed up tight. So let me repeat myself. You like this girl. She's the one you've really got the hot nut for, and now that she's legal and there's no repercussions from anything you might do with her if she's willing, you need to make a move. Screw thinking you're gonna hurt her, break her or destroy her. I bet you're doing that as we speak, which is the real reason you're calling. Instead of worrying about what *might* happen, worry about what *is*. You're falling in love, jackass. Let yourself do it. If not for yourself, for me. Because I'm getting sick of having to be your moral compass. I can barely keep my own shit together. How can I be expected to do it for you too?"

"I can't."

"Don't make me bang this phone off the wall next, Matty. I swear to god. I can't afford to get another one. This is the third one already. Shove that shit down. Talk to someone. A professional or something. Deal with your shit and move on. Be happy. No more fucking excuses."

"She's dating Gavin."

This gives me the opening I'm after. It seems to stop him cold. The only sound to be heard after I've dropped it, a heavy whistle followed up by the sound of his breathing.

"Well, shit. Forget everything I just said. Walk away. Run if you have to. But do not put your hands on anything that son of a bitch has touched. You won't make it out alive. Ask Merrick."

Jackson Merrick and Melinda Richardson's relationship drama is historic shit. Even three years later, the aftershocks are still present. Especially since the very guy she'd chosen to screw around on him with is the very guy that the girl I'm currently obsessed over is dating.

"Smith put us in a tag match. I called that when we talked last week. He's pulling a play from the pro wrestling handbook and attempting to build shit leading into our title match. I'm playing the game, it's all part of the job, but he wants to involve Kimber."

"Wait, don't tell me. He's gonna put the two of you against each other by throwing her in the middle." There's a slap of some kind and then he laughs. "Someone needs to remind him that's been done."

"WWE did it."

"I know!" Bryan yells excitedly. "I'll send you my South Park DVDs and you can show him that one episode where everything Butters wanted to do, the Simpson's already did. Smith needs a wakeup call."

This is why I call Bryan. He can complain about being my moral compass all he wants, but his ability to turn even the most serious thing into a joke is exactly what I need right now. It takes the beating I just put myself through, doing right by Kimberlee, out of my head. He's giving me the distraction I'm really after.

"I told him I couldn't do it."

"Of course you can't. Not when you suck major donkey balls keeping your feelings a secret."

"Thanks, man. You really know how to compliment a guy."

"Anytime, sugar tits. Now, what happened when you told him no for the first time since he made you his bitch in '03?"

"He threatened me with the title."

"So you're calling me because you wanna jump ship?"

Is that why I'm calling?

I mean, apart from the distraction his idiocy provides, am I really thinking about making the move?

I think I am.

"I wasn't sure until now, but yeah. I guess that's what I want."

"Don't do it. Not yet, brother. With Brady pulling the stunt he did a few months back and him coming over, you coming in would overshadow that and you know it. I want you here, Reese wants you here, it's where you belong, but so does he."

"Fair enough. But what do you suggest I do?"

"Say no. Stick to your guns. It's not just about you, so don't back down. Protect her in this. I could give two fucks about Gavin, but you know as well as I do that if you saw this through, you'd open the door to Smith exploiting some very real and painful stuff. You don't want that, and Gavin would demand it.

You might be like a son to him, but he's still a promoter. He'd sell you out in a second to please his golden boy."

It wasn't always that way. In the beginning, before Gavin came in and took over, Smith saw past the physical. He was determined to stake a legitimate claim in the business where the guys, no matter their size, would get the attention they deserved. One look at Gavin though, his ability to pick up a microphone and spit promos on the fly, let alone his looks and ability in the ring, and all of that shit flew out the window. He put everything he had into Gavin and years later, he's still doing it.

Gavin Fortune is making a literal fortune for Radley Smith, and family or no family, there's no way he's going to give it up.

"And if he fires me?"

"Then you come home, Matty. But since we both know he won't, stay where you are. Ride out his temper tantrum. Steal the show the way we both know you're capable of doing. Even if it means jobbing to some green newbie."

I've heard everything Bryan's said, but it's the part about a home that guts me the most.

If you asked me a few months ago, a year even, where my home was, it was here.

CPW is the only home I've ever known since I made the decision to escape the very real one I was stripped of the day my mother was taken. Other than a few visits to Bryan, and the twice a year shows Smith puts on there, I haven't gone back for an extended period of time. I can't. When I walk the familiar streets I grew up on, or worse, head over to the house and just stand outside and take it in, all of the memories flood me and take me clean off my feet.

The very same way I feel these days whenever I get within spitting distance of Kimberlee Parker.

Can I really do what Bryan said and willingly stay with that feeling? Worse yet, stay away from it when even from my place in the locker room, I can feel it calling to me? *Feel her calling.* Her voice like the sweetest, most beautiful siren song. One that if answered, will bring about my demise?

Surviving whatever Smith dishes out is easy. Surviving Kimber, not so much.

"Matty, wherever you're going in your head, don't."

"I'm with you, Bry. I'm just planning my next move."

"Which is?"

"Coming home."

✳ ✳ ✳ ✳ ✳ ✳

Head hung, I reach Smith's door and knock. Making sure as I do to shake off the residual nausea I've been experiencing since the call with Bryan, so the old man doesn't pick up on it and exploit it.

Are you fucking crazy? The monster from long ago returns screaming. *Everything you ever wanted could be yours tonight in that ring!*

No way. He doesn't get to do this now.

After the mirror shattering by my hand and the bottle full of pills I swallowed in an attempt to silence him that damn near cost me my life, I thought I'd finally gotten the upper hand in our twisted relationship.

It appears I was wrong.

"You gonna stand out there all damn night? Get your pansy ass in here already!" Smith's muffled yet bitter filled bark filters through the door.

This isn't just me saying no to something my promoter wants. This is about it being the first time I've even so much as thought of going against him. It doesn't matter that there's a first time for everything.

In this business, especially when you're being kicked around by Radley Smith, you don't say no. You take every scrap he gives you and you run with it because he has the power to make or break you.

Twisting the knob, I push my way into his office and leaning against the door, I wait for him to acknowledge me with a hard nod before taking the steps needed to finally enter.

"You talk to Wycked?" he barks out and it's my turn to nod. "You work it out?"

"There's—there's nothing to work out, Smith."

"What in the blue hell's that supposed to mean?" he looks up, glaring.

"It means, I'm not doing it. I can't."

"Boy," he starts, his normally gruff voice lower and more controlled. "This had better be you pulling the biggest damn rib in history, because if it's not, I will beat your ass right where you stand."

His threat is just that. A threat. He won't touch me. Contrary to what most believe, Radley and I are close. Over the course of the lifetime we've been together, leaning on each other more times than not. Hell, I'd even been his best man when Marie talked him into renewing their vows five years ago.

Making me the only person besides her that Radley Smith actually gives two shits about.

And I'm about to take a gigantic crap all over it.

"I'm not screwing around, Smith. It's not a rib. The guys aren't gonna bust through the door and throw you into a headlock and have a laugh at your expense. I'm serious. I can't do what you want me to."

Where I expect his controlled exterior to break and for him to come leaping over his desk, grabbing me in his meaty paws and strangling the life out of me, he just continues to stare me down. His face unreadable, his expression blank, as he instead slings the chair as far back as it can go, bouncing back off the wall before throwing his massive body down into it and releasing a heavy sigh.

"Matthias, in eleven years you've never once said no to something I asked you to do. You have always, even when my ideas weren't worth the paper they were written on, done what I needed you to do. For you to say no, it means there's something going on here. Something you had the chance to tell me earlier and didn't. So unless you want me making good on my threat and taking your head clean off when I sock you in your jaw, you better spit that shit out."

Where do I even begin?

How do you tell Radley Smith that you can't work with one of his performers because you're so deep in with her you're drowning?

"Five seconds or I promise you, I will pull it from your collapsed lungs myself."

"I kissed her back." I blurt, immediately dropping my eyes to the puke orange carpet under my feet and shaking my head. Wishing I could take it back. "She kissed me, ran, and instead of letting her go, I kissed her back. She was fucking fourteen and I took advantage of her. Put my hands on her. Smith, I can't fucking do this stupid shit tonight because if I do, I'll never come back from it. None of us will."

"Jesus fucking Christ!" he growls, slamming his balled up fist down hard onto the desk. The impact from the force making it wobble the same way I have since he told me about his plan for the match. "What is with you stupid sons of bitches? Head's full of rocks, I'm sure of it. She was what, thirteen?"

"Fourteen." I clarify, not that it makes me feel any better about it. I still fucked up and even though I avoided it for seven years, it's finally time to pay for it.

"I didn't fucking hear this. You know I got a bad ticker. You trying to do me in? Jesus, Matthias."

"Smith—"

"No!" he bellows, cutting me off. "You listen here. Whatever you did back then, you shove that shit down and do your god damned job. No more of this pansy ass shit you're about to spew about feelings."

"This isn't about feelings." I argue, the rise to his own voice now reflecting back in mine. "This is about me not wanting to fuck things up for her."

"Bullshit, boy. I wasn't born yesterday. I can see it in your eyes. This is about nothing *but* feelings."

"Fine! It's about my feelings. I don't *feel* right having her thrown at me after what happened before. I won't do it. Strip me out of the title picture, put me right at the bottom of the line and make me work another ten years for a spot. I don't give a shit. I'm not doing it."

Slamming his hand down onto the table again, he pushes himself back from the desk and stands. Leaning over and looking like death as his eyes harden as he stares me down.

"Handle this shit however you gotta, go out there, and do what I'm paying you for."

"No." I tell him, my voice firm. My decision made.

He could fire me right now and say he never wants to see me again. I'm not changing my mind.

Fuck the monster. Screw Radley Smith. None of them know what's right. Only I do.

I'm not Smith's bitch.

"Matthias…" he sighs, running a hand over his near balding head. "Don't make me do something I'll regret."

"Radley," I repeat back, going with his first name and making my stance clear. "I'm not making you do anything. Just like you're not going to make me do this."

"Pack your shit and get out of here."

"Excuse me?"

"You heard me. Get the fuck out of my sight. You're suspended. Effective immediately. Get the hell out of my building and don't think about coming back until you're ready to play ball."

Kimberlee

I move through the locker room like a ghost, breezing past the girls as they all stand around commiserating.

Cassidy and Hannah giggling over something they're watching on Cass's phone, while Lena, Devon, and Melinda huddle together discussing god knows what in hushed tones. None of them looking at me or silently questioning what Matthias Kemper could have possibly wanted.

None of them giving a shit about me at all.

This should make me happy, but it only adds to the misery I feel.

From the time I decided I wanted to do this at eleven, it's been a road I've had to mostly take alone. There wasn't time for dating, movie nights with friends, or something as simple as catching up over lunch. One by one, my friends dropped off like flies, finding it hard to understand why of all the things I could do with my life, all of the dreams I used to entertain, this was the one I chose.

My need to be the best female competitor in the ring that day and today, I let it consume me. It became everything, which meant no room for anyone else.

I likened it when I went off and did the one ASWA show, to the life of a writer. A solitary existence, even though unlike authors, I'm surrounded by a lot of people.

Unless you were climbing between those ropes every day, locking up with competitors as hungry as you who were looking for their chance to make a mark in a very selective business, you didn't understand me. Until you were pounded on so hard you walked away with two black and very blue eyes and muscle damage to your legs, waking up the next day and doing it all over again, you just didn't get it.

I was alone. The same way that after what happened with Matthias, I'm alone now.

An invisible entity just floating by. Each step I make, taking every ounce of willpower I have to see through. My body feeling like lead, while at the same time splintering and breaking apart like wood.

Tears long gone and left on the arena floor, but the dam of them breaking deep inside where the pain is centralized. Still unable to find my voice. The one that if I could, I would use to beg one of these girls to pull me away from before I'm completely consumed by it.

Championships, accolades, five-star matches, and all of the perks that come when after years of busting your ass you're recognized for it.

None of it matters when the very reason you fought so hard for all of those things is broken.

When you've been stripped of your heart.

Which is preposterous when you think about it. How a guy that only after a few weeks of bonding, one awkward kiss, and a reunion of sorts seven years later, could have that much control over the very valve that beat so strongly for this sport for far longer than I've known him.

When did I relinquish control of my life to Matthias?

Was it the day he called me a little girl and blew me off? The weeks I spent proving I was more? Or was it something more recent? The day he saved me from Gavin? Or today in the hall before he slammed the proverbial hammer down, smashing not only what could have been between us, but also my desire and love for what I do?

The better question being, why any of this even matters at all.

He made his position clear and I need to move on. There will never be anything there, no matter how badly I wish there could be.

I need to move on with Gavin and make the most of it. Stop being so torn between the man I can't seem to move on from, and the one that really wants to own my heart. Openly. For the entire world to see.

"Well, aren't you Miss Popular today?" I hear Melinda sneer and stopping mid-stride, I turn toward the sound of her ire. Meeting her scowl head on as she leans against the open locker room door. My heart springing to life with the hope that like it had been before, it's Matthias on the other side.

It's that bout of wishful thinking that has a spring appearing in my step as I quickly cross the room. And what comes crashing down just as fast when it's not Matty's face I see, but Gavin's.

"What's wrong?" he asks, his brow furrowing. Moving toward me the way a good boyfriend does and wrapping me up in his arms.

"Nothing's wrong. What are you doing here?"

Running a hand over my hair and smiling softly, he steps back.

"Smith had a few words with me about tonight. Looks like there's been a change of plans, babe. Kemper is out."

Kemper is what now?

"What do you mean Kemper is out?"

"Smith wanted you to interfere tonight, but apparently Kemper threw a tantrum and said he wanted no part of it. Smith sent him packing with a thirty-day suspension. Effective immediately."

Oh no.

No. No. No.

He couldn't have. He wouldn't have.

I know Matthias didn't want to do the spot, but I didn't think he would handle it this way.

Smith either.

Those two are family. Even if they're both too stubborn to admit to it.

This can't be true. Gavin has to be playing me.

"I don't think I heard you right. I could have sworn you said that Smith suspended Matthias."

"That's exactly what I said, babe. Are you sure you're okay? You're not acting like yourself."

Again his eyes flick over me, lingering on my face. Looking for something that no matter how broken I feel inside, he's never going to find. No one will. I will never let on the damage that was done in the very hallway Gavin is standing in. It's my secret.

"Sorry. I'm not feeling well." I offer up in an attempt to get him off the truth. My illness, in this case being of the Kemper variety and not a virus. "So if he's out, who's in?"

"You're not gonna like this."

"Why would who you tag with tonight matter? You know I've got a match of my own."

"It's Merrick, Kimber."

"Okay."

I'm well aware of their history. What Gavin has been swearing up and down for weeks he wanted to able to move past, but couldn't seem to make any headway on. Even if he hadn't said a word about it, I would have learned of it just from the amount of gossip the rest of these people do. The guys are worse for it than some of the women. I'm still not getting what bearing any of that has on me though.

"Why would it bother me?"

"Because Smith wants you to interfere."

"And do what exactly?"

I already have a good idea what he's going to say next, which explains the bile now rising in my throat. What if I don't turn my back on him now and run back into the washroom to deal with, will end up at his feet. The plan that Matthias couldn't handle because of the way he feels—*the way we both feel*—Smith is going to put at Jackson's feet instead. Taking whatever good Gavin wanted to do in terms of their personal history and blowing it to shit in the process.

Yeah, I'm definitely going to be sick.

"Stop!" I cry out at the exact moment Gavin goes to speak, stopping him cold. "I can't do this. I need to talk to Smith. I need to get him to change things."

"Kimber, what are you talking about? You don't even know what he wants yet."

He's confused and he's got every right, but this isn't just about Smith wanting me to screw around with Jackson anymore. It never really was. I could do that blindfolded. It's not like there are any feelings there. No, this is about Matthias. This is about the suspension. It's about us. I can't do any of it.

Not this spot. Not Gavin. And definitely not Matthias walking away.

"Gavin, I can't do this anymore."

"You can't do what?"

"This." I motion between us and down the hall, encompassing everything all in one shot. "I can't do any of this anymore. I'm sorry. So damn sorry. I need to go."

Not giving him a chance to respond, the buildup of saliva forcing its way to the surface quicker than I'm able to control, I turn and make a break down the hall. Turning the corner and straight toward the waiting recycling bin.

Lifting the lid in time, I empty the contents of my stomach and remaining hunched over long after the last dry heave takes place, I just continue to breathe and swallow until the unease begins to fade. Moving back after a few minutes, my head and heart clearer than it's been since I arrived here four months ago, I ready myself for what I have to do next.

It's time for me to talk to Smith, and maybe, hopefully, save Matthias.

Before I lose him for good.

Chapter Nineteen

Matthias

Shoving my bag into the trunk of my rental, I slam the lid closed. But instead of moving toward the door and driving away the way security is waiting for me to do, I lean back against it. Letting everything I've done tonight really sink in.

Bryan's words mixing in with Kimber's plea for me not to do what she knew deep down I was about to like a car crash on repeat, and culminating in the anger filled growl of Smith as he demands I get the fuck out of his sight.

I've had a real bang-up night so far and it hasn't even begun.

What the fuck was I thinking?

I'm a fucking idiot.

Yes, you are. You just threw everything away for a piece of fucking ass.

Smooth and calculated like the snake he is, my nightmare is back in full effect.

It's all her fault. In being apart all this time, I silenced him. With her back and shoving her relationship with Fortune in my face, laughing at me as not only did she play him fantastically but also played me, I'd awoken a beast. One that now that he's returned, there would be no stopping.

At least not until I left her and this godforsaken place behind for good.

"Matthias!" I hear the voice call, only this time louder and decidedly more female in comparison. My involvement with Kimberlee and just how deeply she's affected my thoughts obviously making it morph into the one version I wouldn't be able to swallow down and ignore.

"Matty! Wait!"

It's only when I've closed my eyes and begged the monster to leave me be and the voice calls to me, closer this time, I realize it is, in fact, Kimber calling.

Looking in the direction of her voice, I see her running. Pausing after a few seconds and starting again, her destination clear. One that she doesn't stop fighting for until she's standing in front of me. Her chest heaving up and down pulling my eyes from hers and straight down to her tits.

Eyes up, Kemper.

Delivering them to their destination but unable to voice the very real struggle taking place inside my head, I revert back to the way I handled things before and plead silently.

I can't do this with you right now, little one. Please go away.

A message she clearly doesn't get as she ends the silence and starts in.

"Don't do this. I know what you said back there, and I get why you can't see this through. But, Matty, Gavin told me what you did."

Of course, he did. I bet he couldn't wait to run and tell everyone about the epic meltdown the lunatic had on his boss before being thrown out of the building.

At least Smith got his wish of having an unhinged superstar.

Between the voices in my head and those eyes haunting me, I'm the perfect damn candidate.

"I didn't do anything but say no for the first time in eleven years."

"Then why are you out here instead of in there," She points back toward the building. "Where you belong?"

Hasn't she had enough? Wasn't what happened in the hallway enough? What is it with her? Is she just a glutton for punishment?

"You know why," I state evenly, though with her proximity right now and the way my heart feels as though it could beat clear out of my chest, I'm anything but calm.

"You don't have to do this. We," she switches gears. "Don't have to do this."

"Kimber..."

God, even saying her name is a struggle. One I don't need right now if I want to get out of here with what's left of me intact.

"No, Matthias. I know why you're so against what Smith wants. It hurts, but I get it. We can find a way around it though. Make it look like we kissed. Other people do it all the time." Stepping forward, she reaches out and when her hand brushes across my arm, all thought of restraint flies out the window.

It's like we've gone back in time.

Only this time, I'm the one on her with lightning quick speed. My lips catching and gripping onto hers as if they're the very thing I need to survive. As though she's my lifeline.

She's both angel and devil as her lips part, giving herself over. Moaning into my mouth, the sound vibrating off when I capitalize on what's she giving and allow myself to drown even deeper in the sea that is her.

My hands of their own volition coming around and pulling her even closer, until just like in the hall before, we're one singular being.

Her heartbeat also mine. Her breath—her very life force—all mine and mine hers.

"Come back with me," she pants breathlessly. "Stay with me."

Yes, Matthias. Do that. Stay with her. Take what you should have all those years ago. Forget that she's with Gavin. Take what's yours.

What could have easily been the moment I finally give in and ignore my fears, becomes something else the second the nightmare rises. Like being doused with a blast of ice water, I'm shaken awake. Acutely aware again of just how wrong all of this is. Not only because she belongs to Gavin, but also because of what will happen if I selfishly give in. What I'll do to her.

"I—I can't." I awkwardly stammer and then try to explain. "Gavin."

"No, Matty. You've got it wrong. That's part of the reason why I had to find you before you left." She whispers against my face. "There is no me and Gavin. Not anymore. There never really was."

Bringing my hands around to rest on her shoulders, I gently move her back. Giving us both the space that right now, especially after the way every cell of my body just sprung to life with her admission, we need.

"No."

"No, what?"

"You can't break up with him." *Shit, even to my own ears I sound like a prick.* "He's a bastard, but he's still better than me."

"You're wrong." She argues with an emphatic shake of her head. "No one is better than you, Matthias. Not for me."

Pressing her body so close to mine I can actually feel the erratic beating of her heart against my chest, I give into the need again. Gripping her tightly and spinning her around until her back is the one leaning against the hood of the car. Hovering over her, my shadow bathing us in our own private darkness, I push her back and take. At least until her own need for control has her pushing back and taking just as much as she submits.

Giving me everything she has. Everything she is.

Her surrender.

Starting at her neck and running my tongue over the glistening droplets of sweat as they bead there, I taste them all and press my lips down harder and suck. Responding to the squeak of a moan that turns into a sigh she lets escape as I continue my mouth's assault, marking her body. Moving lower, just above her breast, I graze and nip her with my teeth before moving back up her neck to her jawline. Begging her to breathe when I hear the sharp intake of breath and upon getting it, smashing my lips down onto hers hungrily. Nipping her with my teeth before sucking on her lip, tasting every delectable yet sinful inch as she pushes back and gives me more.

Our tongues coming together and fighting for control of the moment. A control she'll never have as I just continue to assault her mouth with my own. Drowning the further I push her.

In her taste, her smell, and her feel as her body melts into mine.

Grinding into her when I feel her hand begin to move down over my arm, brushing ever so lightly against my torso before finding and gripping the crotch of my jeans. The only part of me at the moment fighting harder and stronger to block out my mind's fight over how wrong this is. The part wanting the monster to win.

Bringing her other hand around, she begins playing with the clasp of my belt, unhooking it and moving toward the button, it happens again.

"Kimber," I struggle to get out, her name falling breathless and choked.

"You want me, Matty. So take me."

It would be so easy to lay her out over the hood of my car, stripping layer upon layer of her away until all that was left was the bare body she's hiding underneath. The sinful curves that would be absolutely impossible to ignore if it wasn't for the attachment I have to the one part of her I can never truly hold.

Her heart.

It's goodness, its purity, even now as my breath is labored and I'm completely struck stupid by just how fucking hot she is looking up at me, bringing me back down to earth.

"Not like this. Not on the hood of a car, and for damn sure not in the fucking parking lot. You deserve better than that."

"What I deserve is you. Whatever way I can have you. It's okay, Matty, I want this."

What the fuck has gotten into me? I want to feed into what she's said and take her the way she wants. Bare, with nothing between us. Give myself over to her.

The first and only in twenty-nine years. I'm lost in her and the way she makes me feel. How easily she makes me forget the promise I made.

Releasing my hold, I jolt back as if burned and start shaking myself free of her control. Fanning the flames of not only her need and desire, but mine.

I meant what I said.

Even if I wasn't so fucked up in the head, I still wouldn't want my first time, *our first time*, to be like this. She's better.

So much fucking better.

"Love me, Matty. The way you said you would if this was happening in a different time." Curling her fingers around the edges of her shirt when I chance it and look to her again, she begins pulling it up. Exposing her midriff before lifting just high enough for me to make out the lace trimmings of her bra. Black, like the color of my soul, and what has my breath catching and holding as she exposes the rest of it, pulling her top clear off and laying it on the hood before focusing her gaze back on me, pleading. "Please, Matthias."

I do love you, Little One. I tell her. My heart not yet willing to admit the truth of the statement aloud, but still wanting to get it out before it consumes. *I love your honesty and the way your eyes dance whenever you talk about what we do. Your smile whenever you're put into a match. How in control you always are, even in the most uncontrollable of situations. I love the way you're unapologetic for feeling, and the way you allow your tears to fall without thought. How open and ready you are, even now as I'm about to break your heart again. The same way I did when you were fourteen. I love everything about you.*

Groaning, the sound of which appears more like an animalistic release as it vibrates against my chest cavity, I look away. Focusing on the pavement and the surrounding area. Anywhere but at the vision standing before me giving herself over so unabashedly.

Slipping out of my jacket, I fist it in my hands before handing it over. Not so much as taking my eyes off the pavement as I wait for her to take it.

"I want to. Fuck!" I curse at the ground when she makes no move to take the handout. "I want nothing more than to bend you over the hood of my car and shove my cock so deep in you, you'll never forget me. Forget how it feels. How we feel. Love you the way you fucking deserve! It's all I've been able to think about for weeks!"

This isn't me. I don't do this kind of thing. Admit things that have been only mine for years.

She's changed me the way I always knew she would.

"Then do it." She practically purrs, lifting her body higher up onto the hood as her eyes begin to skirt around, finally becoming as aware as I am that out here, we're definitely not alone.

"No." I repeat, attempting to remain calm despite how out of control I actually feel. "Take the jacket, Kimber. Cover yourself. This can't happen."

It's when I finally feel the weight lift in my hands a few seconds later that I chance looking again. Her true feelings on what I've done not even attempting to be masked as I see her resolve break and tears begin to slip out of her eyes. Grabbing her shirt from the hood, she jumps down and wrapping my jacket around her hourglass frame, she does as I need her to and covers up.

"Thank you." I whisper and am unprepared for the cold raw laugh she lets escape.

"I can't believe I actually thought it was me." She mutters.

Stepping toward her and reaching out, I spin her back around to face me. Her tear-stained cheeks, reminiscent of Avery before her, threatening to unravel me completely.

Pain.

What I caused.

I really am no better than Jonathan.

"What do you mean by that?"

"You're a smart boy, Matthias. Figure it out yourself. That's how you prefer it anyway, right?"

Nothing should sting at this point, given how dead inside I am, but the bite to her words does. Stings like a bitch.

Why does doing the right thing always have to feel so fucking wrong?

"Yes, but I still want to know."

Moving closer, quicker than I'm able to react to, her hand lands in the center of my chest and she's shoving me back with everything she's got. Jamming her finger hard into the center once I've attempted to recover and glaring at me with a fire I haven't seen in her eyes since she was fourteen and determined to prove her place.

"It means I stupidly thought that out of all the girls in the world that talk about you, throw themselves at you, and want to be with the Almighty Kemper, I was it. I was *the one*! I thought I would be the one to have you. Tame you."

"You have. You do. I am."

"You have a funny way of showing it!"

"Little one..."

"Don't you *little one* me! You don't get to do that after what just happened. What's been happening since the moment I got here! I'm not your little one! Not anymore."

"No...you're not." I concede, giving up the fight. She isn't mine to have, so neither should the nickname. It's better this way. "Go. Get the hell out of here. Go back inside that building. Back to the Women's Championship and the role of Queen you share with Gavin. Just go. Run while you still can."

"Screw you, Matthias! You don't get to tell me who to be with."

"I do when it's what's best."

Sensing the movement of her hand but unable to move quickly enough, it impacts with the side of my face, the force stronger than a slap. The reason for it and the lingering ache that remains, clear once I've pulled myself away from the shock.

She punched me.

Catching the swing of her other hand as it moves, I reach up just in time to stop it. Holding it in place above her head, my own ire now on full display as I glare down at her.

"You only get one free shot with me, little one. No more. Get the hell out of here."

Yanking her hand roughly out of mine and bringing her other hand around her wrist and rubbing once it's free, she attempts to glare at me through the tears that are now falling at a more rapid pace.

This is it. The moment of truth.

The moment as she turns her back without as much as another word spoken, I know I've both won and lost.

It's the end of us.

Chapter Twenty
February 2015

Kimberlee

I've seen a lot of crazy shit since I got here, heard even more with all the stories everyone has, but this has got to be the craziest.

Smith, *Radley freaking Smith*, is actually giving us two days off.

His reasoning?

Marie says we deserve to spend some time with the people we love.

In other words, she's damn sick and tired of his stance on love in the locker room and is putting her foot down. That, or she just wants the old coot home for a holiday I'm sure he's spent more years missing than actually present for.

Either way, his news has livened up a locker room that for the last couple of months has been coasting by on fumes.

Match after match, day after day, weeks coming together and turning into months in the time it takes you to blink, without so much as a good night's sleep to carry us over.

I'm not complaining. I've been enjoying the run. The more time I spend in matches and then helping shape other parts of the show, the less time I have to think about him and the hole his leaving has caused where my heart used to reside.

Even with us not being together, I miss him.

I can feel the loss of him down every corridor, in every new building we're in. I can see the loss evident in the main event title picture. It turning back into more of the same with him gone.

Jackson and Gavin. Back and forth. A move that by now, Smith has gotta be just kicking himself over.

You can only do the same program so many times before the fans start bailing.

It's a lesson I learned real early on once I started working full time for my dad. They're gonna get bored and lose heart over having to come up with a million new ways to put on the same match, and the crowd? They're just gonna give up. They're gonna take their money, find a place where they don't recycle the same damn shit over and over, and put it there.

Where it belongs.

Matthias leaving. Smith suspending him and not listening to any of us that pleaded with him over the last few weeks to change his mind, it's everywhere.

The entire locker room is feeling it.

"Hey babe." Gavin appears, wrapping his arms around me and pressing his wet lips to the side of my face. "You ready for two fun-filled days off?"

That's another new development.

Gavin and me.

Don't look at me like that. It's not what you think.

This time, unlike the last, there's no secrets between us. He knows the score. He knows about Matthias. God, he knows more than I probably should have said when I finally unloaded it all on him a few days after Matty left. And even though, I didn't see it happening the way it has, especially with him, he's been a bright spot in an otherwise dark existence.

The one light in this long and winding tunnel of despair I've been riding around saddled with since everything happened.

He's made it easy to agree to what's going on between us.

A relationship. Only not one for us. One for everyone else.

Okay go ahead, roll your eyes. I want to. But he's offering me something that even though I've tried doing it another way, I desperately need if I'm going to survive my time here.

Friendship.

Someone to confide in when like earlier this morning, the ache was so prevalent again, I made myself sick.

He keeps me from losing myself to the loss.

Gavin Fortune—THE Gavin Fortune, is the best damn fake boyfriend I've ever had.

"If by fun-filled you mean, going home and having my dad put me to work with special appearances and bookings, sure. Can't wait." I smile weakly before finally giving into the truth and jamming a finger down my throat.

Laughing, he pulls me even tighter into an embrace. "It can't be that bad."

"It's not." I admit with a resigned sigh. "I love going home and seeing everyone. Even if we're down one member of the family with Zach out of town. I guess I'm just raw still."

"Because he lives in the next city over?"

That's another change. We don't even say his name anymore. He's just always a *he* or *him*.

Never Matthias.

"Yeah."

"I know you said you wanted to go our separate ways for the two days, but if you need me, I can go home with you. It's not exactly a hardship hanging with Renegade."

It doesn't matter how long I'm here or how accepted by most of the locker room I've become. It makes me giggle every time I see one of the guy's fanboy out over my father.

Gavin coming in second only to the man who I'm not supposed to be naming.

"Thank you, but its fine." Leaning into him when I catch the party making their way around the corner and down the hall toward us, I sling my arms around him as per the rules and snuggle in. Always putting on the best show possible so no one is any the wiser about the way things really are.

Keeping my past with Matthias a secret.

"Who is it?" he whispers so covert, I can't help smiling from my position in his neck.

"Ortiz, Reid, and Melinda. I think there's someone else too, but can't make them out from my position. They're taking up the entire damn hall."

"Not for long." Gavin laughs under his breath before bringing a hand up under my chin and pulling my face up to meet his. "I'm gonna kiss you now."

God, it's so planned out. Uncaring and lacking feeling, but with the catcalls that come once he does as he says and places his lips to mine, there's no denying that it works.

Appearances are being kept up. We're still King and Queen Darling of CPW, just the way Smith wants us to be.

"I'm gonna need to let you go." He groans once the group has finally passed by.

"Why?"

Stupid question. I shouldn't even care why, but with how quick he is to voice it once we're out of the woods, I'm curious. He's never done it before.

"I forget what happens when I kiss you, Kimber. That's why. If I stay this close for much longer, the guys are gonna get to see more of me than they want."

Ohhhhh.

Laughing, I tap him on the nose and do what comes easily to me. Moving away. Creating distance. Giving him what he needs as he turns away from the direction more people seem to be streaming out from in order to adjust himself.

"I'm sorry, Gavin."

Turning back with a quick look down to his crotch, he looks back up to me before sliding over closer.

"What for?"

"This, what you're doing for me, I know it's not your speed."

"You," he brushes his own finger across my nose, bopping it. "Are my speed. You keep me grounded and you're fun to be around. Not to mention the banging body you're sporting with all that time in the gym. It's definitely *not* a problem."

"You really wouldn't rather be off with a girl that's actually willing to sleep with you?"

This gives him pause, but not for nearly as long as I expect.

Maybe Gavin isn't the whore he's been made out to be after all. He's sure as hell been different with me over the last six weeks. If what Matthias warned about before he left is actually true, he's one hell of an actor. I'm not seeing him slip at all. He's been good to me.

"You do sleep with me, Kimber."

"That's not what I meant and you know it."

Wiggling an eyebrow, he grins and all traces of the serious attitude I was about to give fades away. I can't stay mad at him when he looks at me like that.

Fortune has gotten under my skin.

"If you're asking if I need to get fucked, the answer is no. We talked about that remember? I do what I need to do when the need calls for it. Otherwise, you're stuck with me."

You see how messed up this is?

We're supposed to be dating, yet here he is, freely admitting that when he needs to get with a girl, he does. He cheats on me.

Clearly I've become completely dysfunctional in Matty's absence.

"So basically you're getting laid the second you land back home, right?"

Grinning bigger and winking, he brings a hand up and rubs my shoulder.

"Not the second I land, and not if you need me with you, but yeah."

When I haul off, slapping him hard across the chest and he flinches before flashing me those saddened baby blues, I buckle and laugh.

"Hey! You kissed me! What the fuck did you expect to happen?"

"Nothing, Gav." I manage to get out through another round of laughter. "Absolutely nothing."

"You ready to blow this place before Smith has a change of heart?"

"I am." I admit, a bit unsure. Knowing what's coming when I finally make my way out of here and head back across the border.

"Next time you try to convince me of that, you might wanna make sure you're convinced first."

I can't get anything past this guy. He knows me a little too well with all the time we've been spending together in an attempt to make this whole thing look legit.

Maybe it's time to take a few steps back.

The last thing I need is one of us walking away hurt when we're done with this stupid game we're playing.

I've been hurting enough for the both of us.

"Oh no! She's thinking. Evacuate! Find cover! She's about to blow!" Gavin hollers at the top of his lungs, raising the eyes of a few of the women making their way down the hall and effectively turning my cheeks a fantastic shade of red.

Idiot.

"You're crazy."

"For you, darling. Only for you." He leans over and pinches my arm with a grin.

"Let's go before you do something really crazy like getting down on one knee."

"Wait!" He stops me before I can move away. "That's actually an option?"

"No, Gav, it's not. Now knock it off. If we don't get out now, we're gonna be stuck here. It's Smith we're talking about, remember?"

Slipping my arm through his, I shake my head at him and begin pulling him toward the door. It's time to blow this joint. Shows over.

At least until the next one comes when I land at home.

It would be so easy to take Gavin up on his offer of keeping me company, especially with the allure my dad seems to hold for him, but I can't do it. Because what's coming when I get home, no one can know about. Not even Gavin, even knowing he's the only one that would understand.

I have to see Matty again.

Matthias

Two weeks.

I've been hiding out for two weeks longer than my allotted month-long suspension. Dodging calls, deleting emails, turning my phone off and blocking numbers for days when the texts come rolling in.

Turning my best friend, whose sofa I've practically been living off of for the last six weeks, into my own personal secretary. A job that for the first week, he didn't actually seem to be too bothered by, but now he's shoved his boot up my ass about.

He's done, and honestly, so am I.

It's time to face this.

Face Smith and what I know is coming.

"You come to your senses yet?" he growls when after slipping into his office, I throw my body down into the chair without a word.

"If by come to my senses, you mean I'm willing to be put into a long-running feud with Gavin Fortune over the affections of his girlfriend, then no."

"Boy, I've had about as much as I can take from you about this."

That makes two of us, old man.

"I'm not changing my mind."

Shoving the chair across the room until he's leaning over the desk, he pounds his fist down hard. And where in the past, the move would shake me, it doesn't so much as make me flinch this time.

He doesn't get to win here, so he can bring me back in and punish me while I'm here, or he can rid himself of me altogether. I'm done caring either way. It's not like I can't go back and spend another six weeks on Bryan's sofa or the gym.

"Do you have any clue the trouble you're causing?"

Before I can even come up with a response, he's bringing his other hammer down across the tainted wood and filling me in. "No you don't, because you got your little panties in a twist over a woman and can't see past it in order to play ball. This little stunt you're pulling, it's bad for business, boy. I've had enough of it."

"I don't know what to tell you, Smith. You were the one that suspended me because I wasn't going to be your little bitch."

"It was about more than that and with your attitude right now, son, you're reminding me why it was the right thing to do."

My attitude. *Right.* It's gotta be me at fault here. God, this guy is no better than my old man. I thought for a while he was different, but he's not. He's in a position of power over me, just like Jonathan was, and he's not against using it. In this case, blaming me for his own decisions.

Based on the amount of seats I put asses in alone, he had to realize booting me off the upcoming shows was going to be a hit to him monetarily. It would be the same way if Merrick, Ortiz, or god forbid, Fortune, were yanked out of nowhere.

He's gotta own that choice. It's not my burden.

"Spare me, Smith. I'm not at fault for your choices. Isn't that what you always taught me? We gotta own our shit. How about you start owning yours? Or does all this sage advice you growl out all the time not apply to you?"

Leaning back on his feet and expelling a heavy breath, he shifts and pulls the top drawer of his desk open, and after a few seconds of shoving papers around, pulls out a packet. Tossing it down hard onto the table between us.

"Go on. Read it."

Scooting my seat closer to the table, I reach out and pick up the papers and after scrolling through the first two pages, it becomes apparent very quickly just what this is.

A new contract.

"You wanna lock me into a guaranteed contract for the next five years?" I ask in disbelief. "Do you even have the money to do this?"

Radley Smith isn't exactly poor, but guaranteed contracts, one that keep superstars for a set period of time for a locked in amount of money, is something he's never done.

The last time it was even brought up between him and Marie at dinner one night, he damn near flipped the table on her with how adamant he was against it.

Believing more in the system already in place and not wanting to change.

"Don't worry about the damn money. You never have before. You live off canned spaghetti for fuck sakes."

Can't argue that. I live cheap.

Comes with the territory when you don't know when or even if your next meal is going to come.

"I'm not signing this. You don't even believe in this shit."

"Times change."

"You mean, you've changed."

"If that's what you take from it."

"Still not doing it. I know you. I know what you're about." I argue. "Tell me, did anyone else on the roster get one of these?"

"No." he wastes no time grunting out and that's all I need to know.

I know what this is about now and I definitely don't want any part of it.

I respect the hell out of this man when we're not at each other's throats, but I can't do what he needs me to here. I can't sign the next five years of my life away knowing there's a risk of it just being more of the same.

I meant what I said before. I can't be his little bitch boy.

"In that case, let me do you a favor." Reaching across the desk and picking up the contract again, I watch as his eyes spark to life. Probably assuming it means I'm gonna sign it and give him what he's after. What changes when he sees my fingers land in the middle of the paper and he's given the reality check.

"You do that and you're as good as done here."

"Then I suppose this is goodbye." I quip, pulling my fingers back and ripping the paper. Shredding it straight down the middle and then taking each individual half and continuing to tear, letting it all fall to the floor like confetti.

Shoving himself out of his chair and making his way around the desk, I'm off my ass and being slammed against the wall before I can so much as blink. The old man still packing one hell of a punch despite the years he's spent on the sidelines, and completely taking me off guard.

Hand gripping me tightly at the neck and my now lax body frozen in place, he leans in as close as he can get, his smoke drenched breath covering me when he speaks again, spit flecks flying.

"You and me, we're done. Get the hell of this office, out of this building, and don't you ever think of coming back. You're dead to me."

Releasing his hold, I catch myself, and with one final look in his steely brown eyes, I give him exactly what he wants.

Even though as I open the door to the room and walk over the threshold, it physically kills me to do it.

This isn't just me standing up for myself and walking away from my job.

I'm walking away from the only real father I ever had.

Son of a bitch. This one is gonna sting.

Nodding to a couple of the mid-card guys as they're leaving with their bags slung over their shoulders, I pick up the pace until I'm breaking into a full jog. Not stopping until I've reached the exit door and am blasted by the shot of coolness as I hit the outside.

Sucking in a deep breath, I let everything that just happened settle and after a few seconds of wrapping my head around just how alone I've now made myself, I look up and that's when I see them.

Kimber and Gavin.

Great.

Chapter Twenty-One

Kimberlee

"Don't do it, Kimber." Gavin tugs at my arm, attempting to turn my attention from the enigma now making his way from the same building we exited and put it back on him.

He's right.

I know I said I needed to be around him again, but now that I'm being faced with that very thing, I'm not sure it's the right thing at all.

My heart doesn't seem to agree, though.

The jolt to it, waking up for the first time in six weeks, it knows exactly what it wants.

Matthias.

"Please." Gavin's pleading now. "Just get in your car and drive to the airport. It doesn't matter what he's doing here, but this isn't the place for another go round."

Every single time Matthias and I are together, it turns into a battlefield, and in the end, I'm always the one walking away wounded. So I should walk away the way Gavin wants, but I can't.

He's here and he's just as mesmerizing as always. His heart, the same way it's been doing since those few weeks when I was fourteen, calling to mine. Pulling me to him even though we're physically nowhere near each other.

"I can't, Gavin. I'm sorry." I finally turn and tell him weakly.

All my previous fight, the sass my dad says I was born with, now stripped away to nothing.

I've got to see this through.

Six weeks apart was long enough.

Squeezing my shoulder supportively, he again tries to pull me away from the train wreck that after a few seconds of pause himself, seems to be making a beeline straight for us.

For me.

"Go, Gavin."

"No. If you think I'm leaving you here with him so what happened before can happen again, you're crazy."

Silly man. Of course I'm crazy.

We wouldn't be in the position we're in if I wasn't.

"It won't happen again. A lot has happened since then. I'll be okay."

"Kimber..."

There is something so wrong about this picture. After all of the warnings I've had about him, he shouldn't be the voice of reason right now. The one standing here protective.

He should be the one exploiting and I should be laying him out for it.

Oh how the mighty have fallen.

"Gavin, go." I hiss as Matthias crosses the parking lot, a few feet away from being in arms reach. My body tensing, readying for his arrival.

"Son of a bitch!" he exclaims with a hard drag of his hand through his hair in clear exasperation. "If that piece of shit hurts you again, I will end him. You're finally doing okay."

Oh, Gavin. I sigh to myself. *I was never okay. I'm just as good an actor as you are.*

"It won't get that far, I promise." I lie a little too easily. "I just wanna know what he's doing here."

"That's bullshit, Kimber. That's as likely as me wanting to dress up in drag and win the Women's title."

Shoving at him playfully as the laugh falls, I pull him in for a quick embrace before whispering again his need to go. Something that thankfully after returning the hug, he concedes and gives.

"You'll call if you need, yeah?"

"Yes."

"Be careful, girlfriend." He whispers.

"Always, boyfriend."

With another quick embrace he's off, just in time for me to turn back to garner Matthias's closeness and find myself damn near face to face with him.

"I see you took my advice."

"Yeah," I agree, weaker than I was going for. "I guess I did."

"He cares about you."

"Yeah, he does." I say, this time more confident. Gavin does care. "What are you doing here?"

"Dealing with things."

"Like?" I ask, curious. A question I want to completely rescind when his face lowers, crestfallen. "Matty, what happened?"

"I'm done here, Kimber. For good. Smith...well, it's over."

No way! They're family for Christ sakes. You don't give up on family. Even when they're like Smith and Matthias and they butt heads more than they actually get along.

"That can't be true."

"Afraid it is, little one."

Little one. Damnit. Focus, Kimber. Don't let him see that it still gets to you. Fake it the way you have been for months. Sell it.

"Matthias, he didn't mean anything he said." I make excuses. "Things around here have been falling apart since he suspended you. He knows it. Hell, the entire locker room knows it. He's not doing what's best for business. Neither are you, staying away as long as you have. Whatever he said that's making you leave for good though, I know for a fact he doesn't mean it."

"Maybe, but it doesn't change that it's happening. I can't be what he needs me to be."

"So, you what? Take your ball and go home? Tuck your tail between your legs and run again?" *Like you did with us.* "If you walk out of here and leave things the way they are right now, you're no better than he is."

"Never said I was better than him, Kimber."

"Don't do this."

God, I swear every damn time we're together, I'm offering up the same plea. I'm getting sick of it.

Just once, can he listen and not do what I know he's going to regret later?

"Kimber—"

"No, Matthias. You belong here. I told you that before. It hasn't changed. This entire building, all of the performers in it every damn night, we're better when you're here. Stronger."

"Half of those guys in there don't give two flying fucks whether I return or not. Hell, if I leave right now it gives them an opening. They can be Smith's next pet project and get the attention they actually deserve. It's a win. Don't make it out to be something else when it's not. I'm still the same anti-social bastard I've always been."

"Not to me."

Way to go, Kimber. Just lay all of your emotional shit out again. Let him see that even with six weeks passing and him pushing you away, you're still fucking invested.

"You always did see me better than anyone else." He admits, a flash of a smile appearing before it quickly falls, admiration in his tone matching the look that sparks at the same time in his eyes.

"I always will."

Silence falls after my admission, but where it should be uncomfortable, it's not. It's one of the most peaceful moments I've had with this man since he was thrust into my life over nine years ago.

"I miss you." He whispers, breaking the silence and nearly blowing me off my feet from the weight of his statement. "I fucking tried not to, but Kimber...You. Just. Won't. Go. Away."

"Matty..."

Here's where I should tell him he doesn't have the right to say those things. That he lost that chance when I was giving myself over to him on the hood of his car and he rejected me.

Instead, I close the distance between us, pausing when my chest brushes against his and lift my hand to his face. My fingers cupping and beginning to stroke his cheek.

God, I've missed the way he feels.

Unprepared for the way he leans into my move, giving himself over so easily and the way his eye closed as he does it, I'm struck stupid.

"The way we left things...I haven't been handling it well."

"Me either. I miss you too, Matty. It's why I don't want you to leave again."

"I'm starting to think I'm never going to be able to completely leave you, little one. Not when around every corner, in every match, every damn dream I have, you're there. You're everywhere. I can't..."

"You can't what?"

I just know that the Kimber that's been masked for the past six weeks is gonna regret asking this, but it really is like I've been accused of by Gavin. I'm a glutton for punishment.

I *need* to know what he's too hesitant to say.

"I can't escape you."

"Then don't."

"It's not that easy."

It's low, barely there really, but the backbone that's served me well coming up in this business, it awakens with his newest attempt to pull away. Growing leaps and bounds with each second that passes with only the sound of our collective breathing between us. As easy as it would be to ignore, to delve deeper and really get into it with him about, I can't this time.

This is one of those defining moments my mom used to tell me about whenever we'd have relationship talks as a kid.

I can choose to accept what he's saying and waste my breath again, like I feel like I've been doing every damn time we're together, or I can do what I probably should have been doing all this time with how allergic to bullshit I am, and put an end to it once and for all.

What I have with Gavin may be as fake as the two people acting it out, but even that fake relationship offers me more than this mess with Matthias does.

I need more.

I *deserve* better than this.

I can't be the only one fighting. Which means, this is where the fight, at least for me, really ends.

"Nothing worth having is easy, Matthias. It's messy as hell. That's supposed to be what makes it worth it."

"Kimber..."

Here it comes.

"No, Matty. You know how I feel. How I'm pretty sure I'm always going to feel. But for both our sakes, I can't do this with you anymore. You're either with me or you're not."

I can see by the way his eyes lower from mine and he pulls back from my touch that I've gotten my answer. Unspoken but loud. His message, through his body language, is louder than ever.

I just can't believe it took me this long to see it.

Summoning up every ounce of strength I have, I prepare myself for the goodbye that's coming. One that no matter where we go from here, has to stick.

Hot and cold may work for some people, but the scalding nature of the heat when I'm with Matty, and just how frozen and hard I become when it's cold, is debilitating.

Life—love—shouldn't be like that.

Not for anyone.

"I'm sorry for what happened with Smith, but I'm sure you'll land on your feet wherever you end up. It's been nice seeing you," I offer robotically, the pull to him just as great as it ever was, but being shoved down by what is for once my stronger mind. "But I have a flight to catch."

As I pivot on my heel and turn to walk away, there's a small part of me that wishes history would repeat itself.

That instead of having it be me calling out through tears when I was younger as he walked away from us, he's the one that collapses to the ground and does it.

That he makes me understand that his words aren't just that. Making me feel the epic love we could have shared. What I thought if I broke down his walls, we could share.

But as I open the door to my car and slip myself down inside, all I'm filled with is the dead air of him letting me walk away.

Only this time, it's not him letting me go, but me doing it.

It's time to move on.

Part Three
What Goes Up...Must Come Down

Chapter Twenty-Two
May 2015

Matthias

"Holy shit!"

Ears honing in on the voice, my head jerks up and even with the significant distance between where I'm standing and his place in the ring, the side of my face quirks involuntarily with the knowledge of who's there.

Brady Raines.

Otherwise known as the only other person in the world right now who understands a little of what it's like to be me.

You know, living under the black skid mark of pain delivered by the one and only Radley Smith.

Moving toward the ring, he holds a hand up calling time to his opponent before making his own way over and leaning across the ropes, Cheshire grin firmly in place.

"You know, when Bryan said he was bringing in an old dog, I had no clue he meant you. Shit, you passed old a long time ago. Ancient is more like it."

Jamming my middle finger firmly in the air, I pause at the apron before jumping up and into the ring to join him.

"Funny you should say that. I could say the same damn thing about you."

Brady, along with Jax and a few of the other lifers of CPW like Ron and Cameron, we all came in around the same time. I was first, having two or three years on the other guys, but considering everything we've been through since, on the road and off it, at this point, we're all a bunch of dinosaurs.

"According to Bry, you do. Every damn day." He laughs, slapping me across the shoulder before motioning across the ring to his opponent. "You come to help me school this one?"

The *this one* he's referring to being a baby faced and boney legged midget, who looks like he would fit more with a boy band than with the bunch of freaks he's currently being subjected to.

"Nope. I'm actually here to see you."

Moving over to the corner, he leans down and snags a bottle of water, cracking the cap and draining it before tossing it down and turning his attention back.

"What do you want with me?"

"A chance to work with you if you're game."

My revelation obviously surprising the hell of him with how quickly his brow lifts.

"Since when do you wanna work with me? I would have figured if you're here, you've got your heart set on a different prize."

He's not wrong. Coming in, my ultimate goal here is the Heavyweight Division, but since I'm well versed in working my way up from the bottom of the pile, I've got to start here.

Hell, if I was small enough to make it work or could guarantee dropping the weight needed, I'd be going for the Lightweight Division. It's how I operate. I refuse to come in and steal someone else's place.

"One day, but since I'm the new guy, I figure I'll come for you instead."

"Tell me something, honestly."

"Sure."

"Did you loan Bryan the money to get this place off the ground?"

How the hell did he find out about that?

"Yeah, I did. How do you know about it?"

"Your friend has pretty loose lips when he's wasted."

Of course. There's a reason I used to keep Bryan close when I first started working with Smith. He's horrible when he's out with the boys and getting his drink on. Filter fades away entirely. He'd give up state secrets if he had them. Loose lips is an understatement.

"Yes, he does." I say, chuckling softly. "But if you don't mind, I'd like it if that little piece of dirt didn't go any further than here. This is Bryan's thing. I just helped make sure it happened."

"Don't say another word," Brady says, bringing a finger across his lips. "My lips are sealed."

"Thanks."

"So I assume Bry and Reese know you're here. They also aware you're downgrading?"

Since his own admission means he doesn't get it, here's the skinny on Brady.

He's pound for pound one of the best mat technicians in the ring. Where others shine through their aerial performance, Brady's the opposite. He can't take risks the way Gavin, Jackson or even myself have done in terms of the ropes, but he will take ones square in the middle of the ring that would make you weep. He's also the last person I'd ever call a downgrade.

In fact, from where I'm standing he's the best.

"I'm upgrading and the Brady Raines of old damn well knows it. To answer your other question, yeah, they know. Bryan is the reason I'm here. He told me he's having a rough go of finding you a solid guy to work with. So here I am."

"You wanna put me over?"

"Why is that so surprising?" I laugh, confused yet amused at the same time by the change in a guy that not two years before had been one of the cockiest sons of bitches on the planet. "This isn't Radley's show, Brady."

Lifting a hand in surrender, he laughs awkwardly.

"I know it's not. I guess I'm just getting used to the way things are run here."

"And you can still hear that SOB's voice in your head breaking down your every breath. Yeah, trust me. He's invading on this conversation right now."

After another round of laughter and a held up finger in my direction, he turns toward the other guy in the ring and gives him his walking papers. Waiting the guy out before turning back to face me, game face on and at the ready.

"What are you waiting for? Let's get to work."

✶✶✶✶✶✶

If having a CPW reunion with Brady was expected the second I landed, being launched straight at another person from my past there as she breezes her way through the doors, albeit slower and carrying a hell of a lot more weight than she was the last time I saw her, wasn't.

"Why are you staring at me like that?" she eyes me once she reaches the edge of the ring. Lifting her leg up onto the first ring step and heaving out the heaviest sigh I've ever heard. "It's because I look like a beached whale, right?"

Avery is pregnant. Very fucking pregnant judging by just how round and protruding her belly is, but there's no missing the glow that her being this way provides. She looks…well, she looks beautiful.

Merrick can kill me for thinking it later.

"I was thinking that I like this look better than the one you had when we first met. If it didn't mean you being flat on your back for the duration, I might actually advise you keep it up."

"Aww, Matty. You always know the right thing to say." Smiling serenely, she makes her way up the final two steps and jogging over, I squat down on the rope, allowing her entrance and accepting her arms and the loose embrace she provides once she's in.

"It's so nice to see you." She admits softly before taking a step back and letting her arms fall back to her sides, her eyes never once distancing themselves from mine. "Brady doesn't fill me in nearly as much as he should about what's going on up here."

"How's life in California? Jax? He about ready to shit himself over this whole baby thing or what?"

Moving over to the turnbuckle, she leans herself against it as laughter spills out.

"As a matter of fact, I think he's more ready for this than I am." Looking from me to her abdomen and back again, her cheeks flush as she points. "Twins."

"No way." Though, with as close as she looks to popping any second, it does make a hell of a lot of sense. "Congratulations."

"Thank you." She smile blushes, bringing her hands to her cheeks as she attempts to hide it.

I was right before. I definitely like this look more than the first. The days of mascara and eyeliner marring her bronze colored eyes, thankfully long gone.

"So what brings you here? Brady got a call a little while ago and took off." I fill her in, leaving out the part that with the grin he was sporting before he damn near flashed his way out of here, there's no doubt who was on the other end of the call.

"Would you believe me if I said I was here to talk to you?"

"I would. I'm just not sure why."

"Bryan called my boss, which lead to my boss reaching out to me because it seems since I made the move, no one else has come close to taking my place." She laughs softly. "Or rather, Bryan wouldn't accept anyone else."

The first part I already believed just based on the little I did learn about her through her time in CPW with Merrick, but the second part definitely seems factual. Bryan, after meeting her while she and Jackson were split, had done nothing short of gush over this girl. There's no doubt in my mind that even with babies on the way, he still is.

"What does that have to do with me?"

"He told me about CPW, Matthias. Well, no. That's not true. I get the feeling there's a lot more to what happened with you and Smith, but he told me enough to make me wanna get on a plane when I quite possibly wouldn't even fit through the doors."

"You'd fit just fine. So stop that or I'm telling Merrick." I attempt to joke, swallowing down the urge I have to admit that she's right and there is a hell of a lot more to my decision to part ways with Smith and CPW then what she's been told.

Pulling herself slowly back off the turnbuckle, she grips the middle rope and lowers herself down to her knees, before letting her hands fall to the bottom ropes as she maneuvers her way into a comfortable sitting position. Patting the mat when she's down and beaming a smile along with the nod of her head in order to get me to join her.

Taking her up on the offer, I fall to the mat and lean back against the ropes right at the exact moment her next question slips.

"What happened, Matthias?"

"I couldn't do it anymore."

"I already know that. Bryan told me that much. But what *exactly* is it you couldn't do? You seemed at home there, and with the number of times we've had Smith and Marie over to the house for dinner and were subjected to hearing about you, I know he was happy to have you there too. So what really happened?"

Do I dare tell her? Admit that it wasn't a spot on the show I couldn't handle doing that made me run, but in fact the woman I was scheduled to do it with that had me disappearing with my tail between my legs? Would she even understand?

For all of the issues her and Merrick faced, he never backed down. He never gave up hope of the two of them ending up where they are now. Our situations are nothing alike.

Hope isn't a word that even exists in my vocabulary these days.

"Jackson took me to one of the shows last week. Smaller venue, slower speed. It was different, but solid. I missed you, though. No one told me you made the move."

"I'm sorry." I apologize. "It was a spur of the moment decision."

"Why don't I believe that?"

Because you can see I'm lying.

"If you talked to Bry about this than you know the real reason I left. He likes you so I can't imagine him keeping his mouth shut."

"She looks great." Avery admits, proving my point. Bryan had in fact spilled all to the reporter. "Jackson says she's not the same as she was when she first came in, but that she's really dived right into making the Women's Division something again."

Six months. Six long months I tried my hardest to put her out of my head when she came in and got with Gavin. Forcing myself to tune her out entirely in the month suspension Smith had given me. And respecting her final goodbye to me outside of the building six weeks after. Keeping my distance. Not in any way shape or form ready to deal with the onslaught of feeling—a lot of which was regret—I knew would appear when she so much as entered my thoughts.

Sure, I thought about her. There wasn't a time when those eyes weren't there, just on the periphery in my mind, threatening to do their worst. But for the most part, I'd kept it all at bay.

Until now.

Until Avery made it all come crashing down again.

The agony I experienced when I pushed her away that day and drove to the airport. The pull I had the entire flight to turn right back around and go back. To beg her to help me fight my demons. To stay with me when I knew deep inside the reality was, she needed to stay away. The pangs of regret and remorse over something that had never really come to be even though we'd flirted with the idea more than once.

Her eyes the day she made the decision—the smartest one she's ever made—to walk away from me, when like it always seems to with us, we were brought together again like moths to the flame.

It's all just there ready to boil over again, as if no time has passed at all.

"She lost the title, but got it back a couple of months ago and has been like a woman on a mission since. Destroying all comers. Jackson's words. She's totally immersed herself into the job it seems. Reminds me of some other people I know."

There's no missing the dig. She means me, probably Jackson too with as much as he threw himself into the job before they got back together.

"Does she seem happy?" I blurt out, but before I can take it back and kick my own ass for caring enough to ask in the first place, she's shaking her head.

"No."

"What about Fortune?"

Even getting his name out guts me, knowing from the little bit I managed to syphon from Bryan that she did indeed do what

I told her and had gone back to the two time champion. The two of them and how happy I'm sure they are together enough to make me wanna puke all over my own wrestling boots.

"They're still together, but you know Gavin."

"Is he cheating on her?"

Slow your roll, Matthias. This isn't any of your business anymore. You walked away.

"I refer you to my earlier statement. He's Gavin. You tell me."

That would be a big fat fucking yes.

Damnit. I don't want to care about this. Shit, with the way she talked about him when he first asked her out, she made him seem so different. I was hoping, even though it shredded me to do it, that he had changed and was willing to be better for her.

Being right shouldn't feel this shitty.

"Does she know?"

"Know what?" I finally look up from my lap and acknowledge, the sickening sight of myself being reflected back through her eyes. "No. Yes. Maybe. Shit, Avery. I don't know anymore."

"Do you remember the night we met?" Shooting her an 'are you kidding me' look, she laughs. "Okay then. Well, do you remember what you said to me that night?"

On a good day, my memory is great. Most of the time though, it's a miracle I can even remember the conversation I had right after I've had it. An issue I could say is because of the amount of hits to the head I've taken over the years, but that I just know runs deeper than all that. My ability to block things out stemming from the past.

A past that until this woman chose to enter today, I was keeping buried where it belongs.

Just like Kimber.

My Little One.

Always mine.

Pinching the bridge of my nose, I attempt to take myself back in time to the night I found her crying in the darkened corner of the hallway and after a few minutes of going over the gist of how it all came about, I groan. Loud. Thankfully, the sound making her fill in the blanks for me.

"That night, I told you about Jackson and me. How close we seemed to be to turning a page and reuniting, but what a certain interruption with a person who shall remain nameless for fear of making my blood pressure spike, prevented. That ringing any bells?"

"Yeah, of course." It's not exactly like I could forget Melinda. "But what does that have to do with whatever it was I said?"

"You said that what I really needed to hear was standing behind me."

Right, because Jax at the time was standing behind her.

"Still not following, Avery."

"If you take away the literal meaning behind what you said, I think you'll get it. My advice to you is what you gave me. What you opened my eyes to."

Okay, here goes. Stripping away the literal meaning and looking deeper.

What is a lot harder than I thought when after a couple more minutes of absolute silence where I'm sure any second, a billow of smoke is going to come pouring out of my ears, I'm still not getting it. What could she possibly be getting at that I'm too stupid to see?

"The night you consoled me, Matty, you lied to me. You said the only relationship experience you had was the one you were in with your hand. And even though I think you were being kind of literal there, I also think she was already under your skin at that point. Am I right?"

Unable to come up with the words to either confirm or deny, I merely nod and she smiles lightly.

"She's been there the entire time hasn't she?"

Again, I nod.

"Then that means she's here now too. She might not be standing behind us the way Jackson was that night in the hall, but she's here. And if what I've seen and what Jax has told me is to be believed, you're there for her too. She's never given up even if appearances show differently. I misread what was going on with Melinda and deep down, I know you know, wise guy that you are, you're doing the same with Gavin. So what you need to hear Matty, it's standing right behind you. Just turn around, shut everything else off, and listen to it. Listen to her."

Chapter Twenty-Three

August 2015

Kimberlee

Oh, how the mighty have fallen.

Of all the places I would have imagined landing after the train wreck that derailed my life, HFWA wasn't one of them. Hell, it didn't even make the list.

Reason one?

Gavin talked non-stop during our wonderfully fake relationship about his desire to go there and dominate the way he has everywhere else when his time with CPW was up.

Reason two?

I damn well know who runs the show. Or rather, who I'm gonna risk bumping into based on his personal relationship with said guy that runs the show.

Yet here I sit on a plane, about to embark cross country to that very promotion, and whoever and whatever is waiting for me once I land.

Being summoned by both owners during what was originally supposed to only be a couple of months off to deal with my personal feelings after being *'jilted'* and *'dumped'* by Gavin, but that had turned into something more. Culminating in me requesting my release from CPW and the legacy I'd built there in favor of starting over somewhere new.

A place without memories.

A new start.

A new Wycked while Kimber stayed the same.

It's been a few weeks since the conference call in my apartment with Reese and Bryan, and I still can't get over just how easily I let myself be talked into this. Especially knowing that at the end of the day, I was going to be taking one hell of a pay cut to do it.

Three weeks since I decided it was time to get back on the damn horse. Or given my one real connection to Bryan, what could be considered walking from the fire in one pan straight into another.

Matthias Kemper.

A name synonymous with making my heart race and my soul bleed. A name that contrary to what the girls in CPW knew and what I let everyone else around me believe, I'd been following religiously since his abrupt departure a little less than six months before.

Every day, the stomp he delivered to my heart that resulted in cracks, and the salt he then poured into them until the cracks turned into a full-fledged gaping hole, never far from my mind even though for a while, I really tried to make it appear as though it wasn't.

Crap. This was a bad idea.

What's only made worse when my phone rings, signalling a text, and I'm met with the man's best friend.

When you land, head straight to the training facility. Reese will be waiting.

Training facility? *Say what?* Since when am I going there?

I realize that it's been a couple of months since I've actively participated in a match, what with the very publicly broadcasted breakup with Gavin and Smith giving me time off, but that's not long enough to garner ring rust. I'm fully prepared to get back into the gym routine once I find one in the area that suits my needs.

No way am I being treated like some newbie.

Why do you want me going there?

His answer is immediate and only serves to bother me so badly, I'm bordering on pissed the hell off.

We're delaying your debut.

Why would they promise me a spotlight to shine under, a real push, only to shelve me before I even get there?

It makes no sense.

Unless…

This has to be about Matthias. Bryan is the one delivering the news. He's Matty's best friend. It's the only thing that makes sense. His friend knows I'm about to come in and he's doing everything in his power to make sure I'm as uncomfortable as possible.

I can't believe it.

That's right, Kimber. You can't believe it because it's not true. Matthias might be a lot of things to you right now, but the type to intentionally try to bury you? It's not his style. Nor has it ever been.

The voice of reason is right. This isn't Matty's style.

So what the hell is going on?

I thought you said you wanted to bring me in to strengthen the Women's Division? When did that change?

I can't believe I'm having this conversation in text. Couldn't he have at least waited until I was safely on ground before blowing my entire world apart?

So much for a fresh start. I'm as stuck in bureaucratic bullshit here as I was in CPW.

We still want that. But we have other women that could benefit from working with you. So for the first couple of months, we want you to be there to work with them. Nothing's changed, Kimber. We still want you. *I* still want you here.

Before I can come up with a reply, another text comes through, this time, from his partner in crime. The two of them obviously attempting to save themselves by double-teaming me with praise.

You belong here, Kimber. Nothing's changed. Don't overthink it. Just get here in one piece. I'll explain more when you land. See you soon.

Yeah. Okay. I text back quickly to Reese before bringing up Bryan's window again. Staring a hole into the screen and tapping the top of my phone as I attempt to come up with a response.

One that doesn't end up with me asking the question I've gone months not asking, even though it's been on the tip of my tongue to do it the entire time.

Asking how Matthias is. If he thinks about me the same way I do him, and if he's happier now than he was when I last saw him. If he misses me as much as I still miss him.

Shit. Whoever said walking away and cleaning the slate was easy, needs a reality check. I've done a lot of things over the last ten years that were physically hard and mentally draining, but nothing quite like what's happened since I walked away from the man who still owns my heart.

I know it was the right call. That I was right doing it the way I did, but it hasn't shut any of it off. Not the feelings, not the memories. Nothing.

All it's really done that has been beneficial is throwing me headfirst back into what I've loved doing since I was eleven.

Fake it 'til you make it.

That's what they say, right?

Well, I've certainly done the faking part. My relationship with Gavin was solid proof of that and pretending every day that I don't care about Matthias was another bang-up performance.

Now, when I land and head off in Reese's direction, coming face to face with him at some point in the process, it's time to see if I've done the other part.

To see if I've made it.

With the voice of the flight attendant coming over the intercom, I swallow down the question and all thoughts of Matty and focus on what has to happen now. Texting Bryan and shutting my phone off.

Plane's about to land. I'll see you soon.

Harbour Front Wrestling Alliance here I come.

I just hope my heart survives.

Chapter Twenty-Four

September 2015

Matthias

I should have seen this shit coming.

All that buildup from Reese and Bryan, setting me up for the title reign they said I earned in my short time here.

I should have seen it for what it really was.

Bullshit.

"You've got to be shitting me."

I can't have heard them right. When they called me in here, I thought it was to finally tell me that they were elevating Brady up the ladder.

That instead of tearing the house down with me on every available occasion, he was going to move on to Sniper and finally have the belt the way he deserved.

It was supposed to go that way.

The way I wanted it.

Not this way.

Fuck. Raines is going to hate me.

"Matty, I know this is out of left field, but we've talked it over with Brady and even he feels this is the right move. This isn't his time. He's comfortable holding the Middleweight Championship. He doesn't want to move up."

Bullshit. I know better than that.

The world title is all any of us want.

Brady Raines may be a stand-up guy, but at the end of the day, he's just as hungry as the rest of us sorry fucks chasing this crazy ass dream.

"You wanna put the title on me five months in?" I scoff, swimming in their bullshit. "And you also want me to believe Raines is okay with it?"

I'm not hearing this. I can't be.

I told Bry the day I got here what I wanted to do during my time here. This isn't it.

This isn't even close to it.

I'm not ready.

Fuck, I spent the last eleven years with Smith and in that time he never even thought I deserved it. If he didn't, this has gotta be about more than my body of work in the ring.

It's got to be Bryan talking his partner around and giving into our decade's long friendship.

I can't let it go down like this.

"We've been watching you since you got here, man. I thought for sure that the toll of what happened with Smith was going to hinder your ability to do business here. That at the end of the day, you would go off the rails what with the differences in the way things are run, but you haven't. You've been working with heavyweights as much as you have the mid-carders and jobbers, brother. When you're not working with them, you're in the gym busting your tail. Proving yourself."

I can't exactly sit here and argue with Reese. That is what's been going down since I got here in May. Me putting everything I've got into what I do, in order to not only drown out the past and the nightmares, but her too.

Apparently, it didn't go unnoticed.

I hate this.

On the one hand, this is exactly what I've been striving for since I sat my stubborn ass down in the middle of an arctic cold front outside Smith's gym, waiting for some acknowledgment. But I also know that there are a lot of people here deserving of the shot to go against Sniper. Ones that have been here working a lot longer than I have.

More than all of that, like a third god damned hand, I don't think with the frame of mind I've been in since I got here, what really drives me, I can carry the title and make it mean what it should mean regardless of who holds it.

I don't think I have it in me anymore to be the man.

Bryan knows this better than anyone.

"Guys," I start, ready to feed them the same argument I'm having internally with myself, but pausing when I see the jubilant glisten that pours from my best friends eyes. "Are you sure this is the direction you want to go in?"

"Yes, Matty. Reese and I have been going back and forth over this for a couple of weeks now. Hashing out every possible alternative. We've come to the conclusion that there is no one better than you for Sniper to drop the title to."

Stepping forward, Bryan reaches out and with a hard pound across my back, he grins.

"All you gotta say is you're on board and the title is yours for the taking this Friday."

Friday.

Our biggest show of the week.

Shit.

"How long?" I manage to choke out once Bryan's done me the solid of moving back and taken some of the pressure off. "How long are you going to want me to hold it?"

"We're going to let you determine that, Matthias. People come to see you. I know it, Bryan knows it, and we damn well know that you know it. So as long as you want to carry it, it's yours. When you feel you're ready to drop it, when you really believe someone is deserving and you're willing to work to make it happen, we'll follow your lead."

"Take a step back, brother. You're not thinking straight right now."

Of course, I'm not right.

It's been two days since they put the title around my waist, two days since I captured what I've been working my whole life for, and now they're sitting here telling me they wanna strip me of it and put it on the man that should have had it.

On Brady.

How the hell did they think I'd react pulling this shit?

I really did buy into their having faith in me and letting me determine the way this was going to go.

But you did determine it, didn't you? You're the one that said yes and then fell apart. You brought this on yourself. Just like you always do.

"Fuck you." I hiss, realizing too late as Reese's eyes go wide that I've spoken aloud.

They've already figured out there's something off with me and as the voice rears its ugly head, I'm sitting here giving them more proof instead of dispelling it the way I should be.

Son of a bitch.

"What the fuck did you expect to happen when you put the title on me? Of course, I was going to embrace it and run with it."

"We sure as shit didn't expect that you were going to cram a month's worth of partying into a seven-day binge." Reese hisses through clenched teeth. Obviously as done with me and my 'antics' as I am with this conversation.

"So this is about me being late to the show last night?"

"No," Bryan steps forward again in an attempt to intervene. "Matty, this isn't about you being late. It's about you walking out of here the day we told you our plans and seemingly forgetting everything we talked about."

"I didn't forget anything."

"Yeah, buddy, you did. The first night, I had to pick you up at your mom's grave, where a caretaker found you passed out at six in the fucking morning. The next day, you didn't even bother showing up to help train the way you have been for months. We shrugged that one off because after the state we found you in, we figured you needed to sleep it off. But it kept getting worse. The police were involved in the last altercation for fuck sakes. Or are you so far gone you've forgotten that?"

Fuck sakes is right. I don't need a damn play by play of the last week.

"We should be suspending your ass for the shit you're pulling, but since you're the reason this place is even here, we're choosing to go a different route."

Of course, it's Reese delivering that blow. Reminding me again what a stupid move it was fronting my best friend the cash.

"I don't want you doing me any favors." I sneer and that's when it happens. I see my best friend finally break and lose what's left of his self-control. Shoving his fist down onto the metal desk the same way Smith used to when he was pissed.

I've really stepped in it now.

Too bad I don't give a shit.

"You wanna suspend me? Do it. Hell, take your fucking belt and shove it. I'll go out there and do business the way I always have and drop it to Brady, Socio, whoever the fuck you want to carry it and you can be rid of me. Hell, fire me, Reese. I know you didn't want me here in the first place. Make things easy for yourself."

"Shut the hell up, Matthias," Bryan growls and not backing down, he comes at me. "We're trying to do what's best for you."

"What's best for me? Right." I laugh. "That's always been your thing, hasn't it? You've got a real savior complex. Too bad you can't save someone who doesn't want to be. Must really piss you off."

"Matty, I'm begging you. Stop talking."

"But I thought we were just getting started? Why the hell should I stop right when things are getting good?"

"You're in a bad way. It's like night and day from the man who walked in here months ago. There's something wrong with you, and in order to protect what we've built here, we've gotta get you right."

"By taking away the only fucking thing that matters to me? That seems fair?"

There. I've told them the truth. It's the only god damned thing that matters anymore. I've lost everything and everyone else that mattered. My mom, my dad, Smith. Her.

Fuck. Now's not the time for her to haunt me.

She can do that, laughing as she does, when I'm licking my wounds later.

"You're standing her smelling like a fucking brewery, Matthias. You have a match in less than six hours and you're shit faced. Weaving on your feet and acting like an indignant little shit. Do you really think that's fair to us? To the two people that believed in your ability, your talent. God, your fucking heart? Is it fair that we have to have a drunk ass champion representing our brand when we're trying to get a damn foot in the door?"

"You don't know what you're talking about, Harrison."

"If I come over there and blow on you, you'd fall like a house of cards. You're unstable. I'm sorry if it hurts your pretty little feelings, but I'm not having someone like that as the face of my company. Not even if you're the reason we can even call ourselves that."

"Matty, please. He's not trying to be an asshole, but you need to hear what he's saying. What we both are. Why we're doing this."

"I'm a…liability." I pause, giggling to myself when Bryan's done. "Don't worry, *bro*. I've heard that one before. I got you loud and clear."

"No, Matty, you don't." He argues, trying to be my best friend again. "You don't get it at all, which is the problem. Go home."

Washing his hands of me, he brings his hands together and steps away. The first time in years he's ever backed away from me and as his back turns, also giving me a first there too.

I'm not just ruining my run here. I'm ruining my relationship with the only brother I've ever known too.

"Get out of here. Go sleep off your latest bender and be back here for show time."

A show that after tonight, I have no doubt if Reese has his way, I won't be a part of. And leaving me as alone as I was when I started this whole journey, to begin with.

My grip on the brass ring that I was so honored and yet so god damned scared to hold, it's slipping. The moisture of my hands releasing it until I close my eyes, take a breath and upon opening them, see it gone completely.

As if I never even had it.

Kimberlee

"Kimber, what are you doing back here?"

Such a silly question.

I was asked to be here.

Okay, so maybe not *here*, here. But I was asked to be a part of this tonight, by the man asking me the question now, no less.

Besides, it's not like there's anywhere else I need to be for this match.

Matthias's title match.

A newer development but with the way he's using the ladder to his advantage right now, a weapon even more dangerous than the ones his body already contains, a development that should have been afforded him a long time ago.

"I had to…" I attempt to explain but pause with a sigh instead. "I don't know, Bryan."

"He's good, isn't he?" He ignores my comment, making his way over and stopping directly to my left, eyes as focused as mine had been on the enigma that is Matthias in the ring.

"The best," I admit proudly, albeit sadly. "He deserves this."

Tapping his finger against his lip, he releases a sigh of his own and despite the pull, I have to go back to watching Matthias facing off against Brady, I turn to Bryan instead.

"What's the sigh for?"

"You're not going to like the way this turns out, Kimber. It doesn't have a happy ending."

Something tells me that with everything I know and have experienced with Matthias, nothing ever does end happily. It doesn't take away from this moment though. How into what he's doing he is.

Just the way he's always been.

"He's not the same guy you knew. I don't even think he's the same guy I knew." Bryan muses and now he's got every part of my attention.

The pull to watch the man I love giving his all in the ring, now erased and filled with concern as to what Bryan's really getting at.

"What does that mean? What are you saying without actually saying it?"

"You'll see."

God. Men. It never ceases to amaze me just how annoying they can be. What kind of answer is that really? I mean come on! Just spit out what you really wanna say already.

"Why are you back here? It can't just be because you wanted to confuse the hell out of me."

"But it's so much fun." He jokes.

"Yeah, I bet."

"I know I said this before, but Kimber, for more than just wanting you here because of your talent in the ring, I'm really glad you agreed to do this."

"You're...welcome?"

Stepping up to the monitor and running a hand over Matthias's moving form as Brady hits him repeatedly in the head with shot after shot from their position on the top rope, he sighs again, turning back to me, his eyes forlorn.

Like he's lost the only thing that matters. Or maybe, in this case, the only person.

"I'm sorry for this. For all of it."

"For what?"

Stepping back and walking away without so much as an acknowledgment that he heard me, I spin on my heel and turn to go after him, pulling him to a stop before he can make his way back out and disappear.

"For what, Bryan?"

"You'll see, Kimber. You'll see."

Shrugging out of my limp hold, he drags himself away. His shoulders slumped. His body obviously feeling the loss.

Turning back around and focusing my attention again on the match, despite the confusion of the last few minutes, that's when it all begins to make sense.

What Bryan means, it's happening right before my eyes.

Brady, having gotten the upper hand, has tossed Matthias down off the top rope and onto the table Matty set up earlier like a bridge from the announce table to the ring. Matty's lack of movement in the moment making it appear as though he's been taken out indefinitely, but I know better. Moving slowly but his every step deliberate, Brady heads to the other side of the ring and after grabbing another ladder, sets it up in the middle of the ring. And in the time it takes Matthias to shift from his place on his own piece of unforgiving metal, Brady is climbing.

Blinking and praying to god as I do that I don't miss a thing, I watch with bated breath as he climbs his way halfway up the ten-foot ladder, pausing for what looks like a breath or two before moving again.

Matthias, moving with a speed that given the brunt of the hit he took, shouldn't be possible, dives for the one Brady is now climbing and begins inching his body up, flinching as he goes. My heart breaking when halfway up, he slips and barely catches himself. My breath lodged in my throat as I silently cheer him on while Brady reaches the top and looks down on his opponent with a sadistic grin.

Laughing when Matty continues to use that will of his that I know lives for these matches—this business—and continues to inch his way up to match him.

The two of them sharing blows, Brady chopping hard across Matty's chest as Matty's seem to connect with the man's face. Not so much as shaking Brady as he barks out the deepest cackle I think I've ever heard a man make. Brady smirking when after one final blow, one that connects with the side of Matthias's head, he knocks him clear off the ladder. Giving him the opportunity to reach up in a matter of a few seconds and pull the title from its binding. Claiming it as his own.

This is what Bryan meant when he said I would see.

And watching him now, as Brady straps the belt around his waist and celebrates as his entrance music plays, I see the moment I'm pretty sure with his first question Bryan asked when he caught me back here, he never wanted me to.

Matthias's loss.

Hands in his hair, gripping it tightly and pulling, tears pouring from his eyes, Matthias leans back against the rope and does the one thing I never thought I would see.

He breaks.

This isn't just the loss of the title. The loss of being the guy at the top of the mountain.

This is more.

It's going to be the true loss of him.

The last seeds of the Matthias I knew, the Matthias Kemper I know, pouring out of him as water continues to pour from his eyes for the camera's enjoyment.

The only question I have now as I watch him lose what matters, is why?

Why did he lose it?

Chapter Twenty-Five
Title Loss Aftermath

Kimberlee

It always ends up this way.

No matter how fast or how far I run from it, we always seem to end up right back where we started.

Not alone the way we clearly intended, but together.

Matthias and Kimber.

Two damn halves of the same whole, but too damn stubborn to admit to ourselves that it's meant to be this way, let alone admit to each other.

Going from adversaries, to what I like to think was friends, and having it turn into something more until it all comes crashing down.

Round and round we go like a freaking Ferris wheel.

I'm not sure what we even are to each other at this point.

Judging by the hardened look in his eyes now, especially with my admission of wanting to save him, I'm sure we're right back in 2006 again and adversaries.

"You want to save me, huh? From what exactly?"

"Yourself."

I don't know if it was my arrival a little over a month ago, the pressure to be the man or something else entirely, but it was easy to see right from the second I landed here and threw myself into the thick of things that Matthias wasn't the same guy he was under Radley's tutelage.

He'd gained more of an attitude. More of an edge.

Watching his matches on closed-circuit monitors in the back when no one was around to see and catch the fire in his eyes, an animalistic rage I've never witnessed, he was definitely not the man I knew.

Even if my heart wanted to believe otherwise.

Backstage talk swirling that he was drinking more and showing up to events reeking of alcohol. A smarmy smirk etched into his normally broody features that didn't seem to fit. In all of my quiet attempts at watching him from afar or listening in on others that were much closer, he still kept to himself. The only thing that did remind me of the Matthias of old.

Everything else was new. Different.

Wrong.

It was easy to escape him. There was no real ducking or dodging to try and stay out of his path because when word spread he was going to have the belt put on him, it was Gavin all over again. He entered into a new plateau and we weren't even on the same planet, much less the same galaxy. It also helped that with Reese and Bryan wanting me to work with some of their greener acquisitions, we never really ran into each other. My time spent in the training center and his on the main stage.

But it didn't stop me from watching.

I drank Matthias Kemper in, despite all of the months and distance between us, because it was what I always knew deep down I was going to do.

He was it for me even if he didn't feel the same.

And tonight, after what happened in the ring; what none of us in the back really saw coming, there was nowhere else I had to be but here.

I meant what I said. I want to save him, even if it's from himself. We may never be anything, but I will make sure he knows *he is* something.

"Bryan send you to do his dirty work?" he finally speaks again, bringing me out of my thoughts and awakening me again to where we find ourselves.

"No. He has no idea I'm here."

"How'd you find me?"

Okay, Kimber. Here's where you tell him that despite your walking away when you last talked to one another, you've actually developed quite the stalking streak.

Ugh. Even to my own ears I sound deranged.

"I followed you."

Where I expect him to laugh in his inebriated state or hell, get pissed that I'd taken things so far, that's not the response I'm rewarded with when he does acknowledge my response. There's a playful curiosity, maybe even a little surprise, dancing in his eyes.

"Why would you want to follow me around? Don't you have better things to do, Miss Next Women's Champion of the World?"

Hmm. Looks like I'm not the only one that been keeping tabs.

For someone that hasn't so much as passed me in the halls since I got here, he sure knows what's coming.

"Actually, you're making me miss out on a really important call with Zach. It's been exactly three days since I heard about his latest lay."

Zach is a common thread between us. My sometimes idiotic, often man whore like, but loyal as hell brother, trained almost as much by the man sitting in the barstool as I had been.

"He really tells you about that shit?" Matthias laughs and the sound, after so long not hearing it, does more good for me than I'm sure it's done for him. Filling me with a hope that when I walked in here and caught him downing shot after shot of hard liquor, I didn't think I'd have.

"Unfortunately yes. I mean," I quickly attempt to save my admission and joke. "Yes, but that's only because he knows I *love* hearing all about it."

God, even I can't bullshit well enough for that and I fake dated a dude for almost a year.

"He's better than that."

"I know." I agree, reminded again of just how many times I've told Zach the same thing. "But he's an adult out from under my dad's eye, being given a push that has put him on top of the world. This is how he chooses to handle it."

"You didn't."

Shoving myself down onto the stool beside him and motioning to the bartender for a beer, the raw attack on my throat from the whiskey definitely not feeling the best, I turn into him.

"I'm not Zach, Matty."

"No." he whistles low. "You're *definitely not* Zach."

Fourteen year old Kimber rises at what appears to be his jab, but before I can let him have it, he's speaking again and the argument falls away. As usual, I've taken him the wrong way.

"If you were, there wouldn't be so much bullshit between us."

Us.

Well, so much for this going smoothly.

"There's no bullshit between us, Matthias. Once upon a time I thought there could be something," *There still is something you little liar.* "But it just wasn't meant to be anything."

Except it could have been everything and something tells me with the way his head hangs in his hands now, he agrees.

Whatever this is between us, nothing is going to be able to stop it. Not even us.

It's just too bad that nothing's changed. He's still shut off, and I'm still refusing to take it. Even if my being here might say different. I can't just turn off caring. Whether it's Matthias, Gavin, god, even someone like Melinda, I'm always going to give a shit and not want to see them hit rock bottom.

"My whole life, all I wanted was to be one of them." He practically whispers, his face still angled perfectly toward the bar his elbows are leaning down hard onto. "One of the top guys. *The best guys.* To make that championship mean what it always did to me as a kid. The pinnacle of this sport. Proof that you were the best in the world at what you do. What made all of the sweat, the pints of blood and boatload of injuries worth it."

"You were one of them." I inform him, equally as softly. The other patrons around us no longer privy to our conversation. "You *still are* one of them, Matty."

"Right. I'm so damn good that the belt is on someone else tonight, and I'm in a bar with someone who feels obligated to be my guardian angel."

It should sting, being relegated to that but it doesn't because in a backwards way, it's true. Feelings aside, history aside, I'm here to make sure that what happened tonight in the ring, what was taken, doesn't destroy him.

The loss of the spot at the top already claiming more than a fair share of performers in this business.

Matthias not needing to be the latest casualty.

"Did they tell you why they pulled the title off you?"

Cursing under his breath, he nods, and lifting his eyes from the bar he turns and places them straight on me. The pain reflecting back in them telling me more than I wanted to know.

"My behavior."

The drinking. The attitude he has whenever someone does talk to him. The changes he made once it was decided he was going to be the champion. It ended up costing him the only thing he's ever wanted.

"So you thought the best way to handle that was to continue it?"

"You got a better idea?" he barks out before tapping the bar and signalling to Saul for another round.

Slipping my hand around my own bottle, I slide it over to him and motion for Saul with a hand across my neck not to give him anymore. I'll let him drink, I'm not his mother, but he's not gonna be drinking that hard shit anymore.

Not if I want to get him out of here in one piece.

"I do, actually."

"I'm dying to hear." He slaps the bar and smirks, and after swallowing down the urge to smack him the same way I'd done in the past with Gavin when he tried this shit, I let him have it.

Maybe what I did with Gavin that first night in CPW can work here too.

"I would take what I was told as constructive criticism and change things. I would work on it and myself so I could come back stronger. Not rush from the building, drive halfway across town, and get blasted in a bar."

"Well, we can't all be perfect like you, can we, Kimber?"

Shoving him in the arm, I grab the bottle before he has a chance to bring it to his lips and put it to my own, taking what has to be the longest swallow before slamming it back down and motioning with my hand for him to have a go.

"What the fuck was that?"

"Little miss perfect trying to see how the other half lives?" I answer sarcastically and my breath catches when his lips genuinely seem to quirk up into a smile.

Not the fake ones he's been wearing since I showed up. Not even the one he wears around the shows or even at the gym. A real one.

Showing shades of the boy I once knew.

He's still in there.

"I didn't think you had it in you."

"Did you already forget I stole one of your shots when I got here?"

"Cute, but no. It's just after that speech, I didn't expect you to come over so quickly to the dark side."

He's not so different after all. The dark side he's speaking of isn't the bar, it isn't even the booze. It's him. It's always been him. He's still warning me off in his own stupid way.

"Here's what I know, Matty. You're better than this. I don't know what's happened to you since you left Smith and came down here, but it's pretty obvious that whatever has, it's not working in your favor. You have to deal with that. Bryan and Reese love you. They wouldn't have brought you in and given you the push they did, if they didn't have faith you could do it. Problem is, you don't have it in yourself. You never have. And now you're paying your ultimate price for it."

"My ultimate price?" he interrupts right as I take a breath, readying myself to continue. "What the fuck is that supposed to mean?"

"It means, there is nothing more important to you than the title. Than being recognized for all of the years you've put yourself through this. Your ultimate price is the belt. Even knowing how many people see your greatness, you still didn't. So when you were handed the brass ring, it fell. You fell under the weight of it."

"I don't need this." He responds, his resolve wavering as his voice shakes. "If I wanted another fucking speech, I would have stayed with Bryan."

"You do need it, though. Don't you see that? You might not want it, but you do need it. Someone needs to break through this wall you've built and make you see reality. You're spiralling. So if you won't save yourself, someone else needs to do it."

"Someone like you?"

"Don't see anyone else here taking it on, do you?" I motion around the bar with a wave of my hand. "So yeah. I guess that leaves it up to me."

Eyes softening, he reaches out across the bar. Pausing right before his fingers have the chance to brush against mine and almost thinking better of it, pulls his hand back until it's wrapped safely around his bottle.

"Why are you doing this, Kimber? After everything I said, the way I treated you, and the things I did...why is it you here?"

Because I'm in love with you, you big dumb buffoon.

If he was clearheaded, I'm sure he'd know this. As it stands, knowing that he was drinking before I walked in and he'll probably drink long after I'm gone, it's not something I'll ever utter aloud. He wouldn't care.

He didn't before. Can't imagine it would start now.

"Because I know you, Matthias. You're going through something, a lot of something's if I had to guess. No one, not even you, should ever have to go through that alone. Not when they have someone that cares."

Combative Matthias, I've seen him. The stubborn side of him, often times outweighing the broody and quiet parts and making itself known in a pretty impactful way. It's what I expect from him after everything I've said. But as I'm coming to learn the more time I spend here tonight, never expect, because people, mainly Matty, will surprise you.

"I messed up with you, Kimber. I didn't see what was really there when I had the chance. I saw what could be, but what was actually happening? The feelings, the need and the reality? I didn't see it. I fucked up."

Whoa.

"You following me here and being the only damn one that gives a shit about how I might be feeling after what happened tonight, what I caused because I wasn't as ready for this as I thought, I appreciate it but I don't deserve it."

Reaching around his back and slipping his wallet out, he slaps a few bills down onto the bar top before shifting and lowering himself off the stool, righting his jeans and situating his jacket before finally finding my eyes again.

"I don't deserve you. I never did."

Oh god. Not again. This feeling of living in some kind of sick time warp has got to stop.

I came in here not with the intent of feeling something for him again, or even reactivating what was already there. I only wanted to help. Do right by him because of who he is to HFWA. To wrestling as a whole.

The last few things he's said though, they've changed the landscape. It's like we're back in CPW all over again and he's getting ready to leave in order to save me.

Moving around his own stool, he leans over into my own personal space and placing another, much smaller bill down onto the bar, paying for my drink, he pauses before he can pull all the way back, his next words warm as they brush across my ear.

"I'm sorry, Kimber. For everything."

"You're forgiven."

"No I'm not. Not really. Not yet anyway." He whispers against my hair, the faint trace of his lips causing me to shiver. What he catches and uses to his advantage in this newest emotional assault as he fingers a tendril of my hair.

"What are you doing?"

"Just what you told me to do."

"W-which is?" I stammer, the feel of his fingers still in my hair shaking what's left of my earlier resolve to keep this entire moment feelings free.

"Saving myself. Taking what was said and using it to come back stronger so I can earn back the one thing that matters."

"What's that?"

My head betrays me as it aligns itself with my heart, both of them sitting and waiting with baited breath for him to admit what I've known to be true ever since I met him.

That even though this business is what we were born and bred to do with our lives, titles and reigns important and our livelihood in terms of our longevity, there is still one thing that could override it all. One thing that matters more than all of it combined.

Love.

"You, little one. I'm going to come back stronger for you."

Matthias

"I gotta admit, when you said you wanted a sit down to discuss where we go from here, I wasn't entirely sure I should accept. Especially when you wanted it alone."

After my altercation the night after the loss of the title with Kimber, and what she said, this was my first stop.

Reese Harrison is only half of the faces that run this place, but with my personal relationship with Bryan, the friendship that's spanned decades and what a lot of people around here like to think played a part in my rise and epic fall with the title recently, it's him I need to hash this out with.

I can fill Bryan in later. This has to start with Reese. He's the one I've got to win over if I want this rise from the bottom to work the way I see it in my head.

Kimber was right when she said that the title was my price to be paid.

Being at the top of HFWA was my ultimate goal and I reached out and grabbed it. But like with everything else in life, when you're not ready, take it for granted, or with me, when you're not at all in the right frame of mind for it, you will screw it up.

You will fail.

The nights I spent in bars all over the city trying to drink the memories away, drink her away, along with the ache that was ever present in my chest since Kimber put the ball in my court and walked away from my latest round of stupidity. The way I threw my entire being into the matches, even taking unnecessary risks to my own person in order to put on the best damn show. The devil may care attitude I had, almost suicidal to anyone looking at me from the outside. They were all signs that I wasn't ready for the position I found myself in.

But instead of reaching out to Bryan, Reese, Brady, hell even Avery and admitting I wasn't in the right place, I'd taken it on and made a mess of it myself.

This, where I find myself now, a result of all the choices I made. Ones I've got to own if I want to do what I said and be better.

Not only for her, but for me too.

"I would have understood if you didn't take the meeting. It's not like I've done much in the last little bit to deserve it."

"That's not true though, Matthias. If you hadn't displayed everything we wanted in our champion, we never would have made the collective decision to put the title on you. We would have left it on Sniper."

"It's better where it is now."

"Brady's stepped up, I'll give him that. He's definitely a good choice. You just have to realize that he wasn't our first choice."

"I know."

"What happened, man? Where did the guy that was hungry to prove himself and win over the boys go?"

He drowned in the sea of insecurities, fears of the present and the past, along with the truckloads of booze he'd been drinking.

That's the honest truth and the answer that Reese should definitely hear, but it's not at all what I say when I do speak again.

There's only a select group of people that know about my past. About my parents, the tragedy that seemed to wipe out anything in my life that ever mattered, and who I became because of it. Reese isn't one of them and even though I trust him to a degree, it's still not to the level where I feel I can get into it.

I'm not sure I'll ever hit that level of trust with anyone ever again.

Except Kimber. You want to tell her everything.

For once, the irritating voice of the monster as he rouses, doesn't bother. This time, he's right. For her, especially with what I know I'm always going to feel for her, I'd give it all over.

"I let the pressure to be who you all needed get to me. I didn't say shit about it, just kept swallowing it down. Determined to do what I needed to do. I started drinking to take some of the edge off and before I knew it, I had a problem I couldn't contain."

"This got anything to do with Smith?"

There's a name I haven't heard in a while. With the chill that makes its way through me at Reese's mention though, obviously still one that seems to have a hold over me.

"Yeah, I guess in a way it has a bit to do with him. His way of doing things, the relationship we had for all those years, it's harder to shed than I thought it would be."

"Why couldn't you just admit that before we put you over?" Reese asks and my answer, having expected this to be one of the first things he asked, is right on the tip of my tongue.

"Because I thought I had a handle on it. I didn't, but I didn't wanna let you down. I thought that once I had the title on me things would change, but instead the noose around my neck got tighter. You both did the right thing making the judgement call you did, stripping me of the title. I'm not the right guy for the job."

"You are when your heads in it, Matthias. That hasn't changed."

"Thank you."

"Don't thank me for stating facts that deep down, you know to be true. Don't cheapen yourself that way. Just get right with yourself. Straighten your head out."

"That's kind of what I'm here about."

"You want to have a go at Brady?"

"No." I tell him honestly, knowing that in this fresh start, I'm in no way ready for something that huge. "I want to be pulled off the shows entirely for a while."

"Excuse me?"

"You heard me."

"You're right, I did hear you. I just don't think I understand what you're saying. Bryan and I, we don't want to punish you for what happened, Matthias. It's not like you broke any rules. You were just self-destructive. We were trying to help you."

"I know. And now that I've had time to think about things and get my head screwed back on somewhat straight, I need to do things a different way."

"And that way is?" he asks, finally backing away from the window and finding his way to the chair, sitting.

"Let me work behind the scenes."

"We already have a crew for that shit, man. I don't need to tell you that you're better qualified to be in the ring."

"Not what I meant." I laugh and when his brow pulls in and he begins rubbing across the bridge of his nose, I only go harder.

"I'm glad that my lack of understanding amuses you."

"It does, but only because Bryan looks the exact same way when he talks to me these days. I know you have a backstage crew. I'm not looking to go back to putting rings together."

"Then what are you getting at?"

"I wanna train some of the people you just brought in."

"And why would you wanna do that when you could easily be in the main event?"

"Because I'm not quite there yet. Someone told me recently that where other people had confidence in my ability to carry this promotion and get it to heights you want to reach, I didn't have it in myself. So doing things this way is my way of achieving that."

Not going to bother telling him that the last time I found myself in a position like I am now, being thrown into Renegade's promotion had been what had turned me around. That's for me only.

It's time to get that feeling back.

Get me back.

"You sure about this?"

"I'm positive."

"You know that most of the people we brought in are girls, right? That gonna be a problem for you?"

"Nope." Not when the other reason for me wanting to do this is a part of that group he just brought in and is going to get me one step closer to achieving what I really want. "I'm good working with whoever."

Tapping his fingers on the desk before bringing his hand up and over his hair, he breathes out a heavy sigh before finally looking back to me with a quick nod of his head.

"You've got yourself a deal."

✶ ✶ ✶ ✶ ✶ ✶

"You did what?!" Bryan yells when after coming in the door a little over an hour ago and finding him in the kitchen making dinner, I drop my meeting with Reese on him.

"It's the best thing for everyone."

"Like fuck it is! You should be the one with that belt strapped around your waist, Kemper. I love Brady, and I've got all the faith in the world in his ability to carry it and make it matter, but you and I both know it's not his time."

No, it's not his time. Not with the feud he set up before they made a new plan for the title. But it's what they've got now, and unless they want a repeat of the person they had a week ago, Bryan needs to get on board with this and fast.

"You never should have put the title on me in the first place, Bry. So either elevate Marcus so you can keep the feud going with those two, or put the belt back on Sniper."

"I'm not hearing any of this shit right now. I'm still upstairs passed out. I have to be. This is the stupidest shit I've ever heard come out of your mouth, and brother? You talk a lot of crap."

"'Fraid not, man. You're actually here and we really are having this conversation."

"I hate this conversation."

"Not exactly a fan of it myself, but when you told me to come home and took me on here, I made you a promise. I would do whatever it took to make HFWA the best damn promotion on the planet. I let you down, and as bitter a pill as that is to swallow, this solution is the best way I know to make it right."

"Minus a couple, a lot of the people Reese scooped up are still green as fuck. Maybe one or two matches to their credit. You really wanna subject yourself to working with them when you could easily be in any damn title hunt you want?"

"It worked before." I say, referencing the time with Renegade. A time I know he remembers just as well as I do. "It can work again."

"Is it really that bad?"

"Yeah, Bry, it is. If I don't do something to change things, it could be worse."

There hasn't been a match since what happened with Grant where I ever put my opponent at risk again. My lesson was learned during my time with Renegade and his family. There's just no denying with how deep I was burying myself in the bottle in order to push out the voices in my head and the memories that continually haunt, it could easily happen again.

A truth that scares me more than anything else because it's a way I never want to be again.

"Shit." He hisses before full on cursing me. "Fuck, Matty! I thought we were past all this shit. Why now? Is it because Reese wanted Kimber here? Is that what this is about?"

"No." I deny even though it's not entirely the truth. "It's about me doing right by the one guy that despite my every attempt to make him do it, has never left my side."

"Bullshit. You've already done right by me. You helped me realize this entire thing to begin with. Or have you forgotten that?"

"I didn't forget the way you seemed to forget that I wanted it kept quiet, if that's what you're getting at."

"Shit. He fucking told you?"

"He did." I laugh. "I'm just waiting to see who else does."

"I'm sorry, Matty."

"Don't be. Just tell me you're okay with this and you won't go after your partner for making a judgement call without you."

"Reese is safe. I'm just not sure you are. I still think this is the wrong move."

My best friend is loyal, even to his own detriment. He can't see that what he wants for me and what I can feasibly handle these days are drastically apart. He just wants to do whatever he can for me.

It's just too bad that in this one way, the decision is made and he doesn't get a say.

Bryan is owed a better Matthias. He's been there through it all and despite my piss poor attitude, never left. He's the closest thing I'll ever have to a brother and it's about damn time I acted like it.

Did what it takes to show him what I've never been able to admit out loud.

"You're sure I can't talk you out of this?"

"Positive."

"And you're gonna be able to handle working with her?"

"That's actually the other reason I wanted you to know."

Pulling the pan off the burner, he places it on the counter, flipping the knob on the stove off before leaning over directly across from me at the bar.

"If this is where you tell me you can't work with her and you wanna be kept as far away as—"

"Stop." I interrupt the speech I can feel is coming. "That's not what I was gonna say."

"It wasn't?"

Shit. If Bryan automatically goes there, I can only imagine the way Kimber is gonna react when I show up. I've got a long road ahead of me if I want to make things right.

I really wish I could erase minds.

"No, it wasn't. I was going to ask you to make sure that out of all of the people he brought in, you let me near her."

"Matthias, she's one of the best damn women's competitors we acquired. We need her here just as much as we need you. I don't want you fucking with that. With her. There's been enough of that between you two."

"I wasn't planning on it." *At least not in the way he's thinking.* "You told me to handle my shit with her before, and well, this is my attempt at doing that. The right way this time."

"Who are you and what have you done with my best friend?"

Can't exactly argue that response. He's been wanting me to act like this for years now. I think we've gotten to the point, the both of us, where we actually believed it was never going to come.

My head was going to permanently take up residence in my ass.

"Your best friend got left behind in that house ten years ago."

"And now?"

"He's here."

When no response follows, but he doesn't turn away or put his attention back on the food, I tell him the only thing left to say.

The truth.

"I care about her, Bry."

"Jesus. You really did pull your head out if you're admitting that." He whistles softly. "Sorry to say I've known it for the last nine years though. You're a little late to the Kimber-Matthias party. Pretty sure the entire world knows how the two of you feel."

"No shit."

"Get your girl, Matty. But this time when you do it, make it last. Don't let her go."

He doesn't have to tell me that. I already know. This time when she's in my arms, it's going to be forever.

I don't think any of us will survive it being any other way.

Chapter Twenty-Six

Kimberlee

Stepping through the doors of developmental, geared up and ready for more of the same, I'm met by the complete opposite of what I expect.

It's not the parade of girls I've been working with over the last several weeks climbing the ropes and taking dives off. It's not even the four guys I've been working with.

That is natural. Expected. Just another day.

What I was looking forward to.

This is anything but.

Someone's clearly in the wrong place.

Moving toward the ring, my feet moving of their own volition even though I'm in no way prepared for another losing battle in our never-ending story of them, I pause when I hit the steps, and for lack of anything better to do, I watch him as he attempts his earlier move again. Waiting only until his feet hit the ground before clearing my throat and announcing my presence.

Which the second he hears it, has his head lifting and turning, his eyes with no flutter in between, landing straight on me.

Matthias, ever the hunter, with his prey in his sights.

Sucking in a breath and swallowing, I harden myself against the pull of his penetrating stare, keeping my mind focused on what's most important.

Getting answers.

"What are you doing here?"

"Trying out some new moves. Shaking off some of the rust."

This guy. God. He's only been out of the ring for a couple of weeks. Rust? Really?

"Okay, but you could do that anywhere. Why here?"

"Isn't it obvious?"

"Not really, no."

"You."

"Me?"

God, Kimber, have your communication skills lapsed so much that the best you can do is repeat everything back?

Swallowing hard, I move up the steps, and even though I'm moving slower than when I first arrived, I make quick work of them. Pausing for a breath, maybe two, before slipping my body through the ropes. Caught and unable to move another step when he shifts and moves toward me with a smile.

There's no way in hell I'm letting him see how affected I still am. I can't do it.

Pausing as I take the first timid step in his direction, I notice how still he is now. Watching and waiting as I make my way to the center of the ring, but making no move to continue his earlier movement.

Head held high, eyes staring him down, I attempt to exude as much confidence as I can. Praying as I do that my knees keep their hold and don't betray me the way the rest of me wants to, with the proximity I now have to him.

"Yes you, Kimber." He returns easily to our conversation. "You're right. I could have trained anywhere, but those other places don't have what I want."

God help me. I know why he's saying it like this. The question he wants me to ask.

And despite my resolve to stay away from all things Kemper when I walked away from him on Valentine's Day, I'm going to give it to him.

I *want* to give it to him.

"What do you want?"

"I want you. More specifically, I want to work with you."

Willing my heart to slow and shaking off the residual sting it experiences hearing it's not something more, I nod.

"The others will be here soon."

"No, Kimber." He shakes his head emphatically. "They won't be. It's just us today."

Just us.

I need to tell him to stop talking. My heart is still invested despite my every attempt not to let it be and the way he's talking, the way he's making it sound, is giving me hope.

With Matthias Kemper, hope isn't something wise to have.

Hope with him leaves you broken.

"Very funny."

"It's not a joke."

Of course it's not. Yet really, when you think about it, it is. It's the funniest thing I've heard all day. Working with Matthias? It's got to be a cosmic joke.

"I don't think that's a good idea." *Because despite wanting to hate you, I love you and can't trust myself with you.* "We should probably stick to the way things have been."

Studying me, the air falling silent around us, he rubs a hand across his chin before his eyes lift and see straight through me and my lies.

Not a damn thing has changed. I'm still as transparent as I've always been.

"Are you sure about that? Something tells me you're not a huge fan of the way things have been lately."

Does he mean us or my place in HFWA?

"If you're talking about being here training instead of on the main stage where I think I should be, you're right. The difference between me and you is, I know this is where I'm needed."

Bringing a hand to his chest, his lip quirk ups in the most delicious yet devilish smile and my heart thumps its approval.

What I wouldn't give to reach out and touch it. Feel the grooves and changes evident in his face as he wears it.

Biting into my lip as hard as I can, feeling the blood being drawn when I hit pay dirt, I focus on the sting and swallow down the urge, waiting out whatever is about to happen next.

"It hurts that you think the worst of me, little one."

Livid, hating myself for reacting but pissed even more with his nonchalant attitude and the name he still has the audacity to call me after all this time, I ball my hands into fists. Keeping them clenched tight and ready at my sides, more than a little ready to haul off and hit him.

After everything we've been through he doesn't have the right to use that name anymore. He lost it the last time he bailed.

Eyes softening, he steps back with his hands in the air. A sure sign of surrender and what only seems to fuel my need to hit him even more.

Who the hell does he think he is?

A question that just as I'm about to put a voice to it, freezes in my throat when he turns his back and heads over to the far ring corner. Squatting down, he picks something up, fingering it in this hands before hopping back up to his feet, turning and showing me.

Gloves.

More specifically, fighter's gloves.

What the hell is going on?

"What are those for?" I motion to the gloves and he smirks before holding them out between us, waiting for me to take them, hope springing eternal in his eyes. Snatching them from his hands, not returning the smile I'm rewarded with when I do, I slip them down over my hands and tightening the straps, familiarize myself with the material, stretching my hands.

The only thing close to this I've used being the tape I wrap my hands in before each match. This is a whole new experience for me. One I still have yet to understand.

"Are you going to tell me what these are for now? Or you just planning on standing there grinning like a cat that caught a canary?"

Chuckling to himself and taking what's left of my hardened resolve and liquefying it, he nods.

"Back before I found Smith and he took me in, I used to hang out at the gym a lot. They didn't have a set up the way a lot of the ones these days do, so I would usually just spend hours wailing away on a punching bag."

"Did you want to box?"

"No, but you make do with what you've got. This gym, well, that's what it had."

"What does that have to do with me?"

Grinning, he steps toward me again and just as I'm about to take a step back, sensing he's going to touch me and not sure how well I'm able to handle it, he slips on a pair of his own, bringing them up between us and staring me down.

Not with desire but determination. Focus.

Whatever he's about to drop, he's taking it as seriously as he has everything else since the day we met.

"One of the last things you said to me has been playing on repeat ever since. It took me a long time to come to terms with the fact that you were here to stay. That no matter how far I ran, you'd always catch me, but now that I have—come to terms with it, that is—it's time for me to give you what I think you've been after since that day."

What I've been after?

"I don't get it."

"For one day, I want you to forget the rules. Well, no. Maybe more than the one day depending on how much of it you need to get out."

"How much what? Matthias, you're not making any sense."

"Hurt. Upset. Fuck, maybe even rage if you've felt anything like I have over the last couple of years."

Ahh. I think I get it now.

This self-deprecating idiot wants me to take out everything I'm feeling on him.

How generous.

"We're not going to fight, Matthias. No matter how badly I want to rearrange your face."

"You're right." he says, shining that glowing smile again. "*We're* not going to fight. You are."

"No, I'm not."

Closing the already too small gap between us and effectively stripping me of the air I need to be able to keep my wits, his hand cups my face, his eyes softening with the move as he leans in as close as he can get.

Well, as close as he can get where his lips aren't attaching themselves to mine.

God help me. How long have I wanted this kind of attention from him? This reaction?

Years. The answer is years.

Keep your wits, Parker. You can't trust that he means any of what he's doing right now.

"I know what you're thinking, wicked one." He plays on my name with a smirk. "You think that I'm doing this because I'm messed in the head."

He's not too far off.

"It's probably true, but that's not the reason. I mean, I do deserve to have you wail on me, I want you to if we're being honest, but there's another reason."

"And that would be?"

"There aren't many areas where you're weak, but when it comes to executing proper punches in the ring, at least ones that look real and have the most impact, you're falling a little short."

He's not wrong. I'm always worried about actually connecting when I'm with the other girls. Not wanting to mess up their pretty faces, I hold back. Giving about twenty percent of what I can do, instead of the hundred that being in this business deserves.

A fact that he obviously hasn't been turned on to.

He believes I can't hit.

This might be fun after all.

"So you want to train me in the proper way to punch?"

His head begins to bob but before he can complete it, I'm on him. Jab after jab. Ones he can't predict or in any way defend against. And just like I assumed he wanted before, the rush of adrenaline that flows through me as all of my pent up feelings spill out and over into the hits, is intoxicating.

"You wanted me to get my feelings out? Fine. This is me getting my feelings out, you stupid, selfish, son of a bitch." I hiss once I've taken him down to the mat and fallen to my knees on top of him.

Not letting up as I land shot after shot to the side of his head and chest, his arms and anywhere else I can reach that's open and exposed to me.

It's only when his hand falls away and I land a punch so damn hard I can actually feel the sound of a crack as I connect with his jaw that his hands are up and grabbing my wrists, halting me.

Out of breath, a fire of his own now blazing strong and mighty through his eyes, he attempts to catch his breath as his words fall.

"I...told you...before. One shot. Just one."

I'd gotten off more than one but with as revved up as I am, as blurry as my vision from all of the emotion I've let pour out of me after being pushed away repeatedly is, I'm not about to argue semantics.

Let him think that last shot was the only one.

"I hate you."

"I know you do, little one." He whispers, releasing another series of worn out breaths.

"I really hate that I still want you."

"I hate that too." he agrees, his voice finding a solid base and coming in stronger. "I really wish you didn't. Wish I didn't want you just as badly too."

Did he really just admit that?

Bringing my knees in tighter around his legs and locking him firmly in place, worried that now that he's admitted to feeling anything, he'll run, I yank the gloves off my hands, tossing them across the ring before leaning down and slamming both hands down into the mat. Our faces so close to each other, my nose brushes against his.

"Matty,"

"Kimber..." he inhales sharply, a rough bite to his voice as my name falls. What he follows up with a shift of his body, lifting until its rubbing as it arches into mine. The explosion of heat mixing with the very real feel of his want as it presses itself against mine.

Hard to my damp.

A flush breaking out across my cheeks cause enough for his upper body to lift, a hand coming out and gripping my face, brushing my hair back and sending shivers through me as he proceeds to smash his lips down roughly against mine.

Hungrily.

This is definitely not the kiss of a fourteen year old. It's what that forbidden moment of ecstasy causes when you deny it as long as we have.

Breaking away and sucking in air but keeping close, I bring my own fingers up and run them over the contours of his lips. Lips that for the third time in years, I've memorized and made as familiar as my own.

"What is this, Matthias?"

"What do you want it to be?" he asks, his voice low, but just as dangerous to my body as he's been every time we've been around each other. His voice like the sweetest sin.

"I want you. All of you."

"You've got it. You've had it for nine years."

He's been mine as long as I've been his.

Isn't this what I've wanted all this time? For his admission that it wasn't one-sided? So if that's the case, why am I not happier about it?

Staring directly into his eyes, the truth of his physical need for me as blatantly obvious as the truth now pouring from his hypnotizing blue irises, I'm still torn.

Getting Matthias to admit things has never been all that hard. Getting him to stay after he's done it has. I might have him trapped between my legs, and he might be present with me in the moment, but once I move back, he'll be able to leave and I don't think my heart can take it if he does.

I need him to be what I said.

All in for good.

No more chances.

If I let him in, give him the part of me that with the way his body moves up and down as he breathes in and out, I'm physically aching to, he's got to do the same.

And this time stay instead of run.

"I'm not leaving, little one. Not this time. Not ever again if that's what's etching that frown so deeply into your face."

"How can I believe that?" I breathe, my voice barely an octave higher than a whisper. "You've left before."

"I'm tired of running. From myself. From you. From the reality staring back at me. I can't do it anymore. I know I've got a lot to prove, but I told you the other night that I'm willing to do it. I will prove myself to you again."

"I don't really hate you." I admit and his chuckle kick-starts my heart.

"It would be so much easier if we could though, wouldn't it?"

"Yes."

It's starting to simmer with the altered tone of our conversation, but it's not gone. It's still there, just humming under the surface the way it always has.

Even now, our bodies intertwined and our eyes, like the rest of us singularly focused on each other, I want to lean down and capture his lips again. Have the feel of them burned into the very recesses of my mind. Feel his hands as they snake their way around my body and pull even more into him,

Pressing us so close we become one being.

I want his callused hands roaming over my skin as he removes every layer of clothing that's now sticking itself to my body with the physical exertion it's been put through. The sounds he'll make as he does. The ones I'll freely give him in return.

I've never wanted to lose myself in someone so much in my life.

And with the way his eyes darken and become hooded, drenched in the same desire and passion fueling me, he clearly feels the same.

"I forgive you." I admit, placing my fingers to his lips. "But I don't think I'll ever forget."

"I don't want you to forget. Never. Remember it all so I never stop working to make it right."

Stripping me of my rebuttal, his hand finds mine and pulls the barrier of it away from us. His lips on mine again, this time softer, moving parts of me that when I walked away from him all those months ago, I never expected to be reignited again.

Our lips moving in unison, the kiss deepening as he releases his hold on my hand and does as my earlier vision depicting and wraps his arms around me, crushing me to him.

Flipping us around until my back hits the unforgiving feel of the canvas, he sucks in a breath before returning to my lips. Nipping them with his teeth as whispered expletives and rough moans filter out from somewhere deep inside him. A place that until this moment, I don't think he's ever allowed himself to go.

What only seems to become more pronounced when I part my lips and allow his tongue to invade not only my mouth, but my senses as his hands begin their own slow perusal of a body that's never been more open to his touch than it is now.

The journey of my own as they connect to his sweat-laden body, frozen when after releasing a soft moan, we're thrust back into the reality of where we are by the sound of a door clicking open.

Hand finding my ass, he cups it and with another whispered curse and nip to my lips, he lifts. Hoisting us until I'm suspended in his arms, my legs wrapping instinctively around his as he guides us across the ring.

"Where are you taking me?" I manage to get out once we've made our way over to the ring steps and he's lowered me back down to the ground so we can make our way out of the ring. The faces of some of the girls I've been working with widened in shock when we both finally turn our attention to the interruption.

"Where we can be alone." He practically barks out, never once taking his eyes off me as he says it. "This isn't over. Not by a long shot. But we don't need the audience."

I can't help it. With the way he mentions audiences and the business we're in, I laugh. It's only after a few seconds of attempting to figure out what's funny, or maybe if I've lost what's left of my mind that the light bulb seems to go off and he gets it.

"Okay, well, I don't want the audience. Not for this. Not for what comes next."

"And what exactly does come next, Kemper?"

Wrapping an arm around my waist and pulling me into his side, he acknowledges the intruders to our private moment with a nod, all traces of his earlier smile gone as he practically races for the door.

"Us. Preferably together." He whispers when we reach the door. "Now let's get out of here."

Chapter Twenty-Seven

Matthias

Right before my first match with Smith, nerves got the best of me and I spent most of the time before it hunched over the porcelain throne.

Confident in my ability in the ring even with the predetermined outcome, and more than a little ready to get out there and put on one hell of a clinic for anyone who might be in the crowd, but no better than the little pipsqueak I was as a kid seeing my own idols in action.

Shaking in my wrestling boots, my gear plastering itself to my body with the sweat draining from every pore. Stomach tied in knots, wanting to make good on the chance Smith gave me taking me on to begin with, much less this match. A shot of fear so heavy it had my insides just as twisted as my outsides, I was finding it really hard to make it more than a couple of feet away from the toilet before another round hit.

This drive back to my place with Kimber, her hand a lot like my gear back then and slick with sweat as she holds onto mine, is a lot like back then.

I'm anticipating what comes next. Eager to get on with it while at the same time, petrified of what's going to happen.

What most guys experience when they're in their early teens, I'm overloaded with now.

A thirty year old virgin. What a fucking joke.

A joke that seems so out of this world, someone made a movie out of it.

I'm a professional wrestler for fuck sakes. People the world over park their asses in seats to see me and the others bust our balls to give them a hell of a show. Countless people lining up outside hotels and arenas in order to get just five minutes in our presence.

The last damn thing I should be experiencing after living with all of that from the time I turned sixteen is performance anxiety.

But here we are.

I want this to be everything she wished for and more.

If she's been with anyone else, which considering how affected I've always been with her, I'm sure she has, I want to be better. I want it to mean more.

When we're together, I want it to be the way I've always imagined it going in my head. I want it to be everything. The beginning and end. The first and the last. What my mom always said it should be when I was with someone for the first time.

I want it to be magic.

Even better than what we deliver when we slide between the ropes. The rush we experience as the lights come to life over us and the spotlight is on. The adrenaline that spikes when the bell sounds and we lock up the first time. The need and desire that drives us as we take risk after risk all to hear the crowd erupt.

It's got to be better than that. Earth shattering and moving. Cataclysmic.

When I've got her pinned beneath me or she's on top doing the same, I've got to deliver the performance of my life. I've got to drop my walls and let her in. Giving her every damn piece of me there is to have. Well, what she hasn't already captured.

Who am I kidding? She's already captured it all.

I just need to man up and make sure that now, she knows she has.

Jesus. It really is like that first match. I'm gonna be sick before we even get there.

"I'm nervous too." Her soft voice pulls me from my anxiety and cutting my eye in her direction, I take her in.

No part of her screaming her fear of what comes next. Instead, Kimber looking the most relaxed I think she's ever been.

Head leaning back against the headrest with eyes closed, and lips quirked up in a smile that given how I feel, would have me shooting my load here and now if I wasn't so riddled with the awkward road my thoughts are taking.

She looks at peace. Secure.

Happy.

"What makes you think I'm nervous?"

"The grip you've got on the wheel for one. If you hold on any tighter, I'm pretty sure it's coming inside with us."

Quickly looking to my hands on the wheel and being met with exactly what she's seeing, I ease up and without so much as opening her eyes after I've done it, she laughs.

"Cute, Matty."

Great.

Leading into the moment where I bury myself inside her for the first time, she's calling me cute.

"Not helping with the whole nervous as shit thing over here, little one."

"Wasn't trying to." She opens her eyes and grins. "Just telling the truth. Do you always move that fast?"

God I hope not.

It's only when she slaps her leg and her laughter fills the car that I realize I wasn't as quiet and for my ears only as I thought I was.

Settle your shit, Matthias.

Hitting the light that will bring me to my street, I pause and wait for it to change before turning and slowing down the closer I get to the place I rented. The car at my hand going slower than I think I've ever gone as I attempt to set myself right. Swallow down the anxiety and fear over what's to come and just follow my heart.

Be selfish and give it and my body what they've been craving since it was twenty-one.

Pulling into the driveway, I let the car idle for a minute before flipping the key and filling the car with silence.

"Kimber," I pull off my belt, shifting to face her. "There's something you need to know before this...well, before we go inside."

"You're overthinking this."

She has no fucking idea how right she is.

"I've never done this before and—"

"Yeah, I get that. I've never done anything like this before either."

Okay, hold the fucking phone. Is it possible that what I thought about her was wrong?

Could this be her first time too?

No way.

Kimber is, well, she's fucking amazing. I can't imagine there not being a line of guys, both in her dad's promotion and other places she's worked, that didn't want to be with her or didn't experience her the same way I have over the years. She's gotta be reading what I said wrong.

"No, Kimber. I mean, I've never done this at all. With anyone. Period."

"Yeah, I know. That's why I said you're overthinking, Matty. This is the first time I've ever done something like this too. It's why I admitted I was nervous before. This is new to me."

"You're not getting it, little one."

"Yeah I am, Matty."

"I'm a virgin." I shout, reeling back at my own admission, disgusted.

This is not the way I wanted things to go. I just knew that it needed to be said before we step out of the car. I can't let her think that whatever happens when we get inside, or how damn quickly it's all going to happen with all the years I've managed to go without, was a reflection on me, or worse. Her.

"Oh."

Unbuckling her belt, she slides it off and turns toward the door, and before I can call out and question what the fuck is going on, she's sliding out and slamming it behind her. Her body a blur of movement until she's walking over to my side and opening my own door.

"What are you doing?" I finally summon up the words when she reaches in and grabs my hand with hers, attempting to pull me out.

"Shutting up the voices in your head."

If she only knew how true that statement is.

Shifting my legs out of the car and letting her pull me up, I shut the door and that's when she's on me. Lips on mine, her body attaching itself to mine until we're chest to chest. The differences in our height noticeable but manageable as she lifts herself up on her toes, wrapping her arms around my neck and holding on for dear life.

Anxiety beginning to drain away with each passing second, and disappearing entirely when she uses all of her weight to push me back hard against the car as her tongue presses for entrance. Access I easily give her as my lips part and my tongue is there to greet her.

An innocent distraction kiss turning into a whole lot more when the heat that flooded me at the performance center forces its way forefront and takes over. The need to have more of her, to feel her body wrapped around mine, driving me as I hoist her body up and swing her legs around me, making a beeline straight for the door.

Hunger subsiding when after climbing the steps, I attempt to finagle my keys out of the pocket I slid them in when I pulled them from the ignition, a strangled annoyed curse falls after my second attempt and I admit defeat.

Why did I have to lock the fucking door?

Releasing one of her arms from its place around my neck and sliding it down until her hands are brushing against my thigh as her hand finds its way into my pocket, she does the impossible and rescues the very bane of my existence, biting her lip and failing as she giggles before handing them over.

"We make a pretty good team." She admits as I slide the key into the lock and after twisting it and stepping in, slam it shut before pushing her back up against it.

"We do." I answer roughly before snagging her bottom lip with my teeth and bringing it into my mouth.

Seconds turning into minutes that feel like hours we stand there, our bodies pressed into one another, the friction of us moving and our clothes rubbing together as I grind and she answers back, making my dick swell to the point of explosion. What I need to prevent with everything in me if I want this moment to last longer than the two seconds I damn well know it's going to.

A feeling she must understand when she finally breaks the connections our lips have maintained, moving down, biting into the flesh of my neck with a nibble before sucking gently and giggling softly.

"What's so funny, little one?"

"The truth?" she asks, pulling back and meeting my eyes.

"Of course."

"It never stops, this thing between us. I thought the time apart and the distance for all those years would diminish some of the flames, but whenever I get within a foot of you, it's like every part of me comes alive. Everything is so incredibly easy. Natural." *Yes, little one. It is.* "I know what you're worried about, Matty. I get it now, but I think I'm going to be the one with the problem if we don't do something soon."

She's going to be with the one with the problem.

Fucking hell.

That's not happening while I've got her pressed against the god damned door. Hot as fuck as it might be, she's better and worth more than that.

"You room, Matty. Where is it?"

Upstairs.

Shit. I can last that long, right?

Shifting her, craving the feel of her against the hard thickness of my cock, she moans softly again and that's when I shut down my head and move.

Making a beeline for the stairs, taking them as quickly as I can until we're both practically crashing through the door of my room. Pausing when I eyes my bed. What I've been avoiding actually sleeping in since I moved in, the largeness of it leaving something to be desired when it's just me coming home to it, never looking as appealing as it does now with her here.

The only one I ever want in it.

"Matty," she murmurs, nipping my lip with her teeth. "Put me down."

What? Was I so far in my head that I missed something?

Shit. I have no fucking idea other than mechanics what I'm actually doing here.

How the hell do guys do this shit every day? What the hell am I missing if she already wants this to be over?

"Why?" I choke out, insecurities on full display as my voice cracks.

"Put me down and see." She kisses me softly, easing some of the edges I can feel beginning to creep up.

Doing as she asks, she releases her arms from around my neck and I slide her legs around, lowering her to the floor, but before I can ask what comes next, Kimber silences me as her eyes stay fixed on mine, but her hands slide down to the fringes of her shirt and she begins to lift.

Moving slowly, which only serves to make the need running rampant inside me that much worse as the fabric moves painstakingly slow up her skin, I resist the urge to reach out and rip it off her when I see it pull over head and fall to the floor.

The seductive smile she's wearing, the one lifting her entire face only seems to grow as her fingers fall to the lining of her jeans. Watching transfixed as she pops the button, followed quickly by the zipper until she's shimmying them down her legs and off, I'm stunned. Struck stupid by the beauty now standing unabashedly in front of me in only her panties and bra.

"What," I find my voice, asking. "What are you doing?"

"Seducing you. Are you seducible, Matty?"

Looking from her down to my jeans and seeing just how seducible I am staring back at me, even covered, I meet her eyes again and they're flickering with fire.

Brazen desire.

She's enjoying the tease.

Following her lead, the precipice I'm standing on no longer stable, I pop the button of my jeans. Hearing the tear of the zipper as I forgo unzipping in favor of ripping them down, the need inside of me to be freed reaching a fevered pitch, I watch her eyes lower and follow. Her tongue slipping out and running over her lips.

She likes what she sees.

Jesus Christ. I'm gonna blow my load.

Biting into her lip the way she is, I don't think I can hold out any longer.

I'm gonna lose control and ruin the moment before I've even had a chance to taste her skin, let alone get the opportunity to slip myself inside her and lose myself.

"You tell me, Kimber. Am I seducible?"

Words, they're coming out all clipped. Raw. I've never felt anything like this in my life. I'm flooded and drowning in feeling, but also alive with reaction. Every part of me awake, buzzing, and in desperate need of this woman's touch.

"I think you are." She purrs, her hands reaching behind her until I see the fabric of her bra fall forward. Sliding down her arms until she's pulling it the rest of the way off and stepping toward me. Her body barely brushing against mine enough to make my cock jump and respond at the exact moment her fingers slide over the lining of her thong.

Breathe, Kemper. Just keep breathing.

"Kimber..."

"Hush, Matty." She shushes, finger coming to rest against my lip as she smiles. "Let me love you."

Let her love me.

I know she means with her body, but there's this second when my heart beat picks up where I so badly wish she meant it differently.

That she wanted to love me the way I do her.

A realization that has me closing my eyes the second her fingers brush against my skin as she quickly works the same magic that had me hypnotized, doing the same to me.

Freeing me of my shirt and my heart all in the same breath.

This isn't just sex.

This woman owns me.

Pressing her lips to mine and feeling the weight of her smile as it marks my face, I kiss her back as her hand finds and slides its way into mine.

Stepping backwards, each step she takes slow and deliberate as she guides us toward the bed and what I know is going to happen now.

Us making good on my promise from earlier and coming together.

Yeah, that's definitely not happening.

I'm not even sure I can hold out long enough to get inside her. This damned volcano is ready to blow.

Fuck! I'm going to ruin this. Why the fuck did I wait so long?

Right. Because it's her. My little one.

Allowing my eyes to open, I take her in, paused and sitting at the edge of the bed, seeing me, bare and with no restrictions, the way she always has. A vision, a gift really, that I'm not even sure I deserve, but one that now that it's here and being given so freely, I know I won't ever take for granted again.

One I want to cherish.

Need to love.

My little one is all grown up and mine for the taking.

Dropping to my knees before her, I force the need to have her to the background and let the reality of what's about to happen set in. How it feels to be here with her. To be so open and exposed. A storm of emotions unleashed as I feel the prick of tears beginning to rise and sting my eyes.

Her hands coming to rest on my face, eyes once I lift my head enough to meet them, staring straight into the very depths of my soul. Time stops. All sound fades with only our collective breathing to be heard as we take each other in. Look deeper than the physical to what lies underneath.

All of the pain caused to me, from me to her, all of it is forgotten with the innocent look of love I see in her eyes. What should scare the fuck out of me, but has me sinking even further into the abyss I never want to be freed from.

The one where it's just us and we're happy.

In love.

The place, this moment, where nothing can touch us.

Running her hand over my face one final time, she lowers it to my chest and wiping at my eyes as I feel the feather-light touch of her fingers as they graze across the elastic of my briefs, I give into the need again. Let it lift me back to my feet at the exact moment she bites down hard into her lip.

Oh, I'm definitely seducible.

"Kimber..." I plead, my voice is breathy as I attempt to remain in control.

"What, Matthias?"

"You know what."

"Maybe I do, maybe I don't."

"I've never been," *Fuck, how do I even begin to explain this?* "I need to be inside you. You biting your lip like that, your eyes filled with how badly you want this, I'm dangerously close to ending this before we begin."

Way to go, Kemper. Maybe you can show her the stain beginning to appear on your damn briefs from the lack of control you've got while you're at it.

Leaning back, she crooks a finger at me, smirking and egging me on. Shifting back on the bed until she's resting with her slightly elevated against the headboard, but her body spread and ready. Waiting for me to take what she's offering.

All of her.

Everything I crave.

Her mind. Her heart. Her body.

All mine.

The last time we were in a position like this, I turned her away. The farthest thing from my mind now.

This time, all I want to do is stay forever. With her. Only ever her.

Catching her movement as she shifts and starts to sit up, I see what I've done. The worry I've caused as it seems to fill her whole face, and sliding down my briefs, slowly at first, the way she'd done with her own and earning her smile again, I follow the crook of her finger and lower my knees to the bed.

Not stopping until my body hovers just above hers as she moves her legs around to pull me in and take me down to where I know the most pleasurable destruction awaits.

I've never wanted something—*someone*—more.

"Love me, Matty."

I do little one. I love you so much it hurts. I'm always going to love you.

A silent admission not yet ready to be spoken, with a vow that long after tonight, I plan on keeping for as long as she'll allow.

I'm going to love her until reality takes her away. Drown in her. Succumb to her.

Be selfish with her.

"Once," I murmur against her lips before I capture them. "Will never be enough."

"Then take as much as you need. Make me yours."

Positioning myself at her entrance, slipping a finger down over her slit, feeling the dampness that awaits me, I use my mouth and make love to hers, breaking through not only her barrier as I slide inside filling her but my own. The final wall that was built up so strongly around my heart, crumbling to the ground as her heat surrounds me.

My name falling reverent and breathless from her lips at the same time as hers falls from mine, I do what she asks.

I take her and after nine years, make her mine.

Chapter Twenty-Eight

Matthias

Most of the guys I went to school with happened to be guys heavily influenced by a bunch of different sports. Hockey for the most part, but there were basketball and football stars too. All guys looking to prove they were the best at what they did and looking to make a name for themselves.

Which usually meant girls. A lot of them. Some of them even throwing themselves at these guys just for the scraps of attention they'd get. To be that weekend girl. Forgotten by Monday morning and never to be thought of again.

It was that bad. You had the odd guy like Bryan, who stood out, but it was rare. And if Bryan was rare, I was limited edition.

I noticed girls. I'm not blind. When more than half the population of my high school was female, it's kind of hard not to notice them. They were there, but for me, they were just people.

Not conquests. Not there for my amusement or the equivalent of a blow up doll to get my rocks off with. They were just kids like me.

I wasn't immune to their appeal. There were some really pretty girls I went to school with. Bryan's high school sweetheart is one of the top draws. She had a heart that seemed to match what her outward image portrayed and it was no surprise when after a few weeks of them being together, he'd come back informing me that he'd given it up.

Leaving me alone in the oh-so-exclusive virgin club that for years, I'd never given two shits about being a part of.

And there I stayed until last night.

Until Kimber.

I know what you're thinking. How does a guy with needs and urges like every other red-blooded man on the planet go thirty years without having sex?

It's easier than you think.

Sex, my mom always said, was an expression of feeling.

It meant something even when people abused it and pretended they just needed to release tension. It always meant something, everything to most, and it needed to be treated as such.

Call it me wanting to honor her and not giving it up to some random ring rat or another girl that passed by during my years on the road, but I never felt the need to do it.

That decision to remain a virgin was made even easier by seeing what a sexual connection with someone could mean with the aftermath of my parent's relationship.

Having one parent underground and one as good as with his place behind bars, was a phenomenal deterrent.

Kimber has always been my game changer.

The feelings she would evoke when the moments weren't as amped up and charged as they often are with us, let alone the desire, the passion, and sometimes, even the hot-headed rage she brought out of me just thinking about her with anyone else, they spoke to her being the one my mom would have said that I waited for.

Which means, other than my inability to keep myself together long enough for her to get off, to experience the level of ecstasy she gives me every damn time we're together, I have no regrets about the way things happened.

She's always been the one.

At fourteen, she was the forbidden one, but still the one.

Even after going home to Smith and having to spend the next seven years beating off to any and all pictures and videos I could find of her during that time, she was still there, pumping away inside me. The real blood in my veins.

Seeing her again in CPW and having those eyes digging their way so deep inside that I knew I would never be able to escape it, she was no longer forbidden. At least not in the way she was then. Her age wasn't a factor anymore, and with the sparks that flew, the way just one look heated my blood and made me want to fight better, be better, I knew I could have her. She was just as taken by me then as I was with her, time not seeming to let go for either of us.

She was still mine. My one.

The only one.

I just couldn't give in.

Not when I knew the second I did, everything would change. Life as I knew it would alter and neither of us would ever be the same. Even after spending years directing my focus back into the ring and my pursuits there, I was and still am driven by a darker desire.

A darkness that was born in me on a single night ten years ago. One I was afraid would repeat itself in spectacular fashion given what really ran through my veins if I gave into it. Gave into us the way I so desperately wanted to at that point.

Kimber is it.

Feeling the brush of skin against the side of my face, I look down and I'm met by the heavily sleep-laden, but just as hypnotic eyes of the girl I spent the night loving as she beams a sated smile before burrowing her body into my side.

Warming not only my blood and awakening a more primal urge to have her again, but also doing the same to my heart on a much deeper level. Something about the sight and feel of her this close, giving me something I never expected to find.

A safe place.

The voices in my head silenced for the first time in years.

Further proof that holding onto that stupid ass v-card Bryan spent years ripping on me about was the smartest thing I ever did.

Without it, I don't think I'd be feeling half of what I am.

Complete. Safe.

Strong.

God, I feel the strongest I've ever been and it's all because of her.

"Hey," she murmurs softly, again running a fingertip down the side of my face. "Where are you right now?"

"I'm here."

"I've been watching you for a few minutes and here is the last place you are. Tell me the truth. What's going through your head?"

There's a shake in her voice, one of trepidation, afraid I'm sure of what answer I'll give. But what she doesn't seem to get and what I need to spend as long as possible making sure she understands is, the Matthias that took off, the one who thought he was doing right by her by protecting her, he's long gone.

All that's left is the selfish one.

And he's not going anywhere she's not.

"I'm sorry about last night."

"What part?" she asks, her voice barely a whisper now as again, the wrong choice of words hits me square between the eyes.

"Shit." Sliding my arm around her, I pull her even closer, pressing my lips to her hair and inhaling deeply before kissing her. "I meant that I was sorry for blowing my load when we'd barely made it to the bed."

Sighing heavily, blowing the stray hairs resting in a mess over my eyes out of my way, I bring my free hand up through it and attempt to save this moment.

"I've never you know because...well, you just know."

I sound like a fucking idiot.

"Matthias, yesterday, all of it was everything. You have nothing to be embarrassed about. I knew what I was getting into."

"I waited for you." I blurt, not at all what I wanted to say, but no doubt what she needs to hear. The truth, always so damn easy to spill when I'm around her.

"I know and I'm honored."

She's honored? Fuck. More like the other way around.

With all of the shit I've pulled with her over the years, no matter what my intentions were at the time, the last thing she should ever have given me was herself the way she did. I still have so much to make up for that I don't even feel worthy yet, and I know what's in my heart for her.

Of the two of us, I'm the one that's honored.

"It should have been you," she admits softly and slipping my arm back around, I shift in the bed and pull her up so we're face to face.

"What should have been me?"

I wait her out, and after a few seconds of lip biting and what I'm pretty sure has to be a mental argument taking place inside her head, she shifts her own body closer and laughs.

"It's so stupid. You don't even want to know."

"I want to know everything there is to know about you, little one."

This is a first.

With her face now buried in my shoulder, her own embarrassment obviously keeping her from looking at me the way I need her to, I can actually feel the warmth from the blush she's doing.

I've blushed and been around others doing it. I've just never let anyone else get close enough, or even wanted to be close enough, to actually experience the way it would feel to be this close to someone else doing it.

To actually feel it warming your skin. Burning a hole through you until it smashes straight into your heart and alters you.

When she shifts and attempts to lift herself from her place buried in my shoulder, I stop it. Like a crazy person, I take back my earlier want and will her to rest her face back where it was so I never have to lose the way it feels having her react.

"I can feel your blush. I don't even have to see your face to know it's there and just how deep it runs." I let the words fall out in a rush, needing her to understand exactly what's happening to me, tears starting to prickle and pull at the corners of my eyes with just how heavy a revelation this is. "I don't want to lose it."

"You won't," she states and the strength behind her words, how secure they sound, it's my undoing.

There's not a second of doubt for her. She's letting me know I'll never lose her.

"I wanted you to be my first, Matthias. For a long time, I would look for you everywhere. Venues my dad would rent out and shows I would do apart from him. I would turn down the party invites and dates because all I wanted was you. I knew you were with Smith and CPW and you wouldn't have ventured away from that, at least not then, but I still watched and waited. Hoped really. I thought that once I was old enough, we'd see each other again and that would be it. Stupid, right?"

There's this moment where I get what she's really saying, words she hasn't spoken, where the familiar rage of the past begins to awaken and lift, but I quickly swallow it down. After the way I left things when I walked away from her in 2007, it's my own damn fault it didn't work out the way she hoped for. The fact that she was someone else's, even if it wasn't for long, it's on me.

"It's not stupid, Kimber."

"It was." She argues softly, her lips finding my shoulder and kissing me before her head lifts and we're again caught up in the sea of each other's eyes. "But you're sweet to say it's not."

Cupping her chin and pulling her face to mine, I place my lips to hers, letting them linger instead of pushing for a deeper connection the way my body craves. Letting her feel what I'm about to say next. The reality.

"What you hoped for and what you wanted, even knowing what a jackass I was after the way we left things back then, it's not stupid." Quickly kissing her lips again, I lean my head against hers. "It took a little longer than it should have, but it still happened."

"What did?"

"We saw each other again and that was it."

Laughing, the vibration of which filters straight from her through me, she pinches my side.

"Don't you mean, you let me wail on you and it turned you on so much you finally gave in?"

It's a joke, I can hear it in the melodic lift of her voice as it alters in pitch, but the sting still rises.

I'm a lot of things to a lot of different people, but with Kimber, considering her ability to see right through me, I've never been anything but real. Acting on my urges? That's definitely not real or me.

"You've been turning me on since you were fourteen. If that was all it was, I would have gone against everything I believed in and screwed you back then. Fuck, little one. I wanted to even knowing it was wrong. That wasn't what happened yesterday."

"Then what was it?"

God, those eyes. They're going to be my destruction, especially when they're as wide-eyed and innocent as they now as she searches for answers she should already know.

"Was that what it was to you?" I ask instead, needing her answer to this more than I think I need the next breath in order to breathe. "Was it just a need to get laid?"

In lieu of a spoken answer, she's quick to shake her head in argument.

"No. It was more than just needing to get laid, Matty. I can't lie to you, there was the need. A lot of it. I've wanted to be with you for as long as I can remember, but that's not what made me come back here. My feelings did that."

"And now that you're here?"

God, I'm so fucked right now.

I'm asking these loaded questions praying that when she answers they'll be what I want to hear. In no way prepared for how I'm gonna react if they're not. I need her to tell me that what we shared yesterday wasn't just a one-off. That it's something she wants, like I do, to happen again.

I want her to be my first and last.

She really is what I said before.

My only.

"I'm hoping to stay here."

Tell her. The voice urges, different from before. *Tell her now. She deserves to know.*

"Kimber, I—"

"I got invited to this party and needing the escape, I went. I ended up drunk off my ass and hooking up with some random guy I can't even remember the name of. I don't even know if my first time was any good. It ended up not meaning anything and I crawled out of bed the next morning, complete with a walk of shame that I felt in my bones. It felt like I betrayed you."

Thankful now that I didn't let the words slip, I bite them back, willingly keeping them for a better time and focus my attention instead of what she's just admitted to. What she meant earlier when she said that it should have been me.

This is it.

She feels guilty that last night was our first time—my first time—but that it wasn't hers. I can't let her do it. Not when it was. At least in the ways that matter.

Our first time is just that.

Ours.

"It doesn't count."

"I don't understand..."

"I walked away from you, Kimber. I wanted you to be mine, and you were mine in all of the ways that counted. But you couldn't actually *be* mine, at least not then. It makes sense that you would have moved on. Fuck, I wanted you to move on even knowing it would kill me to see or hear about it. You have nothing to feel guilty about."

"Sleeping with some random guy to block out the one you really want, and living with the guilt of it for years isn't moving on, Matty."

"No, it's not." I agree. "But we're here now. My reasons for waiting, I would have waited forever because I didn't care. Women meant as much then as they do now. Nothing. I didn't need the trouble I knew it would cause. I couldn't be like the other guys. I couldn't be like *any* guy. Rubbing one off in some random dive bar bathroom, motel room, or hell, even on a break when we're roadside, was the way it had to be. I dealt with the urges the only way I was willing to at the time."

There's a draw as she sucks in a breath, clearly surprised by what I've admitted. How mechanical I make it all sound. Like jerking off was some kind of chore. God.

Have I really been that disconnected?

"You really would have gone forever."

"No, I wouldn't have. It would have happened eventually. It just wouldn't have been some random screw. It would have been me and you. It was only ever meant to be me and you. I'm just pissed it took me so damn long. The reason for your guilt is me."

Here it is again. The chance to tell her how I really feel. A way I'm sure she knows even without me saying the words, but an expression of feeling I can't quite bring myself to say because I'm still so petrified of what will happen when I do.

The pain I'll cause.

Shit. No. I can't go there.

Not after what we've shared. What, with her body so close to mine, we're still sharing.

I deserve this. I'm deserving of her and what this could be.

"Matthias, I lo—"

It's fucked up, but knowing what she's about to say, I use our closeness to my advantage and kiss her. Giving her everything I have the second our lips touch, hoping that in the end I don't make her regret wanting to say the words by stealing them from her the way I do.

It can't happen. Not yet. I'm not strong enough to handle what'll come.

So using my body to dominate both of our minds and our hearts it is.

What she easily gives into as releasing the hold I've had on her face and wrapping an arm around her again, she moves with me as I position her on top. Our tongues dancing, our bodies moving, and clothing that had been placed back on during the night, slowly being pulled away and tossed to the floor as we lose ourselves in each other.

A guttural moan escaping from inside as she slides her ready and willing heat down over my cock. Slowly she moves, almost painfully, all the way down and up again, smirking seductively when I curse and hold onto her tighter, keeping myself buried inside, but instead of letting her move up, to release me again, I push myself into her as deeply as I can.

"Matthias...please," she murmurs and the sound has me hardening even more as I use my cock to rub against her walls.

"Tell me what you want."

"Don't stop."

"Wasn't planning on it. This...it's never gonna stop, little one." I admit, even though I know there's a deeper meaning than what she meant. "We're going to be this way forever."

Slipping her arms loosely around my neck, she moves with me as she brings herself closer to the edge, our lips colliding as we lose ourselves in feeling. The friction building until I'm free falling over the edge, surrendering control as I give her everything I have.

Picking up speed, I match her until it's the sound of our collective moans, curses and pants filling the room. Kimber's voice rising much the way it did the night before as her pleasure climbs, reaching its peak as I do again, as I did before.

Make love to her.

Because that, as I take her over the edge into her own personal nirvana, my cock covered in her release, is exactly what this is.

Love.

I'm in love with Kimberlee Parker.

Chapter Twenty-Nine

Kimberlee

There's an incredible peace that exists when everything comes together and you're happy for what feels like the first time in years.

From the years I spent living with my father, watching his moods change based on situations he found himself in. Like the bitterness and longing that comes with not being able to be the Renegade the way he'd been before I was born, along with the anger that would rise at the worst times, making me see a different side of the man I loved more than anything in the world. At any given point, I never knew what I would be walking into. So I was happy, but it was fleeting.

A promise from a boy back then, it brought around a sense of peace unlike any I'd experienced up until that point. It was my first taste of what could be. I could actually see a light at the end of the tunnel, at least until it was taken away. Or rather, he took himself away before he could see what that promise and his impact on my family had done.

There wasn't many times after that where I was settled. I was always living in a relative calm before the storm. Creating magic in the ring, while the people around me talked shit about me outside of it. The calm and the storm in living color.

Busting my ass and putting on the best possible shows for my father and other promotions, no matter how few and far between they were, they were my calm. Where I felt as though nothing could touch me even though I was still walking around with the memory of what real peace could be from the one that got away.

When I got to CPW and I knew we would end up face to face again, I was as prepared as I could be. Hopeful, even though years had passed, but needing to experience the peace I found with him again, even if just for a few seconds. His turning away, the boy now a man that had perfected running, it stripped me of that calm and ended up turning me into a shell of my former self that not even Gavin with his 'let's give the people what they want' idea could fix.

Everything about my life was fake from that point on.

I finally understood Gavin and his ability to make the world believe he really was the man he portrayed, because I had turned into the same thing. I was Wycked, not Kimber.

I left her with Matthias on Valentine's Day, even if I was the one walking away.

Jump forward to the present, where I've gotten to experience this man in the most intimate way possible. Seen layers to him that the rest of the world doesn't get to see, and had my heart filled with a plethora of emotions, and all I feel is the peace I've been searching for.

Matthias is a hurricane on his best day, but in the moments we've managed to share over the last forty-eight hours where we've been completely shut off from the world and enjoying each other, there is no storm. No tumultuous wreckage from the destruction his running and hiding has caused in the past.

No sign of him running again.

There's just peace. Calm. Serenity.

He's trying. Making good on his newest promise. And I've never been happier because I'm where I belong.

Matthias Kemper, for all of his faults, is my happy place.

"Now who's the one drifting off?"

Looking down to his hands position on my leg, as his other one holds the wheel in a grip different from the tension-filled one the first time we'd been here, I smile.

"Just wondering where you're taking me."

After waking me up with coffee and a toe-curling kiss that had me wanting to pull him back to bed where he belonged, he told me about his plan for the day. A place, he explained that he wanted to show me, which now, a few hours later, brings us to where we are now.

Driving.

His grip on the wheel, relaxed and at ease a few moments before, now tightening the closer we must be getting to what is still to me, a mystery destination.

Wherever he's taking me, clearly not a happy place.

"I made a lot of mistakes with you, Kimber. Promises I wanted to keep but couldn't. If I want you to believe me when I tell you I don't want to this to end, that I want to be with you, I have to do what I've spent years avoiding. I have to let you in."

This, the Matthias talking right now, is the reason my heart never gave up when the rest of me wanted to. It's in his honesty.

How determined he is to do things right that keeps me coming back for more.

"You have nothing to prove to me, Matty. I'm here no matter what."

It's the truth, but with the way his head shakes, it's clearly a truth he's not ready to hear. His mind still firmly planted in the belief that he's in some way undeserving and needs to prove himself worthy.

What he should already know he is by one look in my eyes.

"It's not about proving myself, little one. It's what I said. I'm letting you in. You're the only one I want to let in. To make understand."

If I didn't already know I was in love, even if I'm holding back from admitting it aloud, this would be the moment where it happens.

As it is, I'm already feeling myself falling deeper. Dangerous to say the least, but welcomed.

I want to love him the way he deserves.

"Okay..." I murmur before allowing my eyes to close and enjoy the ride as he takes us to our destination. A ride that ends quicker than I thought when what feels like a minute or two later, he's pulling to a stop and announcing we're here.

"Where is here exactly?" I ask, popping my eyes open and taking in the residential street we're on.

"Where it all began."

Unclipping his seatbelt and pulling it off before leaning over and doing the same to mine, he exits the car and I follow him as he makes his way over to the passenger side and opens the door, his hand extended for me to take.

"Are you sure about this?"

Slipping my hand into his and letting him help me out, he twines our fingers together and walks us across the street. Pausing on the sidewalk, his expression changes as he looks toward the house he's stopped us in front of. His face sunken, his eyes sad.

A house that judging from the length of the grass on the lawn and the dilapidated and worn down look of the frame, has seen better days. The porch wood stained and not by the paint that was previously there, but by weather damage and time. The wooden door leading into the place looking to be barely hanging on by a thread.

"What is this place?"

"It's where I grew up." He easily gives up, his tone clipped, his eyes masking a pain I can only imagine based on what he's already let slip, has to be threatening to drag him under.

This is where it happened. This is where he lost his mother.

He really is taking me back to where it all began. The place where everything went bad and the very reason he's so reluctant to give in to the very real feelings between us. His fears and anger. His loss. Maybe even his happiness at one time.

It's all wrapped up in this broken down palace.

"I was so pissed off when they moved me here. We used to live in this small little apartment across town and I had made a couple of friends. The place was shit. I mean, there were bugs and rats and mold seeping through every crevice. It was hell for everyone that lived there, but it was my hell and I was comfortable there. Happy even. Things were good. It hadn't fallen apart. We hadn't fallen apart. So when they said they got this place, I was livid."

"Did it go bad right away?"

"That's the thing. It was still good at first. They argued, but they never went to bed angry. They involved me in almost everything they did. Took me places, accepted and even involved themselves in my love of wrestling. It was just as good as it was at the apartment. I was pissed about leaving my friends and the school, but everything at home was still okay."

"When did it go bad?"

"My mom used to tell me it happened when Dad lost his job. Thing is, I remember everything from back then," he pauses, squeezing my hand as he allows himself to go back in time. "It started years before that. Small stuff. He would verbally attack her, saying some of the meanest shit you can think of. It was when he started heavily drinking that it changed though. Became physical, verbal and emotional. After a while, you could actually see how much he enjoyed the fight because he just got into it with her all the time."

"Matty..."

"The first time he laid his hands on her, I was too fucking little to do anything. I didn't even really understand what was going on. For the first few times after that, I thought it was normal. Every relationship was like this. Combative. They would still have moments of peace and my mom was still smiling, so I thought you know, everything is okay. We're still good. Turns out, you can smile through the pain. You can and you will fake it for the people you love. That's what she was doing for me that entire time. Faking it because she loved me and wanted to keep her family together."

I want to end this. Yesterday when we made love, he cried. I saw the prick of the tears in his eyes first and watched frozen as the first ones began to fall. He showed me a side of him that I'm not even sure he knew existed. I'm seeing it happen again now, but for a completely different reason. His body is filled with tension. Hard to my soft. The both of us opposites in the moment.

I want to end it, end *this*, for him.

Take it all away until all that's left is the Matthias I experienced last night.

"I eventually picked up on how wrong it was. She would cook me dinner before him and it would turn into a physical assault. The same shit happened if the laundry wasn't done. If his work shit wasn't pressed and ready, but my school clothes were. She'd do her best in front of me to chill the situation out, but it never worked. So I started getting involved. I was small, fucking puny really, but there was no way I was gonna sit by and watch him break her."

"He hurt you." I state, not even bothering to ask. I suspected based on the little information he had given me about the way the relationship with his parents turned out that it was bad, but I just never realized how bad.

And with the nod of his head, he's confirming my worst fears.

Matthias was abused by the one person that should have loved him.

"Repeatedly when I was younger. Not so much when I got big enough to fight back." Laughing, the sound of it so distant it sends chills down my spine, he finally pulls himself from the place he'd gone and finds me again. "I don't think he ever thought I would do that. Fight back. I guess the jokes on him. All the years he spent calling me a little girl came back to bite him."

Slipping his hand into the pocket of his pants but never looking away from me, he pulls out a key ring with two lone keys on it and motions with his head to the front door.

"Come on. Let's go inside."

Oh no we're not.

We're not going anywhere until I get answers.

Like, what the hell is he doing with the keys to this place? And more to the point, what is so important inside that we have to walk into the house of horrors in order for him to show me?

There's nothing here I want to see. I've heard more than enough to last me a lifetime.

"Matty, what are you doing with the keys? Did the owners give them to you? Does anyone even live here? Has anyone lived here since?"

Question after question pops into my head as I continue to ramble, only stopping when his finger brushes across my bottom lip. My eyes in the uncertainty falling from his but easily finding their way home again with the simple touch.

"I own the house, Kimber. People have lived here before because I've rented it out. I bought it with the money left behind from my mom's insurance policy. No one lives there now. They haven't in a while. I guess when you find out that someone was murdered in cold blood inside, it kind of loses its appeal."

"Why did you buy it?"

"The truth?" he sighs. "I bought it because in some twisted way, it was a connection to her. Happier times *and* the really fucked up ones. This was the last place she existed. I couldn't let the bank or anyone else take it. I was barely old enough to know how to sign my own signature at the time, but I knew I wanted this place. I wanted her."

Looking from the house and back to me before lowering his gaze to our hands, he traces swirls over my skin and speaks again. His voice barely there. Almost too quiet. All of his will, the fight I know is there inside him, missing.

"Will you come inside with me?"

"Of course."

Making our way across the front lawn and up the stairs of the porch, he pauses at the door, his free hand rising until it's running over the broken and protruding slivers of wood near the hinges. Rusted metal that upon closer inspection is barely keeping it standing upright. My earlier thoughts proven correct.

"During one of their last fights, I did this to the door. I damn near broke it off when I shoved my way through it after getting her out. I wanted to end his life that night, but I didn't. Biggest mistake I ever made. I kept the door the same because I wanted the reminder. The next time I'm in a position like that, no one gets out alive."

I have a feeling this isn't going to be the only visual reminder that Matthias kept around after what he lived through, and that scares me. With the way he's reacting to the door and how easily he recalls what caused every indent and every break, I just know there's more of these waiting around the bend.

The need to take him by the hand, drag him back to the car and take us back to the place where we were happy has never been as strong as it is now.

Unlocking the door, he pushes it back and taking a timid step inside, he releases a heavy breath before heading further in, finally allowing me entrance to see what looks to be the complete opposite of the way it looks from the outside.

The entryway, what leads off into a kitchen and a living room, is immaculate. Every item, every inch, clean and neat. As though none of the pain that was evident from the outside and even the front door has ever touched it.

What the hell is this?

"Matty..."

Turning around to face me, his head crooks to the side.

"Yeah?"

"Why doesn't the inside look like the outside?"

"Because she wouldn't have wanted it to."

Okay, clearly he's talking about his mom, but with her not here to enjoy the way it looks, to enjoy anything at all, I'm not understanding why it seems to matter to him so much.

"I don't understand."

"My mom furnished this place. Sure, it was on my dad's dime at first because he was the only one working, but even after she got a job, she paid with her own money to make this place a home. Even if it was the furthest thing at the time from what a home is actually supposed to be. It was a mess that night, the night he..."

I can't take much more of this. The way his voice trails off and his body seems to sag as he attempts to come up with the words to tell me of the night she died, it's hurting me almost as much as it is him. I can actually feel the bandages I placed over my own heart when he walked away, breaking off and falling to the wayside as he loses what little control he managed to use to get him here.

He's not the god-like figure he is when he's in the ring anymore. Here, standing in this entryway, he's just the scared kid he was before. The one that took it all on himself when things turned tragic.

He's lost.

"I get it." I attempt to soothe as I step into him, wrapping my arms around his back and pulling him into a sideways embrace.

"I didn't want her to come home and see it like it was. It took a long time, trying to get all of the same things back again, but I did it. I wanted her to come home to something beautiful whenever she was ready."

He redid the entire inside of the house to honor her.

Breathe Kimber.

"She never came home. She was gone before I even did any of this. I'm not so messed up that I don't realize it was all pointless. But wherever she is now, she has to be able to see it. She has to know."

Tears that are now visibly falling from his eyes as he begins to break and sink even deeper into my embrace are now lifting and spilling from my own. The sniffling and my lame attempts at stopping them in order to be the stronger one in the moment, failing as it can still be heard from my place buried in the side of his shirt.

Emotion, a sea of tears falling like rain into the fabric, creating another reminder for him. One that when we leave here and he eventually strips the shirt off and washes it, won't ever go away. It'll stay, like scars do. Forever. A reminder of the day he gave everything he had to the woman that loves him just as much as the one he lost.

Everything he did, the beauty he wanted to create, and the love he wanted to show, it's all here. He achieved it. My heart breaks knowing she never got to see it. It breaks for him and for her.

She should have been given the chance to see just how much her son really loved her.

"I'm sorry, little one. I never should have brought you here. Into this shit. Into my mess. But I wanted...I don't know what I wanted other than for you to see me. The real me."

Pressing my lips into the fabric lining his shoulder, I let the last of my tears fall before pulling back and moving around until we're aligned. Face to face. Heart to heart.

"Thank you for letting me see, Matthias. For trusting me with your memory of her. Of your time here."

Bringing a hand up, he brushes the hair back from my face and cups my cheek, smiling every so softly as he leans down and presses his lips to mine. All of the pent up and unreleased emotion, mixing with the dampness of his face as he puts everything he has, everything he feels, into his kiss.

Giving it all to me.

Giving himself.

"No one else, little one. Only you. Only ever you."

And I know, beyond all doubt and reason that he means it.

I am the first and the last.

I'm his only.

Matthias

It physically destroys me to separate from Kimber, but with what I know has to come next and how after I broke down on her, the first question out of her mouth was to ask if there was more she needed to know before we left and went back to our lives, I know it has to happen.

There is more. So much more.

Things she needs to see, words I need to tell her in order to make her understand where I've been for the last nine years. Why I wasn't with her when every part of me wanted to be.

Releasing the grip I've got on her body, my eyes fall on the living room and what awaits beyond the threshold I have yet to step through. Everything as put together and in its place as the rest of the house, but the flickers of still video firing up in my head, momentarily making me forget that it's not 2005 and we're actually in the present.

"It happened here. A lot of their fights did." I explain lightly before crossing the room. Waiting until I've stepped deep in with the sofa behind me for support before finally turning to face her.

Our eyes connecting, hers alive with understanding mixed with sympathy, mine breaking because standing here, even with her support and strength guiding me through what comes next, I can still smell the faint traces of blood and see the stains of it on the floor. The visuals still as real as they were then.

Grabbing onto the edge of the sofa as my legs weaken, I feel myself begin to fall, and with little regard to what Kimber's going to think seeing it, I drop to my knees as guttural, heart wrenching sobs begin to pour out from the place I've had them buried for the last ten years.

My hands easily finding the place on the carpet where I held her in my arms as she bled out. Using what was left of her strength to repeat how much she loved me when she should have been saving it to fight to stay alive. Running my fingers over a place long since scrubbed clean, a sea of red surrounds me. Calling to me. Begging for me to succumb to the darkness that was born from it that day so long ago, but what a few seconds later with the presence of her body as it connects around mine, has me pulling back from.

Shifting my body, I maneuver hers around until I'm pulling her into my lap. Reminiscent of the way my mom was, but different. Allowing myself to completely break on Kimber after a few unsteady attempts at regaining control. Leaning on her the way I should have forever ago, but was too much of a dumbass to take advantage of when it was offered.

Her touch giving me strength, and crushing her to me, hanging on for dear life the way I am, I expect her to run, but she doesn't. Further proving why she's the one here. The reason she's the one I ran so hard from, but fell so hard for. Holding on just as tightly to me as I am to her and making what has to come next bearable.

It's time to bring her into my darkness, but not to join me in it. To light the way so maybe, just maybe, I can finally be set free.

Be a part of the light that for nine years, Kimber's been bathed in.

"I made sure the piece of shit couldn't move and I went to her. Held her in my arms. She was talking. Babbling really. I told her to stop, pleaded with her to keep her strength because I knew I needed to leave her to call for help, but she wouldn't do it. She kept telling me she loved me. Over and over. Kept forcing herself to do what I knew was killing her. I couldn't get past that. I still can't. I blame myself. If she hadn't have been so focused on making sure I knew how she felt, maybe she'd still be here. Jonathan may have dealt the pain, but I was the final blow. I'm the reason she's not here."

"Matthias, that's not true."

Deep down I know she's right, but it doesn't make it any easier to believe in.

"This is why I couldn't do it, Kimber."

"Do what?" she whispers, sniffling before burrowing her face into my neck, leaving the softest trail of kisses all the way from my neck to my cheek. Not stopping in her attempt to soothe, to be here and let me feed off her strength, as she reaches the corners of my lips and repeats the gentle gesture.

"Why I couldn't get close. If the two of them could start out so well and fall so deeply, and then have it all turn so twisted so quickly, who's to say I wouldn't do the same? I mean, I am their kid. Who's to say I wouldn't be something worse than what Jonathan was? It was already happening, even before I found Smith. I met Bryan by unleashing my anger and taking out the guys trying to hurt him. It got worse after she died, and I don't have to remind you what I did to Grant. I couldn't take the chance it would happen again. I couldn't hurt you too."

I'm not stupid. I know every time I walked away or pushed her to Gavin, I hurt her. I also know that's how it starts. What eventually turned my dad into the monster he became, were instances like that. Emotional attacks. Hurting her heart. Breaking it.

But in my head at the time, every single time it happened, I thought it needed to be done.

I was an idiot because it wasn't right. This, what's happening in this house now, what happened the day before, and what I've been experiencing since the moment I decided it was alright to be selfish, that's what the right move was.

It's what I should have been doing all along.

"I know I hurt you. I've been hurting you for years now. I also know there's nothing I can say or do now to make that right. Not really. I can try and be different, I can do more than try and really make it happen. Love you the way I told you in CPW that I would if I just let myself. But it would never erase what I've already delivered. The real damage I caused. The damn darkness that lives inside me because of who I am. All I can do..." I pause, swiping at my face as years of unshed tears continues to fall like rain. "All I can do is say I'm sorry and show you the reason."

"You were afraid." She murmurs and all I can do is nod.

Afraid is an understatement, but it's as close to what I'm feeling as it gets. I'm petrified.

The monster under the bed, he's not there anymore because he lives inside me. A monster that I want to protect her from at all costs.

Even at the expense of her heart.

"I'm scared too, Matty."

"You...you don't show it."

"I do, but until two days ago, you never stuck around long enough to see it."

Her truth hurts but I need to hear it. I need to take the pain I caused and carry it. Do whatever it takes to make it better.

Make sure it never happens again.

"You scare me, Matthias. This with us, it scares the hell out of me, but I think it's supposed to. It would be weird with the connection we have, if we weren't always aware of just how fragile this is and frightened of what could come. Afraid of taking the wrong road and sending it off into a ditch or losing it entirely. Losing ourselves."

She gets it. Who the hell am I kidding? She's always gotten it. She's always understood.

Me, my bag of emotional shit, what we do.

Kimber has always seen it all.

"I don't want to hurt you. I don't want the same hands that spent the last forty-eight hours memorizing every inch of your body, to be the ones that bring you pain. I don't want these lips," I bring my hand to her lips, touching them softly. "To ever feel the sting of hate-filled words. Experience the heartbreak that she did every time he opened his mouth. I want them to feel nothing but love. Devotion. Surrender. Because when I kiss you, little one, that's what I feel. What I've always felt. Even when it wasn't allowed."

"You won't, Matthias." Her words fall softly against my fingertips. Like her blush against my skin before them, breathing new life into what I thought had been long dead.

Making me feel and do it without the one thing I've lived my entire life by.

Fear.

"You don't know that."

"I do know that. You're not him, Matthias. You could never be him. He may have played a part in creating you, but so did your mom. You're not him. You're you. But you're also the best parts of her. I've seen it."

Shifting her weight in my lap, she moves until her back is against my chest and bringing my arms around her, she leans back into me, releasing a sigh when her face connects with the side of mine.

"What do you mean you've seen it?"

"The first time was a few days before you left our place to go home to Smith. I mean, you'd already shown that side of yourself to me when we were hanging out talking, and when you made me promise to tell you if anything happened with my dad while you were there, but this, it was different because I wasn't seeing things through that little girl with a crushes eyes."

I have no idea what she's talking about. I remember the promise I made her give me, the one I fully intended to act on before we kissed and I let fear send me packing. I remember everything that happened with her, but everything else, especially then, it's a blur.

"You were in the house, the kitchen actually. I had come in after helping Zach set up for the show, heard voices and headed straight for you. I stopped before barreling on in and interrupting though, because I heard you talking to my mom."

*

"I worry, Matthias. Even knowing this is the life I chose for myself, I worry for her moving on from here. It's selfish of me, but as her mother, I want more for her. A different life than one that lives or dies on whether we can perform to a certain standard every night."

I've been here before. Heard these words. My mom might not have been a wrestler, might not have understood a damn thing about why I loved it so much, but she did understand wanting the best for her kid. Just like Kimber's mother now. There was many a night when I first told her what I wanted to do and actively set out to make it happen where she sat up at night worrying about me. Even when there was nothing to fear. It never went away.

Just like if Kimber chose a different path, I know it wouldn't go away here. She'd still worry and want more for her kids.

It's called being a parent.

"When William and I first started out together, it was a good day if we got a meal, let alone one that didn't consist of a bag of raw potatoes and the ninety-nine cent peeler he stole for us because we couldn't afford to even spend that much if we wanted a roof over our head for the week. Make no mistake, I realize it's a different time now and things aren't quite that dire, but it's still not where it could be and for that, I want more."

She's right. It is a different time. We've graduated from potatoes to Rahman noodles because the damn potatoes are too fucking expensive.

This dream of ours, what lives and runs so easily through our veins, is not for the weak. It will bury you if you let it. For some of the guys I've worked with, it'll kill you. There is no guarantee, but for people like me, Kimber and Zachary, none of that matters. Wrestling claimed us and there's no going back.

We're all in.

"Are you the reason Renegade is going so hard at her?"

"How do you mean?"

I find it hard to believe that she doesn't know what I'm getting at, but for now I'll play along.

"He's harder on her than he is the other girls. When he's paying attention that is, which honestly, isn't all that often. When he does though, it's like he's trying to purposely hurt her. I don't think that's the case. I think he's trying to open her eyes to the reality of what can happen in the ring, a worst case scenario kind of thing, but it's having the opposite effect."

"She's digging her heels in and becoming more determined, I take it?"

"Yeah. If you both want more for her, you're going about it the wrong way. Right now, you're securing her place in this business."

"She's his little girl..."

"And she's one of the most well rounded wrestlers I've ever worked with. Including guys. She's hungry, like a lot of us are when we first start out, and desperate to prove herself. You did this for a lot of years, even when you were pregnant with her. I know you remember that hunger. The desire."

"I'm afraid there's more than one desire at play as it pertains to Kimber, Matthias."

"Whatever it is, you and Renegade created her. Created this. Brought her into this life. And no matter how badly you wish things could be different, you're left with the end result of that. She's made for this, the same way you and Renegade proved you were."

"You care a great deal for her, don't you, son?"

Loaded question but one that with as on the spot as I am, I can't not answer.

"Yeah, I do. Which is why I'm in here talking to you about this, instead of out there where I belong. She's amazing. You two are a big part of the reason she's that way. But you can't turn back the clock or beat her into giving you what you want. She's already proven she's just going to come back harder. So let her. Whatever happens, however this plays out, let it happen. She might fall on her face, she might soar, you'll never know. But one thing is certain. If you do it this way, she will follow the path she's meant to and you won't lose her in the process."

"I knew you'd soar if they stopped trying to clip your wings."

"You remember..."

"Of course I do. It was about you, little one."

What I also learn from my walk down memory lane is the point she's trying to make. If I had been Jonathan, I would have worked alongside of both her parents in order to get the result they wanted. I would have broken her spirit and left her to find her own path doing something her parents found more acceptable.

In going to bat and putting my mom's pep talks to good use, I wasn't him.

I was her.

"You did it again the night of the showcase. I heard you talking to a girl. I didn't know it was you until you rescued me from Gavin, but she was there again, Matthias. She came out through you."

Avery.

Her tear stained face with the dark makeup streaks all too familiar. Like going back in time. Complete with the desire I used to have then to erase it all and make everything better. Jackson at the time making it surprisingly easy.

Erasing her lines and loving her the way she deserved.

The way they both did.

"I've met the girl, you know. Avery. She's nice. What you did for her that night, the way you sat on the floor and talked with her, he wasn't there. It wasn't him at all. It was all you."

She's right.

Jonathan never took those makeup lines away. He was always the one putting them there.

"The person making you run, Matty, it's him. That's what he wants you to do because deep down, he was never happy and he wanted everyone to be as miserable as he was. Her light was too much for him. He couldn't dim it enough so he did the unthinkable in order to make it happen. He's doing the same to you now. Dimming you. Making you think love caused what happened, when it was him. Love had nothing to do with it. He's been erasing whoever you were meant to be in favor of what he could make you become...and you're letting him."

Never again.

Jonathan Kemper doesn't get a say anymore.

"I'm sorry, little one." I tell her regretfully. "Sorry for being scared and not admitting that's what it was from the start. For believing in something that wasn't real. For every tear I ever made fall from those breathtaking eyes. But mostly, I'm sorry for running and letting him win."

"Promise me something."

"Anything."

As the word falls, the fear I expect doesn't come. I've never meant anything more.

Right here in the middle of the floor, in a house that has haunted me for the better part of twenty years, on what has got to be the worst first date in existence, I'm ready to promise her the world.

Because with her by my side, I can deliver.

I can be someone worthy.

Worthy of love. Worthy of her. Worthy of the life my mom wanted for me before my father dimmed her light for good the way Kimber said.

I can do it all.

I *want* to do it all.

"This isn't going to be easy, but whenever he wants you to run and you think you have to because you'll be keeping me safe, find me. In the ring, out of it. Backstage or at home. Find me. Don't let him win. Don't let him take you away from me again."

Promises are tricky for me. My need to keep them and deliver on the ones I make others give. It's never been something I'm good at, but for this beautiful, amazing woman, I want to be good.

I want to be the best.

Which is why when I'm finally able to speak again, it's not fear of failure or screwing up that answers for me.

It's love.

"I promise."

Chapter Thirty

Kimberlee

Three weeks.

It's been three weeks since Matthias stood across the ring from me holding out a pair of gloves, asking me to pummel him.

Three weeks since we faced his demons together, and three weeks since he made good on his promise not to let the darkness of what happened in the past win.

So many changes, but all of them good. Changes that are nothing short of happy.

Date nights that he claims every time I bring it up, he's doing to make up for the horrible first one he took me on. The one to his childhood home. The one I happen to think was the best first date I could have ever had.

My first date period.

Our relationship a series of nothing but firsts, but different in comparison to the way others have started, because they don't know going in that this one is *the one* the way I do.

Matty the one for me, and me, Kimberlee Parker, the one made specifically for him.

Dinners with Bryan and rooms filled with laughter of the crying kind, as Matthias walked slowly out from the darkness that's been his home for too long, and straight into the light that's been waiting for years to see him.

Leaning on me in the moments when the fear got the better of him, strengthening the bond we share, and letting me help him the same way he did for me so long ago.

Stolen moments at shows, where it's just the two of us locked away alone giving into the feelings we have for each other. The passion that's always been there from the first moment and the feelings that seem to only grow infinitely larger with each passing day. Culminating in the nights where instead of spending them on his sofa sleeping the way he explained he's been doing forever, we're together in his bed, loving each other instead.

It's been the best weeks of my life.

"Give it back, Matty." I dive at him when after stealing my phone he flaunts it in my face laughing. My father's name flashing across the screen, big and bold much like the man himself. "Don't you dare answer it!"

"Why not, Kimmie?" he taunts, making me sock him in the arm when in his laughter he gets close enough for me to grab. "Shit!"

"You deserved that," I smirk, using his stillness as he rubs his arm to snag the phone back and quickly hitting ignore on the call. "You know why. I have a match, and you know him. He's gonna wanna talk. Especially with you here."

That's the only thing that hasn't changed in three weeks. My father doesn't know about Matthias. Well, he knows about Matthias, I mean, they've talked, but he doesn't know about us.

When I told Matty I was scared too, I meant it.

Everything with us is still so new, and there's always the nagging fear in the back of my mind that at any given moment he'll up and bail again.

So for the last three weeks, other than Bryan and a few of the other more trusted people around HFWA, we've kept our relationship under wraps.

Especially with my dad.

I know how he feels about Matthias and the impact he made before heading back to Smith all those years ago. The last thing I want to do is destroy the bond they seem to have created if this thing between us happens to fall apart again.

"I didn't say anything!"

"You talked to him out of the blue. That was enough. He's not as dumb as you think."

"Little one," his voice lowers as he takes a step closer, fingers ready to grab my phone when he hears it start going off again.

"Don't little one me."

"Tell him."

"No."

I don't mean to hurt his feelings, especially when I know that he's here and he's trying, but that's exactly what happens when I answer. The pain evident before he attempts to shake it off by looking away.

"Do I make you happy, Kimber?"

Shit. See?

He's calling me Kimber.

Abort, Abort!

"Deliriously, Matthias."

"Then why we are we dancing around telling him? Telling any of your family?"

We've had this conversation before and with five minutes left until show time, it's not the time to be getting into it again.

I thought he understood. That we were on the same page.

So much for that.

"Is this about him?"

I don't even have to ask who he means. With the latest acquisition to the HFWA roster being none other than my fake ex-boyfriend himself, and the past history between the two leading into him coming here, I knew it was only a matter of time before Matthias brought him up.

I just wish it wasn't when I have absolutely no time to assuage his fears.

"No. It has nothing to do with Gavin. I told you that was over and done and I meant it."

"Then if it's not Fortune, why are you so afraid to tell your dad?"

"Everyone that matters already knows, that's why. We hardly ever see Dad anyway, and it's not like his opinion matters. Bryan, Reese, Brady and Emery, they all know. And I'm sure half the guys know too with the way you've been the opposite of broody bastard lately. Isn't that enough?"

"But they aren't him." He argues, his feelings on the subject evident no matter how softly the words fall. "They aren't your father."

This isn't a fanboy moment for Matthias. It's not a desire to tell my father because I just happen to be Renegade's daughter. It's about respect. He wants to show my old man respect, and damnit, I want to let him even with this being so new.

It's not really all that new, Kimber. You've been in love with Matthias for years.

"This weekend, okay?" I acquiesce. "We'll go up and see them since Zach is heading home too. I don't want this coming over the phone, and I know you'll agree with my reasons for why that is, so just give it a few more days."

"A few more days." He concedes, meeting my eyes and letting the smile that for the last few minutes has been missing, be found again. Reaching out and instead of plucking the phone from my hands, yanking me to him instead.

His lips finding mine, his excitement over my compromise bleeding into his neediness as his tongue parts my lips and wraps itself in mine. A moment that as I melt into his body, I never want to end until the clearing of a throat does exactly that.

"You two are so gonna get caught one of these days."

Cursing under his breath and making me giggle, Matty releases me and turns glaring toward our interruption.

"And you have horrible fucking timing, as always."

"You always say the sweetest things, baby. Love you too." Blowing a kiss Matthias's way and earning another string of curses, he laughs and turns his attention to me. "Don't you have a match?"

"Yeah," I admit as Matty cuts back in.

"Another interruption planned by you."

"I'll take that one, but it's your fault. You're the one that told me to get her the fuck out of developmental. You're your own cock block."

He doesn't have a leg to stand on and he knows it, but it doesn't stop him from huffing and acting all pissed despite it.

Matthias did go to bat for me, making both Reese and Bryan see the benefit of bringing me up now and giving me a run at a few of the girls before heading straight for the Women's title.

If he'd kept me working with all the new talent, we wouldn't have this problem. We'd have already been home by now.

In bed.

Okay, yeah. Not going there right now. I've got a match. Wrestling with Matty in bed is going to have to wait.

Crap. That's not helping.

"Yes, Bry, I've got a match. Which means it's time for me to love and leave you." Flashing my boss a smile as I pass, I pause when I get to Matthias and pressing my lips against his cheek, watch as all the tension from our early conversation, Bryan's interruption, and everything else floating around in his head evaporates, like a balloon being freed of air as he melts into me.

My effect on him alive and well and just as surprising as the first time it happened.

"Own it." He whispers and nuzzling my face against his, nodding as I do, I pull back just in time to see his eyes closed and a smile rising.

I'm never going to get tired of seeing him this way.

Not ever.

"I will. Play nice."

"No promises, little one."

"Okay," I laugh, pressing a quick kiss to his lips before finally breaking away and heading to the door. "Just don't kill him and I'm good. He still has to sign our paychecks."

Skipping through the door, I giggle when the muffled sound of Bryan's voice questioning what the fuck I said follows.

I was right before.

I've never been happier.

Matthias

"Feels good, doesn't it?"

As soon as Kimber left and Bryan threw a shit fit wanting to know what she said, my eyes glued themselves to the monitors and if I had my way, nothing was taking me off them.

He could do whatever he wanted but I was going to watch my girl in her first match since being brought up out of developmental hell.

Where she never should have been in the first place.

I'm bias, but who cares. She still has more talent in her pinky finger than most of the girls Bryan and Reese have been pushing. She deserves to be where she is now.

Sure it's not in the title picture yet, but it will be. I can feel it in my bones. The same way that even though she's making her way out to the ring now, complete with that godforsaken song that's haunted me since our CPW days, she's there. In my veins, my bones. Shit, she's in my heart and what's left of my fractured soul.

She's everywhere all at once.

"Depends what you're talking about." I grumble, pissed off that I've got to take my eyes off her in order to really focus on whatever Bryan wants to talk about.

"Her, of course. I know it's the only thing you're willing to get into these days." He laughs, and following his hand as he points to the monitor where the bell is sounding and Kimber and Raven are locking up, he snickers. "Keep watching. What I want to talk to you about can be done while you drool."

"Fuck off."

"Pretty sure you've been doing enough fucking for the both of us, brother."

I knew it was a mistake telling him about Kimber. *Shit.* He's never gonna stop riding me about it now. Especially considering how unbelievable it is.

Kemper actually settling down with a girl when he swore off them? Big fucking news for my best friend.

For anyone really.

"What do you want, Bry?" I mumble, doing like he said and not even bothering to pull my eyes off the screen as my girl hoists Raven up from the mat and powerbombs her back down hard.

Jesus. She's a hell of a lot stronger than I thought.

"Reese and I were talking."

"You're business partners. Doesn't that come with the job description?"

"About you, dumbass." Bryan scoffs, and from the corner of my eye I catch his eyes roll at the exact second his tongue comes out.

Some things never change. Not even with us hitting our thirties. He's still the same brat he was at sixteen. That tongue move as old as time.

Idiot.

"What about me?"

I've gotta admit, there's not much that would make me pull my eyes off my little one right now, but them talking about me is making me want to. If it's about my place here, especially after the travesty of what happened the last time they gave me a legitimate push, maybe I need to take a step back from my girl and deal with it.

Kimber would want me to.

"How would you feel about getting another shot at the title?"

Yep. There it is. Sorry, little one.

"How do you feel about it after the last time?"

"Pretty good, honestly. But since it was Reese's idea and not mine, I've got to give him the credit here. He wants you in the top spot. He's seen you lately man. The good you made on your conversation with him a month ago. He thinks you're ready."

Am I? Am I really ready to take that road again?

Better yet, am I strong enough to handle the load this time? Can I strap that title around my waist or hoist it up over my shoulders and declare myself the man? Be the face that runs the place?

Yes. The answer is yes.

Letting my eyes fall to the screen and watching as Kimber kicks out of a lame rollup pin attempt, resisting the urge to fist pump the air as she turns it around and pulls Raven into a standing reverse figure-four leg lock, my answer becomes even more secure.

Things are different now.

I can do it this time because I'm not alone. I don't have to carry it and walk the road as champ by myself. The amount of guys that will come for me, hungry for their shot, and of those, the ones that Bryan and Reese will want to groom in order to do it when I'm done, don't have to be dealt with alone.

I've got her.

I've got them.

Kimber, Reese, Bryan and Brady. They're with me. Even when I'm not.

"When does he want this going down?" I again apologize silently to my girl, turning away from the screen to focus on my best friend.

"A few months from now. We want to establish Brady as a capable champion, so we're gonna throw a lot of different people his way. One's he'll elevate at the same time as he goes over. But you're the one that's gonna be his biggest challenge."

"You've got the whole feud planned out in your head already, don't you? You already sound like you're reading off a script."

"I've been ready for a while now, man. This feud with the two of you, what will be a fight to the finish to see who the best man in HFWA is, it's been there since Brady got here."

That's news. I was still happily planted at CPW when Brady decided to go out to the middle of the ring and blow his entire career with Smith to shit by breaking storyline and shooting straight. Real.

I'm kind of blown away that he thinks that much of me.

"For real?"

"Yeah, for real, Matty. I've wanted you here from the time I said I wanted to run my own promotion. You were supposed to be my guy. The one putting asses in seats. I just knew back then that you weren't where you needed to be. You were loyal to Smith and all he'd done for you—for us—so I had to go at it from a different angle. Times have changed though. It's time now."

"Time for me to be the one putting asses in your seats..." I mull over, confident still in my ability to work, but shaky on whether I'm ready for the pressure that doing it brings.

I'm finally getting my head to a place where it's safe. Where it feels like I'm who I'm supposed to be. I'm not sure if doing this right now will help or hinder it. The last place I want to end up is right back in the hole I was when I forced them to kick me out of the title picture altogether.

"We believe in you, brother. So if the reason you're damn near biting the inside of your mouth to shit is because you don't think you can handle it, stop it. You, Matthias Kemper, god among wrestlers, are ready for this shit. Ready for what is rightfully yours."

Right. Okay. I'm not alone. Gotta remember that.

"Let's do it." I finally concede, swallowing down all of the reservations and really focusing on what he's said. "You just gotta promise me something first."

"Shoot."

"If it's too much, or you see me running off the rails like I did the last time, pull me. Pull it from me. Put it back on Brady or shit, Fortune, now that you've brought him in. They'll carry it and do it well. But don't hope I'll come out of it if it happens. Don't wait and see. What you did the last time, it was the wakeup call I needed. I'm gonna need to you to promise you'll do it again."

"Of course. Our friendship hasn't crossed boundaries before. It won't now either. You're what's best for business, but if you cease to be that, we'll find someone that can be."

It sounds like doubt, making him promise me this, but it's not. I know I'm not the same guy I was when they first decided to put the belt on me. I've come a long way in a short period of time. But there's still a long road ahead. So before I go out there to either soar or fall flat on my face, I need to know Bryan, Reese, and the entirety of HFWA is protected.

I wouldn't be right with any of this if I didn't do it that way.

"Don't kill me, man." Bryan sighs, and pulling myself out of my head and really looking at him, seeing his eyes angled toward the monitor and what is now an empty ring, it makes sense.

He made me miss the rest of little one's match.

Son of a bitch.

"Go. We can talk specifics later."

With a quick slap on the back, one of understanding and not of annoyance with what he made me miss, I waste no time doing what he said.

Blasting my way through the locker room doors like my god damn pants are on fire. With everything that just happened, there being only one place in the world I need to be. Three little words she's waited long enough to hear.

I've got the Championship in my sights again and it's all because of her.

Kimber.

My little one.

With her by my side, I can do anything, but not until I lock things with her down first.

Slowing as I round the corner, my heart jumps when I see her leaning against the wall outside the women's locker room, glowing in all of her post-match exertion. Her lips, even from this distance, listed into the sweetest, more beautifully serene looking smile.

My little one at her most glorious.

Only, the reason for that not being at all the ones I think it should be when my eyes fall on the interloper to our moment. The acknowledgement that she's not alone, like a punch to the gut given the news I have and the admission she's waited long enough to hear.

The stability I've felt over the last month, the security I've found in myself and with her, slipping away and fading fast when the bastard leans in with a smile on his smarmy face and brings my girl—my fucking little one—into his arms. An embrace so intimate, the reality of why she's been so reticent to bring me home to her father becoming all too clear.

It's him. He's the reason.

Her argument to the contrary before her match, complete bullshit.

It's always been him.

Gavin fucking Fortune.

They're not over.

Spinning on my heel and heading quickly back the way I came, I heave out a breath and let my body collapse against the wall once I'm sure I'm out of their line of sight. The reality of what I just walked in on, the way he looked as he took her into his arms and the smile that played on her lips as he did it, all flashing in clips like the goriest horror film inside my head.

Slide after slide of the embrace, laugh lines, and happiness lighting both their faces enough to have me bending over and expelling the contents of my stomach all over the floor.

Ridding myself of her with each remaining wave that rumbles through me.

How could I have been so stupid?

My old man was right.

And after dropping to my knees with little care to the mess beneath me, it appears as though he agrees as he breaks his silence.

It's about time you realized it. Welcome back, son.

Chapter Thirty-One

Kimberlee

Can he be more of a pain in the ass?!

Matthias is the most infuriating man I've ever met, and trust me, I know infuriating. I was raised by William Parker and I fake dated Gavin Fortune.

"Alright. Show's over, honey." I make my presence known, telling the girl who must have been a koala in a past life with the grip she's got on Matthias's neck, what's going to happen now.

When she makes no obvious attempt to untangle herself, I reach out. Slapping my hand down hard around her wrist, I roughly yank it off. A move that earns me a death glare before she starts rambling belligerently.

"Who the hell do ya think ya are? Get your hands off me!"

Yeah, it's official. I'm a glutton for punishment. One that this big dumb idiot is gonna owe when I finally drag his drunk ass out of here.

But first, since she's moving her hands back again, it looks like I'm gonna have to beat a bitch.

"Did you not hear me the first time?" I seethe, stepping forward and using my body to bump her away. My movement so fluid and quick, she's reaching out to the bar in order to catch herself as she stumbles. "Back off."

"There she is, ladies and gentleman," Matthias finally slurs. "My knight in shining armor."

"More like personal protection." I lean in, hissing in his ear. "Trust me, you might not get it now, but you'll be thanking me later."

Lip quirking up when I pull away, I swallow down the urge to reach out and touch it.

Now's not the time, Kimber.

After spending the last couple of hours searching for him in a near-empty building and coming up with nothing but an annoyance, the last thing I need to be doing is falling into that trap again.

Something happened, obviously. Something pretty big if we're playing this bar scene out again. I just wish I knew what the hell it was.

I thought things were great. Better than ever. I won my match and continued the feud with Raven the way Reese and Bry wanted, more than a little ready to celebrate with him.

So what the hell happened in the time it took me to wrestle, shower, and go off in search of him?

"God, you're fucking beautiful." He mumbles before bringing his hand up in what I can only assume is an attempt to touch my face. A move that based on his current level of intoxication just sits in the air before dropping down hard on the top of the bar. "Fuck! That hurt."

"Matty, tell this bitch to get lost." The girl that I could have sworn took the hint the first two times I gave it to her, demands. Sidestepping around me with a smirk and attempting again to make herself at home on his other side.

Even knowing I should let him handle this crazy shit himself, my body acts of its own accord as I reach over him and grab onto her again. This time twisting her wrist back in order to get my point across as I hiss out another, much quieter warning.

"The only bitch here is you. Now, why don't you back the hell off *my man* and go find one more your speed? You know, willing. Easy."

I hate when I have to get catty. It's not really my thing. This girl though, and I'm using the term as loosely as she is, bringing it out of me quick.

"Eww! You two are together?" she whines, gagging as if I haven't already figured out how gross she finds the idea. Resisting the urge I have to knock the look off her face permanently, I just smile as sweetly as I can.

Matthias thankfully having enough wherewithal to shift his body around and pull me to him, strengthening my words.

He may be sloshed off his ass, but at least he knows how to put on a show.

"You're damn right. So do what my girl said and get lost."

"In that case," she glares at me. "You should know that your boyfriend offered to go back to my place before you got here."

I glance down to Matthias just in time to catch him rolling his eyes before he looks up and shakes his head.

"The only thing I came on to was the shot you offered."

"Whatever. You two deserve each other!" The girl shouts, yanking her arm from my hold and making her exit. A curse of 'crazy bitch' coming across loud and clear before she finally disappears to the other end of the bar.

"You can go now." Matty dismisses me, pulling his arm away and placing it back on the bar in an attempt to distance himself.

"I'm not going anywhere without you."

"What the fuck do you want from me, Kimber?"

"Besides you pulling your head out of your ass, you mean?"

"And here I was thinking you liked my ass."

Don't even go there, Kimber. That's exactly what he's after.

"Matty, I do like your ass. I just don't when you're acting like it."

So much for not going there.

A mental admonishment that doesn't mean shit when the earlier lift to his lips comes back even higher than before.

God, I'm a sucker for that smile.

"How many shots did you have before I got here?"

"Two."

"Bullshit." I scoff, knowing better and lifting his hand, he flips me off.

"It's not bullshit. I had the one I ordered and then one from her." He motions toward the front of the bar where I can now see the girl talking to a new group of guys.

Damn. She moves quickly.

"You were slurring your words when I got here, Matty. Try again." I say with a wave of my hand through the air. "And if you haven't figured it out for yourself yet, you stink."

"Thanks, Mom." He sneers. "I always smell like booze when I drink. Doesn't matter how many I have."

He can attempt to explain things away all he wants, but just because he might smell when he drinks doesn't erase the slur that even now I can hear just under the surface when he speaks.

"Matty..." I say, finally expelling the sigh that's been building. "I grew up with a dad that was drunk more times than he was sober. I know the signs."

"That makes two of us then, but you already knew that about me, didn't you?"

I did, but the edge in his tone tells me that admitting it right now isn't the way to go. I didn't come here to make things worse.

And any mention of Jonathan Kemper is as bad as it gets.

"Do you want me to call Bryan to come to get you?"

"You call him and you can kiss your job goodbye."

There's the Matthias I know and love. We're right back where we started.

"You're a fucking asshole."

"So nice of you to notice." He sneers again before slamming his hand down onto the bar and cackling like what he's said is the funniest thing in the world.

Crap. He's farther gone than I thought.

Our relationship might be in the beginning stages, but I've been around Matthias when he's drunk before and this, if his two drink comment is true, is something else entirely. Two shots wouldn't make him sound this bad.

There's more going on, but whatever it is, it's going to have to wait. There's the more pressing need to get to the bottom of why he's even here to begin with that has to come first.

Let alone getting him out of here safely.

"You shouldn't be here, Kimberlee...Parker." He pauses, with a purposeful draw on my name. "You're better than this. So do us both a favor and go. I got this. I don't need a double d." Snickering to himself for a second, he starts up again. "Designed driver. Not tits. Though that wouldn't be so bad right now, I gotta say."

Ignoring the majority of what he said, I hone in on the driving comment and let him have it.

I'm done with whatever this is.

"Like hell you don't. You smell like a brewery and you're belligerent."

"You know what I can't figure out?" he flips himself around on the stool until he's facing me, his glossed over eyes landing on mine with ease. "What the fuck you're wasting your time following me around for. Sure, we had a good time together. I rocked your world or whatever. But babe, you gotta let it go. Especially with what you've already got going on."

Danger. Danger. Do not respond to this or you'll live to regret it. And what the fuck does he mean by what I've already got going on?

I can see the warning signs all over this, but despite them, I still react. My hand coming out and connecting with his face. The sound of the smack so loud it's rolling in waves through the entire bar.

Stupid drunk, son of a bitch. How dare he take what happened between us and make it dirty?

The way he looked at me that night still haunts my dreams weeks later. How tender he'd been once we got past the initial awkwardness. How he so easily admitted that night that it was me he waited thirty years for.

Our night of passion, his first time, one that made me feel like the most important person in the world.

In *his* world.

Screw him and his attempt to belittle it.

"You're lucky we're in public or I'd lay you out the way you deserve. Go ahead and pretend that night didn't mean anything to you. But if you think for a second I'm gonna sit here and take your bullshit when I see through it, you've got another thing coming."

"You don't know shit, little girl."

"Oh no?" I shove him. "Do I need to remind you which one of us cried that night?"

"Fuck you." He spits, lowering his eyes away as he attempts to turn himself back toward the bar. A move I catch and prevent by gripping onto his arm so tightly, he's forced to look at me again, no matter how much he hates it.

"No, Matthias. Fuck you."

Giving me back as good as I'm giving and again making me question his earlier statement on the amount of drinks he's actually had, his arm comes out around me hard and swift, yanking me to him. Our bodies pressed so closely together that our noses bump. His eyes falling to my lips at the same time as mine drop to his, realizing almost instantly just what his little move has done.

"Maybe that's our problem." He whispers, licking his lips when he catches me biting into mine.

"What is?"

"We need to fuck."

Shaking my head and attempting to pull out of his arms in order to create some distance, he holds on tight, making it impossible for me to go anywhere. Least of all away from him the way I need to.

"Tell me you don't feel it, Kimber. The current between us. It's so strong it's damn near sparking."

Of course I feel it. I'm in love with the buffoon. I feel everything when it comes to him.

I'm just not about to admit it with the mood he's in. I'm not going to allow myself to be vulnerable. Not to this. And not to him when he's like this.

"You're drunk."

"No, sweetheart; I'm fucking buzzed. There's a difference, ya know. You wanna know what else I am?"

Yes. No. Oh god, he's so damn close my head's all scrambled. I don't know what the hell I want anymore.

"Going home."

"Huh?" he asks, genuinely taken off guard.

"You asked if I wanted to know what else you are. The only thing you are right now is going home."

Even though I don't want to give into it, the second those damn lips of his raise again, this time the half smirk really reaching until it's straight up making his eyes dance, I'm the one needing to grip onto something stable to stay upright. The look doing what it did that night and every damn night since the first one together. What it's done from the damn start.

He makes me weak.

Matthias

I'm the world's biggest asshole.

Time and again this woman finds me and somehow manages to save me from myself, and all I do is flip the god damned table instead of just turning it like normal people do, and make her feel like shit for it.

Make her curse me. Hate me.

While I sit here *in-fucking-love* with her.

Thirty damn years I spent focused on one singular pursuit.

I see wrestling, I do wrestling. I become wrestling.

It's that black and white. No outside influences need apply. Least of all members of the opposite sex. But this woman. God.

This fucking woman.

She pushes every one of my buttons. Makes me want things that in a million years I swore to never desire, much less crave so heavily the way I do when I'm with her.

Kimber makes me want to go back on every promise I ever made myself. Reset the hardware and given her cry comment, my software, making all of my future promises be to her only.

Only, I can't tell her. Give her the three words she deserves to hear. I have to make her despise me instead. Especially with what I caught a few hours ago.

There's only one problem with that plan.

Whenever she's in the same room, all I want to do is break my vow. Be near her.

Sin with her.

Our first night together, along with every night since, is still so fucking vivid, I can actually feel my skin burning the way it did then. And even a drunk person can figure out why that is.

Kimber is my weakness.

Even when like right now, she's looking at me with fire blazing in her eyes.

"There's only one home you're getting me into tonight, and it's not mine."

There it is. The need we share. She can pretend all she wants, but that current I was talking about earlier is there for her too. She can feel it the same way I can.

The only question now is, how long am I going to have to wait for her to give in to it?

Give into me.

From the time she reappeared in my life when I was in CPW and I ran like the piece of shit I am all the way out of the country, we've been doing this dance. Back and forth like a pendulum swinging. Together, not together. Ready and willing to dive straight into the deep end, and on the flip side, scared as shit about the horrors that will be unleashed once we do.

It's mainly me causing this, but despite my every attempt at distancing myself, I just can't seem to.

Kimberlee Parker has gotten under my skin and weaseled her way into my heart and I don't think there's any real way to get her out. Even after seeing her and Gavin together the way I did earlier.

The catalyst for me even being in this dive, to begin with.

Jealousy, heartache, maybe even heartbreak, turning me into even more of a pathetic loser than I already was.

"I saw you." I finally admit, cringing as I hear the slur.

Damn. I really am drunker than I thought.

Something isn't adding up. I can't be this blasted off two drinks.

What the hell is going on?

"So happy your vision isn't impaired by your stupidity."

"No, Kimber. You're not hearing me. I didn't say I see you. I said *I saw you.*"

"Saw me? What does that even mean?"

"Earlier in the hall. I saw you."

This piece of news gives her pause. I can actually see the wheels turning in her mind as her eyes squint with the determination she has to figure out just what I'm getting at. If what I was getting at wasn't the damn reason for me being so on edge, and if I wasn't overrun with concern over just what the fuck was in my drink to make me feel this loaded, I might find her expression cute.

God knows I have before.

"Bryan talked to me about the championship. How he and Reese want me to go over again, but this time, have me hold it longer. They've seen the changes over the last few weeks and felt that I finally had my head screwed back on straight. I wasn't a risk anymore. I was ecstatic. All I could think about, with you and me being in such a good place, was hunting you down and telling you. Imagine my surprise when I turn the damn corner and see you," I pause, giving her a chance to take in everything I've admitted. "With him."

It's small, but there's no missing it. The tiny gasp she lets escape right before her eyes go wide. Caught like a deer in headlights.

"He had his arms around you. On you." I mutter bitterly, feeling my blood pressure beginning to spike with the visual reminder of the way they were touching. "You were in his fucking arms. Like you'd never left. Like you belonged there. So you wanna know why I'm here drowning my sorrows, Kimber? Look in a fucking mirror."

"Matthias—" she attempts to explain, but the loss of my arms is all the answer I can muster before I cut her off.

"You were it, Kimber. I knew it. I've always known it. I was ready to tell you as much. Admit that night what I should have told you the night we slept together. I'm *in-fucking-love* with you. You're all I think about. *All I see.* I was ready to ask you to help me beat the fear. Not only the fear about us, but the fear of being the fucking guy in HFWA. I didn't want to do it alone. For the first time in fucking years, I was ready to tap out and admit defeat. Love beat me. I guess the jokes on me, huh?"

Turning my back to her, I jump down off the stool and after tossing money down onto the bar, start walking. The sound of her voice calling my name the most beautiful song, but also a song that the more you listen to the words, begins to slowly break your heart. One that despite everything I've seen and now know, is still damn near impossible not to turn back toward.

Reaching the door of the bar, I twist the knob and push it open, finally allowing myself the perverse pleasure of seeing the face of the woman who now understands what it feels like to be me. Swallowing hard as I take her in one final time, I push down the urge I have to run back to the bar and sweep her up into my arms.

Take it all away.

What I can't do.

So I do the only thing I can.

I open my mouth and let the shit fall out.

"Give your real boyfriend my best."

Chapter Thirty-Two

Matthias

I got out of the bar and halfway to the highway, pulling off onto one of the lesser known side streets, before reality kicked in and I realized what I'd done.

How badly I screwed up.

Walking out of the bar, even after what I witnessed between Kimber and Gavin, was wrong, and all it takes is the voice of a fourteen year old to see it.

"Don't do this, Matthias. Don't leave me."

I was breaking yet another promise I made pulling the stunt I did.

Parting shot and heartbreak aside, I told her I was in this with her. That I wouldn't leave again. Yet here I am doing exactly that.

It doesn't matter if I meant every word, if I still mean it. I'm still leaving.

I can't let it go down like this. I've run for far too long as it is.

I'm not the same guy anymore and the last three weeks are all the proof I need of that.

I need to go back, even if it ends with my heart being ripped out.

She deserves it. She deserves the real me.

The one who keeps his promises.

Squinting and staring out the windshield attempting to make out what's coming and going, the lack of visibility down this way making it incredibly hard to make out much of anything, I take a deep breath, close my eyes and send up a silent prayer that what I'm about to do isn't going to cost me.

Putting my foot down hard on the gas, I coast forward for a minute or two before grabbing the wheel tight and doing what has got to be the widest U-turn I've ever done. Waiting until I've completed the turn before releasing the breath I'd been holding since I made the decision to turn back.

I can already feel the weight on my chest, and the ache that's been present since I saw caught her in the hallway, lifting.

I'm doing the right thing.

Finally.

The look in her eyes when I walked out of the bar, a look that when I finally got her back in my life I swore I'd never put there again, I can't live with it. I can't live with myself knowing I'm the one that put it there. Like I put it there at fourteen, and again seven years later when I walked away from her and willingly broke her heart. Distancing myself from what would have and should have been when we ended up together in CPW.

It was always meant to be me and her.

"I'm sorry, little one. I know I fucked up again, but I'm gonna make this one right too." I whisper to the air, hoping it carries to her as I put my foot back down on the pedal and push down on the gas with all I've got.

Picking up speed until just in the distance I can make out the road I'd turned off in the distance. Lights beginning to illuminate the area but doing it too late.

Just as I start to adjust to being able to see past the pitch black darkness that's plagued me in every possible way, something darts out in my path and I'm yanking the wheel. Swerving to avoid whatever it is, but what doesn't seem to even be there anymore as the car pulls off the road.

Slamming the brakes as hard as I can, regret at shoving my foot so hard on the gas flooding me, I'm not quick enough. A long block of gray—the guardrail—coming into view and my dulled senses doing shit for me as I yank the wheel again, but two seconds too late.

The next sound I hear the impact as the car crashes straight into it. A crunching sound, along with the cracking and shattering of the glass loud and violent as the impact throws me forward and I actually feel the crack of my skull hitting the dashboard before bouncing me back hard like a ping pong ball against the seat. A sharp pain making its way from my neck straight down my spine paralyzing me in place.

With my head beginning to spin, my eyes instinctively beginning to shut themselves off from the nightmare I'm experiencing, I will them to stay open and force my body to connect with the door. Slamming as hard as I can into it and failing as after I attempt to hit it again, shaking the lock with even shakier hands, I feel the car beginning to teeter.

Fear of what happens next, what lies on the other side of the guardrail, making the fight or flight responses that kicked in right before the impact fall away until all I feel is heavy. Weighted down. Summoning up the last bit of fight I've got, I slam myself into the door and again fall victim as nothing happens. The car weaving up and down with the force of the wind outside, but the door stuck and not budging.

I'm fucked.

No! It can't go down this way!

Not when I realized I was screwing up and was doing things differently. Going back to her. Determined to make my word count and not repeat the mistakes of the past.

Not running when things got real, but fighting.

For her.

For us.

For love.

I have to keep this promise.

Every other promise failed, but this one can't. I can't let it.

Wiping at my eyes, pushing my hair away and attempting to rid myself of the water that now seems to be pouring down straight into them, that's when I make it out.

It's not water.

It's blood.

Thick, oozing and dark, followed by the pungent smell. One I'm all too familiar with having swallowed enough of it in matches over the years.

Only as I stare at my hand, it's not my blood I'm seeing. It's hers. Wounds all seeping the same coloring, thinner, but never-ending, no matter how much pressure I put on the wounds in order to stop it. To save her.

I'm covered in her blood.

No. That's not right. She's dead. She's been dead for years. It's not hers. It's yours. You're hurt.

Attempting to snap myself out of the past, I close my eyes, shaking myself free and that's when it happens.

A shot of loud, boisterous cackling fills the entire car. The precipice I'm on, teetering even more from the force of it.

This is it. This is how I'm going to die.

I was too late.

Again.

No wonder you couldn't save her. You can't even save yourself.

The chilling voice of my monster—Jonathan Kemper—the last thing I hear before my eyes finally give into the weight being forced down on them, and the world, along with everything in it, fading completely to black.

Part Four
The Aftermath

Chapter Thirty-Three

Kimberlee

"You were it, Kimber. I knew it. I've always known it. I was ready to tell you as much. Admit that night what I should have told you the night we slept together. I'm in-fucking-love with you. You're all I think about. All I see. I was ready to ask you to help me beat the fear. Not only the fear about us, but the fear of being the fucking guy in HFWA. I didn't want to do it alone. For the first time in fucking years, I was ready to tap out and admit defeat. Love beat me. I guess the jokes on me, huh?"

How long have I been waiting for that admission? For him to finally stop running, realize what was going on between us and admit that despite not wanting anything to do with it, it happened anyway.

Admit that he was as in love with me as I've been with him?

I'm starting to think that fourteen year old me was the smarter of the two of us and knew this, when after our first meeting, I kissed him.

She knew it was going to be this way.

That Matthias Kemper would sweep his way into my life like the tornado he is and make it impossible for me not to love him.

I just wish I'd listened to her sooner. If I had, maybe we wouldn't be here now.

Matty, on the other side of those double doors, busted open on some operating table as they attempt to save his life. And me in this godforsaken chair, waiting for answers.

Waiting for them to tell me that they got him here in time and I'm not going to lose him.

Lose us.

"This is all my fault."

Hanging my head in my hands, I finally let go of the tension and allow the tears to fall.

If I had just stuck to my guns in the bar, run to him the second I saw him starting to walk away, maybe I could have done something. Prevented him from getting behind the wheel of the car, intoxicated as he was. Gotten him home where he'd be safe. Where we both would.

Instead I'd stood there, completely frozen in shock after everything he admitted to and what he mistakenly saw and let eat at him, and done nothing.

The same way I'd done nothing the last time he walked away almost a year ago.

I should have told him he was being stupid. That if he just focused on what was really happening between Gavin and me, he'd see it was innocent. Just a girl, head over heels in love with a damaged boy, giving the other man she'd mistakenly strung along for months, his life back.

"No, it's not."

Dropping my hands and twisting around in the chair, I'm face to face with the only other person on the planet that cares as much as I do about the man now fighting for his life.

"Yes, it is, Bry. You weren't there. You didn't hear the things he said. What I was too stunned to do anything about. If I had just gone after him..."

I can't even finish my thought. I know it's my fault, but admitting it out loud is too much. I won't be able to handle it when he blames me too.

"He's in love with you," Bryan answers, matter of fact. Like he's known the truth I've just learned tonight, forever. As if it's just another day.

How? How can he so calmly admit something that just thinking about it, has the bandages being ripped off the cracks in my chest and allowing the blood of my broken heart to seep through?

"He's been in love with you for years, Kimber. But love for Matthias is loss. The second he put a voice to it, he knew it would be done. *He* would be done. What happened tonight? I know how easy it is to blame yourself. Hell, I blamed myself for bringing this whole thing on by bringing him on board when he wanted out from under Smith. I get it. What you don't get because you weren't there when everything happened is, it's not on us. It's not our fault. It's his. He's so determined to not become his old man that he's allowed his mind to become a minefield and in the process, for the very real people and feelings he has to become skewered."

"I don't understand..."

And I don't. None of it. I know I wasn't there when his mom died, but I didn't need to be to know how hard it hit him. How the sins of the father became his to take on, the fear of just who he would become keeping from enjoying the simplest of pleasures in life. I was privy to all of that. The first time at fourteen, again at twenty-one and now. None of it explains what Bryan is getting at, though.

"I've known him for almost fifteen years, Kimber. Not once in that time has he ever let anyone get close. It's a hard limit for him. If he keeps them at arm's length, he's keeping them safe. So tonight, after admitting what he did to you, he did the only thing he thought he could do."

Protect me.

"Bryan..."

No. Protecting me from himself is one thing, but taking himself out in order to do it? No. Matthias wouldn't do that. No matter how messed up his head was. How much of a minefield it is.

He didn't try to end his life tonight. I refuse to believe that.

"He wouldn't do that. Not to us. He knows how we feel about him."

"He does, but he also knows that in his world, love is death. So if he admits he's in love with you, what do you think has to be going through his head after?"

His mother.

His guilt.

Oh God.

"He thinks...he thought," I stammer over my words and moving around the small loveseat, Bryan lowers himself down beside me and pulls me into his arms. Warm, strong arms. Safe ones, but not the ones I want. The ones that could turn this nightmare around and make things right.

Bryan isn't Matthias.

"He thought Gavin and I were back together."

"I know," He admits softly. "He told me what he saw before he bolted out of the building. I tried to talk him around, but he wouldn't listen. You know him. Nothing you say gets through if he's already made his mind up."

"I do know that." I laugh softly, the sound so foreign it feels wrong. Sitting with Bryan and laughing about Matthias's stubbornness while he's a few feet away fighting god knows what, is just so damn wrong.

"You were never really *with* Gavin though, were you?"

Gavin and I were together for a long time. We put on a damn good show. No one so much as suspected it was just that. How does Bryan know the truth?

"No."

What I really want to say, scream really, is no I wasn't because I've been Matthias's since that first kiss at fourteen. But

I don't say that because while Bryan may know a lot, that's just for me. It's always been Matthias. It always will be. Even if when we're face to face again, we end up right back where we started. He said it himself before he walked out of the bar. He wanted me to help him beat the fear, and that's exactly what I plan on doing. Even if it's the last damn thing he wants.

"He asked me to save him, Bry. I didn't see it at the time, but when he came to see me and found me with Gavin, he was going to ask for my help."

"I guess you know what you have to do when he comes out of this, right?"

"Yeah, I do."

I need to save him, the same way he saved me.

"As much as I hate it, Matthias has spent the better part of fifteen years trying to be everyone else's hero. Not being able to save his mom in time, losing her in the bloody way he did, it changed him. Instead of dealing with his own shit about it, he resigned himself to helping everyone else. I don't think there's a person in HFWA or CPW who hasn't felt the effect of Matty when he's on a mission. When he comes out of this, when he comes back to you, someone else needs to step up to the plate. Be *his* hero."

Heroine.

It's quiet, but there's no mistaking it.

Matthias needs me.

"Bryan says that when you're awake and done with rehab, he's giving you another title shot. You're gonna win the belt, Matty. There's a few of the guys, you know how they are. They've been there from the very start and aren't too pleased that a guy that's best friends with one of the owners comes in and gets the shot." I laugh, remembering the way my time in CPW started. How the very same things were said about me even though I'd been with two other companies before. "I remember the way the guys talking about me used to piss me off. Not you, though. Even when I thought you hated me, you always knew I deserved it."

It's been this way for three days now. I sit here beside his bed, at least since they finally stopped fighting me about leaving, and talk to him about everything he's missing. The stuff I hear from a few of my friends in CPW, and what I learn when Smith himself calls to check in, along with everything happening at HFWA. What the plans are even though he's not awake and things are still so up in the air.

I ramble, for hours it seems, about things that honestly don't mean shit anymore. The only concern I have, the broken and bruised man in the bed beside me and just where he is that's preventing him from coming back to me.

To us.

I guess I should just be happy he's alive. Considering the condition he came in with, the bleeding in his brain and the multiple seizures he experienced, what they still won't know until he does wake up whether he's going to ever be able to come back from, things could have gone a completely different way. But I can't focus on that because I know it's not what he would want.

So I give him what I think I know him well enough to know he would really be after.

His place in this business.

"Smith says that you need to stop ribbing us with this whole coma thing. He knows you're in there and awake. He said if you don't snap out of it soon he's gonna lay a beating on you the likes of which you've never seen before. Direct quote." I laugh softly before reaching over and smoothing out the stray locks of unruly curls that are blocking me from really seeing him.

"I kind of want to see that fight, actually." I whisper against his skin, pressing my lips to his warmth, willing him as I do to wake up and come back. End the suffering for everyone. The entirety of HFWA held captive same as I am. Completely at a loss to where to go from here, knowing one of their own is locked inside his own mind with no signs of escape.

"Something tells me you'd win that one like all of your others, though. It's why I always bet on the unpredictable one."

"No one knows what to make of me, and honestly? I think that's what I like most about doing what I do. I can be anyone I want, whenever I want, and no one will ever see it coming."

"So basically what you're saying is, you're crazy?"

"I prefer unpredictable."

Bringing my hand to my mouth, I cough, muttering crazy again and that's all it takes for him to pounce. Pulling my hand away and taking the word and my breath away as his lips close down over mine.

"That crazy enough for you?"

"Nope. I think you may need to try it again, maybe for a little longer, if you really want me to feel the crazy."

"Longer, huh? If you really want long, I can show you."

His lips are on mine again, reading me like a book, silencing my argument, or rather the joke about his size I was more than ready to deliver. Making good on my request as this time when he takes my lips, his kiss is deeper, more unpredictable as his tongue pushes for entrance and entangles itself up in mine the second it's given. Soft moans quickly following, from both of us, though his hungrier in comparison. His need for me every time we're together like this, unable to be contained.

"Mmmmm," I moan lazily when after a few minutes he pulls back slowly. "That was definitely crazy."

"You make me crazy, little one."

"Are you sure you didn't mean to say I drive you crazy, Matty?"

Nipping at my nose before lowering his lips back down to mine and taking my bottom lip into his teeth, he grins.

"As a matter of fact, you do both. I like it."

"You do, huh?"

"Mhmm," he murmurs, pressing his lips to mine again. Sweeping me up in him so much, I'm not in the least bit prepared for what he says next.

"I wanna be crazy with you forever."

Shaking myself free of the memory, my attention immediately goes to the bed, where as vivid as the memory of the morning after we made love was, I expect him to be staring back at me. Where my heart sinks again when I see him, eyes closed and breathing steady, resting someplace far away from where I can reach, same as before.

It's been happening like this a lot lately. The stolen moments we've shared over the years, memories forcing their way to the forefront of my mind until I'm completely stripped away from the real world and taken back in time to the day they happen. Where they become so much more than memories, but tangible pieces of time that I'm actually able to hold in my hand and relive.

The sights, smells and feel of things just as alive as the day we lived them.

"I know I've been saying it so much you're probably sick of hearing it by now, but I miss you, Matty. I want you to come back because I really want the next time I say these words to be when you're awake and seeing me. So you can witness just how much I mean them. I love you. Please come back to me."

Dragging the chair as close to the bed as I can get it, I slip my hand around his before lowering my head down softly onto his side. Welcoming the combination of warmth from the heated blankets he's covered in and that from his own body and letting it envelope me. Keep me safe in a cocoon only he can create.

Releasing a sigh, I repeat my wish for him to come back, softer this time. The memory from before not doing what the others have done and strengthening me, but instead, the opposite. The fight slowly draining, a little more each minute, until I'm gripping his hand tighter in order to get some of it back.

"I love you, Matty. Don't let me fight alone."

Chapter Thirty-Four

Matthias

"I love you, Matty."
I love you.
Please God, don't let this be a dream.
Please let the voice that's breaking through the haze be hers.
My little one admitting to loving me the way I do her.
Tsk, tsk, Matty boy. You know what happens when you admit your feelings.

No! You can't take her from me yet. You can't take her from me at all! I yell, raising my fist up in order to retaliate, only finding it nowhere to be found.

What the hell is going on? Why can't I feel my arms? Better yet, why can't I feel anything? And where's Kimber? I heard her, I know I did.

The voice may be fast, but not that fast. He couldn't have taken her yet.

But even if he did, I'd find her.

I'll always find Kimber.

"Is there any change?" I hear my best friend whisper, to which I hear the soft clearing of a throat, followed by a low but distinct sniffle, before the voice of my angel speaks again.

"No, not yet. I keep talking to him the way the doctors tell me to, keeping him up to date on stuff happening at work and you and Smith. I've even been reminding him how I feel about him, but there's nothing. Not even so much as a twitch of acknowledgement."

After a pause where I can actually feel my heart seize, she eases it when she speaks again.

"How long is he going to be like this? The doctor said his last scan looked good. So why isn't he waking up?"

"I don't know, Kimber. Maybe his body just needs more time."

What the fuck is he talking about? I'm right here. Shit. Maybe if I wave my hand they'll be able to see that they aren't alone and stop talking as though I'm not there.

Good luck with that.

This isn't happening. No way. I've let this son of a bitch win for long enough. He's not doing it anymore. We've been apart long enough. I need her to see that I'm here. She needs to know I love her too.

She's all I've got. All that matters anymore.

Not wrestling. Not titles. Not even the perks that come along with being at the top of the mountain. It could all fade away tomorrow and it wouldn't even matter because nothing matters if Kimber isn't a part of it.

Focusing everything I've got into lifting my hands, I feel the air move as they start to lift, and after a brief second to take a breath, I'm waving them slowly while hollering at what I hope is the top of my lungs in order to be heard.

I don't know what the fuck is going on, but I'm here, Bry! I can hear you!

The laughing, hysterical and manic, blasts itself over my pleas and when it finally settles, I can see there's been no change. He's gotten in the way again. They still don't know I'm here and I still don't understand why.

It hurts. Everything just hurts.

Her pleading to not let her fight alone, her admission of love, over and over on an endless loop in my mind, and one I'm completely unable to respond to. To let her know we're on the same page with. My body not cooperating and letting me reach for her so I can know that she's real and that she's here.

"*Shut the fuck up!*" I explode, as loudly as possible when just like before, his laughter falls so noisily, I can't even hear my own thoughts anymore.

They're gone, Matthias. Don't you get it? You destroy everything you touch. Everyone you love just withers and fades away. When will you ever learn?

No. They can't be gone. They just can't be. I know he's right. It's why I kept fighting everything. Keeping them at arm's length and never admitting I loved them. It was the only way I could be sure that what happened to my mom wasn't repeated. But this, I didn't do it. I didn't admit how I felt. Not to Bryan and definitely not to Kimber. So what is this really about?

Oh, but you did. You told her that you loved her and now you're paying the price.

Come on, Matty. Wake the fuck up! Remember!

"Brain injuries are tricky, Kimber. The doctor told us that. Maybe this is what he means. Just because other people in his position may have woken up already, doesn't mean he has to. He was in surgery a long time. Anything could have happened."

"You don't think he's going to wake up, do you?" my little one cries, only making the need to fight even stronger.

She's keeping her promise. The one she made when she was a kid. She's telling me here and now that she's hurting and I've gotta do everything I can to protect her.

"Matty is the strongest guy I know. He watched his mom die in front of him, despite what happened at the hospital. He stood up in court and detailed what that sick fuck of a father put them through, him and her both. He's taken so many beatings in and out of the ring since I moved across the street when we were kids. If there's anyone that can come back from whatever this is, it's him."

You're damn fucking right, Bry.

It's just up to me to do what I did all of those other times again.

The time for cowering and bending to the will of the voices that haunt me is over. It's time for me to fight.

For me. For her. For us. For love.

And this time, win.

Kimberlee

"That first night after you lost the title," I pause, remembering the night I came across him in the bar "I came looking for you because I wanted to tell you the truth about everything."

The truth I'm speaking of being the relationship between me and Gavin. How it had turned into the greatest rib of all time when the reality was, I don't think it ever intended to go down that way. Gavin at some point, feeling more than his own rules allowed and breaking it off before he could get hurt, and surprise of all surprises, making me feel a loss in the process.

Not a loss of love. Only the man lying in the bed beside me has the ability to cause that, but a loss of something. Even at its craziest, when we were putting on a show for the media, the locker room, god, even our families because we had to keep up appearances, it was still the one real thing besides my work in the ring that I had.

Gavin and the support he gave me was very real.

So Matthias's warning before he left CPW wasn't warranted.

If anything, I was the one playing a game with him.

"There was never anything between Gavin and me, Matty. I know that sounds like total bullshit, but it's not. He saw me the day you were suspended. He saw what I hoped you could see, but that you pushed away. He called me out on everything. He knew I was in love with you even before I could admit it again to myself."

I don't even know why I'm telling him all of this. I suppose it's because after spending a week in this room watching people come and go, I've run out of things to tell him, other than the obvious ones. The important ones.

I love him. I miss him. I can fight alone and I can win, but I don't want to.

Not anymore.

"You're probably wondering what I mean by again. I guess I should have told you this back then. Maybe it would have made you stay. Matty, when you came to stay with us when I was fourteen, I fell in love with you. It really was true what Zach and my dad were saying. You *were* larger than life. But more than that, you treated me as though I was."

The door to the room slides across the floor, the sweeping sensation as it pushes back, silencing my admission and forcing me as I turn to come face to face with the very man we both walked away from.

Radley is here.

"Smith."

"I can't say this is all that surprising." He remarks, motioning to Matthias and over to me. "Your daddy know about it?"

"Yeah, he knows."

"He know how long it's been going on?"

"Yeah, old man. He knows everything." I answer truthfully. The call I made to my dad, after talking to Zach after Matthias's accident still fresh in my mind. The cool edge to his voice when he learned of the kiss at fourteen, turning into sympathetic understanding when he learned just how deep things really were between us.

My father a lot of things to a lot of different people, but by the time I ended the call, I could safely say, he was the most amazing man I've ever known.

Not the Renegade. Not the infamous William Parker. He was none of those people that day. That day he was who I needed him to be.

My daddy.

"Can't imagine he was too pleased to hear his golden boy laid hands on his princess."

"Oh, you mean like the best friend that knew about it the entire time and never said a word?" I remind him and when he lets loose a boisterous laugh, I smile.

"Still a pain in my ass, I see."

"Always."

"How's our boy doing?"

Up until now, Smith has only checked in by phone or had Marie do it by text. From what Bryan's said, he's told him numerous times he wanted to make the trip out, but with Marie and her recent diagnosis, was hesitant to do it. So seeing him here and freely admitting to what anyone with eyes and ears has known to be true since Matthias landed on his training center doorstep at sixteen, it's strangely soothing.

His dad—the rightful one—is here.

Now all he needs to do is wake up and see it.

Be reminded again that he's not alone in this.

He's never going to be alone again.

"About the same as yesterday when you called. No change."

"When's the last time you got yourself some sleep?"

In other words, I look like hell.

"I got a couple of hours earlier when the nurses came in to check on him and switch out his bedding."

"Not what I asked. A couple of hours is barely a nap. When's the last time you got a full night?"

"Before."

Nothing else needs to be said. I have no doubt that if he's anything like my father, he's going to turn into a growly monster now that I've admitted just how long it's been, but I don't care. I'll fight and argue the same way I did with him.

I'm not leaving Matthias.

Enough people have done that already.

"Calm yourself. I wasn't gonna say anything."

"I don't know what you mean."

"You look about ready to lunge for my jugular, especially if you're anything like sleeping beauty over there." He says, sweeping his hand out toward Matthias again.

Sleeping Beauty. How fitting. Considering in all of the years I've known him, been in the ring with him, and spent time with him out of it, this is the single most relaxed he's ever looked.

The morning after our first time notwithstanding.

"Sorry, it's not intentional." I attempt to excuse whatever expression it is he's pulling from me. "Do you want a few minutes with him?"

"Yeah, if you wouldn't mind."

Well, will wonders never cease? Radley Smith actually has a polite bone in that body of his after all.

"Of course." Sliding the chair back from the bed, I stand and making my way over to where Matthias is still peacefully unaware of what's going on without him, I lean over, pressing my lips to his forehead.

"Go easy on the old guy, he came a bit of a way to see you."

Brushing my nose against his, I give him one more kiss, this time on his lips, willing him as I do to again wake up and come back before finally turning and making my way over to the door where Smith stands.

The look of uncertainty clearly written all over his face as he doesn't so much as acknowledge me, but stares straight through the man he considers a son.

"You too, you hear me?"

"What?" He shakes himself free and turns to me, scowling.

"Go easy on him. Wait until he's awake to tell him how much you wanna beat his ass."

"You just wanna see him respond."

My face lifting up into the first smile in days that feels any bit genuine, I lean in and half-hug him, not wasting a second once I've pulled away to let him know the truth.

"You're right, I do. But mainly, I just wanna see the two of you kiss and make up. I hate when family fights."

With that as my last word, I bolt from the room like my ass is on fire, not wanting to know what kind of comeback Smith has at the ready. Besides, he needs to realize what the rest of us have known for years. Just like Matthias does.

They're both worthy of being loved, and there's no one better for them to learn it from than each other.

Radley

I never had children of my own.

Between the years travelling, being home way less than I was in the air or behind the wheel, it just never happened.

We missed our window by the time I finally did pack it in and head back full time. I've been living with that choice every day since.

How I let Marie down. Stripped her of something I've got no doubt she would've been fantastic at. I mean, she does a pretty good job of parenting me most days. Can't imagine she wouldn't be the same with a midget of her own.

It's one of my biggest failures and trust me, I've got a lot of them racked up over the years.

Matthias walking into my gym that day, that gangly as fuck boy with steely eyes and a point to prove. A boy with one hell of a chip on his shoulder and the same never say die attitude I'd spent the better part of forty years mastering, well, he was change.

He was my chance.

Everything changed that day and from that moment on, I took him under my wing, even trying more than once to straighten him out myself before finally throwing my hands up and sending him to Renegade.

He was my boy. A younger me, through and through.

I'd have done anything to save his life. Keep him with me.

There aren't many ways you can break this old fucker, but between Marie's diagnosis six months ago and then Matthias leaving after doing what every boy does to their dad, promoter or not, I was broken. Torn up and shredded like the contract he ripped to pieces in front of me on the last day.

If I thought I knew what shredded felt like after that though, I'm not sure what this is. What I feel staring at the boy that for all intent and purposes is as mine as anyone that Marie and I might have had if situations had been different.

The sick thing about this entire mess being that other than a bandage around his arm and the monstrosity wrapped around his thick skull—another attribute I'm sure he got from me—he looks peaceful. Serene.

Like he's just sleeping.

I blame myself.

It's why I stayed away. I told anyone with a set of ears that it was because Marie was going through a lot—and she is—but that wasn't it at all.

My wife, I married a strong one. Stronger than me if we're getting down to the brass tacks of it all. I didn't make life easier on her. I didn't make it easy on anyone. If the promoters I worked for during my heyday weren't already six feet under, they'd tell you.

The point is, she didn't need me there. She pushed me for a week to get my ass on a plane and get up here. Be with our boy.

What's happening to Matty, it's on me. I pushed when I should have stopped and listened. He might be like a son to me, but I'm still learning what it means to be a father. A real one. What the boy in that damn bed looking so damn peaceful needed more than anything.

His actual old man, he didn't deserve the boy. Most days I'm not even sure if I do. I just know that where Jonathan Kemper didn't want him, I do.

I want him now, the same way I did when he was sixteen years old.

"Boy," I grunt out, taking a step toward him. "I made so many mistakes with you."

A wave of emotion rolls over me the second I lean over the bed in order to take his hand. With the weight of it threatening to pull me under, I reach for the chair that Kimberlee had been sitting in when I arrived. Throwing myself down into it and dragging it over the floor with a loud screech in order to be close enough to see this through.

"I should have seen what you were going through and done something. Said something. I stupidly told ya to let it out in the ring and you did what I said. Grant happened because you were following orders. You always did that. Did what I wanted without question, even when I was wrong. And, Matthias? Make no mistake. I *was* wrong."

"All I could see was myself in you, and I wanted to push you until you reached your full potential. You were the second coming of Radley the Destroyer. How could I not push you? Real bang-up job I did with that, huh?"

Tapping his hand and wrapping my own around it, I look up, and that's when I see the ugly stain that's seeping through the purity of the bandages his head is wrapped in. The circular stain calling to me, reminding me of every single way I screwed up with this gift I was given.

It may have taken me sixteen years to get him, but I sure as fuck wasted no time helping destroy the next fourteen. It's the reason he's here. If I hadn't put my foot down in a way that was just my anger talking and not my common sense, he'd still be at home where he belongs.

He'd still be safe.

"Before you walked into my place fourteen years ago, I was ready to pack it in." I admit, giving up something I haven't spoken to another soul, not even my wife, since it happened. "The guys I was working with, they were talented, but they weren't 'it'. They weren't what I was looking for. I wasn't sure there was enough left in the tank for me to keep going trying to find that. I was tired. I was back to spending more time apart from my wife than with her, same as my time on the road, and I was just done with the lot of it. Then in walks you."

Laughing, remembering the way he was then, I grasp his hand tighter. Creating a lifeline. Not only for him, but for me.

"You didn't take no for an answer, not even after the hundredth time it was said. No matter how many times I told you screw off, fuck off, and get the hell out of my face until you aged up, you just kept on coming back for more. You liked the punishment even then, Matty. The negative attention. I didn't get it at the time, but I figure it's because you were getting attention period. You'd take it any way you could."

"It was that stubborn ass way of yours, always coming back that did me in. I knew I found what I was looking for. Didn't even need to see what you could do in the ring." I pause, laughing again as I recall the first time his scrawny little body, what he thought was jacked at the time, stepped into the ring. "But boy, were you entertaining. Trying to be something without proper training. Thinking that a few hours with a punching bag and a few VHS tapes made you the man."

I'm nearing sixty years old and even during the biggest run of my life, I never talked this much. Not for a camera. Not even to my own wife. This is new ground I'm covering today and a lot of what I'm saying, I'm not even sure why it's coming out. I just know that for too damn long now, he's only ever seen one side of me.

Smith, the promoter. Smith, the former superstar.

I want him to meet the person I haven't allowed anyone but Marie to see since the day we started dating.

Matthias needs to meet Radley.

"You've been sleeping long enough, you hear me? You're scaring the pants off quite a few people here, wanting to snooze out like this. So if you're hearing this, you need to wake the hell up. I know for a fact there's at least one person here that won't be able to so much as close her eyes until you do. So get the fuck over yourself and get back here, alright? You've got a company to own."

I've given a lot of shit to HFWA. Called them every name in the book, especially recently, with all of my old talent that's jumped ship and gone there, but that's because I've been jealous.

Bryan and Reese putting together something over the border here that I only wished I'd listened to my talent at the time and thought to do myself. Maybe things could have been different. Hell, maybe we could have been promotions that worked together instead of poaching off each other.

But that's the other reason I'm here. It's time everyone, Matthias included, knew why I was so against this. So against him being here.

"I love you, son. You're the best damn thing that ever happened to this washed up has-been's life. I don't deserve you, I never did, but I swear on my daddy's grave that if you'd come outta that place you're in right now, I'd try again. Do whatever it took to earn your respect. Earn the love and loyalty you've given me over the years without me even having to ask. It's long overdue."

"And if I'm not enough of a motivator for ya, or the little pipsqueak out in the hall pacing it isn't, then do it for her. She's in love with you the same way Marie is with me. The real kind, not that fake shit we exploit and use at shows. The kind that even when you push 'em away and break 'em, they still get back up and keep fighting. The kind that don't take the shit you're giving lying down, but don't walk away either. She's got it written all over her face. You need that. She needs that. Take it from me. As much as I hate admitting it, I got lucky with my Marie and you, you're lucky to have her. So do what you've been doing with the girls on the roster for years and give her what she needs. Be the one that makes her happy. Proud. The same way you've been doing for years with me."

Pulling my eyes from the picture laid out before me, that same well of emotion from before, spilled and pouring out and down over my face for the first time in thirty-five years, I push the chair back from the bed, letting his hand slip out of mine in the process.

I've said all I can. Done all I can. Now that I'm here, I'm here and I ain't leaving. I just hope that some part of what I've said gets through and he doesn't keep us waiting much longer.

Don't think the hospital will take too kindly to the ass beating I'll continuously give them if he does.

Pulling my body from the chair and giving into the cracks of my joints as I right myself, the years of abuse taking more of a toll now than they've ever done in the past, my body weary and tired, I do what Kimber did before me. I move to the bed and leaning over, and rubbing my hand over the bandages marred with his blood, I keep to my word.

I do what any good father would and kiss the top of his head.

"We got a deal to make right. I'll be seeing you soon, son."

Chapter Thirty-Five

Matthias

I've managed to piece together what I think happened to me, what with the voices of not only Bryan and Kimber to guide me, but Radley and Reese too.

There was an accident. One that I caused when I got behind the wheel drunk off my ass and ran myself off the road in an attempt to get back to the girl I almost left behind again. There was some kind of crash, the car was apparently totaled and I have facial lacerations, a broken arm, a busted spine and internal bleeding in my brain that the doctors had to operate on me in order to stop.

Internal bleeding.

I guess she really was right. The apple doesn't fall too far from the tree after all. Not even when it comes to death.

Here's what I can remember, even though being here inside my head and unable to move, is keeping things pretty hazy.

I fell in love. And like every other time I feel anything even remotely close to it, I ran because all I could see was the way love can turn tragic. Dark. How it can strip away every layer of you until all you're left with is the shell, the empty skeletal shell, of yourself. I saw death. I saw destruction. I saw fighting, pain, and words you can ever take back.

I saw blood. I saw tears. I saw the end.

I saw the way it would all come to pass if I gave into it.

The thing is, I already gave into it. I did it at twenty-one when I kissed that little girl back, even knowing what a shit storm I was creating. I loved her then. I'm sure of it.

It was hard not to. I mean the girl, she lived and breathed what we do. What *I* was doing. She had so many plans, ideas, and things she wanted to accomplish before she finally stepped away. She had dreams, the same way I did before everything turned bad at home. She was funny. Engaging. She never let a conversation pass without making one of us, sometimes even both of us, laugh.

She was alive and it was electric.

Addictive.

She was beautiful, even then. I don't care how it sounds because at the time she was underage. Those eyes, the emerald old soul eyes that were far more grown than the rest of her. Her body not yet grown into herself, but showing the bare tracings of the bombshell she would become. Soft skin and hair the color of night. The color of my soul at the time. It all accentuated the rest of her.

I was entranced by it, even knowing it was wrong.

I could never understand why she was the one to get through and I told her this repeatedly over the years, but knowing that she had, as scared as it made me, I knew I would never be able to give it up. She did stay with me in my heart through everything. Just like I told her she would on the floor of some piece of crap arena when out of fear, I broke her heart.

I've been in love with Kimberlee Parker for nine years. But fear clouded my judgment. Made me see things that weren't there. Listen to voices that weren't real or buried away in a prison cell the way they deserve. I let it take over my life. Gave myself over to the darkness I was drowning in, letting it keep me from the one thing that even after it was shoved at me more than once, I still believed was wrong.

The one person that no matter the consequences, I had to protect.

If wrestling was my life, protecting this girl and the others I did over the years by not repeating the sins of the past, was my mission.

How many times was I told that the sins of my father weren't my load to carry? How many therapists in the beginning, before I up and bailed on them all, said that I had nothing to feel ashamed about? That I was only a kid and I had done everything I could possibly do to make things right?

God, there had to have been' at least ten of them, not counting all the people in my life since, saying the same.

I never heard it. I listened sure, but I never let it sink in. Never believed it.

Until Kimber.

She made me want to believe. Want to be different. Be someone worthy of her, then and now. She made me want to be better. Acknowledge that the voices weren't real, that the pain wasn't mine to bear anymore, and try and move on.

And I did it. I moved on with her. I was happy.

Fuck. Happy isn't even the right word.

I was at peace. I found my happy place. A soft place to land. It was like coming home to my mom when I was a kid. I was wrapped up in this blanket, a cocoon even, of understanding, support and love, and much like I became addicted to Kimber, I became addicted to that too.

Until just like every other time, the voices—*the past*—won out.

Making me see something that wasn't there.

I heard her tell me her truths, even though I couldn't acknowledge them.

I just need to figure out how to fight this newest demon, what's keeping me locked up tight in my own mind, so I can find her and tell her that I believe.

Believe in her.

Believe in love.

That I want it with her.

I want everything.

"It's about time."

Turning at the sound of the voice, I see her. She's standing a few feet away, still out of my direct vision, but there's no mistaking who it is.

Who she is.

"Mom?"

"You're not meant to be here, Matthias. You need to leave. Go back."

"I don't know how. I don't even know where here is."

"You were in an accident and your mind has put you in limbo. You're on the cusp of life and death right now. You need to make a choice."

Well, that's easy. I already have.

"I want to go home."

"Then do as your family has told you and fight. Focus on that as hard as you did all of those tapes as a child and go home. Go home to her."

Her? My mom knows about Kimber?

"Oh, Matty boy." She laughs softly, moving toward me quicker than my eyes can keep up with. **"I know everything. I've seen everything. I've been watching."**

How can something so amazing, be so wrong at the same time? I know the way things have been since she died. I didn't want her to ever have to see that. I thought her being dead and all, she wouldn't have. She wouldn't see the monster her son became.

I think I'm going to be sick.

"Why did you go back, Mom? You knew, same as I did, it was always going to end this way. Why would you willing put yourself—put me—through that?"

"I loved your father, Matthias. For all of his faults, I loved him. He wasn't always the beast you remember. He was soft-hearted. Kind to a fault. Driven, but in all of the best ways. He was tender, caring and romantic. He listened. Helped everyone, regardless of who they were to him. That's the Jonathan I kept returning to because I truly believed that as long as I kept fighting, we would and we could beat this part of him."

"You thought you could save him."

"In the beginning, yes. Toward the end, once I realized that his issues extended far beyond just the anger of losing his job, it was more about saving you."

Saving me? I've had one foot out the door for years. Even wanted her out the door with me. She didn't have to worry about saving me. I was saving myself.

"No, sweet boy. You weren't. You were doing everything in your power to save me, with little regard to yourself. You were being the parent when it should have been the other way around. For that, I'm sorry. I'm sorry that I didn't see what was really wrong. That I didn't force his hand years before to get the help I think everyone, his family included, knew he needed. I failed you."

No! She's wrong. She didn't fail me. All she did was love me. She loved me so much it got her killed.

"Matthias, you must stop blaming yourself. This is the very reason you're here instead of where your heart wants you to be. What happened is on your father. It's on me. Not you."

No way.

"I was there, Mom. I could have done more, pushed you harder. Don't tell me this isn't my fault when I damn well know it is."

"Your only job was to be a child. Instead, you were a boy that had to grow up far too soon. A son that had his hand in adult issues that his parents should have known better than to let him get involved in. The fault here lies with me and your father, Matthias. The sooner you come to terms with that, the sooner you can go home and make your own mistakes right. Be the man I know you are deep inside. Be the best."

Is it really that simple? I admit I wasn't at fault for what happened and everything will go back to normal? I'll wake up, say the things I should have been saying to Kimber and Bryan, and move on?

It can't be.

Everything I've been living with, being swallowed whole by, there has to be a reason for it. It can't have been for nothing. Everything I've done, the person I became, believing that it was the way things had to be, it can't be wrong.

No one else died.

I did what I needed to do.

"Life isn't about sacrificing yourself to prevent death, sweet boy. It's about loving and hurting. Rebuilding and reclaiming once you've lost it all. Learning from it and carving out a better, more fulfilling future. It's about feeling. Happiness, sorrow, and everything in between. Life, Matthias, is about living. Something that based on everything I've witnessed since I passed, you haven't allowed yourself to do."

She's right. I haven't. I haven't allowed myself to live because from the moment I walked into our living room and saw her bleeding out, time stopped and I forgot how.

"You were happy once."

Say what? "When?"

"When you came home again."

I came home a lot over the years. Most of the time it was just passing through for shows with Smith, but I never settled back into the city until I came back to HFWA and Bryan.

Is that what she means?

"It seems you're getting it. Yes. That is indeed what I'm getting at, but there's still one crucial piece you're missing. That's what I need you to focus on, Matthias. Once you do, you'll find your way back."

One crucial piece.

There's only one thing that could be and it's not a thing at all. It's a person. What my mom is standing here telling me is, if I want to go back, I need to focus on the last time I was happy and who I was happy with.

It's in her that I'll find my way back.

"Now you've got it. I can see it by the light that's being returned to your eyes. Focus on that, sweet boy. Focus on her and the way she makes you feel. That's where you'll find the strength to live again. Live the way I always wanted for you. Relinquish the control. Stop trying

to save everyone else and this time, let someone else do the saving. The same way you did with me."

"How do you figure that?"

"You loved me, Matthias. Love, you'll soon learn, has the power to transform everything. Heal it, change it, even save it. You saved my life. Gave it purpose the second you were brought into it. Your love was life-changing for me, and now it's her turn to do the same for you."

"You really believe she's the one."

"I wouldn't have worked so hard to get the two of you together if I didn't. She's yours, Matthias. She's always been your one. I know it and she knows it. Now it's time for you to know it too."

In the second it takes me to blink, she's moved. Now standing, floating or whatever people do in crazy ass dreams like this, in front of me. Her eyes as blue as the sea, mirroring my own. Irises dancing as her face lifts up into the brightest, most beautiful smile I've ever seen. One that over the years, I've lost track of her even being capable of with as often as the pain overrode it.

She looks happy. At home.

At peace.

"I love you, Mom." I choke up when I feel her brush against me, pulling me into an embrace I didn't even know I needed.

This. Why I'm here. It's for this.

I need this embrace because it's going to give me the closure I never got when she died. Closure I never allowed myself because all I could see was her in my arms the day she lay dying.

The last touch I ever allowed.

Until Kimber.

"I love you too, my sweet baby boy. I always will. Fiercely."

Separating herself, she steps back, and that's when I see it beginning to happen. She's fading, or maybe I am. I'm not sure, but whatever it is, as much as I want to call out and make it stop, keep her with me just a little longer, I don't.

I've gotten what I came for.

"Tell Kimberlee your mother says hello." She calls out, a gentle laugh escaping as the final traces of her fade away. The shrill sound of a collection of beeps taking over and dominating what had been the quietest, most serene moment I've ever experienced and bringing me back to what has to happen now.

It's time to go home.

Chapter Thirty-Six

Kimberlee

It's small, a twitch really, but there's no mistaking it once it happens.

Matthias is coming back.

Wrapping my hand around his and rubbing, I swallow down the painful stabbing sensation in my chest, hating that I've got to sever our connection because the stupid call button won't work. Someone needs to know there's been movement, even if leaving him is the last thing I want to do.

What I've been avoiding for the week I've been here.

"Kimber, what's wrong?" Bryan calls out, taking a mad dash toward me from his place by the elevator a few feet away. "Did something happen?"

Yes something happened! I resist screaming.

"His hand...it um—it moved." I explain before looking from his concerned face to the nurse's station again. "I need to tell them it happened."

"I'll do it." He assures me, squeezing my shoulder. "Go back in with him. I'll handle it."

They've been doing this a lot, the men in my life. Bryan, Smith, god, even my dad. They've been going out of their way to make sure I've got everything I need without having to leave his side.

My position and place as clear as it's always been.

"Okay, yeah. I'm gonna go back in. I don't want him to be alone."

"I know, Kimber. Go. I'll find someone."

Moving from his position, he heads for the nurses station and I turn back to the room, pushing my way inside faster than I think I've moved in weeks. An energy level that's been non-existent for sure since I got the call.

Lowering back down into the chair and dragging it over to the bed, my hand instinctively finds his again. Only this time when I take it and squeeze, I'm not met with emptiness. It's not nearly as strong as I know it can be, but he's holding on too. He's squeezing back and when my eyes dart to his face, it's not closed lids I find, but a sea of sharpened, albeit, tired blue.

"You're awake."

"Seems..." he barks out roughly, shaking the cobwebs from his inactive throat as he clears it. "Seems like it."

"You scared the shit out of us. We didn't think you'd ever wake up. You have no idea how scared I was. I thought I'd never see those eyes again. I'd never see you again. I don't know whether to hug you, kiss you or slug you."

I'm rambling, I know, but with no sound coming from him, just the feel of his penetrating stare letting me know he's still here, I don't know what else to do. Words just continue to tumble out until after a few minutes his thick dry laugh stops me cold.

"Little one, stop. Don't want you ending up in the bed next to me."

Ignoring his joke, I look to the door and scowl.

Where the hell is Bryan? Better yet, where is a nurse? A doctor? Anyone?

There was no shortage of anyone coming in and out when he was out cold, so where the heck are they now? Surely Matthias waking up would mean everyone should come running.

"You're scowling."

"I'm sorry." I respond softly, turning from the door and back to him again with a squeeze of his hand in mine. "Bryan said he was going to get someone so I didn't have to leave you. I thought he'd be back by now."

"I don't..." he starts, shifting in the bed and groaning when his body stretches and his bones begin to crack. "I don't want anyone else here."

"But you need to be checked out. You've been out a long time."

Fisting the blanket with his free hand, he pushes it back and looking from the blanket to him, my stomach flips at the sight of the lift to his face.

"Then check me out."

"Never mind. Now I'm sure I wanna slug you."

His laugh, while lightening the somber mood I've been living with since the accident, pains me to hear because it's just another reminder of how long it's been since he's spoken.

"I'm going to get you some water. You sound like crap."

Shifting my hand over his, I begin to pull it back and that's when he shifts with another groan and stops me. His other hand moving over and coming down hard over the top.

"Don't. Not yet."

"But Matty..."

"I heard you, Kimber."

"You what?"

"I heard you. You said you loved me."

When I don't so much as flinch, his hold begins to loosen as his brow tightens and his eyes move from my face down to the bed.

"Did I imagine it?" He asks after a few seconds, and just as the no falls softly from my lips, the door pushes back toward us and Bryan walks in, followed by a nurse and the same doctor from before.

"Holy shit!" Bryan whistles, moving quickly around to the other side of the bed and wrapping Matty up into the biggest bear hug I've ever seen. A hug that has Matthias's entire body tensing and his face flinching in pain.

"Bry..." he chokes out when after a few minutes, Bryan is still holding on tight.

"Let him go, Bryan." I attempt to admonish and when he finally does pull back, he grins.

"He deserves that for the shit he pulled."

"Be that as it may," the doctor interrupts. *Thank God.* "He's spent the last week in a coma. I'm going to ask that both of you step out of the room so I can properly examine him without risk of further injury."

"No." Matthias loudly barks. "I need them to stay."

I'm not sure where it comes from, but there's a plea in his voice that's matched by a look of desperation in his eyes that glues my feet to the floor.

For whatever reason now that he's awake, he's afraid to be left alone. If he's willing to admit it, show it so openly the way he is now, there's no way in hell I'm doing what the doctor wants.

I'm staying put until I'm physically removed.

"It's cool, bro. We'll let them do their thing and we'll catch up when he's done. I've got another dozen or so bear hugs I've still gotta deliver from the boys."

Looking from Bryan's smiling face to mine, he pleads again, but this time, only for me to hear. His mouth forming the words I've been desperate to hear since everything happened.

"Please stay."

Matthias

The first thing I think after opening my eyes and seeing her there is that she's never looked more beautiful. Even if once her head lifts and her eyes meet mine, it looks as though we were both victims of the same accident.

Her eyes tired, her body looking ready to shut down, and her hair matted to her head. But even taking all of that in, she's still the best damn vision for these sore eyes.

Everything I heard and what I fought to come back to, it's all real. She really was here the entire time I was out. She did admit she loves me. It wasn't all a figment of my imagination the way I thought.

But instead of being able to act on what she admitted, her no confirming it, I'm having to watch her from across the room as she lowers her head reverently in what looks like prayer.

Not the first one I'm sure she's done since everything happened.

Details are still a little hazy, but I know from everything that happened while I was out, what I'm doing here. What I was doing that night a week ago. The night I was almost taken away from her—from love—forever.

What my need to drink caused. What I allowed the stupid girl at the bar to slip into my drink because I wasn't paying attention.

I need the doctor to hurry the fuck up and get out of here. I need time alone with her.

I need her to know I love her too.

That I always have. I always will.

Tell her I'm sorry that I didn't handle things better. Apologize as many times as I have to for all of the pushing away, the running, and every other misstep I've taken since we met.

"When you were brought in, you lost a significant amount of blood. We expected that you would wake within a couple of days, but when that didn't happen, we attributed it to you needing a few extra days to heal."

Shut up, Doc. I don't care about any of this.

I also don't want the reminder but looks like I'm gonna get it anyway.

I remember the blood that night. Believing it was my mother's until reality set in, or rather, I forced myself to remain in the moment and realized it was mine. I don't know how long I was stuck there on the road after I passed out, but I do know it's no surprise that I lost a lot of it.

Between my fight to get out of the car, the impact of my head on the dashboard, and whatever else may have happened afterward, I'm amazed I'm even here at all.

"How are you feeling? Pain level on a scale of one to ten?"

"I feel fine. My body hurts, my head is throbbing, but I think that's from being out. So a six, maybe a seven?"

I'm going to tell you whatever the fuck you want to hear right now so you can leave. There's only one person I want to be with right now and it's definitely not the nurse in the green scrubs or you hovering over me with your hands all over my head.

All I need is her.

Alone.

"That's to be expected. The nurse will administer some medication to help with the pain and we'll let you rest." As I nod, he continues his poking around, working from the base of my skull all the way up and around before speaking again. "Everything is how I expect. We'll need to run a few tests, but we'll postpone that until you're feeling a bit more up to it."

"Okay."

Turning my attention away from the doctor as I hear the scraping of the chair from the corner, I see Kimber stand and something about the way she doesn't look my way but instead seems to hone in on the door, has my stomach dropping.

She can't leave.

"Kimber," I call out weakly in an attempt to stop her. "Come here."

Tapping the bed with my hand, I plead silently when her eyes meet mine for her to do what I want and not bolt the way it seems she wants to.

"I'm going to get you something to drink."

"No drinks yet." The nurse cuts in, pulling away from her place around the bed in order to prevent Kimber from moving.

Thank god. Looks like I've got an ally.

"I'll get him something after I administer his pain medication."

Moving back into position, she does as she says and after setting me up, moves to the corner of the room to confer with the doctor.

"Little one," I plead again. "Please come here."

"I can't."

Swallowing the sting her rejection causes, realizing just how much work we have ahead of us, I nod and lower my gaze to the blanket, balling my hand into a fist and tightening my grip around them.

I deserve this. I know I do. It doesn't matter that I was coming back to her. I never should have left in the first place. I should have taken the look on her face and seen it for what it was.

She loved me. There was more to what I saw between her and Gavin. I should have given her the chance to explain.

"I don't want to hurt you." She admits softly, motioning to my head.

"It hurts more having you all the way over there than it would be having you near me, little one." And when I'm sure we've been left alone, the doctor and nurse taking their exit, I confess even more. "In bed with me."

With that admission, her feet move and even though it takes longer than I want, impatient bastard I'm becoming since waking up, I'm able to breathe a little easier when she finally makes her way over.

Shifting when she touches the blankets I've still got balled up in my fist, I wait patiently as she sits and when she pulls her legs up and stretches out beside me, that's when I summon up every bit of strength I have, no longer wanting the emptiness that comes from being separated from her and pull her to me, bringing her into my side. Burying my face in her hair and inhaling deeply before pressing down with my lips and giving her the softest kiss.

"Matthias—"

"I love you, Kimber."

Chapter Thirty-Seven

Kimberlee

I've waited nine years to hear him admit what my heart has known all along. Admit the three not-so-little words that he's just said so easily it's a wonder what took him so long.

But now that he has and we're here together, away from the prying eyes of others, I don't have the first clue how to respond.

"There's something wrong with me," Pulling my face to his and giving me a full view of the truth lying so openly there, he smiles wistfully. "Before you argue and say there isn't, there is, and I can't run from it anymore. I'm not okay. I don't think I've been okay since the day I came home to find her bleeding out on the floor."

"Matthias," I attempt to interrupt, but the brush of his finger against my lips gives me pause.

"I told you I saw someone after what happened. The court appointed it because they wanted me right in the head in order to testify. I saw it at the time for what I thought it was, so I just said whatever they wanted me to so I could get out of there. Grief counseling. Therapy. All of it. I did it because I had to perform for them, and not for the reasons I should have. Not because I needed it. That was the first mistake I made."

Pulling his hand away, the one from my face falling and covering his mouth, he coughs before moving back, continuing with what is starting to eerily sound like a confession.

"I made a lot of mistakes because of that first one. You, Grant, Smith, god, even Bryan and Reese. Instead of dealing with the tsunami I experienced after she died, I just let it fester and grow until it overpowered and overshadowed the real guy underneath. The one that deserved love. Wanted it. The boy who lost the only person that ever cared."

"She wasn't the only one."

"I know that now, but back then she was. Sure, I had Bryan, but where you had your mom and Zach, hell, even Renegade when he wasn't acting like my old man, I didn't. I was always jealous of Bryan and you for that. You had blood and they were there for you. All I had was the blood on my hands, and the voice of my old man that no matter how fast or far I ran always seemed to catch me. I didn't see it for what it was. I'm not even sure I'm seeing it clearly yet. I need work. Help with it. But I do know that the way I was doing things wasn't right."

I've always felt special when Matthias shows me parts of himself I know for a fact no one else has ever seen, but the moment where he admits he's not well and does his best to explain why it's where I see just how much I mean to him.

He's showing me the same way he told me he loves me.

"Kimber, I'm sick."

"Then we do whatever it takes to get you well."

Where his love declaration seemed to give me pause, my response to this latest confession does the same to him. Clearing his throat again he searches my eyes. Lifting a hand and stroking the side of my face, he leans in until our foreheads are touching and releases a heavy breath.

"Are you sure?" he asks, his voice barely a whisper. "It's going to be a lot of work."

"Looks like your head injury is worse than they thought. You've clearly forgotten who it is you're talking to and forgotten who you are. We live to work, Matty."

Releasing a low chuckle, he meets my eyes again and smiles. A sight that for a week now, I thought I'd never see again.

"I could never forget you, little one."

His admission, how easily he's giving in to what's going to happen now, accepting it instead of running from it has got my lips parting and admissions of my own pouring out to match.

"I was so scared when I got the call. It got worse when they finally let me in to see you. I tried to pretend things were okay and you were just sleeping, but I was so scared I was never going to see you this way again. Scared I would never get the chance to tell you the truth."

"I was coming back to you," He admits before I have the chance to explain about Gavin. "The second I pulled out of the bar, all I heard was every promise I ever made you in my head. I couldn't break another promise, Kimber. I told you I wasn't going to run anymore and I meant it. I'm petrified. Scared out of my fucking mind about being with you. Loving you. But I'd rather be afraid for the rest of my life, then face life without you in it."

"Gavin and I were never really together, Matthias." The truth, what I should have told him weeks ago, pours out again. His hold as they fall loosening as he takes in what seems to be a never ending flow of verbal diarrhea. "We faked it. For Smith. For the fans who enjoyed us ruling CPW. The media and their need for a story. It was all fake."

"I know."

"What do you mean you know?"

"I heard you before. It's a little hazy now that I'm awake, but I could hear you. Telling me about your day, admitting you love me, even the truth about you and Fortune. I heard it all. I just couldn't come back. I had to deal with something first. But I heard it. I just thought most of it was a dream."

"What you saw—"

"Wasn't what I thought. I know, little one."

"It's only been you, Matty. Only ever you."

"He took care of you."

As much as I hate talking about Gavin after everything that's happened, if this is what he needs, I'll give it to him.

"Yeah, he did."

"He loves you."

When we first started this pseudo-relationship, I would have said no. Gavin, while not at all the way I imagined him to be when we first made contact in CPW, was still Gavin. He was still the character more than the man. Love wasn't even in his vocabulary. Now that it's done though, I can't say the same. I have no other choice but agree.

Gavin loved me.

"He does."

"I still...fuck. I still don't trust him, Kimber. I don't. But he took care of you when I couldn't. When I wouldn't. So for that, I owe him."

This is it. With the admission of owing Gavin Fortune anything, he's proven to me that he's not the same man he was. He's the guy he said was buried underneath the weight of what he lived through.

This is the Matthias that no matter what seems to be thrown our way, I'm never going to stop fighting for.

"Who are you and what have you done with Matty?" I joke, but instead of getting the lift I want to his face, the one that over the years and our time together I've come to live for, his lips purse and straighten.

"I saw my mom, Kimber. I talked to her. I don't know how much of it was real or just my minds way of handling everything I've been shoving down, but she was there. As real as she's ever been. She made me realize some things. A lot of things. What Bryan, Avery, Smith, god, even you, have been telling me all along. Showing me. I'm tired of running. So what I wanted to tell you that night after your match, I'm saying it now. I need your help, little one. Please help me be better. Be someone who deserves you."

God, he's breaking my heart.

He really is the boy that was left to pick up the pieces.

"You already deserve me. You always have."

"No, I didn't, but I will. When I told you to never forget anything I've done, I meant it. I need you to remember so I can keep working to make it right. Make sure it never happens again. Make us better. Because when we're better, I'm better. I'm stronger with you. Stronger than I've ever been alone."

That makes two of us.

From the very first day he walked into my daddy's gym, got in the ring with me, and went out of his way to sell my abilities, he left an imprint on my soul. He made me better. Stronger. The best.

Matthias Kemper was my hero then, and now it's time for me to be the same for him.

Be the one that stands by his side lifting him up when he's too weak to fight. Be the person that takes his hand and walks him through the fires I'm sure are coming now that he's admitted needing help with his demons.

It's time for me to be his heroine.

"Tag me in." I whisper and when his brow furrows it's my turn to lean in and rest my head against his. "I haven't been in one since the day we met. Maybe this is why."

"You know how well me and tag teams go together. I walked away from my last attempt."

"Then let's do it. When you've had enough and you don't think you can go on, tag me in, and I promise you, I'll do the same. Whatever is coming, whatever demons we have to stare down, let's do it together."

"As a team."

"Not just any team, Matty. The best one."

Matthias

"Just give it to me straight, man. Will I ever be able to get in the ring again?"

The question has been swirling for days now. Only compounded by the amount of time I've spent locked in this bed with Bryan and Smith hovering over me like getting out of the bed to take a piss was actually going to do damage.

Can't wreck what's already been busted wide open, and besides, I'm sick of the fucking piss bag.

Yeah, you heard me. It's a fucking bag that hangs off the side of the bed making it impossible to have a conversation with someone—to get close to anyone—without their eyes flicking to it.

Gross is an understatement.

So the first order of business was to take control of my life back, getting up and taking a piss like a grown ass man should be able to.

I did it. I've done it multiple times in the two days since, but apparently, that's still not good enough for these people. Even taking the short walks around the wall, Kimber by my side and holding me up the way she promised to, has their god damned panties in a bunch.

My little one, she's a fighter.

I always knew she was, but these days, as I sit here pondering my future, wondering if I'll ever get to slip inside the ropes and do what I love again, there's been no one better—no one period—I'd rather have at my side.

She really has been the hero of this whole thing.

Kimber saved me in more ways than one.

Watching and waiting as the man takes a breath, my hand is covered in feeling. A tight squeeze to most, but a lifeline for me. Kimber's hand enveloping mine and letting me know in the silent way she does, that she's here and not going anywhere.

No matter how bad the news is.

Things are different since I woke up. I want back in the ring. I mean, it's what I've always known I wanted to do and what I'm damn sure good at, but it's not everything anymore. If he tells me that I can't compete, will it hurt? Sure. It'll sting like a bitch. But it won't kill me.

There's only one thing these days that can do that, one thing I think has always had the ability to do that and it's her. The loss of her. Something that if I have my way, I'll never have to experience again. Not for five minutes, five hours, days or even years.

I'm in this. I'm always going to be in this as long as at the end of the day, she's there. My little fighter standing her ground and not backing down.

"Your scans since the accident have all come back with positive results, Matthias, but I wouldn't go so far as to say they're enough on their own to approve a return to the ring in the near future. Only time and your body will be able to tell us that."

So not a complete brush off, but not exactly a winning endorsement for getting back to HFWA either. Okay.

See what I did there? It's real and it's happening.

It's as though admitting that I have an issue, speaking with the doctors along with other support staff here at the hospital, and getting the ball rolling to actively fix myself once I get out of here, the weight that was strangling me for years has begun to lift.

I'm not getting back to what I love because what I love is right here beside me.

"Was it the impact from the car that caused the bleed?" my angel speaks up and leaning into her side, my head resting on her shoulder, I close my eyes and let her do her thing.

"Based on what we now know from the medical records sent to us regarding prior head injuries he's suffered, we believe it was a combination of those and the impact from the accident that made the injury you suffered as severe as it was. Having not heeded medical advice in the past with those injuries, we're inclined to believe that was the true catalyst for the bleed."

"So even if I hadn't been in the accident, any hit to my head would have caused it to happen?"

"We believe so, yes. Nothing is one hundred percent certain at this point, but after all of the evidence we've obtained from the accident and your past, my colleagues and I are all in agreement that it could have."

"And there's concern about that moving forward, which is why you said only time will tell right?" Kimber inserts herself again.

"That would be correct."

Okay. Looks like I know how this is gonna play out. Time to take my lumps and deal with it.

"Then it's settled. I just don't do it."

"Matthias—"

"Kimber," I laugh, silencing the argument I know is coming. "We've been over this. I'm okay with however this plays out. I know what matters. I've *got* what matters."

There it is. The flush brought on by what I've said. Nothing beats my little one when she's blushing. *Nothing.* She knows she's it for me and the way she responds to that, well, it's everything.

I'm a lucky bastard and not because of what I survived.

I'm lucky because I have her. Because out of all the easier guys she could have chosen to be with, she wanted to do things the stubborn ass hard way. And I'm determined until the day my heart beats its final beat to not make her regret that choice.

"Don't count yourself out, Matthias. You've shown remarkable progress since coming out of the coma. With everything we've seen thus far, we have every belief you will be able to wrestle again. It's just too early to say for certain right now. We've got a long road ahead of us."

He's not kidding.

Between the therapists, the rehabilitation nurses, physical therapists and neuropsychologist I've got lined up for when I'm sprung from this godforsaken hell and sent home, along with the therapy I asked Kimber and Bryan to look into regarding the reason I even ended up here in the first place, it's going to be a long road.

But a road that when I finally do reach the end, will be rewarding.

I'll be okay.

For the first time in years, I'm going to live. Survive. Thrive the way I should have, but was too screwed up to do.

And I'm going to do it with the people I love by my side.

Kimber, Smith, and Bryan.

Two men that I owe everything to. Two men that for so long I was scared shitless to admit I loved, but who haven't gotten me to shut up about it since I said it for the first time to them both after getting them alone yesterday.

I love them and loving them openly, it doesn't mean the end.

If anything, it's a beginning.

Radley Smith, the ornery bastard, well, it's true what Grant said years ago. I am a son to him and that's because he's my dad. In all of the ways that count, he's mine and I'm his.

And don't even get me started on Bryan Michaelchuk.

If you pull love out of the equation, I'm pretty sure he's my soul mate. If not that, because really, I'd much rather have a soul mate I enjoy seeing naked, he's the other half of me. My conscience when I'm about to do something stupid and my biggest—okay, second biggest—fan when I'm about to reach for something great.

He's better than blood.

He's my brother.

"Hey, you're pretty quiet. You okay?"

Shit. I did it again. Completely zoned out and worried her.

"I'm great."

"You're not just saying that?"

Burrowing my face into her neck, not even caring if the doctor is still around to see, I place my lips to her skin and kiss her. Too comfortable in my position to even dream of moving it, no matter how badly I miss the taste of her lips.

"We promised we wouldn't just say things, so yes, little one, I mean it. I was just thinking about things since it seemed like you had control of the conversation."

"Things?"

"Bryan and Smith. How freeing it's been admitting how I feel about them. Telling them to their faces for the first time."

"They love you."

"Yeah, they do."

"But not as much as I do."

Resting a hand on my chin she presses into my skin and lifts until my eyes are on her. Green orbs I used to think were the signal of my ultimate destruction, dancing and doing the opposite.

Healing me.

"Thank fuck for that. There's only so much Radley love I can take."

If love by threats, barking orders, and a whole lot of growling is a thing.

Have I mentioned I love the ornery bastard?

"I'm pretty sure Marie says the same thing every day."

"Yet they've been married longer than the both of us have been breathing." I remind her. "You think you'll love me like that in forty years?"

Pressing a soft kiss to my nose, she nuzzles it with her own as she smiles.

"I'll love you like that after fifty." Pausing, I see the flicker of light begin to dim from her eyes and swallowing hard, prepare myself for what's about to come. What's inevitable now that I've seen the doctor. We're going to get into what he said. "Are you sure you're alright with never wrestling again if it comes to that?"

Tapping my chin with a wiggle of my brow, I grin. The lift to my face after so long without it, so new, but one I wouldn't give up for the world now that it's there and as permanent a fixture as she is.

"I don't know. I suppose that depends if you're gonna be alright not wrestling once I knock you up with a little Kemper."

Smacking me lightly on the shoulder as her laughter fills the room, she rests her forehead on mine, making both our heads move when she lifts it up and down.

Jesus.

I really am a lucky bastard.

"I love you, Kimberlee Parker."

Shaking her head against mine, I pull back just enough to search her eyes, looking for answers.

"That just won't do, Matthias Kemper."

"Then what will?"

"You know what."

"I love you, little one."

"You got it. Now we just gotta make sure you don't ever forget it."

"No chance of that happening. You'd whip my ass if I even tried."

"You know me so well." She laughs, pressing her lips to mine and letting me experience it. Another thing she's given me without even trying. Her happiness infectious.

"You know what I think?"

"Oh, I do, Kemper. You're thinking I'm the best in the world at what I do, and you can't imagine your life without me in it."

"I was going to say you're the crazy one, but you know what? I like your answer better because you're right. I do think that."

"In that case, you know what has to happen now, don't you?"

"You lock the door, throw me down onto the bed, and have your wicked way with me?"

"It really is as bad as you said, isn't it? All this time on your ass staring at the walls really has made you lose your mind."

"That would be you causing that, little one."

Earning myself another playful slap, I put us back on track.

"What do we need to do?"

"We need to be crazy together. Forever."

"Deal."

And just like that, all thoughts of my career and what may or may not be left of it are gone. And using all the strength I can muster, I flip her in the bed. Hovering over her, like an animal stalking its prey, I do the only thing I can.

Smiling down at her, I seal our deal with a kiss.

Chapter Thirty-Eight

Matthias

It took a lot of time, a lot of back and forth with a certain raven-haired little one, and breaks because of the pain that even weeks after being released out of the torture chamber known as the hospital, but it's done.

Finally fucking done.

Now the two people that need to see it in action need to get their asses here so I can see through the rest of the crazy ass plan of mine.

I've been giving it a lot of thought with all of that time I spent locked to a hospital bed.

So much has changed in a short period of time, and with what I've looked into and found out since I've been out, it's fixing to get a whole lot worse for at least one person I care about.

And in true form, even though it's motivated differently these days, I've gotta do everything I can to make sure that doesn't happen.

"Put the bag down and back away slowly!"

Doing as he says, I drop the bag to the ground and step back, earning the laughter that since I came back, I enjoy almost as much as Kimber's.

"She have any idea what the fuck you're doing when she lets you out of the house?"

Smirking, I don't even dignify his question with an answer.

Of course Kimber knows what I'm up to. How stubborn I was right from the moment I dropped my plan in her lap to see the majority of it through myself. Taking a page from all of the years I spent building myself into the best wrestler and proving again that no injury is going to keep me down.

Sure, the jury is still out on whether it will keep me permanently out of the ring, but with each passing day, that seems to matter less and less. If that last match I pulled off before the accident is the way I have to end things, so be it.

I've got everything I need. Here in the room with me now, with the clearing of another throat entering the equation, and with what I've got waiting for me at home.

I'm in a good place.

"If you're just gonna stand there with that cocky as shit grin, then maybe you can tell me what this place is and why you were so determined I meet you here."

"I'd like to know the answer to that myself, boy." The gravelly voice of my father interrupts and I can't help myself with the laugh that escapes.

These two actually agreeing on something is the strangest thing I've ever heard.

But definitely working in my favor with what I've got planned.

"It's a gym." I laugh when I realize how much work there still is before it's actually what I'm claiming it as. "Okay, so it's going to be a gym when I'm done with it."

"But why are we here?" Bryan questions, motioning around. "What does this have to do with me and that old fart?"

"I'll show you an old fart, pipsqueak."

"Not if those cataracts you're dealing with finish you off first, old man." Bryan laughs before turning back to me and narrowing his eyes. "Before we end up getting into an all-out brawl, I think you need to start explaining some shit, bro."

"It's mine." I admit first, waiting them out as they take in my admission and what with the way Smith's eyes close, I know has to be making them think I'm announcing my retirement.

"The fuck you saying, son? You giving up on the plan to get you back in the ring?"

See? There it is.

"No. I'm still as determined to get back to work as I was the last time we talked. This is something else."

"Which is?" Bryan asks, motioning with his hands for me to get on with it.

"You both know the way shit was for me growing up. How much the gym helped before I ended up landing on your doorstep." I nod to Smith. "It was an outlet for me. An outlet that I still need as much today as I did then."

"Okay, so you want to open up your own gym. Got it. But what's with the name on the outside? That yours?"

Heroes.

Thinking back on all the years I spent looking at a lot of the guys I watched in the ring as larger than life inspiration, heroes for lack of a better term, it seemed fitting. Then when I told

Kimber and she agreed without so giving it so much as a second thought, it was done.

This place is for kids like me to go. To let off some steam, to keep their noses clean, maybe even just to free themselves of the demons that might be haunting them. A place they can come and feel safe.

But also a place that just like everyone was fond of telling me before my accident, can create heroes of the future.

At least that's how I see it going in my head.

"Yeah, it's mine, and if you even think of giving me shit for it, I'll help Radley kick your ass."

"For real? You're choosing him over all of this?" he rakes a hand down over his body before cracking up and howling in laughter. "God, that was lame as hell."

"Kind of like you, pipsqueak." Radley adds with a chuckle of his own.

I've never been surer of what I'm here to do now. What, now that they know about the gym, I need to get on with.

"I wanted to show you both the place and let you know it wasn't the end of the line for me. That it's just a new beginning. A fall back option no matter what happens next."

Turning to Bryan and catching his eyebrow-raising at my choice of words, I just nod and smile.

"You can finally tell your parents I got one of those."

"Planning on it. But you ready to tell me what it has to do with us?"

"This place doesn't have anything to do with why you're here. I wanted you both here on neutral ground for an entirely different reason."

"Boy, if you don't stop pussy footing around, this kid won't the only one on the receiving end of a Radley fist."

Throwing my hands up in surrender, he coughs in an attempt to cover up what has to be rawest sounding laugh.

"Times are changing. I know you know they are, old man, because you've spent weeks talking to me about it. The losses you're suffering. How you're ready to pack it in if any more of your guys end up flying the coop. And Bry," I turn to my best friend. "You know it's changing to. HFWA is growing. Becoming bigger than I think you ever imagined it being when you came to me with the idea years ago. So I was thinking, back when I had nothing but time on my hands and a piss bag attached to my leg, that maybe we need to stop being so stubborn and just accept the change. Move with it."

"What you got in mind?" Smith asks and I've never been happier to hear him ask the question. The one so set in his ways I was sure he'd never change, being the one to ask this means that what I want really can be a reality.

"A merger."

"Fuck sakes." Bryan curses and holding up a hand, begging him silently to let me finish, I start again.

"Smith is ready to pack it in. He's still got a wealth of knowledge that we can capitalize on. That you can capitalize on if would just stop looking at yourself like a competitor. He could be a huge benefit to you, especially with the powerhouse he turned CPW into. It rivals the multi-national promotions and you can't argue that."

"No, I can't." he reluctantly concedes.

"And Smith, Bryan is young and hungry to make a name for himself in the business. He reaches the guys on a level that despite believing you still got it, you haven't been able to do in years. That guaranteed contract you tried springing on me solid proof of how far you've fallen. Not to mention that with what they've already put together in the short time they've been at this, he's proven he knows how to run a place in a way that puts asses in seats."

"That he has."

"I've already talked to Reese about this, because he's just as important in this move as you two are. He's on board. I don't think the guy has ever accepted something as quickly as he did this, because he sees what I do. What everyone will once we see it through."

"You want us to work together?"

"Yes."

Both men turn to each other, staring each other down. Neither one backing down in their stance. But where in the past, I know this would have turned into an all-out pissing contest, they do the opposite. Bryan first, but Smith quick to follow.

Their faces lifting before Smith's hand comes out from its place behind his back, extended to my best friend—my brother—and Bryan quickly taking it.

Sealing the deal the same way I did with Kimber.

"You've both wanted to run your businesses and you succeeded in doing it by created a family atmosphere. It's time for that to become one entity instead of two."

"I need to have a talk with Kimber, man. She's turned you into a pussy."

Closing the distance between us, I wrap my arm around Bryan's neck and slap on a headlock, earning a thumbs up followed by a booming laugh from Smith.

"Right about now, I'd say you love the shit out of this pussy." I argue. "But maybe I'm wrong and you're just jealous because you don't have anyone turning you into one."

"It's not my fault all the good ones always end up taken."

Can't exactly argue with that, but that's another issue for another day. Right now, all that matters is that the two men I care about most, my family, are on the same page and my plan is going to come to fruition.

"Well, if that's all you got, I've got me an annoyed woman waiting back at the hotel who wants to get out and see more of the place then the four walls I've kept her cooped up in."

I think I know Marie well enough by now to know that her annoyance probably has more to do with Radley than it does the hotel, but since the only piece of business still at hand has to do with my best friend, I'm more than okay letting him sell the line of bullshit.

"Wouldn't wanna piss off Marie."

"That we don't. And if you haven't heard me barking it at you for the last ten years, make sure you hear me now. Don't get married. You gotta cut your balls off and hand 'em over the second you do."

Oh, is that all? Sign me the fuck up.

Kimber can have my balls if it means I get her wearing my name for the rest of our lives. The Kemper last name these days not carrying the same stigma it did before.

This time, meaning only the best.

Me and her forever.

"Yeah, you know, I don't have the whole wife problem, but I should probably get back to work. Those paychecks your girl keeps going on about don't sign themselves."

"Actually, Bry, you think you can stick around?"

Giving me his silent acceptance, I turn to Smith and meet the knowing look reflecting back at me in his eyes. He knows better than anyone, after the talk we had in the hospital what's going to happen now.

What's been long overdue.

"I know we said a lot of what needed to be said weeks ago, but there's some stuff that with as crazy as everything was when I woke up, I couldn't tell you." I admit, having sent Smith on his way and spending the last ten minutes pacing back and forth preparing myself for a conversation fifteen years in the making.

A conversation that up until I asked him to stick around, I thought I was prepared to have.

So much for that.

"I know you love me, Matty. I also know how hard it must be having to spend every day with Kimber knowing you can't act on those feelings."

As funny as he is, I can't wait for the day when he's ready to admit to himself just how much these little jabs he makes speak to a bigger issue. If I can man up and finally admit that I'm not right in the head, he needs to do the same.

The reason he can't find someone to settle down with and has been as alone as I have since his relationship with his high school sweetheart crashed and burned, won't be hidden from everyone much longer.

But again, another issue for another day.

"I'm sorry man." I start, knowing that I've already apologized more than enough times, but needing to make sure given what comes next, he hears again. "My behavior. The way I've been treating you for years. There's been no excuse for it. You were there every damn step of the way and I shit on you for it."

"It's cool, Matty. We've been over this already. I know you weren't right."

"No, Bry, it's not. It wasn't just what happened with my old man that caused the rift that was building with you. I'd love to blame that piece of shit for the way I've been treating you, but I can't. It's all on me."

Cocking his head to the side, eyebrow quick to follow, he crosses his arms across his chest releasing a heavy breath, waiting me out.

Here goes nothing. It's time to admit what I was too damn hard headed to do when it mattered. What I waited fifteen years to even admit to myself.

"I was jealous. Green as fuck over everything you had, and instead of just coming clean about it, I let it sit and fester. Every time something good came your way, it just kept growing. Your parents, the way they were with you, how happy and how invested in your life they were. Your ability to be rational in every damn situation we ended up in, when I was to explode. I spent years thinking you were the golden child and got everything you had handed to you on a silver platter. Even when I was the one holding the platter with the HFWA start-up."

"That's why you wanted me to stick around? To rehash shit I already knew?"

Wait, what?

"You knew?"

"Matty, for such a smart guy, you're a fucking moron sometimes. I've always known. I just didn't care. Still don't. I knew what it was. I also knew that once you finally yanked your head out of the permanently jammed in your ass position, you'd change it. We'd get back to the way things were before shit hit the fan."

Fuck sakes.

Apparently I'm as dumb as everyone keeps telling me I am because I did my best to bury that shit, even at my own expense.

"You've always been my brother, Bry."

"And you mine, man."

"If it wasn't for you, I don't know..."

"Oh, for fucks sakes. Not this shit again. Don't make me call Kimber. I will, you know. I'll call her and tell her you're being a complete dumbass and she'll kick your ass. She kind of loves me that way."

She does. If I'm the brother he never had, she's definitely the sister.

"You'd be right where you are now, with or without me. And you wanna know why that is? Because you, Matthias Lee Kemper, are a fighter. A survivor. You survive and you thrive. No matter what shit life throws your way, or how much of it you let yourself be buried by, you always come back. You're like a fucking cockroach. You don't die."

What he's saying might be true, I may have survived and even come out stronger without him, but it's speeches I know come straight from his heart like this one, that make me so damn thankful he's my brother and I get to live life with him.

"If we're offering up apologies though, I owe you a pretty big one too."

"How do you figure?"

"You weren't the only green mother fucker in the room back then. When I got hurt and couldn't join you in taking over the world in the ring, I hated you. There were weeks back then if you remember, where you had to drag me with you because I was so stuck in my jealousy and heartbreak, that I didn't wanna do shit.

But, you turned that around for me too. Accepted my stupid ass idea at the time to run a promotion, to be more than just your fake handler, and helped me achieve it. The hate was hard to hold onto after that."

It's like Kimber all over again. Bryan saying basically the same thing she did about back then. The way I just accepted her for who she was, what and who I knew she would become in the business and went to bat for it in the only way I could at the time.

Shit. I do have a hero complex.

"Problem is, it still must have been there underneath because when you came to work for me finally, I exploited the gift you gave me. I exploited your friendship. I knew you weren't ready for that first run. I could see how close you were to going over the edge and I pushed you into it anyway. It was like in some sick way, I needed you to fall flat on your face so I could stop living in your fucking shadow."

"Bry," I don't even know what to say to him, but I know I've got to say something. Because even finding all of this out, things I never knew at the time, it doesn't change anything. He's still my brother. Still my best friend. "It's all good."

"No, Matty, it's not. But now that you know, now that I've admitted my own damn fault in the way everything went down, it will be. We can both move on from the shit that haunts us."

Now that I can definitely get behind.

"You really wanted me to fall on my face?"

"Yeah, man, I did."

Damn.

"What we talked about in the hospital. You and Reese wanting me to have another go at the belt if I can come back from this, how much of that was my best friend and how much was the promoter?"

"Are you asking if I still want you to fail?"

"Yes, but no. I just need to know if this is my brother or my boss."

"Reese is the one that wants the belt on you, not me. He's looking at this from a business standpoint. The money we'll generate off you and Brady. He thinks if booked the right way, for the right amount of time, it can be one hell of a draw. I happen to agree, both as the guy that signs your paychecks *and* as your brother. But to answer your other worry, it's not because I want to see you fall anymore. This time, when you're back and ready, I want to see you soar."

✳✳✳✳✳✳

So six months, one medical clearance, and with my little one by my side, her own gold resting right where it belongs around her waist, that's exactly what I do.

I soar.

Epilogue
Six Months Later
2016

Matthias

"Little one..."

The car filling with her spilled over laughter, I can easily imagine her shaking her head as she does it before she answers. Reading my mind without me even having to say a word.

"No, Matthias. You can't take off the blindfold. I never ask you for anything, so come on. Humor me for a few more minutes."

I've already been wearing this damn thing for three hours now. I think I'm well past the point of humoring her, and just like I have in the past when I've taken her to places without saying a word, she's being just as evasive now. All I've been able to do for the entire time we've been in the car being to let my mind work overtime trying to figure out what she could possibly want kept such a secret that she's willing to go to this extreme.

Blindfolds should only be for one thing, and that's definitely not what's going on here.

Trust me, I'm being reminded by the serious amount of adjustment I'm due when I finally get the hell out of this prison known as my car.

I should have screwed her plan altogether and taken her to bed the second she teased me back at her apartment after we were done packing everything up for her move into my place. God knows I wanted to, but those damn eyes of hers.

They did what they've been doing for years.

Made me putty in her hands.

"Can you at least tell me how much longer?"

"About ten minutes, I think." She answers as she brings the car to a full stop and after a few seconds pass, flips the key in the ignition.

Ten minutes my ass.

Lifting my hand, more than a little ready to rip the damn thing off my eyes, I reel back from the sting of her hand as it slaps itself down hard on mine.

"Son of a—"

"Don't you dare finish that statement or you'll get worse than a slap."

Goddamnit. Little one wins again.

"Fine, but you've ten minutes starting...now." I tap the watch on my wrist. "After that, I'm ripping this off and I don't care where the fuck we are. I'm taking you the way I should have before we left the house."

"Promises, promises, Kemper."

"Oh, I'll show you a promise."

Laughing, I hear the click of her seatbelt and within seconds the brush of her body as she leans over into my space and presses her lips to mine.

"We're actually here, but since we still gotta walk for a few, just keep it on. I'll make it up to you later if you do."

Well, In that case.

"I'm gonna hold you to that."

Pressing her lips to mine again before creating a breeze that blows over me as she moves back quickly and opens her door, leaving to my imagination of just how she's going to make it up to me later, I lose myself in it until a few seconds later, she jolts me back to reality when the door opens and her hands are over me, unclipping my own belt.

"You know, normally I'm all for wanting to know where you went just now, but I'm pretty sure this time I can guess."

Shifting in the seat as her laughter again spills out, it doesn't take me long to figure out what she's getting at. What I knew before I even started imagining her on top and riding me but stopped giving two fucks about pretty quick.

I'm hard.

Who the hell am I kidding? I'm always hard when she's around.

"Your fault, little one. You teased me and made promises."

Slipping her hand over mine after successfully freeing me of the belt and hoisting myself from the car, I breathe in the air. What I haven't felt in what feels like forever.

Clean and fresh. New air. The way it's felt for the last six months.

Since I admitted what I knew all along.

I'm in love with Kimberlee Parker.

"God, I never get tired of it." I admit, sucking in another breath and releasing it with a contented sigh.

"Never get tired of what?"

"The feel of the air. The taste of it. It's even more powerful with this damn thing on." I finger the blindfold. "It's like everything else is pushed away and all I can feel is it."

"I never figured you for waxing poetic, Kemper."

"Well you should have, since it's all your fault, Parker." I laugh, the feel of her last name on my tongue, strange, but right. I've been calling her little one for so long, it's a miracle I even remember she has any other name.

"The way this feels, it's the way I feel when we're together. The exact same."

"Awww, Matty." She sighs sweetly. "I guess this means I'm forgiven for earlier?"

"Fraid not. You're still on the hook for teasing me the way you did in the shower and then running off before I could finish it."

"Damnit." She curses softly and I'm done. I can't take anymore.

Pulling her to me, I spin her around until her back is against the door and leaning in, press my lips to hers. Not in the hungry way she's expecting with the way her nails dig straight through my shirt and down into my skin. Hunger isn't guiding this at all.

Need to connect to this amazing girl I've been lucky enough to call mine though?

It's definitely that.

"I need this blindfold off, so we're going to pick this up later, but that taste wasn't enough."

"It never is." She admits breathless and my chest puffs out a little more knowing I'm the one that made her that way. That one kiss, just one taste, caused that reaction in her.

A reaction that no matter where we go from here, will never get old.

"Okay, cranky ass. Time for your surprise. God forbid you have to wear that blindfold a second longer than the ten minutes I said." And with that, I let her hand slip its way into mine and guide me where she's determined to go.

Where my supposed surprise awaits.

What when we finally do pull to a stop a couple of minutes later and she hand squeezes mine, has me tuning in to the breaks in her breathing pattern, the sweat that now slickly coats our hands. Her reaction not at all like she'd been by the car or even at the house before we left.

Something's off.

"Kimber, where are we? You're acting weird."

"No, I'm not." She scoffs in an attempt blow me off.

I'm not having it. Something about where we are right now is making her nervous, and I damn well wanna know what it is. She's not supposed to be this way. Not when she seemed so happy about it when she announced it this morning.

"Truth, little one. You blocking me from seeing means I'm focusing on everything else, and you're nervous. I can feel it."

"Take the blindfold off, Matty." She murmurs and that's all I need. My hands easily finding the tight fabric of the headband she's wrapped around my skull and ripping it down over my neck at the exact moment she starts speaking again. "You'll get your answer to that question when you do."

Meeting her eyes and seeing the sheepish expression she's wearing, I brush my hand across her cheek until her eyes begin to flutter closed and that's when I take in where we are.

The answers she said I would get now that I can see again.

From the sidewalk, all the way up and over the newly mowed and freshly planted lawn, to the porch that had been painted over. A clean coat of white erasing the darker off white and caked with dirt shade that had once covered it, I take it all in. Pausing when even from where we're standing at the beginning of the walkway, I can make out the front door.

Gone, the one of the past and in its place a white one to match the porch. No indents, no breaks.

All new and as clean and fresh to my senses as the air had been.

"Holy shit." The curse rushes out as what I'm witnessing has me struck stupid and speechless. "What...How...When? What is this?"

"What does it look like?" she timidly asks, pulling my attention momentarily from the house and straight to her.

"It looks like home."

Eyes widening, her cheeks begin to rise as her lips do and it's the most beautiful vision I've ever seen.

It's Kimber at her most innocent. Her heart never more visible than it is now where we stand.

I've said the right thing.

"How do you feel about that?"

"I don't know," I admit truthfully. Needing more time than just the couple of minutes I've had so far to get a handle on exactly what it is I'm seeing. The house of horrors from my nightmares no longer there. A home—a real one—in its place.

What it always should have been, but that never materialized in the years we lived there or since.

Screw it. I do know what I feel.

"It's the way it's supposed to be. The way it should have been. The way I want it."

Releasing a heavy sigh, her smile only seems to grow in size as she throws her arms around me and presses her body into mine.

"You have no idea how happy I am to hear you say that, Matty!"

"Why?"

"Well," she pauses, biting down into her lip. "I guess because that's what it is. Our home."

Whoa. What?

"Little one…"

"Don't be mad."

"I'm not mad, I'm confused. What do you mean this is our home?"

"It's not. I mean, not yet." She starts, her pitch picking up and matching the speed of the words that seem to fall in a rush next. "I wouldn't assume something like that without talking to you first, but since I did all of this work, I thought that if I showed it to you, we could sit down and talk about it."

"Breathe, Kimber. Take a breath and tell me what you're trying to say but still haven't managed to get out."

If I didn't need answers, I'd just sweep her off her feet, kiss the shit out of her, and make her see how cute she's being. As it stands though, the need for understanding wins out.

But make no mistake, she's fucking adorable.

"I want this to be our home."

Okay, maybe she's not the one that needs to take a breath. Looks like that falls to me because I can't have heard this right. She can't possibly want to take the one place I've spent the last eleven years running from and throw me back in it.

She knows me better than that. She knows I'm not there yet. That I might never be there. Not even after I'm done with therapy, we find the right medication, and I've dealt with the demons of the past.

"Kimber…shit."

"I know what you're going to say, but hear me out."

"I'll do that, but you need to tell me something first."

"Yeah, of course. What do you wanna know?"

She's amped up, excited while at the same time, petrified of my reaction. Something she doesn't have to worry about. I'm not running, I'm not bailing, and I'm definitely not leaving this spot until I know exactly what was in her heart at the time she decided to do this.

I want to know it all.

"How did you manage this?"

"Daddy called in a few favors."

Okay. She got Renegade involved. After the last time we saw him, and what I learned during the few minutes we had alone together before Kimber and her mother interrupted, it's not that surprising. He'd do anything for her. For us. Now I just to need to know how far it extends.

"What else did you do besides the front of the house?"

"The Backyard. Most of that was just gardening so it didn't take long. I handled that on my own, just like I'm the reason the front lawn looks so fantastic." she grins, pleased with herself. "I also remodelled a couple of the bedrooms. Well, no. That's not right. I had someone come in and give them an updated look."

"Anything else?" I ask when she finally takes a much needed breath.

"Nope. Everything inside is the same way it was when we were here last."

Jesus Christ.

She left everything I put together for my mom intact.

"One more question and then I swear I'll let you explain."

"Okay."

"Why?"

"I wanted to honor her too."

Jesus. Shit. Christ. Fuck. There aren't enough of these words.

I don't have the first clue what to say, but I do know that with that statement, I just fell in love all over again.

"Looks like you're the one that needs to breathe, Matty."

"Uh, yeah. I'm not sure I can right now. So um, while I try, why don't you explain?"

"Are you sure?"

"Positive. Go, little one."

So she does and I fall even more in love with every word she says.

I've never felt so incredibly moved and loved in the same moment before.

"When we were here last, I saw the way the place affected you. The good as much as the bad. I saw what you wanted to do for her and god, Matthias. It was the sweetest thing I've ever been a part of. What you wanted to do for her, the way you wanted to honor her, it made me want to do the same. I want this place to be our home because my way of honoring her doesn't end by just cleaning up the outside. It's filling the inside with all of the love she never got the chance to because it was stolen from her. If she can see what you did from where she is, then she'll be able to see us fill this house—this home—with all of the love it deserves. The love you deserve."

"We deserve, little one. Always we."

"Tell Kimberlee your mother says hello."

After what I experienced in the hospital after the accident, I have no doubt my mom can see all of this. Kimber right now, and the words she's speaking. The place of love that it comes from. All of it. I also know that what my mom said to me that day is true too.

She brought Kimber to me. Brought us to each other.

Her hand is in every bit of this.

"Matty, are you okay?"

Sucking in a breath as I feel her hand reach out and touch my face, her question makes sense. In listening to her reasoning, remembering my mom and the last time we spoke, it's happening again.

I'm crying.

"I'm sorry. I didn't mean to make you upset. I thought it was the right thing to do. It felt right. Just forget it. We don't have t—"

Oh, hell no.

With the other voice that's now joined our conversation, the one that should have been there from the start, there's no way I can let her think that what she's said and done is upsetting.

It's the opposite.

This is what my mom meant with her last words to me.

"She says hello." I cut her off, slipping my own fingers over hers and pulling them to my lips, kissing them as softly and tenderly as I can.

"Who does?"

"My mom. Little one..."

"What, Matty?"

"Let's do it."

"Say what?"

"You heard me."

"I did, but I wanna make sure I heard you right. My head's still kind of spinning."

That makes two of us.

"I said, let's do it. Let's make this house a home the way it was meant to be. Our home."

"The same way we're meant to be?"

"Yes, little one, exactly like that. Forever. You and me. It's what she wanted. Why her last request was to say hello to you. It's because she wanted this. What you've done, what we've done here. What we'll fill this house with. She wanted it the same way I do."

It's time.

The past. All the things I lived through, what I put others through, and the self-destructive road I took under the misguided belief that it was what my mom would have wanted. None of that is ever going to go away. It's always going to be with me, but instead of looking at it like the demon that it's been for so long, it's time to see it—wear it—as the badge of honor it really is.

I survived.

I'm here, and I'm standing beside the most beautiful woman in the world.

The woman that is my world.

Who was given to me by the only other woman I ever loved.

I can release the hold I've had on the pause button of my life now. Live the life that not only did she want for me, but the life I deserve.

One filled with more moments like this one. Filled with happiness. Filled with Kimberlee.

A life filled with love.

It's time for this story—our story—to have two winners.

And not just any two, but the best damn tag team in the world.

A hero and heroine together.

Forever.

The End

Heroine Playlist
The Music that Inspired the Book

Heroine by *Sleeping with Sirens*
My Demons by *Starset*
Car Crash by *Three Days Grace*
Cut The Cord by *Shinedown*
Broken Road by *12 Stones*
Battle Scars by *Lupe Fiasco with Guy Sebastian*
Parachute by *Cheryl Cole*
Battlefield by *Jordan Sparks*
Black and Blue (Smackdown Theme) by *CFO$ and WWE*
Familiar Taste Of Poison by *Halestorm*
You Call Me A Bitch Like It's A Bad Thing by *Halestorm*
Demons by *Sleigh Bells*
Avalanche by *Bring Me The Horizon*
Monster by *Skillet*
Rebel by *Nikki Flores*
Ready To Change by *Heartist*
Say Something by *A Great Big World*
Breathe You In by *Thousand Foot Crutch*
Close by *Nick Jonas & Tove Lo*
Sucker for Pain by *Lil Wayne with Wiz Khalifa, Imagine Dragons,
Logic & Ty Dolla $ign*
Ashes of Eden by *Breaking Benjamin*
Breaking Me Down by *Escape the Fate*
This Is A Call by *Thousand Foot Crutch*
What's Left of Me by *Nick Lachey*
Break On Me by *Keith Urban*
On My Own by *Ashes Remain*
Cold Water by *Major Lazer with Justin Bieber & MØ*
On The Way Down by *Ryan Cabrera*
Hero/Heroine by *Boys Like Girls*

Acknowledgements

As much as this story was Matthias's journey, even Kimber's and theirs together, it was also mine. His darkness, her strength and their struggle, all interwoven and connected with my own during the writing of this. All three of us growing in the making of it.

So for this round of acknowledgements, what differs from ones I've written in the past, I'm going to thank those people that not only helped shape this book, but the ones that stood by me through my own journey to happy end writing it.
The names, the people listed here, in no particular order, but holding the same place in my very humbled and thankful heart.

My children. Caleb, Noah, Raine and Isabella. Four people that if it weren't for their very existence, their love and support, and the ways they continue to enrich my life and teach me as I attempt to do the same with them as they grow, would leave me only a shell of the woman I've become. Thank you for being the four unique individuals that you are and for listening and heeding my words when I'm not hearing them myself. For never giving up, never giving in, and for never losing your flames. I love you all and I always will.

Pamela Sparkman. The woman who pulled double duty for this venture. Not only being the very strong voice in the back of my head during one of the darkest periods of my life, but the one going over these words, reading my heart, along with Matthias's, as it poured out in buckets over the pages. Your impact, the imprint you left behind and have left behind after every book I write, it will never be forgotten or made light of. It's been a pleasure and an honor to know you. To love you. Thank you for everything.

My beta readers. All of you individually and together as a unit. You took on a book that I know for some of you, would never in a million years be what you read and had faith in me to deliver on what I have with you in the past. Whether as readers apart from the writing process, or the ones scouring over endless chapters making sure it all worked right. You are at the very core of this book just as the characters are. As I am. Your words of encouragement, along with your constructive criticism through every part of this, appreciated, accepted and treasured. Thank you so very much. I love you all.

Joey. Here we are again, guard dog extraordinaire. A journey of our own again taking place during the making of this one that even though we're nowhere near done with, I don't regret taking for a second. Thank you for being my best friend and believing in me when I don't. I love you and I always will. ANF, pretty boy.

Cheryl. I survived! Just like you said I would when in my weakest moment, in the depths of my own despair mixing with Matthias's, I admitted I didn't think I could do it. So for that and so much more, thank you. I love you and your pretty face so hard.

My Autism Family. This isn't a book geared toward the lives we live the way Count On Me was when I wrote it (more specifically my life at the time), but it is one that is just as affected by what you've brought to my life in the time spent writing it. The years even before the idea presented itself. For the hours spent rejoicing over the positive moments in our lives, as well as the ones where we just held each other as we cried and admitted our fears and inadequacies, you've given me something that can never be recreated. Something so pure and so moving that I'm going to carry it with me long after my time here is done. Thank you for loving me, for supporting me and for believing in me when a lot of times, I didn't. I love you all.

Pro-Wrestling.
From the time I was five years old, you've been a staple in my life. We break up and go our separate ways sometimes, but at the end of the day, we always come back together in the most

glorious of ways. The imprint you as a whole and the superstars apart from it have left on me and my heart, will never be made light of. You've changed me. Given me something over the years to believe in when much like I've said to the others above, I didn't have the strength to believe in myself. Thank you pro-wrestling and superstars that for years have been larger than life, for being what I needed you to be then and what you've been today. Much love and respect always. As John Cena says…Never Give Up. Never stop following those dreams you have and bringing everything you have to the ring to entertain your fans. We love you for it.
I love you for it. And I always will. (Even when I hate you lol)

Readers, Bloggers, Book Buyers the world over.
Without you this dream of mine, of any authors, wouldn't exist. Sure, we would still write the stories that you are all so fond of sharing with the world, but we wouldn't be able to reach the masses we do because of you. So for that and everything else you do, from the bottom of this very humbled and honored author's heart…thank you. We appreciate every single thing you do, day in and day out, and we (me) always will. Never stop shouting your love for things that make your heart soar and I swear to you, I won't stop shouting my love for you.

About the Author
Melyssa Winchester

Melyssa is a mother of four from Toronto, Ontario Canada.

She's currently working on the fourth book in the Black and Blue series, **Shoot** and the standalone second chance romance, **Infinity.**

When she's not writing, you can find her buried under the covers with her portable DVD player, watching marathons of Supernatural and Veronica Mars. When those aren't available, she can be found curled up in a corner with her e-reader and a plethora of books, falling in love with characters written so well she deems them her book boyfriends and girlfriends.

If you want to find her, check Facebook or Twitter (@WinchesterBooks) as she may just have an addiction to both. If those don't work you can always keep up with her progress on her personal site.

Books by Melyssa Winchester

Count on Me Series

Count on Me
Hear Me Now
Take Me With You
All My Heart
Here & Now
Unbroken
What Lies Beneath

Love United Series

Holding On to Heaven
No Surrender
Wanted
Stairway to Heaven
A Light in the Dark

Before the Light Series

Hold Onto Me (Michael's Story)
Absence of Light (Ryan's Story)

Black & Blue Series

Shades of Blue
Into the Blue

Heroine
Shoot (Coming Late Fall 2016)

Standalone Titles

The Space In Between
Remembering Sunday